# The

# Rogue Mage

By Ben Hale

To my family and friends,

Who believed

And to my wife,

Who is perfect

# The Chronicles of Lumineia

By Ben Hale

## —The Age of Oracles—
The Rogue Mage
The Lost Mage
The Battle Mage

## —The Master Thief—
Jack of Thieves
Thief in the Myst
The God Thief

## —The Second Draeken War—
Elseerian
The Gathering
Seven Days
The List Unseen

## —The Warsworn—
The Flesh of War
The Age of War
The Heart of War

## —The White Mage Saga—
Assassin's Blade (Short story prequel)
The Last Oracle
The Sword of Elseerian
Descent Unto Dark
Impact of the Fallen
The Forge of Light

# Table of Contents

# Map of Lumineia

# Prologue: End of a Bloodline

Commander Othan leaned back in his chair and examined the parchment. After six years they were finally closing in on the bandit known as the Soldier. Now it was only a matter of time before the man hung from a noose—or died on a blade. Commander Othan smiled as he imagined the impending execution and rose to his feet, stepping to the cabinet that contained his private stock of ale.

Situated below Dawnskeep, his office curved across the edge of the foundation, one wall transparent to allow an unbroken view of the massive training hall. His collection of elven blades hung on the wall, while blue banners interspersed the weaponry. Light came from a pair of gremlins that prowled the ceiling. Conjured by his own hand, they guarded his office when he was not present.

He picked up a crystalline glass and selected a bottle. Meressa, second oracle on the Eldress Council, had made the ale personally and gifted it to him for his service as captain of her guard. Pouring a glass of the amber liquid, he stepped to the window and surveyed the training hall.

The hall filled the breadth of the fortress, extending all the way to the foundations of the outer wall. The vaulted ceiling made the cavernous space majestic and open, while ensuring the Runeguard with magic had room to train. Although the hall contained the requisite training circles, forges, and armories, his gaze was drawn to the secret that made the Runeguard legendary, the Requiems.

Othan took a sip and savored the drink, his thoughts returning to the Soldier. Six years ago, the Soldier had launched a private war against the guild of Verinai. Comprised of mages with multiple talents, the powerful guild should have crushed him with ease, but the man proved elusive. Those dissatisfied with the guild flocked to his banner, joining his band of Defiant. He wore a mask and kept his identity hidden, even from his own people. Othan scowled, wondering how the man had evaded the oracles' magic.

Since the Dawn of Magic, five oracle bloodlines had guided kings and commoners alike. They could use every type of magic, granting them farsight, the ability to see glimpses of the future. Revered for their power, wisdom, and benevolence, the oracles were the protectors of the peace, the voice of reason between nations. They had never failed . . . until the Soldier.

Othan's scowl deepened and he returned to his desk. He was a Runeguard, sworn protector of the oracles. But he was Verinai first, and he'd taken secret oaths to the guild that superseded his rank and office. He took a final swallow from the ale and placed the glass on the desk. Then he reached for the quill to sign the orders.

The ink rippled.

Othan paused, his eyes on the ink as it stilled. Dawnskeep had been built by dwarven artisans and the guild of Verinai, and he'd never felt a tremor. He frowned as he watched the inkwell, wondering if the earth was shaking as it sometimes did on the South Sea islands.

His desk shuddered again, more violently than before. The vibration passed through his chair and into his body, bringing him to his feet. He had four talents to his credit, and sent a burst of magic into the stones at his feet, searching for the source of the tremor, but the trembling did not come from beneath.

It came from above.

He came around his desk as the entire room shook, the inkwell sliding off the desk and shattering on the floor. Confusion and urgency filling his veins, he reached the door just as it swung open.

"Commander," Lieutenant Jallow exclaimed, breathless, "an oracle has been attacked."

"Where?" Othan demanded.

A piercing shriek shattered the calm. Through stone and flesh the sound reverberated throughout the fortress. The unholy sound carried

11

the timbre of anger, pain, and fear. Othan pushed past Jallow and sprinted for the stairs, fear spiking in his gut.

The curving steps brought him to the main level of Dawnskeep, a great hall for receiving dignitaries and kings. Marble pillars rose to the ceiling, their polished curves reflecting the enchanted figures dancing on the walls.

Othan sprinted toward the dwarven ascender at the edge of the room, other guards converging from the wings. Dressed in the flowing white and blue armor of the Runeguard, they rushed for the dwarven ascender that connected to the upper floors.

"Which oracle is under attack?"

"No one breached the wall!"

"Is it the Soldier?"

The questions were laced with fear and desperation, punctuated by more tremors through the citadel. Five oracle bloodlines had existed since the Dawn of Magic, but currently only one had a daughter. If an oracle perished without an heir, an entire lineage would be extinguished. Othan skidded to a stop at the ascender as the men yanked on the controls. A grinding of gears came from the machinery but the platform did not rise.

"It must be damaged!" one of the guards shouted.

A great cracking came from the ceiling and Othan's head snapped up. He shoved Jallow out of harm's way and launched himself in the opposite direction. He landed hard and rolled as an enormous section of the ceiling came free and plummeted to their former position.

It struck the polished floor with brutal force, sending cracks spiderwebbing outward. Fires and molten stone lined the surface of the fragment. Coughing in the dust and smoke, Othan came to his feet and looked to the hole it had left.

Visible through the gap, the bookshelves of the library were wreathed in flames. Glimmers of light sparkled in the inferno, charms activating to protect the valuable tomes. A bookshelf succumbed and collapsed, sending sparks and books tumbling into the great hall. Another scream echoed, furious and defiant.

"The other ascenders are blocked!" someone shouted. "We need another way up!"

Othan stabbed a finger at the gap. "We have one. Fire mages with me, stone mages, lift us up!"

He darted to the great ceiling fragment and caught the side, scaling the broken stone to the top. When he encountered flames he extinguished them with a burst of his power, the flames answering his will.

Guards ascended with him, reaching the top as other Verinai surrounded the burning rock. They cast their collective magic and used the floor beneath to lift the section of ceiling. Then it gradually rose into the air.

"Who's the attacker?" Othan demanded, but none had an answer.

As the fragment of ceiling lifted toward the opening, another crack echoed. Someone shouted in warning and the guards scrambled away as another chunk of the ceiling tumbled down, bouncing off a pillar before embedding into the floor.

"Lieutenant, reinforce the ceiling!" Othan barked, and guards leapt to the pillars.

As he neared the opening Othan gathered the magic beneath his feet, reaching into the stone. Instead of rigid and heavy, it felt smooth and liquid, and he bent it to his will. The stone flowed upward, carrying him on a finger of rock through the hole and depositing him on the floor of the library.

He shielded his eyes from the flames and spread his other hand, drawing the heat into a tight ball, condensing and shaping it so it could be extinguished. As the brilliant light faded, his eyes widened in shock.

Bookshelves were demolished and broken, leaving the floor littered in burning tomes. Those not protected by charms were charred beyond recognition. Tables and chairs were shattered, the wood snapped like kindling.

One of the great trees that had graced the interior had been uprooted and turned into a treewalker. It now lay on its side, its trunk on fire while the branches were broken and twisted, extending through a broken window.

Shouts of alarm echoed from outside, and he realized the entire city would be watching the fire and billowing smoke. He glanced back and called an order to close the fortress gates. Then he advanced through the fire, searching.

A giant lightcast bird glided through the smoke, its wing broken, causing it to list to the side. The entity collided with a bookshelf, knocking it down. Othan flinched as the bird burst into sparks. Spotting the ascender doors blocked by debris, he picked his way through the piles of ruined books and burning shelves, listening for signs of combat that would indicate the oracle was still fighting. The crackle of flames and shouts from the other guards filled the library, until someone cried out in dismay. Othan whirled and leapt toward them, sliding to a halt when he saw the body, joining those who stood in stunned horror.

Othan stared at the twisted form, numb with disbelief. The other guards converged on the location, their questions falling on deaf ears until they saw the body and joined the silence. Tears flowed, and hardened warriors trembled with shock and rage.

"An entire bloodline, gone," one muttered.

"Who would do this?" another asked.

Othan could not tear his gaze from her lifeless form, his questions unable to find his tongue. There were no bodies around the oracle, indicating the oracle's killer had been alone. Few had the power to stand against an oracle and all were powerful mages. All were sworn to protect the oracles.

"Who could kill an oracle?" a guard asked.

"A betrayer in our midst," Othan said, finally tearing his gaze from the body to look at his lieutenant. "A rogue mage."

14

# Chapter 1: Oracle

## Six Months Earlier

Alydian leaned back in her chair and rubbed her eyes, struggling to contain her irritation. Like all oracles she'd spent the first fifty years of her life in study, and then assumed the role of apprentice oracle. Thirty years later and her mother continued to assign exhaustive lists of tomes for her to read. She knew it was due to her mother's failing health but still found the weight to be stifling.

Leaving the desk, she stepped to the table and poured herself a glass of mint water, draining it before turning to face the desk once more. Leather-bound tomes lay scattered across its polished wooden surface, obscuring the parchment with her notes.

Her quill shifted when the wagon bounced on a rut, a subtle reminder that she was moving. Unlike traditional wagons, hers had been constructed by magic. The wheels were encased in aquaglass, softening the bumps and ruts of the road. Spacious and long, the wagon contained a private bedchamber, a study, and a dining area at the rear. Windows allowed the afternoon light to cascade into her study, and she stepped to the largest, gazing wistfully at the passing terrain.

She'd left Terros days ago and entered the rolling hills of southern Griffin. Trees dotted the rocky slopes, and mountains rose into the distance. Spring had drawn flowers and brush from the earth, brightening remaining patches of lingering snow.

A soldier rode past her wagon and he turned the reins to ride up a nearby hill. She felt a spark of envy over his freedom. The tattoo on his neck marked him as Verinai, a mage with multiple magics. The powerful guild of Verinai now controlled much of the magical industry, even directing the lower guilds that trained mages with single abilities. The wagon she rode in had been built in one of their cities.

Turning away from the view, she stepped to the center of the wagon and blinked into her magesight, and the wagon burst into color and light. Energy filled her vision. The darkwood floor was a dim brown, the water in the pitcher a shimmering blue. Her own body reflected a grayish hue, contrasting with the bright red of the fire in the small hearth. The light orbs bracketed into the walls cast a brilliant yellow.

As an oracle she could see and manipulate all types of magic, but her skill in each varied. She reached for the fire in the hearth and drew on the flames, causing them to twist and curl. Extending from the hearth, the flames shaped into a tiny soldier bearing a sword. The entity of fire swung its blade and bounded to the table, pacing about as if eager for battle.

Alydian lifted the pitcher and poured it on the table. Instead of splashing about, the water flowed into the shape of a beautiful woman. The fire soldier noticed her and strode forward, bending down to offer his allegiance.

The woman smiled and shook her head, raising her hands to craft a sword of shimmering blue. Lunging forward, she swung a playful swipe at the soldier, who reluctantly blocked. Goading the man forward, the woman swung again, and the soldier parried. Then the man recognized her desire and began to teach, leading the woman through a training regimen.

Alydian sighed as she watched the two entities duel. She was not supposed to train with higher order spells until she entered her second century—still twenty years away. She sank into a seat, watching the duel but not seeing it, wishing she could learn more of the battle magics.

Entities were the most common spell for combat mages, and involved casting energy into a shape that mirrored consciousness. It was temporary and linked to the caster's will. The larger the entity, the more discipline was required to cast it. Most mages gained enough discipline to cast a wolf, lion, or bear, while the more disciplined could cast a warrior to fight for them. An entity with a sentient mind like a human or reaver made it far more versatile, but also more difficult to conjure and control.

Alydian's mind was drawn to her mother, the only one to ever cast a phoenix entity. The image of Elenyr wreathed in light and fire was awesome and inspiring. The sight of her soaring into the sky was a supreme reminder of an oracle's power, but it had been many years since she'd been able to cast such magic.

At eight hundred years old, Elenyr was the oldest oracle on the Eldress Council. The other four oracles each had a seat, with the youngest being well into her second century. As yet, none of the others had birthed a daughter, leaving Alydian to shoulder the weight of instruction from all five on the council.

A knock at the door snapped her from her thoughts, and she guiltily dismissed the entities. The fire dissipated from sight and the maiden flowed back into the pitcher. She'd been on the verge of victory, and cast Alydian an accusing glare as she faded away.

"Next time I'll let you beat him," Alydian murmured with a smile.

She stepped to the door and swung it open to find the captain of her guard on the small porch. Human and grizzled, he was a veteran of countless wars. His grey hair was cropped short, and his white uniform was visible beneath his blue and white armor. The reins of his horse were tied to the side of the wagon.

"Oracle Alydian," he said, bowing, "my scouts have found a suitable camp just ahead. We'll bring the wagon to a halt so you can join the council."

"Thank you, Devkin," she said, addressing him by his first name.

The man's lips twitched with amusement. "You're not supposed to address me so informally."

She grinned. "Yet I do. How are your grandchildren?"

He relented with a laugh. "My newest was born last week in Willowvale, a babe with bright red hair."

"Just like his mother," Alydian said.

17

"Aye," the man said. "Perhaps they can visit you in the autumn?"

"I'd like that," Alydian said.

Devkin smiled and then dropped onto his horse, departing with a final nod to her. Alydian watched him go, grateful that he'd accepted her appointment. Her former captain of the guard had been Verinai, and had sought every opportunity to prove his superiority among the other Runeguard. Devkin's appointment had been at her request, but the guild of Verinai had refused to support the appointment for months until Alydian's mother had stepped in.

"Do you trust him to guard you?" she'd asked.

"He may not have magic," Alydian had replied. "But I trust him."

Her mother had smiled. "Then I'll support your decision."

Alydian stepped back into her cabin but a motion drew her gaze. One of the Verinai soldiers had dismounted next to a party of merchants that had stopped to let the Oracle's caravan pass. They craned for looks at her and she obliged with a smile, causing one of the children to wave at her.

The Verinai soldier, a woman with a sword of aquaglass and steel on her back, stepped to a merchant and pointed to a sapphire pendent hanging from the man's pack. The man shook his head.

"It has already been purchased," he said.

"By whom?" the elven woman sneered.

"A duke in Terros," the man said, recoiling from the Verinai. "It's a gift for his wife."

"The human can find a new gift for his whelp," the elf said, reaching out for the pendent.

"Hornan," Alydian called. "Let the man be."

The Verinai ignored her. "This human should respect his betters."

"Hornan!" Devkin snapped, riding into view. "You will obey your oracle."

18

Hornan cast a sullen look at the soldier. "As you order, *Captain*."

Devkin dismounted and stepped to her. "Disobey the oracle again, and I'll have you discharged from her guardianship."

His voice was cold and hard. Hornan dropped her gaze and retreated, muttering under her breath. Devkin motioned to the merchants and smiled, but they scurried away. Alydian noticed the regret in Devkin's eyes and wondered if it was mirrored in her own. The scene would have been disturbing if it wasn't so common.

She entered her wagon again, resolving to speak to the council about her concerns. As she did she caught sight of Hornan riding with a pair of other Verinai, and all three glared at Captain Devkin's back.

The appointment of a human without magical talent to lead a group of mages was highly unusual, especially when there had been several qualified Verinai candidates. Alydian privately enjoyed the anger Devkin inspired. She would have felt guilty if Devkin was ever bothered by it, but the man never seemed to notice the current of hatred directed at him.

She turned away from the Verinai and the annoyance they inspired, reluctantly returning to her studies. Oracles were required to read much of the great library in Dawnskeep before joining the council, and given her mother's health, she would likely join it soon. Diving into the history of the second sentenium of Lumineia, she pored over the records, studying and memorizing events and names of those long dead.

When she tired, she shifted to tomes on practical magic, practicing what she could within the confines of her wagon. Every branch of magic had its weaknesses, and as much as the tomes described them, they could not prepare her for an entity exploding in her hands. Her practice went against oracle tradition, but she couldn't bring herself to let her magic languish while she read from a dusty book.

The wagon rocked and she looked out the window. They had come to a stop on the summit of a squat hill, providing a view of the surrounding countryside. A handful of trees surrounded the hill but the terrain was open all the way to the forest of Orláknia in the distance, home to the elven kingdom. Dawnskeep resided at the border between the human kingdom of Griffin and the elven kingdom.

The supply wagons were drawn into a circle, forming a protective ring around her wagon. Mounted soldiers filed into place and dismounted, gathering to start fires and prepare the evening meal. They were likely going to arrive at Dawnskeep the following night, and the proximity to the elven kingdom caused many of the soldiers to relax and take seats by the fire.

Devkin barked orders, forcing the Verinai and other soldiers to their posts, causing Alydian to grin. Even here, a days' journey from Dawnskeep, he still watched over her. His caution had been a principle reason she'd requested his appointment as captain of her guard. These days few magicless joined the Runeguard. Much to the consternation of the Verinai soldiers, Devkin continued to best many of them in training.

Alydian had also chosen the man because she'd witnessed his loyalty and kindness to his family. She'd seen him embrace his granddaughter with a fierceness that rivaled a mother lion, and realized that if she could gain his respect, he would be a confidant as much as a protector.

The sun hung low on the horizon, indicating the hour of the council. She rose from her chair and chewed on a strip of dried meat before retreating to her bedchamber. A pair of windows allowed light into the small space, while curtains blocked the interior from view. More books rested on a shelf next to the bed, and a pair of light orbs was bracketed into the wood. A desk was mounted to the front of the room. Closing and locking the door, she took a seat at the desk. Then she closed her eyes and used her magesight. Even through her eyelids, the wagon lit up with color. Then she pushed forward.

She saw herself sitting in her cabin, the sun setting outside. Purple clouds swirled across her vision as she pressed forward, the density suggesting her immediate future depended on the choices of others. Given time and focus she could have pierced the veil, but that was not her purpose.

The colors gradually dimmed as the present faded. Unique to oracles, farsight allowed her to see into the future. She latched onto her own energy and willed herself forward until the wagon became obscured by purplish clouds.

Every oracle saw the future differently, but to her it was like a great forest. Her own tree stood in the heart of the trees, an ethereal light illuminating the trunk and canopy. Branches split off from the trunk, each representing a singular future, each fork a choice. Purple fog drifted across the forest, obscuring branches, and at times, entire trees.

Each tree was unique, the boughs reflecting infinite possible choices, the branches so dense it was impossible to see the outcome. Some trees were stunted and broken, the consequence of foolish decisions. Others were bright and strong, marking a long and fruitful life.

The forest seemed to go on forever, the trees lost in the fog and darkness, each representing a different person. As those closest to her, the trees of her mother and Devkin were close to hers, while the other oracles and a handful of friends were also nearby.

Her tree was deceptively fluid, with many branches interwoven between the trees. Other limbs appeared and disappeared, representing the impact of outside choices on her own life. Given time she could trace the foreign limbs back to their owners.

Farsight was a magic like any other, and its weakness was a dangerous one. An oracle could see fragments of fate, but could never know that future for certain, and some had fallen prey to their curiosity, losing themselves in the infinite possibilities until their mind and magic had broken.

She paused, surprised to see a wide fork she would reach in just a few hours. She'd examined her future just days ago and seen her course nearly unbroken. Now she would pass through a haze of indecision before facing a decision that would shape the rest of her life. Someone had evidently made a decision that would impact her dramatically. She hesitated, but knew she didn't have time to delve into the moment further. Her jaw tightened and she made the decision that, whatever path she took, she would meet with the other oracles in one week's time.

The tree began to shift, the two branches bending together and briefly merging into one limb, her decision strong enough to alter her future. Although temporary, her choice rippled across the tree, bending and changing the branches into thousands of eventualities. Ignoring

21

them, she followed the now single path forward exactly one week, the limbs a blur of faces and places. Then she pressed her consciousness into the wood and she found herself standing in the Eldress Council chamber of Dawnskeep.

The enormous room sat on the seventh floor of the citadel, and spanned the entire structure. High windows reached the ceiling on all sides, providing an unbroken view of the surrounding city and countryside. Banners of the five oracle bloodlines hung around the room, situated behind the respective seats of the five-sided table. Afternoon light streamed through the windows, swirling motes of dust and falling upon the center of the table, where the oracle's crest marked the surface.

Five elven women sat around a table, and all looked up at her appearance. The event had yet to occur, but with five oracles deciding it would happen, they could use their collective farsight to meet in private. In the present, the council room lay empty. In the future, all six oracles gathered together. Alydian's mother remained in her seat and smiled as Alydian took hers.

"The Eldress Council is convened," Elenyr said.

# Chapter 2: The Eldress Council

Meressa, second on the council, inclined her head to Alydian's mother. "Elenyr, how is your health?"

Elenyr managed a smile, but even through the purple tint to her farsight Alydian could see the drawn look to her mother's features. She was the only oracle actually in Dawnskeep, but was likely lying in bed in the present.

"Deteriorating," Elenyr said. "Yet I defy the grave."

The others laughed lightly, and Alydian joined in. As often as her mother was ill, she still resisted the call of death. Alydian knew she could not last much longer, but it seemed like death itself feared to claim her mother.

Meressa smiled at Elenyr's comment but her expression remained worried. As Second Sister, Meressa served the dwarven kingdom and rarely made the journey to Dawnskeep, but upon Elenyr's passing she would assume the mantle of First Sister. Alydian knew her as haughty and irritable, both attributes Meressa did not reveal to the public.

"Have you discovered the ailment that plagues you?" Ciana, fourth on the council, asked.

"Age claims us all," Elenyr replied with a wry smile. "But my health is not the topic we should be discussing."

Teriah, in the third seat, shook her head. "The loss of one of our own is always worth discussing."

"Perhaps," Elenyr said, and gestured to Alydian. "But my daughter stands ready to take my place. Perhaps what we should be discussing is your lack of heirs . . ."

The other oracles shifted uncomfortably, and Alydian hid a smile. Oracles usually chose a companion and gave birth in their third or fourth century, allowing their daughters time to assume their respective roles. At six hundred years old, Meressa was long past the time to have a child, and her features tightened at the admonishment.

"You didn't have a child until your seventh century," Meressa said.

"Not by choice," Elenyr said with a regretful smile.

Alydian looked to her mother and their eyes met. Four unborn children had died before Alydian had survived, and the losses were still inscribed on Elenyr's face. Then she shook herself and gestured to Raine, the youngest and fifth on the council.

"What is the status of the guilds?"

"No conflicts to report," Raine replied. "I managed to resolve the dispute between the weaver and farmer guilds with the aid of the Verinai. Alydian's suggestions were very insightful." She threw Alydian a smile, which Alydian returned.

"And the northern conflicts?" Elenyr asked Ciana, who was currently in Terros guiding the human kingdom.

"King Talin has agreed to the treaty offered by the rock trolls and is prepared to honor it. The Verinai have offered to enforce it."

Alydian's eyes lingered on Ciana. The woman was shorter than the other oracles, but conveyed a disturbing aura that many commoners noticed. She always had the fewest patrons asking for aid, and those that did speak to her always seemed more fearful than grateful.

"And the rock trolls?" Elenyr asked, shifting to face Meressa.

"They have agreed to King Talin's commands," she said. Then her features tightened in disapproval. "But they continue to deny the Verinai's request to enter their lands."

24

Alydian grinned. "The rock trolls trust their instincts."

Meressa turned on her. Stunning and beautiful, the elf's eyes darkened with irritation. "Do you have something to say, *child*?"

Alydian suppressed a surge of irritation. "The rock trolls have their faults, but they know how to recognize a foe. Perhaps their suspicion has merit."

Teriah snorted in disbelief. "The Verinai have sparked an era of prosperity our world has never seen. Their mages have increased yield of commoner crops, fortified and trained armies, and now advise nearly every king and queen. What possible cause would you have to suspect them?"

Alydian struggled to voice her concerns. "I just don't trust them."

"You may be an oracle," Meressa said. "But you do not yet sit on the council. The only thing we should hear from you is silence."

Alydian flushed. Before she could reply, Raine spoke. "Alydian may not sit on the council, but she *is* an oracle. We should listen to her concerns."

Alydian cast Raine a grateful smile. They were the closest in age, and Alydian considered the woman akin to a sister. Short for an elf, Raine liked to color streaks of red into her hair, setting her apart from the other blondes in the room. The coloring elicited no small measure of disapproval from the council, but Raine refused to change it.

Meressa regarded Raine with a pensive expression. As the youngest member of the council Raine should have been treated as the lowest ranked, but her wisdom and cunning frequently afforded her more leniency than her two centuries required.

"Alydian's unfounded accusations aside," Meressa said, "the Verinai have a valid request." She nodded to Teriah.

"What is the request?" Elenyr asked.

"The Soldier," Teriah said with a scowl. "He and his Defiant are becoming bolder by the week. I have been unable to locate him with my farsight, so Guildmaster Elsin has requested the Eldress Council pressure the kingdoms to assist the Verinai in locating him."

"She wishes us to force the monarchs into offering aid," Elenyr said, a frown creasing her forehead. "Do you understand the thread you wish you pull?"

Alydian smiled at the reference to her mother's use of farsight, a vivid tapestry. An oracle could follow the fate of anyone—if they knew who to follow. The Soldier kept his face and name hidden, even from his own followers, making him impossible to locate. He could be anyone from any kingdom.

"I know it goes against tradition," Teriah said, "but the Soldier needs to be found."

"We cannot grant such a request," Elenyr said. "We have all used our farsight to attempt to locate him, but there is nothing else the council can do."

"We need to act," Teriah said, slapping the table. "He wages war against the Verinai."

Elenyr shook her head. "But they wage war in return. Who's to say who struck the first blow?"

"You sound like you sympathize with him," Teriah said, her features darkening. "He's killed hundreds of Verinai."

"And they've killed hundreds of his Defiant," Elenyr replied. "One does not simply attack a powerful foe without provocation, and the Soldier may have been provoked."

"How can you defend him?" Teriah demanded. "We need to find and execute him."

"To find the man you must know his cause," Elenyr said. "The Verinai call him a bandit but he does not steal or pillage. He is cautious and smart, and has managed to keep thousands of his Defiant from discovery. He could go after anyone but he kills Verinai, so what did they do to incite such anger?"

"What does it matter?" Teriah asked. "He's a bandit and killer."

"Teriah is right," Ciana said. "We need to step in. If we combine our efforts, surely we can locate him and bring him to the noose he has earned. Perhaps we can have the execution here at the Dawnskeep . . .?"

"We are a council that guides, not executes," Elenyr said, her frown deepening. "Discipline for criminals has always been under the direction of the kingdom in which the crime was committed."

"How many will die before we step in?" Teriah demanded. "The Verinai have requested our aid—"

"Which *you* can give," Elenyr said. "You are the presiding oracle over their guild. But not the council."

"People are dying," Teriah said. "Don't you understand that?"

"We cannot grant Elsin's request," Elenyr said. "We teach and lead. We do not govern. When we cross that line the people will never trust us again."

Ciana shook her head. "He has attacked Verinai shipments in every corner of Lumineia. Can we not dispatch a legion of Runeguard to find him? At the very least they might be able to locate a Defiant camp."

"We cannot use the Runeguard like an army," Elenyr said. "They protect us, and only resolve disputes in small detachments—and only at the request of a monarch."

Teriah growled and looked away, and despite their differences Alydian felt a measure of pity for the woman. As the oracle assigned to the Verinai, Teriah spent much of her time in Verisith, the guildhall city of the Verinai. She'd shouldered the brunt of the effort to find the Soldier, and the brunt of the failure.

Alydian's thoughts turned to the mysterious figure. The Soldier and his Defiant had appeared six years ago and attacked Verinai shipments bound for the kingdoms. The Verinai retaliated and many Defiant were killed. The feud quickly escalated into a private war, one that the Soldier was surviving despite the guild's might.

"There's one thing I don't understand," Alydian said. "Why guard his identity so carefully? Any captured Defiant claim that he wears his

27

mask even among his own people. His lieutenants use masks as well, the ones known as Red and Jester."

Raine's eyes widened. "Perhaps he hides his identity from *us*."

Meressa raised an eyebrow. "You think he anticipates our farsight?"

"It could explain how he has evaded us for so long," Teriah said.

"An intelligent adversary," Raine said.

"Your point is valid," Elenyr said. "But hiding his identity so carefully would only protect him so far. He must be making choices on impulse, preventing us from seeing the effects of his actions until it is too late for us to prepare."

"Such preparation indicates knowledge," Alydian said.

Meressa turned on her but instead of anger it was curiosity in her gaze. "Knowledge of what?"

"Us," Alydian said, sweeping her hands at the table. "He protects himself from those who can see the future, suggesting he knows the exact limits of our farsight."

Raine laughed. "Our sister speaks with wisdom."

"She does," Meressa said reluctantly. "It appears the man studied our magic before becoming the Soldier."

Alydian caught her mother's eye, and Elenyr gave a subtle nod of approval. Alydian realized her mother had let her speak more frequently than in the past, permitting her a chance to gain the respect of the others on the council.

"But how did he gain such insight?" Ciana asked. "Much of the common folk consider our magic infallible." Her comment drew a round of laughter from the others.

"Our magic may be powerful," Elenyr said, "but it is far from perfect. We make mistakes as easily as a common man."

28

"We are anything but common," Teriah said. "We are the council that leads the kingdoms—even if they refuse to listen."

"Our place is not to lead," Elenyr said. "It is to guide."

"But the kingdoms of Lumineia are always in conflict," Teriah protested. "If we *did* lead them, we could bring them peace."

Elenyr straightened in her seat, appearing for the first time as the mighty oracle she had been in her youth. "Your proposal to usurp the authority of the kings has been denied before," she said to Teriah. "Another attempt to speak on the topic will be met with retribution."

The authority in her voice echoed into silence. In the ensuing quiet Elenyr looked between the other sisters on the council, her eyes blazing with power.

"We *protect* the people. We do not *control* them."

"As you order, First Sister," Teriah said quietly, but her eyes burned with anger.

Elenyr seemed to wilt, her power draining as quickly as it had appeared. "Now, how do we deal with the Soldier?" she asked.

"You could encourage the Verinai to place specific guards on their shipments," Ciana said. "If Teriah knows them, she can follow their futures."

"A wise strategy," Meressa said. "If the guards are to be attacked, the streams will be obscured with uncertainty, or death."

With a decision made, the conversation shifted to other topics. Alydian would have liked to return the conversation to the Verinai, but after her mother rebuked Teriah she doubted anything could be gained. Resolving to speak to her mother upon arriving in Dawnskeep, she listened to the other oracles as they addressed other matters.

Alydian was not often invited to sit on the council, but the occasion had become more frequent as her mother's health deteriorated. Alydian spoke little, and sought to learn what she could of the customs of the council. By tradition they each held a rank, with the oldest assuming the head of the council as First Sister. For over two centuries Elenyr had guided the council with a kind yet determined hand.

As Second Sister, Meressa was placed in the dwarven realm, only returning to Dawnskeep a few times a year. Haughty and aloof, she was sharp with tongue and wit, and Alydian had learned to avoid her when possible.

Teriah served the Verinai, and spent the bulk of her time with Guildmaster Elsin. Teriah rarely smiled, her blue eyes dark and calculating. Alydian had only seen her lose her calm once, and the result had been frightening.

Ciana served the human kingdoms, but Alydian got the impression she despised the king of Griffin, a man that Alydian found to be smart and amusing. King Talin had shown on numerous occasions a willingness to defy tradition, a fact difficult for Ciana to accept. Alydian was just now returning from a visit to the human capital of Terros, where she'd worked with Ciana for a fortnight, studying the political and commercial facets of the sprawling kingdom.

Alydian glanced at Raine, grateful to have an ally on the council. Alydian relished the opportunities to visit the woman in her home in the elven kingdom. The short elf maintained an air of delightful mystery that made her all the more interesting, and Alydian had shared many nights with her talking until dawn . . .

—a scream shattered the calm, and Alydian snapped to look behind her. Then she realized the sound had not come from the within the council room, it had come from her present time, at her caravan. She missed what Meressa said as the clash of steel reverberated across the campground, and she heard the distinct cry of a mortally wounded man.

"Alydian?" Elenyr asked, her voice rising with concern. "Is something amiss?"

Alydian struggled to maintain her focus as another scream reached her ears, causing her to flinch. It was happening in the present, that much was certain, but the unmistakable sounds of battle could only mean one thing.

"Someone is attacking my guard," Alydian said.

"Let them deal with the bandits," Meressa said with a dismissive wave. "Unless you lack confidence in your appointed captain . . ."

Alydian scowled. "I trust Devkin with my life. He is—"

—her wagon heaved, knocked awry as an explosion rent the earth. She cried out and lost her link to the future, her sight snapping back to reality as the entire wagon keeled onto its side. = She struck the wall, the glass from the window shattering over her arm, slicing into her flesh. She cried out and reached for the wound, clamping a hand over the cut. Then a shadow fell upon her and she looked up, a man appearing in the window that now faced the sky.

His features were hidden behind a silver mask. Smooth and angular, the mask was spotted with blood. Just his eyes were visible, a startling blue that held her bound. Then he drew a black sword and pointed it to her.

"I'm sorry Oracle Alydian," he said. "But I need the council to hear a message."

"What message?" she gasped through the pain.

"That even an oracle can be killed," he said, and dived through the window.

# Chapter 3: The Soldier

The Soldier dropped through the window with surprising agility, and Alydian scrambled off the side of the wagon, diving through the horizontal door. Snatching at the handle, she swung it closed—but the Soldier reached it first. His booted foot came toward the wood and she flinched, her bloody hand slipping on the handle.

The door fell open and the Soldier's foot met empty air. Unprepared for the lack of resistance, the Soldier stumbled through the opening. Alydian retreated, tripping on scattered books and broken glassware as she sought for an escape.

Terror gripped her breath as the Soldier rose to his feet and stalked forward. Helplessness consumed her and she stood frozen against the back door of her wagon, her hand fumbling for a latch that refused to give.

She sought for her magic with her free hand but her fear shackled her power. Panic engulfed her and she clawed at the handle, willing it to give. The Soldier's mask heightened her horror, the spotted blood of its last victims marring the smooth silver. Soon it would be her blood spotting his mask.

"I'm truly sorry," the Soldier said, raising his sword.

Abruptly the window above them shattered and another figure crashed to the floor. Devkin alighted and rose to his feet, his own blade knocking the Soldier's aside. Blood streaked the side of his face and dripped down his tunic.

"The infamous Soldier," Devkin said, his voice laced with fury, "what kind of deviant attacks an oracle?"

"Do not presume to know me," the Soldier growled, and lunged for Devkin.

Devkin parried and struck back, the wagon echoing the whirlwind of steel. Both men danced across the debris with ease, their blades clanging off armor and nicking flesh.

Alydian felt a surge of relief at Devkin's appearance, but saw that her captain was wounded and slowing. The Soldier seemed to recognize the weakness and drove into it, forcing Devkin back. The captain caught the downward swing of the blade and twisted, slamming the Soldier into the wall.

"Go!" he snapped to Alydian. "Into the bedchamber! Bar the door!"

"But—"

"*Go!*" he roared as the Soldier shoved him back.

Alydian scrambled past the duel, nearly losing her head as the Soldier's blade reached for her throat. Devkin knocked it upward and stepped in, leveling a blow into the Soldier's gut with his free hand. The Soldier grunted and retreated to the back door of the wagon.

"I'll have to kill him to get to you," the Soldier said, panting from the exertion of the duel.

Alydian paused in the opening of her bedchamber and looked back, but Devkin snapped to her.

"Go," he said, the quiet earnestness to his voice sufficient to compel her into the wagon's bedchamber.

The two men closed again as she reached out and pulled on the door. The sound of the latch snapping shut inspired relief—and self-loathing. She hesitated, her hand still on the latch as she listened to the duel, one thought worming itself into her skull.

*I'm a coward.*

The realization surprised her. The Soldier's attack made her feel helpless, but she was one of the most powerful mages in Lumineia, an oracle able to use every type of magic. She did not cower in fear. Yet here she was, hiding while another fought for his life.

She gathered her courage and reached to her arm, sending a surge of magic into her flesh, healing the wound. Bits of glass tumbled to her feet as they were pushed outward, and her skin knit together.

She gasped, the pain bringing a sense of clarity. Then she reached for the handle of the door, intent on joining Devkin in the battle. But a growl of pain and a thud caused her hand to stop on the knob. Beyond the barrier someone had fallen, and she knew who had been victorious. Cursing her fear, she retreated from the door as it shuddered, and a muffled voice came through.

"Your man fought valiantly," he said, "You should be proud."

"Murderer," Alydian spat.

The door shuddered again, and the tip of a black sword pierced through. "When I have to be," came the reply.

Fury burned in Alydian's heart, extinguishing her fear and bringing magic to her hands. She bent the light and cast a soldier, one the size of her adversary. The Soldier's next blow smashed a hole in the wood and his masked face peeked through.

"Perhaps there is some fight in you," he said, his tone amused.

"Kill him," Alydian barked.

The light entity darted to the opening and narrowed, slipping through. But the Soldier drove his black sword through the broken door, the blade piercing the light entity as it passed through the gap. The magic shuddered and disintegrated, crumbling to the floor in golden rain.

Dismayed, Alydian realized the Soldier's sword was fashioned of anti-magic, a gnome weapon that extinguished energy in nearly every form. The Soldier struck the door again, causing it to shudder anew.

Alydian forced down the burgeoning sense of panic and scanned the small room, but the room was bereft of weapons. The blankets from the bed lay at her feet, the mattress leaning against what used to be the

34

wall. A painting had broken against the chair, and glassware littered the wall at her feet. Recognizing that if the Soldier entered she would be trapped, she clawed her way upward, using the light brackets as a ladder. Then she stood on the edge of a gilded mirror and scaled to the window the Soldier had used to enter the wagon.

She ascended to the top and turned a circle, horrorstruck at the devastation that littered the hill. Smoke billowed about her, briefly clearing to reveal the battlefield. Great holes gouged the earth and were filled with lingering flames. The other wagons were also overturned, their bases burning, their wire frames extending like ribs on a carcass. Many guards lay strewn about, their bodies twisted in death. Others lay groaning in pain as blood seeped from their wounds.

The Defiant stalked the camp, each bearing anti-magic blades. They sought the Verinai and paused, plunging their swords into Verinai hearts. Frozen in shock, Alydian watched Hornan die under the blade of a masked woman. She pled for her life as the sword pierced her chest, and her shriek pierced the air.

The sound galvanized Alydian to action, and she jumped over the broken window, bounding across the fallen wagon, searching for an avenue of escape. But the Soldier climbed into view before her, using the window Devkin had entered.

Alydian turned and leapt off the wagon, casting a charm that lifted the earth to catch her. Then she sprinted away. The Soldier dropped into her wake and barked orders. Other Defiant converged on her path, with the masked woman mounting a grey stallion and surging after her. She whipped a black sword into view and angled for Alydian, red hair bouncing on her shoulders. Alydian pointed to the steed and sent a desperate plea for help, causing the horse to buck. The woman shouted in dismay as she crashed to the ground.

Others shouted and closed the gap, and Alydian cast her magic on the earth itself, shattering the surface of the hilltop, sending cracks blossoming away from every step. Men cried out as they tripped on the suddenly uneven ground and fell to their knees. The sheer power of the magic surprised her, and the shock cost her.

A third masked figure stepped out from a wagon directly in her path. On instinct she cast a gust charm, the wind striking the wagon with enough force that it rolled over the edge of the hilltop and tumbled down the slope. The man swung his sword, cleaving the gust of wind in two and stepping into the gap. He caught her arm and spun her about, bringing the sword to her throat.

"I hate to mar such a beauty," he said, his tone regretful. "But you are the target."

"Jester!" the Soldier shouted, slowing to a halt. "Stay your hand. It's my burden to bear."

"Do you have a betrothed?" Jester asked Alydian. He released her but kept his blade at her back, forcing her to walk to the Soldier. "Or are you unattached?"

"You're about to kill me and you want to know whom I love?" she demanded.

"That's a no," Jester said, the smile evident in his tone. "So I have a chance."

Shocked by the man's comments, Alydian threw him a sharp look, and behind his mask he winked at her. His ensuing laughter was light and confident, as if he were speaking to a girl in a tavern. But his sword did not waver.

"You're mad," Alydian said.

"But what would an oracle like in a courtship?" he mused. "Fine cooking? Mead? Or do you have richer tastes?"

He was tall and well built, his armor more expensive than the others, tailor made. Dark and bearing mirage charms to alter color and style, the armor marked him as a man used to subterfuge. In addition to the sword, he had a coiled black whip at his side. Then she spotted the slight indentations on the spine of his sword, each notch a kill. Alydian swallowed as she realized the man was a member of the Assassin's Guild, the very guild the Verinai claimed to have hunted into extinction five years ago. Confusion and fear robbed her of voice, and she turned to the other Defiant, silently pleading for aid.

36

The men and women looked away and would not meet her gaze. She'd expected hatred and scorn, but she was unprepared for the regret and pity. Tears welled in her eyes but she clenched her jaw and straightened, coming to a halt. Jester's blade dug into her back but she refused to budge.

"Whatever you came to do," she said, "do it and go. There's no need to harm more of my guard."

The Soldier raised his sword and approached, and out of the corner of Alydian's eye she spotted the masked woman approach as well. She rubbed her backside, cursing Alydian under her breath. Her mask was red and shaped like a skull, while Jester's was a dark version of a jester's hat, with black and deep red instead of yellow and blue. None of the other Defiant wore masks, and members of the assorted races were dressed in makeshift armor and clothing, the only unifying feature a band of silver on their arms.

"Just kill her," the masked woman growled. "The oracles must learn that they are vulnerable."

"I know, Red," the Soldier said, raising his sword and placing it on Alydian's heart.

"What do you intend for my sisters?" Alydian asked, grateful her voice did not tremble.

Through the mask she watched the Soldier's dark blue eyes. "It depends on them," he said. "If they continue to support the Verinai, they will have to be eliminated."

Alydian's eyes widened. "You would destroy the Eldress Council? They have protected the people for three senteniums."

"And now they oppress them," Red said.

"They do not hunt and kill the helpless," Alydian snapped, her voice rigid with heat.

The Soldier regarded her for several moments, and then he stepped close. Alydian steeled herself for the killing blow, but the Soldier's blade did not pierce her flesh. When he spoke it was with curiosity.

37

"Are you truly unaware of what hides on your council?"

Alydian jerked her head. "The council protects the people and leads the kingdoms," she insisted. "It has always been so."

"Not anymore," Jester lamented from behind her.

Alydian clenched her hands. "My mother—"

"—doesn't know," the Soldier said.

"She is the First Sister," Alydian said, shocked by his reply. "She knows all."

"Even the betrayer in your midst?"

"Who?' Alydian demanded.

"I cannot say," he replied. "I can only say that she exists."

Alydian snorted derisively. "You expect me to believe such a foolish tale?"

Red groaned and swished her sword. "You really are an ignorant—
"

"Enough," the Soldier said, his blue eyes sharp behind the mask. For several moments he stared at Alydian. "Your council may be honorable, but one of your sisters is not."

"I do not believe you."

The Soldier shrugged. "Belief cannot alter truth."

Confused and uncertain, Alydian remained silent, and abruptly the Soldier lowered his sword. Red growled at the motion.

"We came to deliver a message," she said.

"And so we have," the Soldier said.

Red stepped forward, raising her sword. "If you lack the courage . .
."

"No," the Soldier said, unperturbed. "Impulse, not decision."

Red lowered her sword with a growl. "Impulse, not decision."

Jester repeated the mantra, and the rest of the Defiant joined him. Alydian realized that was how the man had evaded capture for so long, making decisions on impulse to prevent an oracle from foreseeing an attack. Then Jester lowered his sword and stepped around her.

"It appears the fortunes smile upon us," he said, inclining his head to her. "And the next time we meet, I'll come to kiss rather than kill."

"I'm not going to kiss an assassin," she said, aghast.

"That's what they all say," he said.

Laughing, he began barking orders for the other Defiant to retrieve their dead and wounded. Red looked at Alydian a final time before joining him. As the bandits departed the Soldier continued to stare at Alydian.

"I wonder, young oracle," he mused, "when you discover the truth, will you join them . . . or will you join me?"

"I will *never* join you," she said.

"It must be hard to see the war from your gilded fortress," he said coldly.

"You are not at war," she said.

"One with so much sight should not be so blind." He stepped close to her. "And when you see the truth, you will have to pick a side."

"I'm not going to side with you," she spat the words at him.

He turned and strode away, casting over his shoulder, "You could pursue us, but I'd suggest you care for your wounded."

The Soldier joined the Defiant and mounted a steed, leaving Alydian and the destroyed hilltop. Her mind burning with confusion, she darted to the nearest wounded soldier and knit his wounds. Moving between the others, she healed them as quickly as she could. She heard a heavy footfall and fear exploded in her heart as she spun to face the threat.

"I thought you'd be dead," Devkin growled, his voice hoarse.

"Devkin!" she cried.

Alydian leapt to him, casting her magic to close the gash in his side. He sighed in relief and his eyes met hers. Tears wet her cheeks as she gently closed his wounds, and she was ashamed to realize her hands were shaking.

"I thought he killed you," she said.

"It takes more than one soldier to kill me." His features were white but he managed a smile. "Why did he spare you?"

Alydian looked to where the Soldier had disappeared, but there was no trace of him or his followers. She wanted to answer but found she couldn't. The Soldier had come to kill her, but decided to spare her life. As relieved as she was, she couldn't fathom why.

Or what he now intended.

# Chapter 4: The Soldier's Refuge

Raiden led the Defiant into the gulley to where they had stashed their horses in a nearby stand of trees. He helped load the wounded and dead onto spare mounts, waiting just long enough for their two healers to ensure no more joined the grave. Then he mounted his grey roan and pulled on the reins to lead them north, back onto the road. They had attacked the oracle close to Dawnskeep, and the Runeguard would mount a pursuit within hours.

"Why did you spare her?" Red demanded.

Jester took his place on Raiden's opposite flank. "She's beautiful."

Red spat on the ground. "Not everyone makes decisions based on the beauty of their targets."

"Says the woman without love," Jester said.

Raiden glanced between them, considering his answer. They had been his allies for years, and although they were frequently at odds, he trusted them completely. They were the only ones that had seen his face and knew his name, even among the Defiant. His caution had kept them alive, and delayed the Eldress Council from finding them. Still, he knew it was only a matter of time until the Verinai or the oracles managed to track them down.

"We cannot last as we have," Raiden replied. "In time they will locate and destroy us, and all of the Defiant."

"Killing the oracle would have shown them they were vulnerable," Red said.

"And incited them to retaliate," Raiden replied.

"You said that killing Alydian would force the Verinai to play their hand," Red argued.

"Perhaps," Raiden said. "But it was a desperate idea."

"Allowing her to live could be just as dangerous," Jester asked. "Just think of how powerful our children will be."

Red snorted in disbelief and looked away. They came to a crossroads and Raiden chose a random fork in the road. His army followed without question, knowing that impulse decisions kept the oracles from watching their future.

Red scowled. "If she marked us with her magesight, she will be able to follow us with her farsight."

"A risk, I know," Raiden said. "But she was terrified and scrambling. I doubt she thought to do so."

"A gamble," Jester mused. "But so was sparing her. The question is, what do we have to gain?"

"An ally," Raiden said.

Red swiveled in her saddle to stare at him, her eyes furious behind her mask. "You can't possibly think she would help us."

"I'm not sure," Raiden said, thinking of the force to Alydian's gaze. "I don't think she knows what the rogue mage is doing, and I suspect she will not approve. Besides, she met Jester, so we know she's in love."

Jester laughed lightly. "True, but I doubt she'd betray another oracle."

"How long until the oracles find us?" Raiden countered. "We've been lucky more times than I can count, and luck is not a friend I wish to trust."

"We will survive," Red insisted. "You've taught us how to avoid their magic."

"We need more support," he replied. "And an oracle on the council would be the highest kind."

"She's not on the council yet," Jester said.

"She will be when her mother dies," Raiden said.

Jester grunted. "You know, I've never heard of an oracle being sick."

Raiden nodded. "That's because between the five of them, they can heal almost anything . . ." His voice caught as a thought crossed his mind. Apparently thinking the same thing, Red laughed slyly.

"You think the betrayer is killing Elenyr?"

"A treasonous suggestion," Jester said, grinning. "How devious."

"I'm a treasonous bandit," Red said, the smile evident in her voice. "It's the only kind of suggestion I make."

His lieutenants spoke as if they didn't believe it, but as Raiden pondered the idea he found it plausible. *Elenyr* was the First Sister, and the council could not act without her express approval—which she'd refused to give on numerous occasions. If one of the oracles thought Alydian would be more malleable, perhaps they'd resorted to poison.

It was a bold move, one that few would suspect. If successful, it would allow the betrayer to assume leadership and openly ally with the guild of Verinai, sealing their control over the kingdoms of Lumineia.

A smile spread on his face as he considered Alydian's response to that. He'd let her go because he's seen fire in her soul. If she discovered the others had poisoned her mother, that fire would burn hot and long. She may not ally with the Soldier, but she would certainly go against the council. Her beauty and youth would draw many to her cause, forcing a civil war that just might bring the Verinai to their knees . . .

He reined in the thought before it could take root. As much as he would love to plan, making decisions would clarify his future, making it all the easier for the oracles to find him. Still, he was grateful he hadn't killed Alydian. Even if it was necessary, it would have been a loathsome task.

"We need to get off the road," he said, and pulled on the reins, leading his steed down a rocky slope.

A permanent camp would be too risky, so they maintained scores of hideouts throughout Lumineia. Before he'd become the Soldier, Raiden had spent two years preparing the locations, and only he knew them all.

He descended the slope and reached a small mine hidden behind a curve of rock. The opening was invisible from the road, while the slope descended to a swamp on the border of Blue Lake. The mine had been abandoned a decade ago until Raiden had purchased the rights under a different persona.

"We're only half a day's ride from where we attacked the oracle," one of his captains said, dismounted and striding to Raiden. "Are you certain that's wise?"

"I don't want to lose any more wounded," Raiden said. "Take them below and cleanse the area of blood. Then start work on the side vein. If a patrol stops you, claim you saw a group of riders galloping north."

The man grinned and began issuing orders to the remaining men and women of the Defiant. Raiden helped a wounded man out of the saddle but the man pushed him away with a growl. Clenching his shoulder, he pointed to the bog.

"We can turn them aside, but not with you here," he said. "Go, before you are spotted."

His words brought a chorus of agreement, and the dwarf that controlled the mine added his voice. "Go, ye blasted soldier."

Raiden relented with a nod. "As you order. Be well, Pathoran."

The surly smith nodded and turned away, helping the wounded man to the mine's opening. Raiden watched him go with regret in his heart. Every member of his small army had been chosen and solicited because of what they had endured. Pathoran had been a smith in western Griffin until a trio of Verinai students had come through. Pathoran had refused to house them for free, and that night his forge and home had burned to the ground.

44

Pathoran had been out on a delivery, and returned to find the smoking husk of his shop. He'd stayed to forge a weapon and then sought the Soldier. Raiden had read the anger in his eyes and allowed him to join the Defiant, giving him the chance for justice.

"Come," Red said. "The others know what to do."

Raiden stepped to the slope and picked his way over the rocks. "I hate to leave them behind."

"I as well," she said, falling into step behind him. "But if we stay, we risk all their lives."

Jester grunted in agreement and took up the rear, and the trio worked their way to the base of the escarpment. When they reached the bog they paused within the darkness and drank from their water skins, filling them from a stream nearby. As they were about to press on, a distant sound compelled them into the shadows.

A patrol of riders burst into view around a bend in the road. They galloped north, pausing at the turn that led to the mine. The leader dropped from his trembling steed and advanced, casting a trio of entities.

Rock rose and ground together, shaping into a hulking soldier. Air swirled and formed the second, while light bent to form the third. The trio stomped to the mine and shoved their way inside. Raiden clenched his fists as he watched the Verinai and his patrol shove the Defiant about, demanding answers. Pathoran folded his arms and stood his ground.

Soldiers and entities disappeared into the mine as the Verinai captain shouted at the dwarf. The muffled sounds of snapping wood and cries of alarm echoed down to Raiden, and he had to reach out to place a hand on Red's trembling shoulder. A moment later the three entities exited and reported to the Verinai masters.

Spitting at the dwarf's feet, the Verinai turned and strode away, remounting his horse and galloping north. Raiden breathed a sigh of relief as the patrol left the mine, and felt a rush of gratitude to Pathoran. If he had not insisted they depart, they would have been spotted in the open.

45

"Let's get moving," Jester said. "It's getting dark and we have a few miles to go."

Jester reached up and removed his mask, revealing a handsome face and a neatly trimmed goatee. A pair of scars lined his nose and cheek, while others were visible on his neck. Rather than detract from his looks, they added an aura of danger to him that made him more attractive. Trained by the legendary Assassin's Guild, Jester had joined the Soldier when the guild had been extinguished under Verinai orders. He was the sole person to ever find Raiden on his own.

Red breathed a sigh of relief as she removed her own mask. She wiped the sweat from her face and smiled, revealing clean teeth and full lips. The woman had been a soldier's wife in northern Griffin until the Verinai ordered her husband's patrol to attack a group of giants. Their force had been inadequate, and Red's husband had been killed. She'd wielded a plow for two years until the Soldier had found her. She'd thrown herself into training with a vengeance, and now her skill rivaled Jester's.

Raiden removed his own mask as well, grateful to release the burden of his persona. Then he stepped into the bog and disappeared. They worked their way past fallen branches and dense brush. Oppressive and dank, the bog was home to alligators, moordraugs, and reavers. Raiden kept a wary eye on the darkness, listening over the sound of their boots splashing through muck.

After an hour they reached a stretch of water and circled it until they came to a gnarled oak rising on the bank. Raiden reached into a pouch and ignited a light orb. Its dim light reflected white off the black water, and he used it to spot an innocuous tree half-submerged in the mud. Striding past it, he stepped onto the water.

His boots plunged into the lake—but came to a stop on a stone pathway. Hidden just inches out of sight, the path provided a secret entrance into the small lake. Striding forward, he spotted the turns and wound his way through the trees rising from the murky water.

Frogs croaked nearby, while a faint splash heralded a prowling alligator. The reavers that stalked the bog did not care for the lake, but he kept a wary ear focused on the sounds of their passing.

46

In the gloom ahead, a large island gradually coalesced into shape, revealing trees and branches rising into the fog. Raiden stepped off the path and ascended onto the dry island. In the midst of the bog, the island and the trees that surrounded it formed a hidden refuge. Raiden's brother had created the path and the refuge before he'd died, and Raiden had added threads of anti-magic into the branches above, shielding them against their adversaries. Surrounded by swamp and mud it reeked of rot, and insects were abundant.

"Welcome home," Red said dryly.

# Chapter 5: A New Target

A small camp lay nestled beneath the trees. A rough-hewn weapons rack sat against one trunk, while three hammocks hung from the larger branches. Raiden strode to the wellspring that drew clean water from beneath the swamp and washed his face. He watched his reflection until the water stilled.

The elf that looked back at him was tall and lean, but a perpetual shadow lingered in his gaze. A thin scar split his lip, the remnant of a hard lesson when he'd joined the elven army. He'd dyed his hair to make his appearance more human, and the brown locks were cut short.

"You know you're handsome," Red said with an amused snort. "Don't be so possessive with the drink."

He allowed himself to be shoved away, unwilling to admit why he watched his reflection. Prior to his becoming the Soldier his eyes had been bright and clear. Now the legacy of Verinai deaths had tinged his gaze, and he wondered if they would ever return to their previous clarity.

"What now?" Jester said, stooping to ignite a small fire at the center of the space.

Raiden removed his pack but retained his weapons. Placing his pack on the rack by his hammock, he knelt and removed food for an evening meal. Then he sank into a seat beside the fire.

Content to let him consider the question, the assassin worked the fire until a spark of flame illuminated the night. Raiden absently extinguished the light orb and returned it to his pocket as Red sat on a nearby log, her red hair visible in the flickering light.

Raiden stared into the flames, consider the various possibilities. He'd always been gifted with strategy, and it took effort not to decide on any of them. They had been raiding Verinai shipments and striking Verinai soldiers for years, but today he sensed a shift in the tide, as if their war was about to escalate.

"Before we attacked Alydian," Red said, "Pathoran mentioned a special shipment bound for the human king. Said it would be departing Margauth in nine days' time."

"What if his informant is wrong?" Jester said. "He has been before."

"It was hard enough to recruit a low level Verinai," Raiden said, leaning back against the tree. "But he's the only source we have. What did Pathoran know about the shipment's contents?"

"Nothing," Red said.

Raiden raised an eyebrow. Most Verinai shipments were standard exports: special clothing, magic-grown food, and enchanted weaponry. The anti-magic blades they wielded had come from a shipment the Soldier had attacked in their first year. For the Verinai to hide the contents of a shipment indicated it was abnormal, and perhaps something they should seek.

"It would be well guarded," Raiden said.

"Not more than we can handle," Jester said. "They may have magic, but they think little of the Defiant." He pulled his whip free and snapped it upward, catching a fly as it alighted on a tree.

"Our advantage will not endure," Raiden said. "They are many and we are few. Until now the kingdoms choose to remain neutral in our little war."

"Aye," Jester said. "But their loyalties might change when they hear we attacked an oracle."

"We didn't kill her," Red said sullenly.

Jester grinned. "You're just mad she dumped you on your backside."

49

Red scowled and rubbed her hindquarters. "I didn't expect her to talk to my horse."

"We cannot underestimate the oracles," Raiden said. "They may be few, but they are more powerful than the Verinai."

Red sniffed and looked away. "*We* could have killed her."

Raiden smiled at that. "Even a fool can kill a king."

Jester, who'd been chewing on a wedge of cheese, guffawed at the reference to his persona. Bits of cheese scattered into the fire as he laughed. Raiden and Red exchanged an amused look before Red conceded the point.

"She's stronger than she looks."

"And will become stronger," Raiden said. "Once she has more training."

"The oracles do not train their magics until their second century," Red said, stabbing a finger at him. "You taught us that."

"She cracked the hilltop," Jester said, picking cheese from his goatee. "She's a powerful one, make no mistake."

"Then we should have killed her when we had the chance," Red argued. "If she joins the Verinai—or worse—the rogue council member, we won't get another chance."

Raiden listened to the two of them argue, wondering who was right. When Alydian did begin her formal training she would learn to harness every facet of her magic. Then she would be unstoppable, and there were already five powerful oracles to deal with—four he corrected. As strong as Elenyr once was, her declining health made her less of a threat.

While his lieutenants argued, Raiden retreated to his hammock and sank into it. Through the canopy, he spotted a sliver moon and watched its dull light until it disappeared behind a cloud. He fell asleep wondering if Alydian already had a betrothed.

He slept lightly, and woke when a reaver coughed nearby. He doubted the beast could breach the enchantments of the refuge, but he listened until he was certain it had moved on. He'd spotted the tracks of a mind reaver, and suspected one had taken up refuge in the bog. Without eyes or nose, the beast was as sentient as any man. It latched onto the minds of its prey and could track them across continents. He wished he could send one after the Verinai guildmaster, Elsin.

When he woke again it was midday, with sunlight streaming through the branches. He rose and prepared a morning meal, the scent of grilled venison dragging his lieutenants from their hammocks. Jester groaned and stretched, joining him to stoke the fire.

"Where do we strike today?" he rumbled.

"We go east," Raiden said.

It was a vague answer, but one that Red accepted with a grunt of agreement. They both knew that deciding to attack the mysterious Verinai shipment would allow the oracles time to foresee it. But simply deciding to travel east would keep them ignorant until it was too late.

"Impulse, not decision," Jester said with a yawn.

They packed for the journey and departed the refuge, using the hidden bridge to escape the bog. Threading their way through the uncertain terrain, they approached the edge of the swamp several miles from where they had entered. Raiden slowed as the trees brightened, and came to a halt at the threshold of light.

Beyond the swamp the ground sloped upward, the hills covered in scattered trees. The strip of earth connected the eastern and western provinces of Griffin. The two provinces dominated the southern and eastern sides of Blue Lake, an enormous inland sea that reached all the way to the dwarven kingdom on the northwest.

Raiden's gaze was drawn to the sprawling city on a distant hill, the mighty tower rising above the trees. Many regarded the Dawnskeep as the capital of Lumineia. The small city that surrounded the fortress was governed by the Eldress Council, and the land did not belong to any kingdom. At the heart of the city the oracle's tower pierced the heavens, its battlements obscured by low hanging clouds.

"So much beauty," Red said, "yet it hides so much filth."

"Not all mages are vile," Raiden said, scanning the road that bordered the bog, wondering where a Verinai patrol would hide. "Do not forget how many single talent mages have joined the Defiant."

As if reading his thoughts, Jester said, "If Alydian marked us, they could be waiting for us on the road."

Raiden stepped out of the trees and strode to the road. When no soldiers appeared, Jester and Red joined him. They turned northeast and Red threw him a curious look.

"How did you know she did not mark us?"

"A guess," Raiden replied, "but a good one. Oracles need time to examine the unique energy within a person, and we didn't really give her time to do so."

"Are you attracted to her?" Red asked, her tone suspicious.

"Of course not," Raiden said, but he recalled her beauty and a smile spread on his lips.

Jester smiled slyly. "Our fearless leader favors a foe. How intriguing."

Raiden forced his emotions away and sidestepped the comment. "We need to stay focused. The oracles are a constant threat."

"Are you ever going to tell us how you know so much about them?" Red asked.

"I don't tell tales of the women I've known," Raiden said, eliciting a laugh from Jester.

Dressed like common folk, with Raiden also donning the persona of a human, few spared them a glance as they worked their way east. The road had been built of fine stone, and connected the two human kingdoms with Dawnskeep. Elves were in abundance, with many returning to their homeland. The elven forest of Orláknia surrounded Dawnskeep and extended into patches of trees all the way to the bog they called home. The fair race represented a large portion of the population in the sovereign city.

Elven, human, and Verinai patrols passed them on the road, some in a hurry. Some of the Verinai rode mounts of light or fire, the riders expressions haughty as they galloped by. Red managed to control her tongue until they had departed.

Merchant caravans dominated the road. Stone and coal from the newly discovered mines in southeastern Griffin were piled onto heavily laden wagons, while cloth and food made their way out of Griffin's western province to supply the eastern province. The people smiled and chatted, and Raiden overheard several whispering tales of the Soldier. Raiden drifted closer to make out one conversation.

". . . attacked an oracle," a man on horseback said to a merchant on a wagon.

The woman shook her head. "I thought he was on our side, punishing the Verinai and all."

The man too seemed discouraged. "Perhaps he merely sought her Verinai guards."

"The Verinai have been nothing but generous," another woman insisted. "Without them we'd never have survived the last winter."

Raiden slowed, allowing the wagon and rider to advance ahead of them. When they were gone Jester spoke in an undertone.

"Many of the people still trust the Verinai."

"How can they not?" Raiden replied. "They only see the hand providing food and shelter, not the one taking freedom and choice."

"And many still believe they are kin to the oracles," Jester said, "and the council is a symbol of benevolence and integrity in spite of the rogue mage."

Red snorted and stabbed a finger at Dawnskeep. "Yet their city is filled with Verinai and the wealthy."

53

"It was not always so," Jester argued. "My father told many tales of the Eldress Council, especially Elenyr. He even saw her once when she cast her phoenix charm."

"Power always corrupts," Red said. "And more power becomes more corruption."

Raiden let them argue, but stopped them before they became too heated. Red fell to seething. They followed the southern road until it reached a crossroads. One branch headed south to where Raiden had attacked Alydian and another went north, passing the mine the Defiant used as a temporary refuge. Raiden took the east path, a much smaller trail that wound between increasingly dense stands of trees. Several miles after departing the road they passed a sign indicating Margauth was six days east.

The traffic on the roadway declined sharply, with only woodsmen and locals using the road. Trappers passed them on their way to Griffin, their packs laden with furs to sell. Raiden nodded blandly but kept his distance, and the other travelers did as well. Foregoing the inns, they slept in the trees.

The road continued to narrow as it climbed into the mountains, until they finally attained a pass and the end of the road came into view. Breathing hard from the ascent, they paused to fill their water skins from a brook making its way into the valley.

"That's the road to Margauth," Jester said.

Raiden followed his gaze across the valley to where the road climbed into the mountains, disappearing into a pass. Margauth was the most distant of the Verinai strongholds, and little was known about the mysterious fortress. Jester had once been contracted to kill a Verinai in its walls, and was one of the few non-Verinai to see the interior.

A wall barred passage to Margauth, and Verinai patrolled the battlements. Outside the barrier, the road forked north and south. The road north was the shortest route from Margauth to Terros while the road south connected past the Lone Vale to Verisith, the Verinai capital.

"What's that?" Red asked.

Raiden peered through the trees at the base of the Margauth road, and just managed to make out a small wagon starting its journey south. Usually Verinai shipments employed two score guards and multiple wagons, yet this one appeared to have a handful of soldiers to protect a single cart.

"That's suspiciously unguarded," Jester said.

"But it's moving faster than a larger caravan," Red said, looking to Raiden. "Asenith and his command are a few days north of here."

"I doubt we have time to gather any Defiant," Jester said. "We'd have to attack it ourselves."

Raiden watched the cart until a stand of trees blocked it from view. He agreed with Jester, but the cart's coloring and lack of guards suggested the Verinai did not want to call attention to it. If they went north for reinforcements they might not make it back in time. If they went south, they would have to face the wagon's guards on their own. Making his decision, Raiden tapped the mask hidden in his pack.

"I think we journey south."

# Chapter 6: An Oracle's Intrigue

For the first time in years, Alydian approached Dawnskeep on a horse instead of inside a lavish wagon. Any other time she would have been relieved at the sense of freedom but, surrounded by wounded soldiers, it was hard to feel anything but worry.

Her gaze lifted to the oracle's tower as they drew close. Fashioned of dwarven stone and crystal, the tower seemed to pierce the heavens. Windows and balconies clung to its surface, and banners of the Eldress Council displayed their crest, a circle bound by a concave triangle on a backdrop of blue.

A circular wall surrounded the council tower. Lining the exterior, five smaller turrets were home to the five oracle bloodlines. As daughter to the lineage of Elsheeria, Alydian resided in the northernmost tower with her mother. The oracles' homes boasted crystalline walls and finely hewn stone. The peak of Dawnskeep absorbed the daily sun, turning the tower into a beacon that lasted throughout the night—a lighthouse to the kingdoms of Lumineia.

The fortress had been built shortly after the Dawn of Magic and a city had blossomed around its walls. Merchants and craftsmen gathered from throughout the five kingdoms to speak with an oracle, and every guild maintained a hall in the city. Dominated by inns, taverns, and shops, the city of Horizon catered to the crowds that gathered to seek an oracle's guidance. Another, smaller wall surrounded the city.

Alydian had always found the sight of the Horizon and Dawnskeep inspiring, but her conversation with the Soldier tainted the view. Unable to dispel her doubt, she lowered her eyes to the city gate. An entire company of soldiers met them at the portal, their Verinai captain riding to Devkin. Alydian recognized him as Commander Othan, a human Verinai in the Runeguard.

"Captain Devkin," he said, "High Oracle Elenyr commanded us to mobilize, and your rider informed us of the attack. Another company has been dispatched to find the Defiant." He signaled his men to tend to the wounded. "High Captain Peranin would like to speak to you about how you let this happen."

Devkin bristled at the veiled accusation, but he inclined his head. "When I have dispatched my duties with Oracle Alydian, I shall answer the summons."

"I have been ordered to assume command of the oracle's guard," Commander Othan replied.

Devkin closed the gap in two strides, coming so close to the Verinai that Othan retreated a step, magic sparking at his fingertips.

"*I* guard Alydian," Devkin growled. "Not even High Oracle Elenyr can remove me from my post without Alydian's express approval."

Othan sneered. "I'm certain that following your failure, she will be more than happy to—"

"Captain Devkin stays with her," a voice called.

Othan's eyes widened in surprise, and he turned to find Oracle Raine striding to join them. "But Oracle, if a Verinai had protected her—"

"The Soldier would have killed them," Raine replied curtly. "Captain Devkin stays with Alydian."

He scowled but retreated. "As you order, Oracle."

When he'd moved to assist the other wounded, Alydian dismounted and stepped to Raine, who pulled her into an embrace. Alydian clung to the sense of safety the woman inspired. When they parted Raine had tears in her eyes.

"When the link was severed, I feared the worst."

Alydian swallowed as she recalled the Soldier's blade. "I'm afraid I did not acquit myself well."

"You're still standing," Raine said, smiling in encouragement. "For that I'm grateful."

"You must have ridden hard to get here before I did," Alydian said.

"Through the night," Raine replied. "It was not until I arrived in Horizon that I learned you had survived. Is it true your attacker was the Soldier?"

"It is," she said.

Raine's features darkened. "I will kill him myself for what he has done."

Alydian grinned at the fierce woman. "I'm sure you will."

"I will care for your guards," Raine said. "Your mother wishes to speak with you."

"Thank you, Raine."

She smiled. "What are sisters for?" They embraced again, and then Raine moved to assist the other wounded soldiers. She moved among them with a smile, healing with a touch.

Alydian swallowed the sudden knot of emotion. Although council members called each other sister, Raine was the only one Alydian thought deserved the title. When Elenyr's health had deteriorated, it was Raine who had shouldered the weight of instruction, and had taught Alydian for her over two decades. Many nights they'd laughed late into the night, exploring the mischief their magic could do. Her presence after the attack was an unexpected boon.

Devkin stepped to Alydian's side and lowered his voice. "I would have understood if you wished to relieve me of my command."

"No one could have stopped the Soldier," she replied.

"Perhaps," he said. "Nevertheless, I'm grateful for your continued faith."

"I cannot stop an inquisition into the attack," she warned. "High Captain Peranin will want to assign blame."

"They were prepared for us," Devkin said, anger and guilt tightening his face. "They buried themselves into the earth so we could not see them, and used anti-magic weaponry to shield themselves from magesight." He finally turned to face her. "They came to kill you."

"Yet they did not," she said.

"But they could have," he insisted. "I will make certain they do not get another opportunity."

She chuckled wryly. "Of that, I have no doubt. Take me home and you can answer his summons."

"As you order," he replied.

He remounted his horse and signaled to four of his surviving command. Although injured, they obeyed without question and surrounded Alydian as she rode through the gate into Horizon. The streets were wide and open, all pointing to Dawnskeep at the heart of the city. Onlookers had evidently heard of the attack and lined the street, craning their necks to get a look.

Shouts and calls surrounded Alydian, and she smiled and raised a hand to them, making it clear she had survived. The Verinai among them cast baleful glares at Devkin, but the grizzled soldier ignored them, keeping his focus on potential threats.

As Alydian endured the inspection by the worried citizens, she found her thoughts drawn to her attackers. They had been dressed in homespun clothing and makeshift armor, while the citizens of Horizon wore expensive apparel crafted by skilled artisans and enchanted by Verinai. Colors were vibrant and varied, a bright aura of wealth that shimmered in the afternoon light.

Her eyes swept the crowd but she didn't spot anyone that resembled the poor that had been present in Terros. The human capital had been filled with beggars on the streets, the sight repeated in the settlements they had passed on their journey. The contrast was disturbing, and she wondered how she'd never noticed it before.

They passed the Verinai guildhall, a gilded complex built more by magic than by hand. A small fortress in its own right, the guildhall encompassed two entire city blocks, and boasted curved walkways that connected the two wings, allowing the Verinai private passage between the two sides of the hall.

Passing under the Verinai arch, she rode to Dawnskeep and entered the Oracle's Gate. Once inside the courtyard, she finally dropped her smile and reigned in her mount. Then she wearily dismounted, wincing at the soreness in her body. Noticing her halting motion, Devkin grinned.

"Your pain will fade," he said, his voice pitched so only she would hear.

"Does every battle hurt this much?"

His grin widened. "Less when you are trained," he said. "You exerted your body to its limit, and it likes to protest."

*Training.*

He'd said it to be comforting, but the word stuck in her mind, a cold reminder that if she had been trained, she could have protected herself, and her guard would not have been killed. All at once the feeling of helplessness returned, filling her body, catching in her lungs. She forced herself to breathe through the panic and pretended to fiddle with the reins of her horse. A hand settled on her shoulder and she looked up to find her mother at her side.

"My dear," Elenyr said softly. "You are safe now."

Tall and statuesque, Elenyr was the pinnacle of grace. She stood calm and serene, giving no evidence that her legs were probably trembling from the effort. Her smile was gentle, her bright elven eyes laden with concern and relief.

Alydian wanted to tell her mother not to worry, that she should not be out of her quarters, but Alydian felt like a child. She struggled with the urge to bury her face against her mother's shoulder. Seeming to understand her reluctance to express herself publicly, Elenyr motioned to her own captain, an elven Verinai named Weldina.

Alydian looked back at Devkin and then followed her mother to the Elsheeria Tower. Upon entering, Elenyr motioned Weldina to remain

60

outside and stepped onto the dwarven ascender with just Alydian. In a whisper of machinery, the small room carried them up into the tower.

"Tears will not be met with disapproval," Elenyr murmured.

"I'm eighty-three years old," Alydian said with a strained laugh. "I'm hardly a child."

"Yet you feel the fear of one."

Alydian was not surprised that her mother saw through her forced demeanor, but she was unwilling to cry like a frightened babe. She stared at the sliding wall of the ascender, her hands clenching into fists.

"He meant to kill me," she said. "And even with all my magic, I could not act beyond my fear."

"Magic or not, one is always bound by fear," Elenyr said.

"But I was *helpless*," Alydian said, her voice harsh as hot tears burned her eyes.

Elenyr touched the ascender controls, bringing them to a halt. Then she wrapped her arms around Alydian and held her. The embrace was frail yet shattered Alydian's reserve, and the tears came freely.

"I felt the sword on my chest," Alydian whispered. "I saw my end."

"I know," Elenyr replied.

"I've never been so terrified."

"Nor have I."

Alydian pulled away and met her mother's gaze, seeing her mother's anguish for the first time. It was not the pain of unknowing, but rather the agony of bearing witness. Alydian wiped at her cheeks.

"You saw?"

"I was using my farsight when the Soldier attacked you," she said. "I felt a tug and followed the thread, and saw the Soldier lean in for the kill . . ."

61

Her voice faltered, and tears appeared in Elenyr's eyes. She blinked them away and straightened, touching the controls on the ascender once again. Alydian managed to regain her composure, and by the time the doors glided open they were both composed. Passing the ascender guards in their white and blue armor, they entered Elenyr's private quarters, contained on the highest level of the tower.

The room was wide and open, with many windows around the circular chamber. A private library extended up the center to a second level, the shelves filled with books on magic and history. Alydian nodded to Weldina and the woman remained at the door, allowing Alydian to help her mother through the door into private bedchamber located at the northern side of the tower.

Alydian helped her mother remove the flowing dress and eased her back into the bed. Light filtered through the aquaglass windows to cascade onto her face, highlighting the contrast between her graying hair and the white sheets. Elenyr finally relaxed, her carefully controlled features smoothing with relief. Then she managed a smile and raised a trembling hand, which Alydian grasped.

"My precious daughter," she said. "Do you want to know what I see when I look upon you with my magesight?"

Alydian raised an eyebrow. When oracles looked upon a person with their magesight they could see emotions, character, and even talents. Doing so also marked the individual so the oracle could follow them in the future, and for Alydian it meant their tree became visible in her farsight. But such an inspection was considered highly personal and not permitted for oracles to perform unless requested.

"When did you look?"

Elenyr flashed a surprisingly sly smile. "On you? Many times."

"But it is not permitted," Alydian said, shocked by her mother's answer.

Elenyr shrugged. "I don't obey every rule."

Alydian laughed. "What do you see?" she asked.

"Power and integrity," Elenyr said. "In time, I suspect you will surpass us all."

"It didn't help me when the Soldier came," Alydian said.

"Have you forgotten the Mage's Mantra?"

"Mother," Alydian said in exasperation, "repeating it a thousand times does not teach me greater magic."

"It is the foundation of all," Elenyr said, grasping her hand. "The stronger the base, the greater the height of skill. Speak it now."

Alydian wanted to protest but could not refuse. "Magic is power, the body the conduit. Might is attained by knowledge and discipline, but cannot surpass honor or will."

Alydian had spoken the lines since birth yet still her mother forced her to recite them. Elenyr seemed to think there were secrets to be had from studying it, even though it was only a few words. When she finished, Elenyr offered a small smile.

"Do not sound so petulant. The knowledge you seek will come in due time."

"Does that mean you will permit me to begin my training?"

Elenyr's smile faded. "If it were my decision, I would have allowed you to train decades ago, but I cannot publicly defy council tradition."

Alydian looked away in disappointment. "I understand," she said.

"I trust you will make the right decision," Elenyr said, patting her hand.

Recognizing the dismissal, Alydian leaned down and kissed her mother on the forehead. "Sleep well, mother, I'll visit you this evening."

Elenyr's eyes fluttered and she nodded before sleep claimed her. Alydian rose and stepped to the door, looking back at her slumbering mother before departing the room. A twinge of fear spiked in her heart and she wondered what she would do when her mother died. She passed

Weldina on her way back to the ascender. Then Alydian absently pressed the rune and descended to her own quarters.

The ascender was positioned on the exterior of the turret, and many of the walls were glass to allow a view of Dawnskeep. She stared at the tower without seeing it, struggling to contain her disappointment. After what had happened, she'd thought her mother would allow her to begin her practical training early. Her lips tightened as she recalled her mother's answer.

*I cannot publicly defy council tradition . . .*

Alydian frowned, wondering why Elenyr had defined her support as public. What other way could her mother support her training . . .

Alydian's eyes widened. Was it possible? Then she recalled the spark of amusement in her mother's gaze when she'd said, *I trust you will make the right decision.* Alydian laughed wryly, grateful for her mother's cunning.

"Thanks for the advice, mother," she said to the empty ascender. "But how do I train in private?"

# Chapter 7: A Daring Plan

Devkin stared at her, and then shook his head. "You are not permitted to start your training until your first century."

"Not publicly," she corrected him, and told him what her mother had said.

She'd found him outside the commander's office and pulled him aside. Her request set the man back and his eyebrows knit in confusion.

"You want me to help you train in secret?" he asked.

"Why train in secret when I can don a persona and train with masters of magic?"

He frowned. "I don't think that's what your mother had in mind."

"The practical training for an oracle is not dissimilar from that of a Verinai," she said. "If I don the persona of a new member of their guild, I can enter their ranks and study with them."

His nose wrinkled in distaste. "You would join the Verinai?"

"Of course not," she said dismissively. "I just want them to train me."

"You may choose the master," he said, "you cannot choose the lesson."

"Please," she said, "the Soldier may come for me again, and I doubt he will spare my life a second time."

His grey eyes flickered with regret. "If you doubt my ability to protect you . . ."

"No," she said hastily. "I just don't want to feel so . . ." She wanted to say helpless but couldn't bring herself to admit it. Still, Devkin smiled sympathetically.

"What you ask is dangerous," he said. "And if your mother finds out . . ."

"She won't," Alydian said. She noticed the sparkle in his eyes and grinned. "You can't deny you like the prospect. And you know I can use my farsight to keep from being detected."

He scratched his grey beard, and Alydian struggled to hold her excitement in check. Then Devkin flashed a wry smile. Before he could speak Alydian embraced him and grinned with delight.

"You have my gratitude," she said.

"If the council discovers your ruse," he said, "we will both be disciplined—severely."

"I'm more concerned about the Verinai discovering my identity," she replied. "I do not know how they would react."

"My loyalty comes with a condition," he warned.

"What would you have of me?" Alydian asked.

"You will not become like them," he said.

"An easy promise to make," she said.

"But difficult to keep," he countered.

She could not contain her grin. "Where do we begin?"

A passing guard forced them away. Alydian struggled to keep the bounce from her step as they made their way to the courtyard outside Dawnskeep. Once they were in the open Devkin spoke in an undertone.

"Do not speak your plans to anyone," he said. "Least of all anyone on the council—especially Raine. I know you trust her, but this is not a secret to be shared."

"I swear it."

Alydian, well aware that the other oracles might look into her future, accepted the warning and made no firm decision on her plans. Her feigned uncertainty would keep her future masked in clouds, ensuring a measure of privacy for her actions.

"I'll see what I can do," he said. "Now return to your quarters. High Captain Peranin rescheduled future patrons to Elenyr. It appears she has already begun to clear your schedule."

"She shouldn't have to shoulder that," Alydian protested.

"She insisted," Devkin said. "She said for you to take all the time you need before returning to your duties."

Alydian nodded, realizing she'd forgotten that her schedule was full. Like all oracles, a portion of her time was given to the people, and anyone was permitted to request guidance. Usually the patrons dealt with family squabbles or fears of a drought, and she would examine their trees to provide insights. Over the last decade Alydian had gradually shouldered more and more of her mother's load.

As she strode to the Elsheeria tower and ascended to her quarters, she tried to ignore the guilt. Her mother needed her, and instead she was exploiting her benevolence. Her mother would never want Alydian to risk training with the Verinai but it would take decades to learn on her own. As much as her books provided, they could not replace the voice of master mage.

The ascender came to a stop at her quarters and she stepped off. The guards were new, likely assigned until Devkin could restore the losses from her personal guard. Their unfamiliarity drew a pang of regret as she recalled the scene of the battle. She passed them on her way to the single door at the end of the corridor.

She entered and shut it behind her before leaning against it. The series of chambers had been hers since her youth and was the only home she'd ever had. After the events of the previous week it felt strange and foreign.

Dominating the whole of the turret floor, her quarters were mostly open. The central space was unblocked by pillar or wall, the vaulted chamber extending to a broad balcony that overlooked the city of

Horizon. The spacious receiving room contained couches around an open fire pit at the center, the transparent chimney allowing smoke to ascend without obscuring the openness to the room.

A door on her right led to her bedchamber, which contained another balcony with a view of the Dawnskeep courtyard. The door beside it led to her office and private library, with a third balcony, also with a view of the courtyard. The door was still open where she'd left it in her hasty departure a month ago, and her favorite mug was visible on her desk. A knock at the door startled her, and she turned to open it.

"I'm sorry to disturb you," the guard said, "but the assistant guildmaster to the mage guild of light has requested an audience."

"Give me ten minutes," she said, abruptly weary.

To her dismay the next few days were filled with individuals seeking to assure themselves of Alydian's survival. The attack on Alydian had sparked a furor in Horizon, and Alydian was not able to speak to Devkin about their plans until the following week.

Each morning she descended to the base of the Elsheeria tower, to the patron receiving hall. Lavish and pillared, the circular room contained a small throne at the center that allowed her to sit and listen to requests for aid. Patrons came from several kingdoms and guilds, some to console, others to manipulate—feigning concern while trying to elicit sympathy for their cause. She smiled at all and answered questions about the Soldier. Those that sought to manipulate her were left wanting.

Gradually, her schedule returned to normal as Elenyr accepted more patrons, which meant a return to her studies. When Devkin directed her to go to the Dawnskeep library and collect two weeks of reading material she knew it was time.

Long after dark, she made her way to the expansive library on the second level of Dawnskeep. She passed through the magnificent great hall, her eyes on the figures of light dancing on the walls. Then she used a dwarven ascender to reach the library.

Taking enough books for a fortnight, she told her guards and her mother she planned to spend the next weeks deep in her studies. Her guards looked at her with pity, interpreting her choice as an effort to hide. She had to work to keep the smile from her face. She returned to her quarters to find Devkin speaking to the newest members of her guard.

"Oracle," he said, opening the door to her quarters and entering with her.

Like the other oracles, the captain of her guard was more than a sentry. Devkin acted as a guide and friend, and was required to be close whenever she departed Dawnskeep. While the other guards lived in barracks beneath the courtyard, Devkin lived in a small room adjacent to her office. When the door shut she put the books on a table, the tomes thudding heavily against the wood.

"Are you certain you wish to do this?" Devkin said.

Alydian made to respond but her voice caught. She dipped into her farsight and looked to her own tree. The tree split down the middle, the impending choice a gaping divide that would forever alter her fate. The choice to remain as she was led to a future of certainty, while the other would be plagued by patches of fog and confusion.

The path of certainty lay with tradition, but carried a legacy of regret. Even with her magic, she could not foresee the outcome of her training. To defy tradition would affect not just herself, but the lives of many. But was tradition the right choice?

She thought of the panic and fear in her wagon, of the terror the Soldier had inspired. Her resolve hardened as she realized the choice was simple. Deny the council. Or deny herself. A thrill of foreboding and excitement trickled down her spine.

"I am committed to this course."

Devkin inclined his head and reached into a pouch at his side, withdrawing a silver necklace. Offering it to her, he said, "A member of the Thieves Guild managed to procure this for me."

"A thief?" she asked, examining the necklace.

"It costs more coin than I make in a decade," he replied defensively. "And you couldn't be seen purchasing it."

"How many thief friends do you have?" Alydian asked, but smiled to take the condemnation from her words.

He grinned. "Two," he replied. "It would be more, but they fear the oracle's power."

"What does it do?" she asked, examining the necklace with her magesight.

"Put it on," he said.

Jewelry was occasionally cursed with hexes and other harmful magic, but she sensed no mark of curse on the necklace. Still, she felt a thrill of nervousness as she placed it about her shoulders.

"Look in the mirror," he instructed.

She strode around the hearth, making her way to the tall mirror situated against one wall. She came to an abrupt halt when she saw the reflection—and did not recognize it.

The woman staring back at her was a young elf, barely out of her fifth decade. Still, she was pretty, her hair braided down her back in the traditional style of elven women. Her clothing and figure remained the same, but her features were altered by the powerful mask charm placed on the necklace.

"Alydian," Devkin said with a smile, "meet your persona, Alethean."

"Isn't that too close to my name?" she asked, releasing a nervous laugh.

He smiled. "It is, and for good reason. Thieves and assassins may be skilled in operating under a persona, but you are not. One mistake will betray you, so having a name close to your own will keep you from revealing yourself."

A thrill of excitement brought a smile to Alydian's lips. Now that she knew what to look for, she slipped into her magesight and examined her reflection. Illusions were complicated enough for light mages, but mask charms were far more difficult. Many regarded it as the highest order of light spell due to the complexity of the expressions it had to mimic.

The mask charm on the necklace was flawless and subtly enhanced or shifted aspects of her features in order to disguise her appearance. The caster clearly had a gift, marking her as powerful in all three aspects of magic: sight, control, and focus. Even knowing the charm was there, she had difficulty discerning her true features.

"It's perfect," she breathed, and turned to Devkin. "When do I go to the guild?"

"You don't," he said. "I managed to get you a slot as an acolyte into the Runeguard."

Surprise bound her tongue. The Runeguard were widely regarded as the best battlemages in Lumineia. To join their ranks was an honor that soldiers from across Lumineia aspired to. Abruptly nervous, Alydian reached up and removed the necklace.

"I thought we decided I would join the Verinai," she said.

"At the guild, you won't just learn how to fight. You'll learn how to enchant clothing and armor, grow and harvest crops, and build structures with magic. You would also be indoctrinated. For now, you only seek to master the skills of a battlemage. Am I wrong?"

"No," she hedged. "I just don't think I'm ready to join the Runeguard."

"We both know you are," he said. "I've seen you practicing your magic when you think no one is looking."

Devkin folded his arms and regarded her, looking so much like a stern grandfather that Alydian laughed. As much as the prospect terrified her, it was a sound plan. She would have centuries to learn every branch of magic, but right now she simply wanted to defend herself. And being an acolyte in the Runeguard would place her in Dawnskeep, making it that much easier to switch between personas.

"It would put me under my mother's nose," Alydian said.

"I told her I secured a storeroom in the cellars to use as your training hall," Devkin said.

The fact that Devkin was now deceiving her mother made her plan seem even more dangerous, and she swallowed against her doubt. Then she recalled her cowardice when the Soldier attacked and her jaw set.

"I'll do it," she said.

"Excellent," he replied. "A training regimen for new soldiers begins in two days."

"So soon?"

He grinned at her worry. "Don't worry, if you fail, they will merely dismiss you from the guard."

She blinked into her magesight and pressed beyond the purple clouds, the world turning into the familiar tree of the future. She followed her own branch and found that there was a distinct possibility that she would be dismissed from the guard, and only a tiny, stunted branch signifying success in the upcoming trials.

Rather than discourage her, the sight of her slim odds strengthened her resolve. Her mother had always said she carried an indomitable spirit. Her tone had been exasperated, but Alydian recalled a note of praise in her voice.

"You're smiling, Mother," Alydian had accused.

"No, I'm not," Elenyr had said. "Now return to your studies."

Alydian grinned at the memory, grateful that her mother had taken the time to teach her. Back then her mother had been a pillar of strength on the council, and led the kingdoms with a perpetual grace. Alydian's smile faded as she realized she would never again see her mother stand as tall.

"What can I expect in the guard?"

Devkin launched into a description of the trials, when the Runeguard would test their knowledge, fortitude, and willpower. Her entry into the guard would begin with four weeks of endurance and

72

combat training, where she would learn to master and use magic she was already expected to know. Low performing students were frequently dismissed.

The second trial would pit her against the other students in a series of duels and contests, culminating in brutal simulated battles. Those who lost would be dismissed and banned from returning. The victors would then enter their final trial and journey out of Dawnskeep to eliminate threats to the kingdoms, such as bandits, moordraugs, or reavers. The triumphant survivors would return to join the coveted ranks of the Runeguard.

As the sun dipped low on the horizon, their conversation shifted to which magics she should manifest as a Verinai. Alydian stepped to a prominent tapestry hanging on the wall, the threads magically woven by Elenyr in her youth. Without seam or knot, the tapestry depicted the circle of magic with its twelve common magics. The rares were placed in a smaller ring, while the handful of known uniques were displayed on the corners. At the center of the piece, the concave triangle in white showed the oracle's crest.

"You can't reveal how many magics you actually possess," Devkin said. "You'll have to pick Alethean's talents and stick to them."

Alydian pointed to the upper curve of the circle. "Fire, mind, air, water, and earth are considered the battle magics."

"True," Devkin said, "but you are already talented with them. You can see spells others perform and practice them on your own. If you display the magics on the opposite side of the circle, they will force you to learn to fight with your weaker magics."

"How do you know I'm weaker with them?" she countered.

He smirked. "Because you don't practice them."

She laughed in chagrin. "All oracles gravitate towards one side of the circle. I take after my mother in that regard. But won't using my weaker magics risk my dismissal?"

Devkin turned to the tapestry and swept his hand at the four magics on the bottom right curve. "If you use healing and body magic you can

73

get away with healing yourself, and trust me when I say you're going to need that. Animal and plant magics will come in handy in the second and third trials."

"Plant mages are frequently earth mages," she countered. "I can get away with five."

"It will draw more attention to you," he warned. "Most of the Verinai have three or four, and being a mage with five talents will draw your trainers' focus and make your peers jealous."

"The Verinai Guildmaster has nine," she said.

"And Elsin is the guildmaster," he said, folding his arms. "Most of the higher masters in the Verinai have four, five, or six talents. Drawing that much attention to yourself will be risky. They will expect more from you, and you will already be starting at a lower level than the other students."

"Earth is one of the strongest combat magics. I need it."

They locked eyes until Devkin growled under his breath. "Stubborn oracle."

She grinned and turned back to the tapestry, her gaze drawn to the lower circle. Now that she had decided, the weight of her plan settled upon her shoulders. She swallowed against the sudden fear.

"I'll have to shield myself from the other mages," she said. "Otherwise the first fire mage to look at me with their magesight will see that I am lying."

"I'm confident you can perform the darkening enchantment," he said.

"How can I do this?" she asked, suddenly nervous. "I don't know the first thing about combat, and the other acolytes are already trained soldiers."

Devkin laughed, drawing her gaze. "Combat is about discipline and focus," he said, "two things that you know a great deal about. Your entities may be limited by your lack of swordcraft, but they will be empowered by your ingenuity."

"Is that how you defeat the Verinai Runeguard?"

"The Verinai's weakness is their power," Devkin said. "They are like a bully with a club. They always think they will win because they only fight those without a weapon. But I wield a sword—and I know how to use it. Master the control over yourself, and the warrior will come."

The words echoed what Elenyr had said regarding the Mage's Mantra. "Do you really believe I can do this?"

"What's the largest entity you can cast?" he asked, folding his arms.

"A bear with fire or light."

"Have you ever pushed them to be larger? Or stronger?"

She shook her head. "I've never needed to . . ." She began to laugh as she realized Devkin's point. She'd never tried to push her limits, and becoming an acolyte would force her to. She inclined her head, accepting the lesson.

"I'll inform the other guards that you plan to extend your time of private study," Devkin said, his voice somber. "After the Soldier's attack, many already assume you are afraid to come out."

"They'll be wrong," Alydian said, her jaw tightening. "And I never want to be afraid again."

# Chapter 8: Acolyte

Alydian slept fitfully and rose early. She would have liked more time to prepare for the upcoming trials, but she was too anxious to wait for the next opportunity. She cast the darkening charms on each of her magics and checked them in the mirror. And then checked them again. And again.

She tried to use her farsight but was too distracted. The only thing she managed to discover was that her mother thought she was training in her own quarters. Alydian felt guilty for deceiving her—especially when she was ill—but was grateful her ruse was intact. Raine visited for lunch and asked how she was, and Alydian nearly told her.

"Just rattled," Alydian finally said.

Raine smiled sympathetically. "Enjoy your personal study. I'll do what I can to give you time to recover."

"Thanks, Raine," Alydian said, relieved her friend did not push the issue.

When Raine departed, Alydian stepped to her balcony and watched the sunlight dance across Dawnskeep. The morning had been a blur, but the afternoon dragged by, each second an agonizing delay. Restless and uneasy, she tried to research more about the three trials she would face, wishing Devkin were there for her to talk to. At night she visited her mother. Then she returned to her quarters and tried to sleep. After several sleepless hours, she rose and stared at her reflection.

"I will not be afraid," she said.

Donning the blue uniform of an acolyte, she added the Alethean necklace and stepped in front of the mirror once more. She looked strong and fit, her gaze hard, her jaw set. Ignoring the slight tremble in her hands, she removed the necklace and pulled a loose-fitting dress over her uniform.

Alethean's supposed family had arranged for her to stay with a cousin in the city rather than in the barracks. The authority for an acolyte's family to do so would invite speculation, but was necessary. Alydian's regular guards would quickly notice if she did not return each night.

Alydian slipped the Alethean necklace into a pouch at her side, gathered up a book, and stepped into her receiving room. She was not surprised to find Devkin and a pair of guards already waiting for her.

"Oracle Alydian," Devkin said, inclining his head. "As you requested, your morning meal has been delivered to the library."

"Thank you, Captain," she replied, falling into step as he strode to the door and entered the hall. The other two guards took up position behind Alydian as they made their way to the ascender. After the losses sustained in the attack on her wagon, she wasn't surprised that she didn't recognize them.

Alydian looked at them more closely. Both Verinai, they glided down the hallway with wary ease, a talent that she had never noticed before, but now found herself envious of. The elven woman noticed her inspection and raised an eyebrow.

"Oracle?"

"What is your name?" Alydian asked.

"Yaria," she said.

Alydian's eyes flicked to the dwarf, and he answered gruffly. "Bathik."

"How long have you been in the guard?"

"Twelve years," she replied.

"Forty-seven," he said.

Alydian smiled. "You have my gratitude for joining Devkin's command."

Yaria's gaze shifted to Devkin and a trace of irritation appeared. "It was not our choice," she said.

Alydian wanted to rebuke her, but held her tongue. Devkin was more than capable of fighting his own battles. Turning her attention forward, she followed her captain to the ascender and waited as it lowered them to the courtyard below. Then they strode across the courtyard to central tower.

Dawn had yet to illuminate the horizon but the tower remained bright, the light bathing the courtyard in a soft glow. It was hours earlier than her usual time to start her studies, but the acolyte soldiers were expected to assemble at dawn.

They reached the main tower and entered one of the side doors. The enchantments of the wall made it appear solid from the exterior but like glass from the interior. As they strode the length of the hall Alydian looked outside and spotted acolytes gathering at the north gate.

She looked away before her nervousness could betray her and followed Devkin to one of the two smaller ascenders in the tower. A large ascender was situated beside the main entrance but was reserved for arriving dignitaries and their parties. Alydian and her guards entered the smaller ascender and the dwarven machinery lifted them to the second level. Alydian surreptitiously watched the gathering of acolytes, struggling to contain the rising nervousness in her gut.

They reached the library and when the doors opened Devkin motioned the other guards to remain at the entrance. Then Devkin led her inside. Aside from the three ascenders, the library had no rooms, allowing patrons a full view of Dawnskeep and Horizon through the transparent outer walls. Comfortable couches and chairs lined the exterior, while towering bookshelves reached to the ceiling high above. Winding staircases climbed up the bookshelves to the upper balconies and terraces, where more books and couches were visible.

Even this early, a handful of patrons walked the labyrinth of bookshelves. The library was open to all, but aside from gawking common folk, the patrons were usually mages. Alydian wound her way

78

to a small staircase near the southern arch and stepped through the illusion of a bookshelf, ascending the hidden staircase to a room ensconced between three bookshelves.

The library may have looked open, but several secret chambers dotted the space, private places of study that enterprising mages had cast upon its construction. Devkin remained outside while she quickly stripped her dress and donned the necklace of Alethean. Then she exited to find him on the staircase.

"Ready?" he murmured.

"As ready as I can be," she said.

He nodded and guided her down the stairs, stepping through the illusion. Then she paused and turned to him, and the grizzled soldier smiled as he regarded her.

"Do not pretend to be Alethean," he said. "*Become* her. Think like her, eat like her, fight like her."

"What if I am discovered?" she asked. She tried to use her farsight to answer for herself, but fear blocked her magic.

"Then you will be reprimanded by the council," he said. "And the incident will forever stain your history."

"That's not comforting."

His smile turned wry. "It wasn't meant to be. Just don't get yourself killed, or it will be my head."

"I'll try to stay alive," she said, and turned away.

"One more thing."

She turned back and saw the glimmer of steel reflected in his eyes. "Make me proud."

She grinned, Devkin's confidence finally stilling her nervousness. He was a veteran soldier and skilled tactician. If he believed in her, who was she to disagree? Inclining her head to him, she turned and slipped away.

As she walked the halls of the library she rehearsed the story they had concocted for her past. She encountered several guards, but they paid her no mind. A moment later she reached the second ascender that brought her to the courtyard. Passing the sentries at the entrance, she strode toward the north gate where the acolytes were gathering.

Two score had already assembled and formed into two groups. All Verinai, the larger group stood apart, whispering and laughing while casting disparaging looks at the smaller group. Their expressions were confident and haughty, and Alydian spotted elves, humans, and a single dwarf.

The second group contained mostly humans with a trio of elves and a gnome in its midst. Alydian noticed that several bore the insignia of the single mage guilds on their shoulders, while a few had no insignia, marking them as magicless.

Alydian would have liked to join them, but the motion would invite more curiosity than she cared for, so she joined the ranks of the Verinai. Several cast her appraising looks until one noticed the insignia on Alydian's shoulder.

"A quinmage?" the elf said, and then sniffed. "But only one combat magic."

"Afraid she'll surpass you, Holan?" another elf teased.

"You've only got three talents, Erona," he said scornfully. "I have all four combat magics. I bet she's practically a barren."

Alydian bristled at the term. "Is your pride a fifth talent? Or is that your stupidity?"

He whirled to face her, but the other Verinai laughed at his expense. Erona stepped to Alydian's side and gestured to Holan.

"Forgive Holan," she said blithely. "He has to compensate for his stature."

Holan flushed. "I'm taller than you."

"But short for an elven male," Erona said. "Perhaps there is a barren human in your ancestry."

80

He snarled at her but another voice barked an order and the entire group turned. Commander Othan strode to them with a trio of Runeguard lieutenants. The elf looked exactly as he had when he'd attempted to take command from Devkin, and Alydian felt an involuntary look of disgust creep onto her features. The commander came to a halt and his gaze swept the two groups of acolytes, his dour expression turning scornful.

"Most of you came from a guild that praised you, where your peers fawned over your talents and power. I assure you, your abilities are meaningless here."

His boots clipped the stone as he paced in front of them. Hard and menacing, the sound made Alydian swallow when his eyes connected with hers. For an instant she feared he'd detected her, but his gaze slid off her face with such disdain that she frowned.

"Of the forty in your party, fewer than a third will join the honored ranks of the Runeguard and have the privilege of killing the oracles' enemies."

Alydian noted some of the Verinai whispering and smiling as they glanced to the group of single mages and magicless. If Commander Othan felt disdain for them, he kept it hidden as he described the trials of endurance, unity, and will.

"Mages, with me," he barked. "The rest of you, with Captain Devkin."

Surprised, Alydian turned and spotted Captain Devkin striding across the courtyard. He motioned the acolytes that did not possess magic to follow him, and led them to the training chambers situated beneath the citadel. Their eyes connected briefly, but the only sign of recognition was a twitch at the corner of Devkin's lips.

When they were gone, Commander Othan strode among the remaining acolytes, looking the mages up and down. "Captain Devkin is the only magicless captain in the Runeguard," he said. "As he measures the capacity of your common companions, I will test your magical limits. Let's see what you're made of."

81

# Chapter 9: The Trial of Endurance

Alydian slipped to the back of the group as they were guided to a set of stairs adjacent to the outer wall. Descending beneath the courtyard, Commander Othan led them past storage rooms and armories to a large ironbound door. Alydian had lived in Dawnskeep her entire life but had never visited the training rooms, and she craned to get a look. Commander Othan pressed on the door and it swung open with barely a whisper, revealing a massive chamber.

Alydian sucked in her breath, shocked to see a room the size of the entire citadel courtyard. Enormous beams arced across the ceiling, connecting the exterior walls to the great pillar at the center of the chamber, the foundation for the oracle tower above. At a hundred feet tall and hundreds across, the hall contained training circles, open armories, and full archery ranges.

A handful of forges dotted the outer wall, and the ring of hammers striking steel echoed from within. Special trees grew beside them, their branches enchanted to grow perfectly straight so they could be made into arrows.

Despite the wonders of the hall, the objects around the central pillar drew her gaze. Giant trees surrounded the tower foundation, their branches dropping to the earth to hold large spheres. The spheres glittered like enormous diamonds, the light dancing off them and shimmering.

"All the training circles have adjacent magic sources," Commander Othan said, gesturing to the training circles. "Find one that matches your talents and cast an entity,"

"What if we have multiple talents?" Holan asked, his expression smug.

Othan stared at him until Holan's smile faded. "Then cast one from every magic you possess."

"At the same time?" Holan asked.

"Is that too much for your frail sensitivities?" Othan asked.

"No," Holan said hastily.

Alydian looked away to hide her smile, her eyes connecting with a human woman nearby. They smirked together and a moment later stepped into training circles adjacent to each other. When Othan had passed on, Alydian appraised the woman.

Slim and short, the woman had black hair and dark eyes. Her tanned skin suggested she spent a great deal of time outside. She lacked the mark of a Verinai, and instead wore the mark of the human guild of sound on the customary left shoulder. When it came time for them to separate, Alydian chose a spot closer to her.

The woman raised an eyebrow at Alydian's choice in position and cast a jungle cat out of sound magic. The orange energy swirled into shape and the small cat began to pace. Alydian nodded in approval. Every magic could cast an entity, but some were more complex than others, and the larger the entity, the harder the spell. Sound magic was notoriously difficult to shape into solid form, and the size of the beast suggested a great deal of skill for one so young.

Alydian cast five entities from the sources of magic around her. Devkin had warned her about displaying her power too early, so she cast a small golem from earth magic. Focusing, she added a golem from the green sphere of energy. She spotted a dark brown sphere of magic and drew on it, shaping its power into a dog. The animal padded around the two golems, sniffing at their legs. Alydian conjured a cat out of healing magic, the pink energy swirling into a tail, back, and legs. Lastly, she reached for one of the silver sources, using the body magic to cast a tiny knight.

She gritted her teeth as she struggled to maintain the spells. Entities were sentient pieces of magic, but their life was linked to the caster. A permanent entity took months or even years of reinforcing the spell until its consciousness became enduring, elevating the entity spell to a sentient. To maintain five entities at once—from different magics—pushed her more than she was used to. Sweat beaded her forehead in seconds, and she fought to keep them from dissipating.

All around her the Verinai struggled to hold their entities in place. Holan had chosen four matching knights, but their heights varied. The fire knight was the largest, and stood as tall as he did, while the swirling knight of air came to his waist.

The single-talent mages displayed the largest entities, until Othan shouted an order and they divided them into two or three. With every mage straining under the weight of maintaining their spells, the area was filled with golems, small soldiers, and animals. Commander Othan strode among them, his disapproving gaze sliding off the acolytes.

"The entity spell is one of the most versatile in your arsenal," he said, passing Erona with a nod of approval at her three tigers. "But a weak mind casts a weak entity." His lips curled in disdain at Alydian's small creatures.

"Small entities can be broken with steel," he continued, "while larger ones can endure more damage unless the blade is fashioned of anti-magic."

He nodded to the gnome who stood before a tiny mouse of anti-magic. Renowned as the most difficult magic from which to cast an entity, the inky mouse shuddered and twitched in the direction of a nearby golem, the gnome struggling to contain the entity's hunger.

Othan stopped in front of the woman at Alydian's side. "To become a Runeguard you must master three simultaneous entities—and be able to lead them into battle. Today we wish to measure your mental strength. Those who cannot maintain their entities will be dismissed at the end of the day."

Smirking, he strode away, leaving the group of acolytes straining to maintain their magic. Other Runeguards in the hall grinned, clearly enjoying the spectacle. After several minutes of solitude it became clear that Othan was not going to return, and whispered conversations broke out. Alydian took advantage of the noise to drift closer to the woman at her side.

"What's your name?" Alydian asked.

"Toala," she said.

"Alethean," Alydian said, trying to keep her dog from attacking Toala's cats.

"Why are you talking to me?" Toala asked bluntly.

"Am I not supposed to?" Alydian asked. Fearing she'd erred, she glanced about for the one of the captains but none were visible.

"Verinai do not talk to single mages," Toala said.

"This Verinai does," Alydian said.

There was a long pause, and then Toala offered a small smile. "Holding five magic must be difficult."

"I've had some practice," Alydian said. "And my mother taught me well."

"Mine taught me, too" Toala said. "She was an Amazon."

"Ah," Alydian said, unsurprised. Many Amazons possessed sound magic. "You're very talented," she said, gesturing to the jungle cats.

"For a single-mage," Erona muttered, causing nearby Verinai to laugh.

Toala flushed, her jungle cats wavering before she regained her focus. Then she pointedly looked away from Erona.

"What do you suppose those are?" she asked, using her chin to point in the direction of the spheres.

"I don't know," Alydian said, and then blinked into her magesight to examine it. "But an oracle helped make them."

"How do you know that?"

Realizing she'd revealed more than she cared to, she shrugged. "A guess. They look like they have every type of magic."

85

Overhearing her words, a nearby Verinai laughed scornfully. "Those are the Requiems. You won't survive the first week, so you'll never get the chance to use one."

Toala's features clouded with anger and she took a step toward him. "We'll see who survives the week."

"Don't," Alydian warned, stepping between them. "He's trying to bait you."

The absence of officers was an illusion, and the Runeguard wanted to see what they would do. Devkin had made it clear they would be using light magic to study the acolytes form a nearby room, the officers evaluating the acolyte's restraint as much as their talents.

Toala heeded her warning and reluctantly withdrew, as did the Verinai, who stepped back with a smug grin. Caught in the middle, Alydian joined the single mages. Her action caused looks of disapproval and confusion among the Verinai, and surprise among the single mages.

"What are you doing?" Toala hissed.

"Standing with a friend," Alydian said quietly.

She would have liked to examine her future for the ramifications of such a choice, but maintaining the entities was taxing enough. Still, Toala's smile was worth any cost.

As the day wore on her entities shrank, as did those of the other mages. All were drenched in sweat, but still the captains did not return. A smattering of conversation broke the labored breathing, but Alydian found it difficult to speak. Magic of any type wanted to dissipate, and it took all her will to hold the entities together for so long.

Shortly after noon a human slumped to the floor. His entities disappeared, and for the first time a pair of officers emerged. Retrieving the acolyte's unconscious form, they carried him from the hall. An hour later another dropped, and then another.

Alydian's vision began to blur, distorting the image of her entities. Several times her dog went after Toala's cats, and she was forced to retreat in order to give them space. Other Verinai did the same.

In the afternoon, the Runeguard in the hall began to call out to each other. Although they spoke to their companions, their scornful words were meant for the acolytes. Devkin had warned Alydian about the verbal abuse, and she kept her anger in check, but one of the Verinai and another single mage began to shout. The effort cost them their focus, and the captains returned to lead them away.

"They're trying to break us," Toala said, her voice strained.

Alydian didn't respond. Devkin had warned that the first trial was meant to test their talent and endurance. But knowing the trial didn't make it easier to listen to the chorus of disdain from the Runeguard. Struggling to hold her magic together, Alydian focused on a single thought.

*Please don't fail on the first day . . .*

# Chapter 10: The Secret Shipment

Raiden and his companions tracked the Verinai shipment for four days, watching for any hint of its contents. Their patience was in vain and they were unable to catch a glimpse of the interior. Jester even risked riding past the wagon to determine if he could see through gaps in the door's window, but the soldiers shouted and drove him away.

Feigning shock and fear, the assassin retreated and took another fork before rejoining Raiden and Red on a hill overlooking the road. Dismounting, he growled his frustration and stepped to Raiden's side.

"They're cautious. A scout ahead and a scout behind, and they aren't letting anyone near the wagon."

"And they're not alone," Raiden said, motioning to Red.

Red scowled and pointed down the road. "While you were gone I scouted ahead. The Verinai have a pocket of soldiers further down the road. They're well hidden, but it's obvious they are here to protect this shipment."

"Then why not ride with it?" Jester asked.

"It's a trap," Raiden realized. "They *want* the Soldier to attack."

Jester motioned to the wagon ambling along the road below. "The wagon is probably empty."

Raiden shook his head. "I don't think so. There's a wariness about the guards that cannot be feigned."

"You still want to take it?" Red asked, her eyes gleaming with anticipation.

"Perhaps they're expecting us," Jester said, a sly smile playing on his face. "I do hate to disappoint."

Of the two, Jester inclined towards caution, but he hated losing a target. He would attack the shipment for the opportunity to shame the Verinai, and then laugh in their face.

"They're expecting a small army," Raiden mused. "They aren't expecting the three of us."

"That's not an advantage," Red said.

"It can be," Jester said. "If they don't see us coming."

"How?" Red asked.

"We don't have to attack the shipment," Raiden said. "We can steal it."

Red's irritation shifted into a wild grin. "I like it. The road passes through a shallow canyon before the road forks. If we steal the shipment in the canyon, we can take the wagon west away from Verinai trails."

"Let's go," Raiden said, and climbed into his saddle.

The trio departed their vantage point and followed the game trail back into the trees. Raiden set a blistering pace. When the trail curved back to the road he let Red take the lead, and she guided them to the group of Verinai lying in wait.

When they drew close, they dismounted and left their horses behind, pressing through the trees to the canyon. The gap had evidently once been a tunnel, and the gurgling creek had bored a hole through the hill, gradually widening the canyon with every spring runoff. The walls of the gorge were shaped like an arch without a keystone, the two sides nearly touching each other above the road.

Breathing hard from the rush, Red kept her voice low. "The Verinai are located there, where the canyon walls nearly touch above the road," she said, gesturing to the top of the cliff.

Raiden nodded, considering the possibilities. The road came from the north and twisted its way through the canyon. Since he knew where

89

to look, Raiden spotted the faint splash of color in the trees, and the shift of bodies as someone moved through them.

"How many?" Raiden whispered.

"Ten," Red replied. "And three sentries, one north, one south, and one across the canyon."

Raiden withdrew the mask of Soldier and donned it, and they donned theirs. He stabbed a finger south. "Red, south. Jester, come from below and take out the sentry on the opposite side of the canyon. The wagon will be here soon, so make it quick. Three minutes."

They nodded and slipped away, and Raiden drifted through the trees, mentally counting the seconds. He slowed as he approached the camp and spotted the third sentry leaning against a tree. Instead of paying attention to the forest, the man had his eyes on a ball of magic in his hand. Clearly bored, he was rolling it through is fingers, a task which required focus and skill. Raiden crept forward, and then heard a low growl at his back.

Raiden dived into the dirt as heat brushed his back, the passage of a fire entity scorching his tunic. In an instant Raiden realized why the man thought he was safe, he had entities prowling the forest around him. Rolling to his feet, Raiden rose and twisted, plunging his anti-magic blade into the wolf's open mouth. Mid-leap, the wolf disintegrated with barely a whimper, its flames turning to ash that dusted Raiden's mask.

Raiden rotated and surged forward, closing the gap to the mage—but the Verinai was already turning, fire sparking in his hands. Another wolf appeared on Raiden's flank, and another on the opposite side. Raiden kicked off a tree, twirling in a full circle, his sword cutting through both entities before plunging into the Verinai's body. The wolves died with their master, and Raiden stepped away, letting him slump to the ground.

He darted forward, bursting into the camp at the same moment Red struck the opposite flank, her sword bloodied from the sentry she'd dispatched. A campfire burned at the center of a clearing while a man stirred food in a pot. Earthen tents had been erected, the ground folded to allow men to sleep beneath.

Jester appeared on the other side of the canyon and leapt the gap, dragging the third sentry with his whip. Then he came to a halt and yanked, the magic of the whip sending the body soaring across the gap to crash into the camp. The heavy form collided with a pair of men at the fire, knocking them both into the flames.

Unprepared for the attack, the Verinai cried out, desperately drawing on their magic. Raiden streaked forward, deflecting a hasty fireball with his sword and whipping his blade down, killing the caster. Then a woman stepped into his path, her face twisting with fury.

"Elsin knew you would come," she snarled.

She sent her magic into the stone at Raiden's feet, and it formed hands that reached for his boots. He danced past them and leapt for her. She relinquished her hold on the ground and drew on the stone around her, summoning a goliath charm. Rock turned fluid and ascended her form, wrapping around her legs, torso, and arms before covering her face, grinding into supreme armor.

Raiden slowed and retreated, wincing as a sound mage nearby shrieked at Red. She raised her blade and cut the banshee cry in two, the sound striking the trees on either side, shattering wood and knocking branches to the earth.

Next to the canyon, Jester fought two Verinai at once, a third dead at his feet. They cast their magic into a pair of golems but Jester spun between them, cutting them into shards of magic that sputtered and melted away. In a deft twist he sent his whip to catch a Verinai by the throat. He yanked, the whip smashing his foe into a second Verinai, and Jester plunged his sword through both their bodies.

"One cut," he said with a laugh. "Two kills."

Red lacked the poise of the assassin, but the farmwoman made up for it in sheer aggression. She charged a huge man, heedless of the asunder hex streaking toward her. The light split on her blade, igniting fires on her shoulders as it streamed past her. Cleaving her way through the magic, she snarled as she closed the distance. The man dropped the magic and tried another tactic, but Red drove him back, hacking at his attempts at magic.

He retreated until he slammed into the trunk of a tree. Red lunged, plunging her sword through his arm, pinning him to the wood. He shrieked, but she stepped in and caught his head, driving her knee into his nose. Then she yanked her sword free and finished him, the savagery causing nearby Verinai to stumble back in fear.

Raiden had a moment of pride but was forced to maintain his focus on his own foe. Evidently the captain, the woman in the goliath charm stomped toward Raiden, raising an arm to form a hilt. Air converged on the hilt, hardening into a shimmering air blade.

The ground shook from the footfalls as she charged. Raiden parried her first swing, but the force of the blow knocked him backward, nearly to his knees. His sword bit into the wind but the woman recast it, the wind healing the gash in her blade before she charged again.

"Your reign of blood ends here," she growled.

"So yours can continue?" he countered, retreating into the trees.

She followed, swinging her sword to sheer a sapling in two. Then she raised her other stone-covered hand, calling on a tree nearby to rise from the earth. The branches bent and groaned, forming into the shape of a narrow man. Roots pulled from the earth and knotted together, coiling into giant feet. The treewalker lumbered to Raiden's flank, swinging a heavy branch at his skull.

Now facing two foes, Raiden retreated further before leaping in and striking at the goliath's leg, his blade slicing through stone and nicking flesh. The woman snarled at him and swung her sword, the weapon coming a hairsbreadth from taking Raiden's arm. Rotating past her, Raiden bounded away.

"You Verinai are so arrogant," he taunted. "Come and get me—if you can."

She growled and surged after him. With the treewalker and the goliath in his wake, he twisted and curved, tracking his foes by the snapping of wood and falling trees. Then he slowed, feigning fatigue, allowing her to catch up. As the sword swung for his back he ducked and whirled, driving his sword into the crack in the goliath's leg.

Her leg crumpled and she went down. Raiden darted to her back and faced the charging treewalker. The Verinai captain came to her feet and rotated—as the treewalker swung a giant limb. Raiden ducked and rolled away, letting the limb smash into the Verinai and send her tumbling backward.

Into the canyon.

She screamed as her feet slipped free, her body bouncing off the stone, cracking her goliath charm before she plunged into the chasm. She fought to cast her magic but the effort was futile, and a moment later she smashed into the road, the impact crumpling the stone armor with the soldier still inside.

Bits of stone scattered away, the rocks clattering off the canyon walls before finally going still. Bereft of the magic that supported it, the treewalker collapsed, its momentum carrying it toward the canyon as well. Raiden just managed to leap away as it rolled into the opening, its trunk going rigid before it smashed into the broken goliath below, the branches breaking on the stones of the creek, sending a plume of leaves outward.

Raiden rose to his feet and stepped to the edge, peering down at his fallen adversary. The Verinai's skilled use of three magics marked her as a master. He'd led her toward the gorge hoping to use it to his advantage, but acknowledged that luck had played a hand in his victory.

Red appeared through the trees with Jester at her side. Both bore the marks of battle, their clothing spotted with blood. Jester approached and looked over the gorge, shaking his head as he spotted the mess.

"I thought you wanted to kill them quietly," Red said.

"She was at least a tri-mage," Raiden said, examining the cut on his shoulder where her air sword had sliced a line through his flesh. "What did you expect?"

Jester grinned. "You dropped her on her head *and* hit her with her own treewalker? Don't you think that's overkill?"

Red laughed wryly behind her mask. "Not against one like her."

"The guards of the shipment will have heard the battle," Jester said. "They'll want to join the festivities . . ."

Raiden turned at the change in his voice and watched the wagon come into view, its guards staring in shock at the damage to the canyon ahead of them. The captain's eyes lifted to Raiden, his expression bright with rage.

"Don't worry!" Jester called, and laughed. "You'll join your friends soon!"

# Chapter 11: The Guardian

The Verinai leapt into the trees at the side of the road, rushing up the escarpment. Raiden and his companions evaporated into the trees. Taking a dozen Verinai by surprise was one thing, but standing against a dozen Verinai prepared for combat would be suicide.

"What now?" Jester asked as they sprinted through the forest.

"Get to your horse and lead them away," he said to Jester. "Red, you're with me. They kindly left the wagon with less guards, let's relieve them of their cargo."

"With pleasure," she said.

Raiden took Red north, curving around the Verinai advance before they caught them. Just as they ducked into a shallow gulley, the mages burst into view. Six treewalkers and several golems had joined their ranks, with a sleek reaver entity at their head.

The entity was of a black reaver, the sheer size suggesting a mage of tremendous power. It was larger than a horse, with the agility of a panther. Although not as deadly as a real black reaver, the entity was fashioned of water, the spines on its back as sharp as steel.

Raiden fought to still his heart as the beast streaked through the trees, grateful he'd insisted they acquire clothing lined with anti-magic thread. The material did little to stop a magical attack, but prevented mages—or their entities—from tracking them directly. When the army passed them by, Raiden grabbed a root and levered himself out of the crevice. Then he sprinted for the wagon.

"I'll draw their focus," he said, "get the reins. You should be able to squeeze past the debris in the canyon."

95

"Wait for you or leave you behind?"

"Don't leave me behind," he said, exasperated.

"As you order," she said, her voice tinged with amusement.

She separated from him and he sprinted through the trees. As he approached the road he spotted the six remaining soldiers standing around the wagon. The captain caught sight of him and swiveled, raising a bow of light.

Raiden twisted, pulling a throwing knife from a sheath on his chest. As the arrow streaked past him he launched his own blade, his aim better than the Verinai's, who cried out as the knife dug into his arm.

The captain stumbled back. "Kill him!" he barked.

Raiden threw another knife but a treewalker stepped in and intercepted it, the blade sinking into its trunk. The treewalker charged, forcing Raiden back into the trees. Five of the Verinai charged after him, and their entities as well. That left just one for Red to deal with.

He dodged and weaved, evading bursts of fire and an asunder lance. Trees burned in his wake while limbs were sheered from their trunks, the heavy branches crashing to the earth. A panther of fire burst into view on his left, and he dropped to his knees and slid forward, allowing the entity to chew on his blade. The sword cleaved the entity from teeth to tail, and it crumbled to ash.

He rolled to his feet and darted south, sprinting up the slope toward the top of the canyon. The Verinai panted from the effort to keep up and Raiden smirked at their fatigue. The Verinai relied on their magic too much, and apart from the Runeguard, rarely pushed themselves to gain any semblance of physical endurance. Still, after the battle with the initial patrol and the shipment's guards, he was tiring.

He reached the lip of the canyon and followed it, sprinting up the slope. A strangled cry rang out, and Raiden glanced back to see the last Verinai fall to Red's blade. Red leapt over his body and ascended to the wagon's bench, whipping the reins to drive the horses forward.

The canyon was narrow, twenty feet deep at Raiden's position. His chest heaving, Raiden spotted the water reaver up ahead and came to an abrupt halt. Realizing he was trapped, Raiden retreated to the edge of the canyon.

Behind and around him the trees parted, the Verinai stepping into view. Treewalkers and entities came to a stop, and the captain appeared, his hand resting on the reaver's flank. The beast snarled at Raiden but the captain merely smirked, his expression one of anticipation.

"Behold the Soldier," he said. "Guildmaster Elsin will be pleased. She planned so carefully for you, but it appears I get to kill you myself."

Raiden growled through his mask. "The Verinai are a plague on the earth."

"We are its conquerors," the captain sneered. "But you cannot understand, for you have no magic, no power. You are *barren*." He spit the word at Raiden. "Your kind must be ruled."

"Magic does not make the man," Raiden replied.

"Oh but it does," the captain insisted, and then took his hand off the reaver's flank and spoke to the beast. "Tear him apart."

The reaver lowered its head and released a chilling snarl—and lunged. It closed the gap in a single heartbeat, its jaws reaching for Raiden's skull. But Raiden took one step off the cliff, dropping into the canyon.

He swung his sword as he fell, cleaving the reaver's front leg from its body. The leg buckled and the reaver could not halt its momentum, crashing into a treewalker and dragging them both into the canyon. Branches snapped as the reaver clawed at the great tree and they plummeted just feet from Raiden. They landed in the road. Raiden landed on the wagon. Catching a section of wood to hold on, he shouted to Red.

"Go!"

Red whipped the reins and the horses surged forward. Raiden looked back and saw the reaver scramble to its feet, but with an injured leg it could not keep up. Other entities gave chase, but aside from a bird of light they quickly fell behind. Raiden swiped at the bird and it fell back a few feet, clearly intent on following them. Raiden reached to his back and withdrew a stock of wood, pressing the trigger on the side.

The bow snapped into place, forming a small hand crossbow. He aimed at the bird and fired, sending an anti-magic bolt into its chest. The bird squeaked once and exploded, the light fading from view. Returning the weapon to its innocuous shape, he placed it back in its sheath and watched the Verinai on the cliff top behind. They shouted curses and gave chase, but the captain stared at him, his expression strangely triumphant.

Raiden stared back until they reached the broken goliath and shattered treewalker. Red managed to navigate past the pile of debris, the wagon wheels bouncing over several smaller branches and the goliath's head. Then Raiden joined her on the driver's bench as the horses reached top speed, galloping around the curve and out of sight.

"Thanks for catching me," he said.

"You should have seen the look on their faces when you stepped off the ledge."

Raiden's smile faded as he recalled the captain's expression, and a sliver of doubt seeped into his gut. The Verinai had clearly set a trap for him, but what if they expected him to escape? What if Elsin *wanted* him to take the shipment?

"Stop the wagon," he said.

"Why?" she asked. "They could still be chasing us."

"Just do it," he said.

She shook her head in exasperation and reined in the horses. Before the wagon had fully come to a stop he dropped to the road and strode to the back, swinging the door open to peer inside. Light shone upon the interior and revealed the cargo.

A man.

Raiden stared at him as the man shielded his eyes from the light, the motion causing his shackles to clink. When his eyes adjusted he saw Raiden in his Soldier mask and recoiled in fear.

98

"You aren't Verinai."

"No," Raiden said. "Who are you?"

"I'm . . . I think I'm Wellen," he replied, and passed a hand over his face. "Or I was."

"Was?" Red asked, stepping into view.

Wellen's features contorted with pain and anger. "They turned me into a guardian."

"A what?" Red asked.

Wellen seemed to stare through them. "They boiled liquid magic and poured it into my body, replacing my flesh."

"Sounds painful," Red said.

Wellen shuddered, his eyes turning haunted. "Most don't survive."

"There have been others?" Raiden asked.

"A few live," Wellen said. "But I don't know where they were taken."

"Soldier . . ." Red said, her voice tinged with warning.

"Get us moving. I'll stay back here."

She nodded and returned to the driver's bench. Raiden climbed into the wagon and it began to move forward once more. Raiden took a seat on the side of the wagon. He made no move to unlock Wellen, and the man did not request it.

"Did you have magic before becoming a guardian?"

Wellen shook his head, his eyes changing before lighting with recognition. "I owned a mill in Nightfall Gorge."

"Family?"

"Wife died from a fever," he replied, looking away. "I didn't have the coin to get a Verinai to help."

Raiden caught the evasiveness and pain to his voice and did not press the issue. Instead he gestured to Wellen's body.

"What exactly does a guardian do?"

Wellen met his gaze—and then the man's body shifted, the skin and bones turning yellow and translucent . . . morphing into pure light. The features and form remained, but the man was gone. As a being of light, Wellen spoke.

"They turned me into this."

He raised a hand and magic curled in his palm, but the power was drawn away by the anti-magic bonds, the dark steel glimmering dully as it sapped Wellen's magic. The brief illumination revealed the size of the chains to be four times what was necessary for even a Verinai.

"May I test something?" Raiden asked.

Wellen frowned. "What is it you wish to see?"

In answer Raiden drew his sword and stepped forward, and Wellen cringed against the corner of the wagon. He cried out as Raiden swung, but the blade merely nicked his hand. Then Raiden sheathed his sword and waited.

Wellen winced at the contact, and abruptly his fear turned to anger. He scrambled to his feet and surged against his bonds, his features contorting into a frightening rage. Magic burst from his fingers as he clawed for Raiden like a rabid wolf. The power came within inches of Raiden's body only to be siphoned away by the chains. Raiden stood his ground and watched the wound knit on the man's hand.

"You're telling the truth," he said.

"*I told you what I am!*" the man screamed.

Raiden retreated from the coach, shutting the door. As Wellen continued to shriek from within, Raiden climbed over the top of the wagon and sat beside Red. He read the question in her eyes.

"I don't know his purpose," he said. "But I know what he is."

100

"And that would that be?"

"A weapon," he said.

# Chapter 12: Requiem

Alydian survived her first week of training. Barely. The first day had been exhausting, but the test of their endurance continued. The second day the acolytes were ordered to cast the largest entity they could.

Alydian chose a bear of stone, and under the constant orders of the trainers, she strained to push the bear's size. Minute by minute it grew before abruptly bursting into dust. All around her the other mages failed as well, and failed again. Under the constant bellowed orders by the trainers they fought to cast more magic. After the silence of the previous day, the verbal assault was shocking and distracting. Each failure was greeted with renewed scorn, and no entity was large enough.

The abuse continued deep into the night until the acolytes were finally dismissed. The following day they cast entities again, this time to battle. The entities smashed into each other, attacking each other in constant, grueling combat. The omnipresent effort to maintain the magic took its toll. Mages began to succumb to magesickness, the impact of channeling so much power through their bodies.

Day after day it continued, with the mages struggling to perform the impossible tasks set by the trainers. Time blended into a haze of fatigue and effort, interspersed by moments spent with healing mages.

Verinai and single mages alike crumbled under the pressure and begged for dismissal, which was promptly granted. Alydian yearned to join them but something inside her refused to yield, and only grew stronger when those about her hurled doubt in her face.

The final day of the trial seemed to never end, and Alydian yearned for the sweet release of unconsciousness. Now forced to push themselves physically, they ran around the great chamber with their entities at their sides, occasionally pausing to force the entities to battle. Sucking in great gulps of air, Alydian struggled to keep her entity alive. Matching the minds of their casters, the two entities resembled drunken brawlers, and barely landed a blow as they stumbled about.

When Alydian was on the verge of defeat she saw Holan's smirk, and her jaw tightened. Then Commander Othan entered and walked among the remaining acolytes, ignoring the stench of sweat.

"A Runeguard could continue all night," he said.

"Yes, Commander," they chorused.

He came to a halt before Alydian, whose head was bowed with fatigue. Through blurred vision she could make out his features but could hardly hear his voice. He snorted in disgust and moved on.

"Your day is complete," he said. "Return to your barracks and assemble at dawn. You may be the worst class of acolytes I've ever seen, but you've passed the first trial. Congratulations."

Alydian released her magic and slumped to the floor, as did the others. One of the Verinai caught the wall and vomited, adding to the stench. Another managed a laugh, the sound laced with weariness and relief.

"To your beds, acolytes!" Othan shouted. "Your second trial begins tomorrow."

Alydian fought to get to her feet and stumbled toward the door, distantly aware that Toala and the gnome were in front of her. When she reached the hall she spotted Devkin nearby, and the man deftly extricated her from the acolytes. Guiding her down a side corridor and into an alcove, he removed the necklace and threw a dress over her shoulders. Then he led Alydian up a staircase to the courtyard.

Alydian kept her feet beneath her but only barely. Never had she felt such fatigue, and darkness rimmed her vision. Devkin seemed to understand and guided her to the ascender that would take her to her room.

"Don't quit yet," he murmured. "Collapse now and questions will be asked that I cannot answer."

Alydian tried to respond but it came out in a mumble. Then the doors opened and he led her past Yaria and Bathik to her quarters.

"Are you well?" Yaria asked, stepping to her.

"Just tired," Alydian said, forcing a smile.

The moment the door was shut Alydian crumpled on the couch with a groan. Devkin pressed the rune in the hallway that led to the bathing chamber. Water heated by dwarven fire bubbled into the tub.

"I don't want a bath," she said. "I just want to sleep."

"The hot water will ease the tension in your muscles," he said. "And if you don't, it will hurt more tomorrow."

She grimaced as he pulled her to her feet. Every fiber of her flesh ached, but she ambled down the hall. Devkin grinned sympathetically.

"Want to quit?"

"*No,*" she said, jutting her chin out as she passed.

"Liar." He laughed and took his customary position near the door. She made her way into the bathing chamber and shut the door before removing her clothes and sinking into the steamy water.

She clenched her jaw at the sting but leaned back and tried to relax, reminding herself that the other acolytes were not getting a bath or sleeping in a soft bed. Resolving to use what advantages she had, she forced her muscles to relax until her fingers began to wrinkle. Then she left the water with a sigh.

Dressing and yawning, she used the adjoining door and slipped into her sleeping room to find a tray of food already laid on the desk. Mentally thanking Devkin, she proceeded to satisfy her ravenous hunger before climbing under the soft blankets. The next thing she knew someone was nudging her on the shoulder.

"Dawn approaches, Oracle."

She blinked her eyes against the light and Yaria's elven features resolved into focus. "Where's Devkin?" she mumbled.

"Patrons were requesting your time," she replied. "He went to schedule them with your mother. He said you requested to rise early for more study. Do you wish to sleep late?"

Alydian opened her mouth to respond *yes*, but the word lodged in her throat. The captain and lieutenants of her guard were more than just soldiers, and filled the role of attendants for the oracles. Devkin's absence could have been avoided, but he'd sent Yaria in his stead, likely to test her resolve.

"I *would* like to begin my studies early," she replied.

She made to rise but gasped as her body protested. Fortunately, Yaria was turning away and did not notice the expression. As the Runeguard slipped from the room Alydian cast a healing charm and magic surged into her limbs, easing the pain. Sighing in relief, she stood and ate the meal prepared for her.

She'd never had a large appetite, but she ate everything on the tray and drained the glass of mint water. Savoring the last of the liquid, she dressed in her uniform and then donned a nice red dress that complemented her hair and blue eyes. Then she stepped into the receiving room, spotting Devkin leaning on the wall by the door.

"Good morning," he said brightly.

"Nice try," she said acidly.

Caught, he grinned. "I thought you'd like to sleep late."

"I wanted to," she replied. "But we both know it would lead to my dismissal."

His grin widened and he motioned her to the door. Again he took the lead and guided her to her private study in the Dawnskeep library. As before, Alydian traded her dress for armor and exited as Alethean, arriving in the courtyard to find Holan waiting for her.

"You had enough energy to study after the first trial?" he asked, motioning to the library.

Caught by surprise, Alydian managed a nod. "I wanted to see if there was any way to make entities easier to cast."

105

He grinned wryly and pointed to the city. "You departed rather quickly last night, but I suppose if I had a comfortable bed waiting for me I would have as well."

"My family arranged for me to sleep in the city each night," Alydian said, stepping around him.

Undeterred, he walked with her. "Perhaps tonight I could accompany you to your home? I would like to meet your family."

Alydian cast him a wary look, and saw the glint of desire in his eyes. Abruptly she realized he now favored her, probably because she'd endured the first trial. But the possessiveness to his smile caused her to drift away.

"I'll make my own way home."

His skin darkened with a flush. "Perhaps another day, then."

He turned and strode away, and Alydian took a different set of stairs to the training hall. Upon entering, she joined the acolytes at the southern training circles. Holan appeared on the opposite side of the hall and joined the Verinai acolytes without sparing her a glance. After the previous day Alydian knew she should attempt to make friends among the Verinai, but as she crossed the floor Toala spotted her and raised a hand.

Alydian smiled and shifted direction, striding to her.

"Alethean," Toala said. "I'm glad you did not falter."

"Our training is far from over," Alydian said, joining her and her companions.

"True," an older elf said. The sword on his back and empty left shoulder marked him as magicless.

"This is Ferin," Toala said. "And the grumpy gnome is Grogith."

The gnome made an annoyed sound but didn't look at Alydian. He stood on the edge of a training circle, his eyes on the Requiems. Shorter than a human, the gnome had large, floppy ears and a triangular head. His eyes were opaque and inscrutable, and his features were lined in a perpetual frown. Gnomes were a reclusive people that lived in the far north, and aside from the occasional merchant group, they did not often journey to the south. Not one gnome was currently in the Runeguard, making his presence a mystery.

"Any other single mages or magicless?" Alydian asked, craning her neck to look around them.

"Just us," Ferin said.

Alydian looked to him in surprise. The magicless acolytes had endured their training separate from the mages, but she'd expected more to endure. Noticing her astonishment, Ferin rubbed his shoulder, wincing with the motion.

"Captain Devkin is exacting," Ferin said.

Alydian listened to him describe the brutal test of his skill, realizing that of the non-Verinai acolytes, all but four had been dismissed during the first trial. Alydian vaguely recalled a blur of faces that had gradually disappeared, and it made her sad to realize she didn't even know their names.

Commander Othan entered the chamber with a quartet of other trainers behind him, including Devkin. The acolytes rushed to form a line, coming to a halt as Commander Othan reached them.

"Knowledge and discipline," he called. "These words will be your mantra, your creed. We will teach you combat skills, and you will master the discipline to carry them out. Pain is a constant in battle, and so it will be in your training."

He guided them toward the Requiems and raised a hand to the stunning trees, pointing to the spheres dotting the branches. "Most of your second trial will take place in Requiems, where you will learn more about combat magics and how to fight as a unit. You may have survived the first trial, but each week forward we will dismiss the lowest two in the group. You want to retain your position? You'll have to fight for it."

Alydian exchanged a look with Toala and they both suppressed a smile. The warning was not idle, but after surviving the first trial it was

107

hard to deny the elation. There was a noticeable shift in the attitude of the trainers, from testing the acolytes to teaching.

They were directed to stand beneath the spheres. Alydian took her place and looked up at the swirling ball of power, awed by the magic being displayed. Mages could only see the energy of their respective talents, so she was the only one in the room to truly bear witness to the vibrant display.

An oak branch reached out and wrapped around her, lifting her off the ground toward the sudden hole in the sphere. She passed through the exterior and entered the hollow interior of the Requiem.

The sphere's surface flowed like liquid diamonds, glittering as the branch brought her to a halt in the center. The wall of the Requiem rippled and images appeared. Trees and mountains, cities and people, all displayed in such vivid detail that Alydian laughed in delight. Then tendrils of light seeped away from the Requiem and curled toward her, caressing her hands and feet and wrapping around her chest.

She gasped when the light hardened on her boots, making her feel like she stood on solid ground. She took a step and the tendrils moved with her, the branch holding her bending to accommodate her movement. But she remained in the center of the sphere.

She leapt to the side and the magic moved with her, keeping her in place but making her feel like she had moved several feet. She spun in place and the branch spun with her, its touch feathery soft.

She sensed the current of earth in the Requiem sphere and drew upon it, summoning it through the tendrils into her hands. She cast a ball of earth energy and saw it appear—but it was merely a mirage charm. The actual power was siphoned away even though it felt like flames remained.

"The Requiem is a tool," Commander Othan said, his voice so close that she turned, thinking he was beside her.

She felt a moment of panic as she realized she'd used a magic outside of Alethean's talents, but a glance revealed the sphere did not contain monitoring magic. As her heart rate returned to normal she realized Othan was speaking through an echo charm.

"The Requiem will replicate any magic you can perform," Commander Othan said, "but saps the dangerous edge to it. You will see and feel your power, but no fire will actually burn, no blade will actually cut. As powerful as this is, the true might of a Requiem is how it links to a memory orb."

His tone lightened at the end, revealing his smile. Then the Requiem shimmered again, the liquid surface rippling with the image of a forest—and the image continued to expand and brighten, filling the whole of Alydian's vision. She tried to widen her eyes but the effort was futile, and the image overpowered her senses.

And became real . . .

# Chapter 13: The Trial of Unity

Alydian's breath caught as she found herself in a bright forest of aspen. Light filtered through the trees, cascading upon the ground, lighting the undergrowth. Birdsong echoed from the canopy, while a rodent rustled in the leaves nearby.

Alydian bent and touched the earth and picked up a stone, astonished to feel the rough texture of the pebble in her fingers. She tossed the rock at a tree and it bounced off, the *thock* of the ricochet echoing into the forest.

The scene was so real that she reached to her waist. She could vaguely feel the limb holding her aloft but could not see it. Then a summer breeze pressed against her clothing, its touch warm and inviting.

"This is stunning."

Alydian turned to find Toala standing nearby, and beyond her the rest of the acolytes were spread out, all equally as enthralled with the Requiem's power. Commander Othan materialized into view and smiled.

"The Requiems can take us into any recorded memory," he said, "and a single memory orb will permit us all to experience the entire event. This particular forest was a memory from Oracle Sana, Elenyr's ancestor and the creator of the Requiems. As much as we would all like to experience such tranquility, it is not the type of scene we experience often."

The scene abruptly changed. Alydian stumbled back when the trees were replaced with burning barricades, a great fortress rising in the distance. The ground was torn and broken and stained by blood. The dead littered the area as smoke darkened across the sky.

110

"This was the final battle of the Griffin slave war," Commander Othan said, "where the slavers tried to usurp the king's authority so they could continue their trade. In time you will have the chance to fight this battle, but for now we'll give you something easy."

The scene changed again, turning into a night forest. Instead of aspen, the trees were poplar and cedar, the branches illuminated by a bright moon. Alydian stood on the edge of a clearing looking down on a small camp. A group of dirty men sat around a campfire, their postures frozen as if time had halted. Behind them, a pair of elven girls were bound and gagged.

Commander Othan strode down the slope and entered the camp. "This is a group of slavers from northeastern griffin," he said. "This memory is from Captain Barrows, who was sent to deal with these on behalf of Oracle Ciana. She located the bandits, and Captain Barrows dealt with them."

He tapped something on his gauntlet and time resumed. Alydian watched as Captain Barrows and two Runeguard burst into the camp. The men retaliated but were cut apart, helpless against just three Runeguard. Time stopped with Captain Barrows untying the elven girls.

"A flawless assault," Commander Othan said, and the image returned to before the battle.

Commander Othan then launched into a description of Captain Barrows' tactics and how he'd used a muffling charm to mask their approach before striking from two flanks, both targeted to avoid the chance of injury for the taken elves. When he finished, he surveyed the group of gathered acolytes while standing beside the dead bandits.

"The endurance trial was just the beginning," he said. "Within the Requiems you will be able to not just *witness* combat, but *endure* it, testing your mettle and ingenuity until you become a soldier without peer." He picked his way through the frozen battle, his voice rising with passion.

"In the next four months you will fight in every war of the last ten thousand years. You will participate in small-scale engagements and large assaults. All of you will die—many times—but death will merely bruise your pride, not claim your life. It will hurt because the Requiems

111

will make it real. The pain will bring clarity and focus, and a determination that will carry you to victory time and again. Here is where you rise from acolyte . . . to Runeguard."

Commander Othan surveyed them for several moments, allowing his words to sink in. Then he began to assign them to acolyte commands. Alydian wasn't surprised when she was placed with Grogith, Ferin, and Toala. She was surprised when Grogith was placed as their lieutenant. The appointment would last throughout their time as an acolyte, with the chance of being confirmed upon their completion of the third trial. Once they were in their commands, Commander Othan swept his hand at the frozen battle.

"Each command will have the opportunity to strike at these bandits," he said, "so prepare yourselves for combat."

Lieutenant Holan went first. He mirrored the tactics of Captain Barrows, but failed in the execution. One of the elven girls was slain when a bandit ducked behind her, allowing the girl to take an asunder lance to the gut. After the battle, Commander Othan froze the memory and shook his head in disdain.

"While Lieutenant Holan considers his failure, each of you will separate into your respective patrols. Today you will repeat the assault on the bandits until they lie dead, none of you are slain, and the captives remain unharmed. We will be watching, and may join your memory to provide direction . . . or rebuke."

He gestured with his hand and his form turned to dust caught in the wind. A moment later everyone else disappeared, leaving only Alydian with her patrol. The memory was also reset to before the attack, and Othan's voice spoke in her ear.

"First patrol to finish will receive extra rations and a night off. Last will clean the barracks—without magic."

Marked by the sudden murmur of voices, the memory began anew. Alydian marveled at how the cool night air brushed across her skin, at the scent of pine and smoke. She could feel the brush of a leaf on her arm and heard a distant snap of a stick.

"Lieutenant," Ferin murmured with a smile, "what are your orders?"

Grogith turned away from them and strode toward the campfire, ignoring the question. Ferin leapt after him and caught his arm, lowering his voice so the bandits wouldn't hear.

"What is your plan?"

"Kill the bandits," the gnome said, yanking his arm free.

Alydian and Toala exchanged a worried look before hurrying after them. They reached the edge of the clearing in time to see Grogith enter the camp. The men jumped in surprise and caught up weapons, the bandit leader darting to the gnome.

Grogith ducked the blow, and in a single motion, drew his anti-magic dagger and stabbed it through the man's throat. As the man clutched the wound and collapsed, Grogith strode toward the others. But a crossbow bolt appeared from the trees across the camp and sank into his chest.

Grogith snarled as he went down. As Ferin and Toala engaged the other bandits, Alydian leapt to a bandit about to slay Grogith. She instinctively reached for fire but remembered that was not one of Alethean's talents. Selecting plant magic, she called on the nearby roots, causing them to shoot out and pierce the man's chest.

Ferin leapt past her but she stood bound by shock, watching the blood seep from the wound she'd caused. The man eyes were wide and open, and she watched them darken, his life draining away. She'd never killed, and the act filled her mouth with bile. The bandit's features seared into her mind, his eyes, his blond hair, his beard. The image sank into her soul and seemed to extinguish a spark she'd never noticed, leaving her dark and hollow.

Recoiling from what she'd done, she dropped to Grogith and tried to heal his wound, ashamed that her hands trembled. Although she knew it wasn't real, the blood stained her hands and armor, and the gnome's features were contorted in pain and anger. The wound knit from her magic but another bolt streaked into the camp, sinking into her side.

113

She grunted, as much in surprise as pain. Aside from minor scrapes and injuries, she'd never endured a real wound. But the crossbow bolt dug into her gut. She gasped as pain exploded from the site and reached to the bolt, but a single touch sent fire into her belly. She stared at it in horror before another bolt plunged into her chest.

She cried out as she went down. Shock bound her tongue as she grasped the bolt embedded in her heart. She wanted to scream and writhe but clenched her jaw, mentally screaming. Then a heavy footfall drew her gaze to a bandit raising a sword over her throat.

"Stupid mage," he growled.

Alydian flinched—and appeared standing outside the camp with her companions. She reached to her wounds but they were absent, only a lingering ache to remind her of her death. She swallowed at the image of the sword descending toward her throat.

"Fifth patrol," Commander Othan barked. "Pitiful attempt. Lieutenant Grogith issued no orders, and Alethean acted as if she'd never been in combat before. Ferin, decent swordplay, but you cannot stand against a dozen men on your own. Don't be a fool. Toala, you should have used your banshee spell earlier to deafen them and stop them from communicating. And someone kill the sentries!"

The voice ended and the sounds of the forest returned. Grogith muttered something under his breath but Alydian stepped in front of him. The gnome snarled and looked up at her, unfazed by Alydian's expression.

"You may not care about my life," she snapped, "but we are a patrol, and I expect you to do your duty."

The gnome scowled and folded his arms. "You expect me to lead you into a fake battle? I'd rather kill them myself."

"*That* clearly worked," Ferin said.

Grogith stabbed a long finger at him. "It would have worked if you had dealt with the sentry."

"Why would I do that?"

"Because you don't have magic," he shot back. "Of course you would kill the sentry."

Toala cried out as a sword plunged into her back. Alydian leapt to her but the bandits had been drawn to the sound of their argument, and they descended upon them in a fury. All four of them went down under a coordinated assault by the bandits. Alydian endured a second death before she returned to the before-battle position.

Grasping the absent wound, Alydian listened to the furious orders by Commander Othan. Grogith remained scornful but they were forced to prepare another assault. They attacked the bandit camp again and again. Sometimes one of them died, but every time the elven captives were killed. With each failure she found herself numbing to the combat, to seeing the foes as objects rather than agents, deserving of the death they'd earned.

After the ninth assault Alydian ground her teeth together, chafing that she could not use her other magics. They were all tired and sore, and Commander Othan had made it abundantly clear that three of the other four patrols had finished.

"Use your mind, gnome!" Othan snapped. "It's sharper than any blade!"

They stood outside the camp once again. Alydian held her side, where a sword had plunged into her stomach. The injury was gone, but the memory remained bright and painful. Grogith stared at them with a scowl on his face.

"How many times does Grogith get us killed before we can get a new lieutenant?" Ferin muttered.

"If you did what you were told," Grogith snarled, "you wouldn't need one."

They fell to bickering and Toala joined in, their voices blending into heated hisses. Alydian endured it for several minutes until she stepped between them.

"*Quiet.*"

Her voice was soft, but the authority behind the word caused them all to fall silent. She fleetingly realized she'd used her oracle voice, but could not retreat now. Turning her back to Ferin and Toala, she faced the gnome.

"You are our lieutenant," she said. "Our lives are yours to disregard, but if you do not lead us we will not survive outside this Requiem. Will you rise to the mantle of your rank? Or carry our blood upon your soul until your own death?"

The gnome regarded her with an irritated expression, but she spotted a flicker of respect in his black eyes. The silence stretched between them and Alydian was grateful Ferin and Toala remained silent. Then abruptly the gnome huffed and turned to Toala.

"Silence your approach and then silence the sentry. Kill him quickly. Ferin, you watch Alethean's left flank while I watch her right. Alethean, cast a pair of stone entities and have them strike the far side of the camp. We strike at their backs when they rise to defend themselves."

"And the elves?"

"Cast an entrapment charm on them," Grogith said.

"On the captives?" Alydian asked. The entrapment charm was usually used to seal a foe in stone.

"You probably can't cast more than two or three at once," Grogith said. "Better to use it on the captives so the bandits can't harm them."

Condescension aside, it was a feasible plan, and Alydian raised an eyebrow to Ferin and Toala. The swordsman grunted and drew his sword, and Toala cast her muffling charm. Alydian grinned and cast her entities, summoning two golems from the ground.

They crept to the camp and waited until Toala sent a whisper to them. Then Alydian used her entities to strike the camp on the opposite side. As before, several leaped to the captives. Alydian darted out of the trees and reached to the earth beneath the elven girls. Dirt rose like jaws of a giant beast, closing around the elves and snapping shut, sealing

116

them off from the bandits. The bandits cried out in dismay when they saw the elves disappear behind a wall of stone.

The entities charged the camp, accepting the first strikes while Alydian, Grogith, and Toala charged from behind. The battle was over quickly, and Alydian's pride at the victory warred with her nausea at her kills. When the last bandit had fallen, she broke the entrapment charm and let the earth fall back to the ground. Then the image froze and Commander Othan's voice came into the Requiem.

"Sloppy yet effective," he said. "Unfortunately, you are three minutes too slow, so you get to clean the barracks. Alethean, you are not excused simply because your family managed to let you sleep in your own bed."

"Yes, Commander," Alydian said.

She caught the tentative smiles from Ferin and Toala before her surroundings faded to the Requiem sphere. She may have performed poorly, but it was the first time she'd been in combat when fear did not bind her. The hollowness of the kills had gradually been replaced with resolve. Commander Othan couldn't know it, but he'd forced Alydian to find her courage. As she exited the Requiem she sensed it deep within her, a slumbering beast that would never be caged again.

She'd never felt so powerful.

# Chapter 14: Rise to Runeguard

Alydian cleaned the barracks late into the night before switching personas and returning to her quarters. Despite her fatigue, she slept with a smile on her face and woke eager for another attempt in the Requiem. The sentiment was matched by the other acolytes as they entered the training hall.

They were summarily tasked with defending a merchant vessel against pirates, a memory from a long dead Runeguard captain. The next day it was dealing with a group of thieves attempting to steal from a castle in western Griffin. By the end of the week they fought in their first war.

Alydian recognized a gradual progression to the training, and the human bandits were replaced by dwarves, skilled elves, and even rock trolls. Beasts were frequent adversaries, with moordraugs and reavers making occasional appearances.

Everyone died.

Everyone learned.

Commander Othan drove them relentlessly, forcing them to fight until the stench of sweat filled the Requiems. No effort was flawless, no tactic completed to perfection. Alydian found her willpower mounting daily, until her entrapment spell could capture more than just a pair of elven captives. Her willpower swelled with each battle, until she was forced to feign weakness lest they discover her.

Holan mastered a fire reaver, a huge beast of churning flames that rampaged across battlefields, rending foes with abandon. Alydian watched the display from afar, resisting the urge to surpass his entity and steal the accolades heaped upon him.

They charged into the right flank of the goblin–Griffin battle. Flanked by a pair of light entities armored in stone, she was followed by Grogith and Toala, while Ferin brought up the rear.

"Holan has become insufferable," Ferin called, sweeping his sword across a goblin and ducking in the same fluid motion.

"He was always insufferable," Toala said. "But you can't deny his increased power."

"He's not the only one that's grown," Alydian said.

Toala grinned and pulled sound from the din, shaping it into several sparrows that she launched into the air. The sound entities flicked across the battlefield, striking goblin leaders in the throat, silencing them. As they choked and clawed in an attempt to issue orders, Toala sent a burst of echo charms into the goblin ranks, issuing her own orders and sowing confusion.

Grogith flicked his fingers into the air. Like spilling a cup of ink, he conjured anti-magic and solidified it into a trio of shackles. Then he barked to Alydian.

"Get them to the mages," he growled. "And cut the chatter. This is our third attempt fighting this battle and I don't want to have a fourth."

Alydian caught the shackles as they fell and cast a speed charm. Her muscles swelled with magic and she surged forward, weaving between the goblins as they desperately sought to stop her. She passed through the maelstrom of battle and threw the shackles at a trio of mages leading the defense. The goblins cried out as the shackles clamped onto their wrists, extinguishing their magic in an instant. Grogith whipped the hand crossbow he'd crafted and took aim, sending three dark bolts into them, ending them for good. Alydian cast a strength charm and leapt thirty feet, escaping the ring of enraged goblins. Another leap brought her to her companions.

As the officers and mages perished, Holan's fire reaver routed the remainder of the army. The memory froze with the goblins streaming out of sight and Commander Othan appeared. He strode among the slain, rebuking the dead acolytes and doling out praise to the victors. He reached Grogith and his eyes swept across them.

119

"Well done silencing their officers and mages," he said.

Alydian shared a smile with Toala. It was the first time Commander Othan had shown a measure of confidence in them. Ferin grinned as well and flicked the blood from his sword before sheathing it. Grogith remained annoyed, and snorted as the commander departed.

"We could have done better."

"Have you lost your wits?" Ferin asked with a laugh. "We suffered no significant injuries and we played a hand in the victory."

"Alethean is holding back," Grogith said.

Startled, Alydian turned to the gnome. "What makes you think that?"

Grogith grunted in response and strode away. Mystified, Ferin and Toala shrugged and followed him. Alydian remained in place and sent a thread of magic into the stone at her feet, feeling the earth all the way to the edge of the battlefield. She tugged . . . and the ground shuddered. The other acolytes paused but the memory was already changing, so no one saw Alydian's smile.

The training had awakened something deep within her. Prior to becoming Alethean she could have conjured a few entities and a handful of stronger spells. Now the flow of magic was as comfortable as breathing, and she yearned to unleash her full power, to test her limits. She couldn't imagine how Grogith knew, and she realized she needed to allow herself to be injured.

Apparently satisfied with their attempt, Commander Othan changed the memory to a new war, this time in the dwarven kingdom. The dark elf incursion was a tale often told to frighten children, and Alydian found the memory surpassed the tales.

In the depths of the earth the acolytes fought the clever dark elves, failing repeatedly. Grogith never mentioned his comment again, but Alydian spotted his gaze upon her, his black eyes inscrutable. Worried he might see through her persona, she allowed herself to be injured, even killed once. She endured Commander Othan's disdain but couldn't be certain she'd assuaged the gnome's suspicions.

Battle to battle the acolytes fought, never lingering after a victory. Each week that passed the lowest acolytes were dismissed, tightening their ranks as they endured the endless study of war. Alydian relished the renewed confidence, but each passing day brought renewed conflicts. Patrons arrived at difficult times seeking to speak with her, forcing Devkin to utilize all his skill to keep visitors from discovering Alydian's constant absence.

Several times her mother decided to visit the storeroom where Alydian was supposedly training. Alydian checked her future often, managing to forestall such visits by going to her mother first. Elenyr never spoke of what Alydian was doing, but her eyes sparkled with mischief whenever they were together. The rotation between personas left her breathless, but the chance of getting caught heightened her excitement. It had the opposite effect on Devkin, who seemed like he'd gained more grey in his scalp.

Throughout the training she thought often of the Soldier, and tried to imagine him as her adversary in the Requiem. But oddly she found the thought of killing him distasteful. He'd come to kill her, and deserved such an end. Yet she often found herself picturing him at her side, fighting as her companion.

She felt guilty imagining him as an ally, but whenever they fought rogue Verinai she gleaned insights from his attack upon her. She realized his strike had been highly specific. He may have slain the Verinai in her guard, but he'd spared the single mages and magicless. All of them. He wasn't a killer without a conscience, for he had a creed, one he adhered to with absolute devotion. And she found a trickle of admiration tingeing her lingering anger.

The acolytes defeated the dark elves and moved on to apprehending a trio of Verinai bandits, all skilled in the very magics the acolytes employed. The trio proved to be the greatest challenge yet, but with Grogith they fared the best of all the acolyte patrols.

Sometimes they were paired with a different patrol of acolytes, other times they fought beside actual Runeguard soldiers. They fought with Verinai and magicless, single mages and even an occasional oracle. Then came the day they fought with someone Alydian knew.

121

Her mother.

It was a battle from Elenyr's youth, when she was the youngest oracle on the council. Resplendent in white armor, Elenyr led a legion of Runeguard, Verinai, and Griffin soldiers to quell a rebellion in the southwestern province.

The rebellion leaders had hired mercenaries and pirates, drawing on enormous support. The Runeguard leading the charge shattered the line and victory seemed assured—until Elenyr was attacked. A small force of gnomes, humans, and mages burst from the trees where Elenyr stood, cutting through the Runeguard and charging the oracle.

Alydian sucked in her breath as the assassins closed the gap, fear spiking despite her knowledge that it was merely a memory. Screaming as they charged, the gnomes cast whips of anti-magic and the mages filled the hilltop with entities.

Sunlight swirled around Elenyr's form, coalescing into giant wings. The very sun seemed to dim as the phoenix came to life, and every soldier on the battlefield stilled at the phoenix's war cry. Then Elenyr launched herself skyward.

Wreathed in the form of a phoenix, Elenyr banked to the side and unleashed a stream of fire from her wings, bombarding the assassins, plunging them into an inferno. Apparently, the insurrection had banked heavily on killing Elenyr, and the moment Elenyr soared above them they surrendered.

The image froze and Commander Othan walked among the acolytes. "How would you describe this battle in a single word?"

"Awe," Toala breathed.

"Power," Erona exclaimed.

"Failure," Othan barked.

The memory reverted to before the battle, and they now stood with the Runeguard surrounding Elenyr. This close, Alydian realized they were watching the battle rather than their ward, their confidence in the impending victory a weakness that the rebellion was quick to exploit.

"Pride has been the downfall of many," Othan said as the memory passed over them. "And here you see the mighty Runeguard on the verge of losing an entire oracle bloodline because they did not think it could happen."

From just feet away, Commander Othan watched Elenyr cast her phoenix charm, and up close the display was all the more impressive. Alydian could not keep the grin from her features.

"The oracles are the pinnacle of hope for all of us," Commander Othan said, his voice soft as fire rained down upon them, passing through the acolyte forms to consume the earth around the assassins. "They can perform magic that dwarfs us all, yet they lack the pride we all seem to possess. We protect them because they can save us—not from death or misery—but from ourselves.

"We must protect them, shield them, and if necessary, give our very lives for them. This is the day you choose to acknowledge that however strong you get, you will never be stronger than an oracle. This is the day you accept your responsibility as a Runeguard."

His voice had risen with passion, and Alydian swallowed against the knot of emotion. She had never taken thought for how much her guards were willing to give for her. Her mind was drawn to the Verinai that had perished in the Soldier's attack on her caravan, and she suddenly saw the attack from their eyes, of their valor and sacrifice. Even the one who'd spoken with hatred to Devkin had stood between her wagon and the Defiant seeking to reach her.

As the memory came to an end it changed again, to a narrow valley with a castle on each end. Sources of magic ringed the walls and stood on pedestals on the floor, while the fortresses themselves held sources inside and out. The red castle was shorter but more fortified, and had thick walls behind a moat. The white castle was taller and boasted war machines on the upper battlements.

"From this day forth," Othan said, "your training will shift. All of you have shown combat proficiency against normal foes, and each morning you will continue to fight bandits and soldiers. But in the afternoon you will fight each other, testing your mettle against those you will fight beside. Patrol members will be shuffled so you may each learn to fight alongside each other, and individual standings will be displayed outside the Requiems. Four weeks remain in the second trial, and at the end of each week, the lowest ranked acolyte will be dismissed. The remaining four patrols will be given the honor of journeying to the third trial. First and fifth patrols, you will begin, and the match doesn't end until one patrol is dead."

His gaze swept across the acolytes. "Welcome to the Crucible."

# Chapter 15: The Crucible

In their first Crucible, Alydian and Grogith managed to kill Erona, while Toala killed another Verinai in their patrol. Grogith ordered them to drift up the right flank, but Holan's reaver hunted them down and tore them apart. The defeat was painful and disappointing, and Alydian ground her teeth in anger as she watched Holan celebrate his victory.

The patrols were changed and they fought again, and again. Alydian disliked fighting alongside Holan, especially when his orders were designed to give himself more chances at a kill. Alydian's disdain for Holan and the other Verinai was evident, and when Holan drew out Ferin's death she snapped, striking at him and knocking him away.

Holan wiped blood from his lip. "I knew you were a barren-lover," he growled.

Othan ended it then, and they fought again. But after that, the behavior of the other Verinai changed toward her. The divide between the Verinai acolytes and her patrol widened, forcing her to pick a side. She didn't hesitate.

The animosity increased daily, and even the Verinai guards joined in. Confused and angry, Alydian found herself in the midst of a rising tide of hatred, and the Verinai acolytes began to target Alydian in every engagement. She died often, but more often than not she was the victor. At the end of the first week, Alydian finished second of the acolytes for kills, a fact which drew even more hatred.

The next week, the daily skirmishes escalated into savage and bloody affairs as acolytes sought to prove themselves. Alydian felt the sting of death more times than she could count, and even after leaving the Requiem she felt the lingering ache. When the Verinai began to strike at her outside the Requiem she voiced her concerns to Devkin, who frowned.

"Are you certain it was Holan?"

Alydian lifted her sleeve to reveal where a fire star had dug into her flesh. The line across her skin remained where she had healed it, and the skin was still tender. The star had sliced into her arm just after leaving the Requiem, and she'd sucked in her breath in surprise and pain. Holan had turned away, a smirk on his face.

Devkin's expression darkened and he caught her arm to examine the wound. "I will have him dismissed for this."

Alydian pulled her arm free from his grip. "You would be forced to reveal your witness," she said. "And if you reveal me, my training will be over."

Devkin didn't retreat from her glare. "They can kill you," he snapped.

"They won't," she said. "And isn't this what we wanted? For me to learn to defend myself?"

"Not at the cost of your life!"

She growled at him, magic sparking in her hands at her fury. "You swore loyalty to me," she said, her voice rising. "Are you abandoning your oath?"

"Of course not," he snapped. "I'm fulfilling it!"

Abruptly the door swung open and a servant entered with a tray of food. She caught sight of Alydian and Devkin with magic in her hands, the tension palpable in the room. Her eyes widened but Alydian managed a smile and stepped to her.

"Thank you," she said.

"Fifth Sister Raine will be returning tomorrow," she said. "She requested to share an evening meal with you."

"Tell her I would be grateful for the opportunity," Alydian said graciously, and then noticed the girl's expression. "Is something amiss?"

"It's not my place," she said, bowing and retreating.

"Please," Alydian said. "Speak your mind."

The girl paused near the door. Under Alydian's soft gaze she relented. "The kitchens fear you dislike their food," she said. "You no longer attend meals with your mother and nothing remains on your trays."

Alydian suppressed a laugh, realizing the cooks would certainly have taken notice of her change in routine, and increase in appetite. Smiling, she gestured to the tray the girl had brought.

"The food is as delicious as ever," she said. "But after the Soldier's attack, I prefer to eat in my quarters."

"That is what I said," the girl said, smiling and bowing before she departed.

The door clicked, and Devkin said, "You're eating as much as I do."

His sour tone caused Alydian to laugh and their previous anger dissipated, but Devkin's eyes were still dark with fury—and fear. He was her guardian, tasked with protecting and serving her at the cost of his life. And she was placing herself in harm's way.

"I will survive," she said. "I swear it."

He scowled. "I don't understand why they would single you out."

"They act betrayed," she mused.

Alydian and Devkin argued deep into the night. Only when Alydian used her farsight to ensure she would survive the next few days did Devkin relent. Even with the assurance, Alydian slept poorly, unable to shake the sense of foreboding.

127

The next morning she joined the ranks of her friends in the mage training chamber, and tried to ignore the baleful glares from the Verinai. The rest of the week passed in a blur of exhaustion and fear.

Although they spent much of their time battling each other, they still used the Requiems for daily training, diving into battles and wars long forgotten. Alydian used the chaotic moments to learn, watching the Runeguard to learn spells for the magics Alethean lacked. Each night she practiced in the confines of her quarters, pushing herself to ever increasing efforts.

But it was the crucible that dominated the acolytes' focus. Each moment in past battles was a chance to survey the other acolytes, studying them, measuring their strengths. Knowledge gleaned was quickly exploited in the two castles of the Crucible. Then Alydian was placed with her three friends to fight beside Holan's patrol.

They stood in the space between the red and white castles, listening to Commander Othan describe the impending conflict. Alydian noticed the scorn in Commander Othan's gaze as he glanced at her, and her lips tightened. "They want us to fail," she said.

"But why?" Ferin murmured.

Before she could answer, Grogith growled. "The Runeguard is no longer a legion of races, and we do not fit."

Alydian frowned, recalling that the Runeguard had originally been a legion of soldiers from every race and kingdom, a symbol of unity among the divided world. But over the last few centuries the magicless guard members, or those with only one talent, were gradually replaced by the stronger Verinai.

Ferin fingered the hilt of his blade, but an easy smile spread on his elven features. "Let us defy their expectations."

"And how do we do that?" Grogith asked with a scowl.

"By surviving," Ferin said.

The elf grinned, and Alydian couldn't help but smile in turn. At four centuries old, the elf was the oldest among the acolytes by a wide margin, but his skill with a sword had caused even Captain Devkin to praise him.

"Patrols one and five," Commander Othan barked, interrupting their conversation. "You will defend the fortress while patrols two and three attack." His boots clicked on the stone as he strode among them, his expression lighting with a dark smile. "One week remains, so every kill counts." Then his form disintegrated, leaving them to their combat.

Holan barked orders to his Verinai and they surged into a sprint, passing through the doors of the white fortress and leaping to the battlements. Alydian followed them to the fortress, but Erona met them inside.

"We have no need for *your* type of aid," she said, signaling a Verinai to shut the gates.

"We will defend the wall," Grogith growled, his raspy voice turning harsh.

Erona stepped close to him but the gnome did not retreat. He folded his long arms as Erona growled, her words laced with profanities and allusions to Grogith's mother. When she was finished Grogith's narrow features were dark with fury.

"My patrol," he said simply, and turned on his heel.

"Stay out of our way," Erona shouted at his back.

Grogith ascended a staircase that wound around a turret, entering the overlook at the top. Then he turned to face them.

"I'd like to gut her myself."

"As would I," Ferin crowed, drawing his sword.

Toala gestured to the battlements, where Holan's patrol had taken up position. The wall curved around the corner of the white fortress, the battlements facing open ground. Two turrets bordered the main doors, while another three clung to the castle's keep.

Bridges connected the rear turrets to the main fortifications. Pathways and stairs wound their way up, connecting the towers into a labyrinth of overlooks, sweeping arches, and alcoves. Cracks and scars marred the stone, some deep enough to threaten the integrity of the fortress.

"What do we do?" Toala asked.

"We let them fall," Grogith said.

"That's it?" Ferin asked, dismayed by the answer. "Shouldn't we at least try to defend the fortress?"

"No."

Grogith folded his arms, jutting his chin out. His small black eyes reflected no hint of compromise. Ferin grunted and looked away before offering his sword to the gnome.

"Will you at least enchant my blade with some of your magic? It will give me an edge against the Verinai."

"No," the gnome said.

"Why are you even here?" Toala demanded, anger seeping into her voice.

"My secrets are my own," Grogith said, and stalked away.

Ferin attempted to follow but the gnome cast a look back that froze him in his tracks. Then he was gone. In the ensuing silence, Ferin turned to Alydian as he ran his fingers through his graying hair.

"What's wrong with him?" Toala asked.

"Did anyone else hear him appoint Alethean as his lieutenant?" Ferin asked slyly.

"I did," Toala said with a grin.

Alydian hesitated, recognizing that, with her farsight, she could lead them in the impending battle with ease. She'd secretly begun using her farsight in previous battles, quickly switching between future and present. But doing so would betray the gnome and likely deepen the divide between them. She shook her head.

130

"Cast entities and prepare yourselves, but do as he says."

Without waiting for a response, she followed the gnome. Grogith had taken a path and ascended stairs to the extreme summit of the white fortress. Nearly touching the sky and capped with broken battlements, it overlooked the wall and the fortress below.

Alydian found him leaning on the battlements and she stepped to his side. She did not speak, even when the second and third patrols attacked, and magic erupted below. Her friends remained in the turret and did not offer aid even when one of Holan's patrol was knocked from the wall, screaming as his leg broke upon the ground.

"Be gone, elf," Grogith said.

On impulse Alydian slipped into her magesight and peeked at the gnome. Anger and pain reflected back at her, so dense that she winced and withdrew. As Holan barked orders and defended the fortress alone, she spoke in an undertone.

"I'm here because at one time I felt weak and powerless."

He did not move, but his black eyes flicked toward her. She continued as if she had not seen the motion.

"Some time ago I was attacked," she murmured. "And they could have killed me. I was helpless and terrified, and sometimes I still feel the touch of a blade on my throat. I never want to feel that way again."

Grogith grunted in disgust. "You do not know your own strength."

"Perhaps," she admitted. "So I need a captain to teach me."

His laugh was raspy and mocking. "You know far more than I."

"About magic," she said. "But who will teach me to be defiant?"

He threw her a sharp look, one of his long ears rising. "I'm not your mother."

"Nor I yours," she said, and smiled.

Below them, Holan and Erona's entities were torn asunder under the combined attack of the other Verinai. Screaming in rage, they

131

retreated deeper into the fortress. The other patrols split up, one going for Holan and Erona, the other ascending after Grogith's patrol.

"Come little barren and I will make your end swift," a Verinai called, his mocking laughter echoing into the fortress.

Toala appeared with Ferin. "Holan couldn't hold them, the fool. Now we have six Verinai coming for us."

Alydian looked to Grogith, and the dour gnome stared at her. Then he rumbled in his throat and pointed to Ferin's sword, an inky substance appearing and coating the steel. Ferin crowed in delight as his sword turned dark.

"It will only last a few moments," Grogith warned.

"It will be enough," Ferin said.

"Are you going to be our captain again?" Toala asked.

Grogith scowled at her tone. "Clog their ears so they cannot work together. Then send an entity to distract them."

"What about you two?" Ferin asked.

For the first time Grogith smiled, but the sight was more disturbing than his scowl. "We punish them for their pride."

Toala grinned and stepped to the battlements. Magic sparked in her fingers and dozens of tiny birds burst from her palms. They spread out and dropped into the fortress, hunting their adversaries. Two found a Verinai just below them. Flanked by lions of fire, the Verinai smirked and pointed upward—and the birds smashed into her ears.

She shrieked and grasped her head, clawing at the birds, but they would not be dislodged. The birdsong was piercing even to Alydian, and she shuddered at the idea of it in her ears. The distraction cost the woman dearly. Ferin leapt down the steps and alighted next to the first lion, plunging his sword into the entity. The lion trembled and disintegrated, while the other lion leapt to him. Toala opened her mouth and sound exploded from her throat in a horrendous wail. It struck the lion on the flank and knocked it from the ledge, and it tumbled into the darkness below. As it disappeared Ferin stepped to the Verinai and struck her on the skull. She folded in half and went down.

The rest of the Verinai's patrol saw the woman's fall and slowed to regroup. United, the five of them charged up the stairs. Instead of multiple entities, they had cast a single giant between them, and the huge entity reached all the way to the battlements where Alydian and Grogith stood.

Alydian sent her magic into the stones of the battlements, and they ground together, rising into a golem that caught the giant's hand. With multiple magics swirling through its form, the giant's fist struck the golem to the ground, and cracked it all the way to its feet.

Shocked by the unexpected strength of the giant, Alydian desperately sought to seal her golem, but the giant swung again. Grogith cast his anti-magic against it but the entity was far too strong, and the fist shattered Alydian's golem, knocking her into the battlements. Alydian blearily stumbled to her feet and saw at a glance that Grogith was dead.

When her vision cleared it wasn't the expected adversaries but Holan who stood before her. His features were bloodied from the combat and contorted with hatred. Little remained of the fair elf he'd been when they first met. All at once Alydian realized Holan had joined the opposing Verinai to strengthen the giant entity.

"Betrayer," he hissed.

He cast a shimmering sword of light and strode to her. Alydian spotted the remaining members of the third and fourth patrols, but they looked on with approval. Without ally or friend, Alydian desperately sought to call on her magic, but the fear once inspired by the Soldier returned in force, binding her power. She stumbled back until she struck the cold battlements. Then Holan reached her and leaned into the blow, driving his lightcast blade through her stomach.

Alydian screamed as the weapon pierced her and plunged into the wall. The searing agony ripped her breath from her lungs. Her trembling hands reached for the blade, blood seeping down her clothing. Holan leaned in, his expression turned savage.

"Betrayer," he hissed again.

Alydian screamed as the weapon was yanked free, and everything went black.

# Chapter 16: Ellie's Refuge

Raiden guided the wagon to a small inn owned by one of the Defiant. He removed his mask and approached after dark, and knocked on the rear door. When the innkeeper appeared, Raiden flashed the sign of the Defiant by raising a fist and tapping the back of it with his forefinger. The man glanced about and then repeated the motion.

"We need to dispose of a wagon," Raiden said, "and we need a new one."

The man nodded. "Leave it in the barn. I'll have a new one here in an hour."

Raiden thanked the man and withdrew into the night. An hour later they transferred the guardian into the new wagon and left the Verinai wagon in the barn. As they shackled him into place the sounds of axes turning the old wagon into firewood echoed into the night. Then they pulled back onto the road and turned north.

Without their masks, they looked like a normal group of travelers. They spoke to the guardian as if meeting him for the first time, and he seemed to believe they were not the masked ones who had rescued him. Raiden still avoided speaking to him on the chance he would recognize his voice.

"What now?" Red asked. "They aren't going to let the guardian go. He's too dangerous."

"He's proof," Jester said.

"Proof that the Verinai are twisted?" Red asked. "We already knew that."

"Proof of their heinous acts," Jester said. "We knew they had secrets and now we can show them. I say we walk him right up to the oracles and poke him with a sword. They'll be shocked and outraged. The betrayer in their midst won't see it coming."

Raiden absently scratched one of his recent scars, lost in thought. "Proof he may be, but the courts are controlled by the Verinai, and we'd never make it into Dawnskeep. We need someone who will believe us."

"What about Griffin?" Jester countered, a smile on his face.

"You want to take him to King Talin?" Red's laugh was scornful. "Have you forgotten he's hunting us?"

"The Thieves Guild gave us pendants that can alter our features," Jester said. "Just bring the guardian and show the king what the Verinai have done."

Raiden cut off Red before she could snap a reply. "It's a bold plan," he mused, "But very risky. The pendants are weak and won't last for more than a few hours."

"You said we need allies," Jester said. "And if we can convince King Talin of the Verinai's true natures . . ."

"He will turn on them," Raiden finished.

"Or he will have us hanged," Red said with a scowl.

"Which is why you won't be going with us," Raiden said. "We only have two pendants, and it will take both Jester and I to keep the guardian shackled."

Red shrugged. "Where would you have me go?"

"We *do* need allies," Raiden said, causing Jester to snort in amusement. "There are many bandit camps in the southern plains of Griffin. Find them and recruit them."

"You get to speak to a king while I talk to bandits?" She shrugged in resignation. "Either way I'm bound to get my throat slit."

Raiden grinned. "We'll meet back at the swamp refuge in a month."

"As you order," she said, and then her scowl turned into a smile. "If I leave now I can sleep in a bed."

Red untied the reins of her mount. Then she stepped off the wagon and mounted the steed. Turning it away, she disappeared into the night. When she was gone, Jester turned to Raiden, his features barely visible in the moonlight.

"I didn't expect you to agree."

"Impulse, not decision," he said, causing the assassin to grin.

For the rest of the night they wound their way north, taking turns on watch. The guardian did not sleep or eat, and made no effort to talk to them. As dawn crested the horizon they turned onto the main highway curving north to Terros.

It was late summer and the road was filled with merchants and travelers. Raiden merged their wagon into place behind a caravan. Although his instincts told him to use back roads, he suspected the Verinai would anticipate that. Instead he chose to remain in plain sight. Several times Verinai patrols passed, but he pulled their wagon closer to the caravan so they appeared as part of it. After a week of hard travel, they reached Terros.

As capitol to the Griffin kingdom, Terros sprawled across a series of hills. The city bordered the great Blue Lake and the waterfront extended for nearly a mile, its docks laden with goods for transport. Large walls partitioned the city into districts, with the king's castle resting on a hill that overlooked the region.

Much of the city was not protected by the district walls, but an expansion was well under construction. Scaffolding rose adjacent to the wall, while stonemasons worked to add height to the already imposing battlements. The district under construction lacked the wealth of the older districts, the houses smaller and of more modest make, but the expansion would eventually reach to the southern end of the waterfront.

They guided their wagon through one of the newly constructed gates and entered the south district. Dilapidated structures greeted them, their occupants dirty and disheveled. As the largest of the districts, the southern district was home to tens of thousands. Rank water flowed in canals that originated clean and bright in the upper districts. The stench permeated clothing and people, and Raiden wrinkled his nose.

He lifted his gaze to the wall under construction. It sloped from the old walls all the way to the ground, the stonework obscured by miles of scaffolding laden with stacks of stone. The hum of hammers and reverberated off streets and homes.

"Ellie can house us," Jester said.

Raiden hadn't decided on it, but agreed with a nod. Ellie had joined the Defiant over a year ago and, although she was too old to fight, she offered her meager shop to any Defiant in need of refuge.

They drove their wagon through the cracked streets, pulling into an alley behind the weaver's shop. Hearing the creak of the wheels, Ellie toddled into view, a smile spreading on her wrinkled face.

"Why does an elf of such beauty grace my home with his presence?" she asked.

Raiden grinned and descended from the wagon, stepping forward to embrace her. "We need a place to hide, and information."

"You know where to go," she said, waving toward the secret room she kept for them. "I'll be there in a moment."

Raiden nodded in gratitude and rubbed his back, grateful to be off the wagon. Then he stepped to the rear of the wagon and helped Jester undo the shackles from the wagon floor, reattaching them so the guardian's feet remained chained to each other.

"Where are we?" the guardian asked, speaking for the first time in days.

"Terros," Raiden said. "We have someone we want you to see."

His features lit up and then darkened. Then he shuffled after them, his hands and feet clinking in the chains. He had not asked for them to be removed, and Raiden wondered if he knew how dangerous he was.

The man looked beaten, his clothing worn and threadbare. In any other setting, Raiden would have assumed he was harmless. But the wild glint to his gaze set Raiden on edge, and he kept his distance.

They guided him into the rear of the weaver's home and opened the secret door hidden behind a section of wood paneling. Then they slipped into the refuge. Although small, the space contained a trio of beds and a tiny table. Raiden sat the guardian on a bed then moved to the table, taking a seat as Ellie entered.

The woman glanced at the guardian but did not comment. Placing a plate of steaming bread and a wedge of cheese between them, she sat on the remaining chair. As Raiden and Jester ate, she talked.

"The Soldier is in real trouble," she said. "His attack on Alydian has set the people on edge, and word is she refuses to leave her quarters."

"She's hiding?" Raiden asked in surprise. He'd thought her stronger than that.

Ellie shrugged. "No one has seen her in weeks, and many are saying she's afraid of the Soldier."

Raiden looked away, struggling to contain his guilt. Alydian had never been in battle, yet she'd displayed a will stronger than steel, standing in defiance of death. He couldn't admit it—especially to his lieutenants—but in that moment he'd felt a stirring in his heart. He couldn't imagine one such as her retreating to solitude . . .

Or had she?

Since attacking Alydian he'd often thought of her, each time feeling guilty for what he'd nearly done. Her features and words frequented his thoughts, and he'd wondered how she was faring. If she was as strong as he suspected, she would not have cared for the feeling of helplessness. She would have sought to arm herself, and do so outside the public eye. But how? Stifling a smile, he resolved to find out, and turned his attention back to Ellie.

She sipped her cup. "It isn't just the Verinai that are hunting the Soldier now. King Talin has dispatched three of his legions to scour the countryside."

"They won't find him," Jester said.

"I know that," Ellie said curtly. "But it's a show of force that will appease the Verinai and the Eldress Council. Oracle Ciana meets with the king daily, demanding that he take measures to protect the people against the Soldier's reign of terror."

"And the populace?"

"Caught in the middle," Ellie said. "Most still think he's a hero, but they also worship the oracles. They fear that the Soldier has lost sight of who oppresses them."

"And the Verinai?" Jester said. "We've heard tales they've become bolder."

"Aye," Ellie said. "They've coerced the weaver and stonemason guilds into allowing them to become advisors. The king, too, has Verinai to guide him. Those who accept the Verinai into their walls see an influx of wealth, while those who refuse see their coffers empty as they attempt to fight the higher quality goods the Verinai produce."

"And Oracle Ciana?" Raiden asked.

"Helps to negotiate on the Verinai's behalf."

Raiden and Jester exchanged a worried look. The news was hardly new, but if the oracles had started publicly allying themselves with the Verinai, it meant they no longer feared the people's ire. But who was the rogue mage? And were they manipulating the other oracles as well?

More and more, soldiers yielded to the Verinai patrols, with the king even replacing his generals with Verinai masters. The Verinai appeared generous, even enhancing other guilds' production with their own artisans. Within a year, the Verinai would have infiltrated every facet of guild and national leadership.

But what were their intentions? Raiden knew little more than the people, but the sheer level of influence and control made his gut tighten.

Supporters of the Verinai were vocal in their claims of the guild's generosity, but Raiden saw the guild as a parasite that hid its vile nature behind a veneer of benevolence.

"Can you get us in to see the king?" Raiden asked.

Ellie's eyes widened. "Why?"

"We have a message to deliver," Jester said, motioning to the silent guardian.

She jerked her head. "The Verinai lead his personal guard. You cannot sneak in to see him."

"Then publicly," Raiden replied. "Surely he still allows the public to speak in open court."

"Only once per fortnight," she replied. "You'd have to wait a few days. But there might be another way. You could don the persona of a visiting noble, but your friend couldn't be shackled."

"I don't want to delay," Raiden replied. "We can go tomorrow as a steward under Viscount Baron."

"You know what he did to my family," Ellie said, her nose wrinkling in disgust. "Why use his house as a persona?"

"Because if it comes to a fight, the king will blame him," Raiden replied.

Ellie smiled, her eyes twinkling with anticipation. "I almost hope it goes sour for you."

Raiden grinned. "We'll sleep here tonight, and then depart in the morning. I don't want the patrols to find us here."

"They won't," she said dismissively. "The street whelps keep me informed of the guard's movements, and no one is smarter than children surviving on the streets."

Jester nodded in gratitude. "You truly are a lady."

The old woman laughed so hard that tears leaked from her eyes. She swept from the room still laughing, and Raiden climbed into a bunk. He slept soundly until Jester woke him for his turn on watch. Taking a seat, he watched the guardian. The hours slipped by in silence until the man suddenly looked at him.

"Are we going to see the king?'

Raiden saw no reason to deny it so he nodded. "We are."

The guardian nodded his head in satisfaction. "Good."

Raiden frowned, disliking the man's tone. But further prodding elicited no response. Resigned to waiting, Raiden wondered if he was making the right decision. The guardian was proof of the Verinai's secret practices, but would King Talin help them? Gaining the support of the powerful Griffin king would legitimize the Soldier's efforts and potentially turn the tide. But his instincts continued to twinge, and his doubt remained.

# Chapter 17: The Accord

They left at dawn, and used the wagon to ascend to the wealthier districts of Terros. The frequency of patrols increased dramatically the closer they came to the king's castle, and they were forced to abandon the conspicuous wagon. Dressed in noble's robes that Ellie had given them and with the pendants, they looked every bit the men they claimed to be. Jester even commented he liked his false goatee better than his real one.

Out of necessity Raiden removed the shackles from the guardian's feet. But he couldn't bring himself to release the guardian entirely. His shackled hands hidden behind a cloak, the man walked between Jester and Raiden.

They passed through Gold District, where shops lined the streets and venders shouted their wares. People from every race strode among the stalls, and coin clinked as it exchanged hands. Raiden spotted a pair of rock trolls and even a dark elf among the crowd. Then he passed into the White District.

White granite formed the pristine homes, their balconies as large as Ellie's entire shop. The District was home to Dukes, Counts, and the occasional Viscount. Patrols passed them, but the rich clothing Ellie had made provided armor against suspicion.

When they reached the castle grounds they joined the small crowd waiting outside the gate. Comprised of various castes of people, they were all there to petition the king's advisors. The guards spotted Raiden and motioned him through.

"The king is expecting you," he said.

"Viscount Baron will be pleased," Raiden said with a smile.

Ellie had learned that a steward of Viscount Baron was expected to arrive in the next few days, and managed to inform the king's advisors that the assistant steward would be arriving early. It was a risk donning the persona of an actual individual, but the opportunity to reach the king quickly was too much for Raiden to pass up.

As Raiden entered the grounds his gaze was drawn to the castle. Set on a hill overlooking the city, the fortress had been built of darkstone, its walls littered with enchantments to brighten the exterior.

The turrets lacked battlements, and instead contained finely carved wood for a roof. The keep rose behind the great hall, the windows glimmering in the sun. More enchantments had been added to the castle grounds, causing the birds to sing and the trees to sway in beautiful patterns.

Statues danced in the gardens around the castle, the stone figures spinning and twirling. Instead of the cheaper light orbs produced by the elven people, the grounds contained birds of light. The entities fluttered from branch to branch, their golden rays further brightening the pristine gardens.

Instead of peace, the tranquility of the gardens inspired foreboding. Raiden hadn't visited the king in years, but he saw the handiwork of the Verinai. He wondered if he was already too late. Perhaps the Verinai already owned the king.

He glanced at the guardian and spotted the gleam of madness in his eyes. His instincts twinged again. Loath to ignore them a second time, he drifted closer to Jester, intent on ordering him to withdraw. Before he could, a patrol of Verinai appeared.

"Viscount Baron's steward?" the captain asked, dismounting his steed.

"Fell ill to fever," Raiden said. "I'm his assistant. Is something amiss?"

"No," the captain replied, "But the king asked to see you directly."

"Of course," Raiden said. "Lead the way."

Jester and Raiden exchanged a worried look as the Verinai took up position around them, leading them toward the main entrance to the keep. Raiden cast about, measuring routes to escape, but they were already committed. Surrounded by Verinai they would never make it to the fortress wall.

"The king is pleased that Viscount Baron agreed to sign the treaty," the captain said. "I assume you brought the signed Accord with you?"

Raiden paused, feigning confusion as he patted the pouches at his side. "I fear I left it in the inn with the servants," he said. "Perhaps I should go retrieve it before I speak to the king."

"We'll send someone to retrieve it immediately," the captain said, and waved to one of the guards. "We cannot allow others to find its contents," he added with a nervous laugh. "Where were you staying?"

Raiden provided the name of an inn as he glanced at the man, marking the Verinai colors on his shoulder and the spark of fear in his eyes. As the Soldier, Raiden had been acting on impulse for years, and knew the signs of an opportunity. He had no doubt his persona would not hold up to scrutiny for long, but perhaps their visit could bear fruit after all, even if it wasn't the flavor he'd anticipated.

He glanced at Jester and the assassin brushed the hilt of his sword. Raiden gave a slight shake of his head, obscuring the motion by rubbing his nose. If the king was signing secret treaties with the other nobles, he wanted to know. But they would need an escape route, and he needed to deal with the guardian.

He glanced back at the man—and his eyes widened. The guardian had begun to fidget, the wild tinge to his eyes bordering on madness. Some of the guards cast him strange looks and instinctively shied away. Noticing the movement, the captain raised an eyebrow.

"Who is your companion?" he asked.

"The Viscount's nephew," Raiden said, and then lowered his tone, leaning toward the captain. "He is unwell, but family."

The captain threw the guardian a doubtful look but nodded. "Every family has its odd ones," he said uneasily. "But I think it best he wait outside. It would not do for your conversation to be overheard."

"My attendant will remain with him," Raiden said.

Jester took the hint. "As you order."

They reached the main entrance and passed inside, where most of the guards came to a halt. Jester caught the guardian's arm as Raiden and the captain passed through another set of doors. Raiden noticed the tension to the assassin's shoulders, the caution in his eyes.

The main hall of the castle was vaulted and wide, with enormous windows lining the walls. Dwarven cut pillars supported the buttresses, and polished marble reflected Raiden's entrance on the floor. Their boots clicked across the surface as they advanced, and at the other end of the hall the king sat on his throne. Surrounded by guards and advisors, the man had been speaking with another steward. Upon Raiden's entrance, the king smiled and stood, motioning to the woman before him.

"Please convey my gratitude to your lord. Thank you for your visit."

"Thank you, your majesty," she replied, bowing before a guard led her out.

The king rose and strode forward, raising his hand in greeting. "Steward," he said, "where's Ibel?"

"Ill with fever, my Lord," Raiden replied, bowing before accepting the king's hand. "I'm his assistant. Viscount Baron appointed me to deliver the Accord personally."

The lie came easily. Stewards and their assistants were known confidants of nobles, and frequently carried out the business for their masters. They were also rarely recognized because they were responsible for the house when the Lord was absent. Evidently the king had not met Viscount Baron's steward's assistant because he smiled.

"Excellent," he said. "But let us speak in private."

146

The king stepped down from his throne and strode to set of double doors behind it. The guards fell into step behind him, keeping Raiden from drawing too close. Now curious, Raiden took the opportunity to examine the king.

Tall and well built, he walked with his shoulders slightly hunched. His gaze, too, carried a burden, and grey lined his hair, a recent addition since Raiden had last spotted him riding in the streets of Terros.

His curiosity rising, Raiden looked around the king and realized that his advisors were *all* Verinai, as were his personal guards. Wealthy nobles in all the kingdoms had taken to protecting themselves with Verinai, but Raiden had thought the Griffin king had resisted that practice.

The king entered a room and a surprising number of guards and a pair of advisors joined him. Small and filled with couches and tables, the room contained the king's private desk. He took a seat behind it and motioned Raiden into the chair across from him.

Surrounded by Verinai in a windowless room, Raiden fought the urge to draw his sword. If they knew he was the Soldier, or even a member of the Defiant, they would kill him before he had a chance to reach the door.

His mouth dry, he licked his lips and forced a smile, his gaze shifting between the Verinai in the room, measuring them, marking the masters. Four were quad-mages, another boasted five magics. Raiden imagined the subsequent battle, where he could move, who he would kill first. Containing the sense of being trapped, he took a seat. Before he could speak, one of the Verinai stepped in.

"Viscount Baron is the eighth noble to sign the treaty," she said. "And we are grateful for his support."

Raiden heard the *we* and his eyes flicked to the king. "I'm certain the treaty will bring increased prosperity to our kingdom," he said, keeping his words vague.

The king smiled but the levity did not touch his eyes. "We can only hope."

The Verinai advisor stepped to the king's side, her stance conspicuously arrogant beside the reigning monarch of the largest kingdom in Lumineia. Raiden's foreboding mounted as he noticed the subtle looks from the other Verinai—even the king—marking her as the one with power in the room.

"I don't believe we've met," she said. "I'm Master Mineva, assistant guildmaster to Elsin."

Raiden thought she looked familiar. The woman was the second most powerful mage in the guild of Verinai, second only to the guildmaster herself. For her to be here—and behaving the way she was, did not bode well.

"There's one thing I don't understand," Raiden said. "How will the treaty help contain the Soldier and the Defiant?"

It was a provocative question, and Raiden watched the responses of those in the room. As expected, the Verinai's expression filled with revulsion, scorn, and a trace of fear. But the king's lips twitched as if he wanted to smile.

"He is a murderer and a thief," Mineva said, her lips curling with hatred. "He should be put down like a rabid dog."

"Easy, Mineva," King Talin said. "He may be a criminal, but he deserves justice like everyone else."

The looks on the Verinai made it clear that the Soldier would never make it to a tribunal if they had their way. Raiden resisted the insane urge to smile as he realized they had no idea who he really was.

"Patrols are hunting the Soldier even now," Mineva said. "And Oracle Ciana has added her farsight to the search. It's only a matter of time until we find him. The new empire will certainly make that easier."

"An oracle besides Teriah is aiding in the search?" Raiden asked. "I understood they did not involve themselves in inquisitions outside their stewardship."

Mineva turned to face him. "The treaty clearly states the oracle's position." Her eyes carried a trace of suspicion.

"I must have forgotten that," he said with a weary laugh. "My duties keep me fairly busy, after all."

Her expression indicated it was the wrong thing to say, and Mineva stared at him. "The oracle's position is the principle agreement of the treaty," she said slowly. "For you to miss it suggests you never read it."

"Of course I did," Raiden said, feigning indignation as he rose to his feet. "How dare you insult me?" He scanned the room and found himself ringed by hostility.

"Where's the Accord?" Mineva demanded, coming around the desk.

The captain answered from behind Raiden. "He claimed he left it at the inn."

"Impossible," Mineva said, and flames appeared in her hand. "No steward would have left a document of such importance."

"He's just an assistant," the king said, also on his feet. "Perhaps it is merely an oversight."

"It wasn't," Raiden said, abruptly deciding to drop the persona. In a fluid motion he yanked his sword free and placed the tip on Mineva's throat. "My regards from the Defiant." The bold motion froze the Verinai in the room, and the Mineva swallowed, her eyes filled with hatred.

"You think to fight a dozen Verinai alone?" she demanded. "You'll be dead before my body hits the floor."

Raiden flashed a grim smile. "I would still see your body hit the floor."

"You are a fool," she said. "Tell us who the Soldier is and you may be spared."

Raiden burst into a mocking laugh. "You don't understand. The Soldier is everyone. He's the common folk that you oppress, the man in the tavern you don't pay, the barmaid you belittle."

"We'll see when he's dead," she replied.

149

Conscious of the Verinai casting lightblades around him, Raiden carefully stepped close to Mineva and wrapped his arm around her, twisting his sword so it rested along her throat. Then he backed toward the door.

"You cannot escape," she snarled.

Raiden backed through the door, and the Verinai soldiers followed him into the great hall, edging closer. He saw the intent in their eyes and gauged the distance, knowing he would not make it in time. They would attack and he didn't stand a chance of escaping. He scowled as he saw death in their eyes, and tensed for a final stand. Before he could move the great hall shuddered, and an unholy shriek came from outside the castle.

# Chapter 18: Madness of the Lost

The Verinai around the king shifted, their eyes flicking over Raiden's shoulder as shouts and screams erupted from the castle's entrance. Despite the standoff, King Talin craned to look past the Verinai.

"What's happening?" the king demanded.

The doors exploded, sending a pair of bodies tumbling into the great hall. Fire climbed from the doors, sending ash and cinders billowing upward. Jester appeared in the opening and sprinted around a pillar, just as a burst of light followed. The light struck the pillar and it cracked, the power searing a line across the stone. Then the guardian stepped through the curtain of smoke, his body phasing between light and flesh.

"What have you done?" Mineva demanded, catching sight of the guardian.

"Don't ask me," Raiden replied, twisting so they faced the guardian. "You created him."

There was an audible intake of breath. "You brought an unchained guardian? Are you *mad*?" She struggled in his grip but he held her fast.

"Tell me what it is," he demanded.

The guardian caught sight of them and began to advance, light blossoming at his fingertips. The Verinai around the king scattered, diving for cover behind pillars and the throne. Shouting for aid, the king darted for the doors leading to the dining hall, and Raiden followed, dragging Mineva with him.

The guardian leaned forward and sent a blast of light through the hall. The asunder lance struck the throne, tearing through it to impact the two Verinai beyond. When the light faded the throne was gone, disintegrated to bits of dust and charred wood. The remains of the men behind were steaming.

"YOU DID THIS TO ME!" the guardian shrieked.

The Verinai unleashed their collective power, striking at the guardian on all sides. Fireballs bounced across his form but he hardly noticed, and he turned on the casters with a surge of vengeance. One man fled, but another searing lance of light blasted him to oblivion.

From within the dining hall Raiden spun Mineva into the wall and placed his sword against her throat. "What is a guardian?" he demanded.

She glared at him. "It was supposed to be chained to a source so it would not succumb to madness—but the Soldier stole it before it could be leashed in Verisith."

"You *wanted* the Soldier to steal it," he accused.

She winced as the blade pressed against her throat again. "Guildmaster Elsin thought you would take it to your camp, where it would destroy you before its magic consumed it."

"How can we stop it?" the king demanded.

"It would take a score of light mages to siphon the power from his flesh," Mineva said. "Enraged as he is, he'll destroy the castle and everyone in it."

The walls shuddered again, and a sphere of light blossomed from the great hall. It exploded outward, shattering every window and door. Raiden ducked as the doors to the dining hall flew inward, the wood engulfed in flames. The burning doors clattered over the dining table, breaking dishes and sending silver scattering. On the opposite side of the opening, the king leveled an accusing finger at Mineva.

"You and your arrogance," he shouted. "You thought you could bring order to my kingdom with *this*?"

"The Soldier brought this upon you," Mineva shouted back. "He steals a weapon he does not understand and his minion brought it to your door."

Heedless of the screams erupting from the great hall, the king continued to shout at Mineva.

"If I survive this I'll tell everyone about your precious Accord. Nobles and commoners alike will turn their fury upon you and your reign will end before it begins. Your Mage Empire will die before it takes its first breath."

"I told Elsin you would betray us," Mineva snarled back.

A beam of light cut the stone wall like a sword through cloth. It cut so close to Raiden's head that it nearly decapitated him, forcing Raiden to dive away. Mineva used the distraction to scramble free, but instead of fleeing she darted to the king.

"Perhaps your daughter will be more malleable," she said, and a sword of fire appeared in her hand. Before the king could react, she drove it into his gut, leaving him to slump to the floor. Helpless, Raiden watched the man fall, his features stricken.

"You kill the king in cold blood?" Raiden growled, keeping his sword between them. "The people will not stand for this."

She sneered at him. "The barren believe what we tell them, and after the attack on the oracle, they will believe the Soldier assassinated the king."

"The commoners are smarter than you think," he said.

"They are cattle," Mineva shouted. "Beasts fit to serve their masters."

"And you're the master?" Raiden snapped. "You can't even master your magic."

"The guardians will be the sentinels of the kingdoms," she cried, straightening in fury. "They will stop wars and crime, and keep all the barren in their place. The era of race will come to an end, ushering in the Mage Empire!"

153

A streak of light sliced through the wall behind her and curved, cutting above her on its way to him. Raiden dived to the floor as the searing lance passed above him, and felt the heat on his back. When he rose to his feet, Mineva was sprinting away.

Raiden stepped after her but a groan caused him to turn and look down, to find the king was still alive. Kneeling at his side, he examined the king's wounds but saw at a glance it was too late.

"Please," the king said, his voice faint. "Stop the guardian before my daughter is killed."

"Why should I?" Raiden asked. "You allied yourself with the people that built it."

The king coughed, his expression twisting with pain. "I gave them control over the mage guilds, and soon they controlled everything. I may have worn the crown, but they sat on the throne."

"The Accord," he said. "How does it create a Mage Empire?"

"The Verinai guildmaster will destroy the kingdoms," he groaned. "The nobles are swearing allegiance to them, and the oracle that leads them. The Empire will replace the kingdoms of every land."

"What about the people?"

"They would be enslaved," the king said, coughing.

"You could have fought the Verinai," Raiden snarled with sudden vehemence.

"They controlled my daughter," the king said, his voice fading. "I had no choice. Tell the Soldier he must save my kingdom . . ."

The king relaxed in death and Raiden laid him on the floor. Then he stood and removed his noble's robe and tossed it into the flames next to the door. The room was empty, the fires having spread to the other openings. Removing his pendant, he donned his mask and turned toward the opening.

He entered the great hall to find it devastated beyond recognition. Pillars lay on the ground, their stone reduced to rubble. Smoke billowed

154

up from scattered flames. Gaping holes littered the walls, revealing patches of light that failed to pierce the smog. Soldiers poured through the front door and fought through the smoke, only to die at the hands of the enraged guardian, who stood in the center of the room unleashing light on anything that moved.

A quartet of Verinai spread out behind him and cast their magic, threads of light striking the guardian like chains. Instead of attacking, the threads glowed bright and began to siphon energy. The Verinai desperately sought to dispel the light, using the guardian as a source to cast entities that darted forward. The lightcast wolves piled onto the guardian, knocking him to his knees.

Raiden saw it coming and dived behind a fallen pillar just as the guardian screamed his fury. He grasped the threads bound to his back and sent a current of power into them, causing them to shatter and launch their casters into the wall. Then he leaned down and punched the marble floor, sending a wave of light arcing away from him. The blast ripped through the entities, tearing them asunder before striking the walls, causing the castle to shudder anew.

Jester slid to Raiden's side. He too had discarded his nobles clothing and donned his mask, and he'd tied a makeshift bandage over a wound in his arm. Blood seeped from the cloth but the assassin didn't seem to notice.

"He shattered the shackles like they were toys," Jester said. "And not even the Verinai could stop him."

"Draw his attention and I'll get close," Raiden said.

"You sure we can't just run?" Jester asked.

"Jester . . .,"

"Worth a shot," he said. He flashed a lopsided grin and then darted into the open.

The guardian turned away from the dead Verinai and aimed a blast at Jester, but the assassin nimbly streaked away. The guardian roared, the sound echoing primal and harsh. Turning with Jester's run, he aimed for him again.

Raiden leapt the fallen pillar and sprinted for the guardian. Dodging rubble and Verinai bodies, he reached the guardian as he turned. Raiden drove his anti-magic sword into the guardian's chest, plunging it all the way to the hilt.

The guardian shrieked, the sound scraping across Raiden's ears like claws. The energy around the sword darkened and the shadow spread like a poison. But the guardian backhanded Raiden, cracking his mask and sending him tumbling across the floor. Light oozed from the guardian's chest like black ink. The guardian stumbled about sending bursts of light in Raiden's direction, attempting to incinerate him.

Raiden clawed his way to his feet and slid behind a pile of debris, the marble erupting in geysers of stone all around him. He huddled behind a section of pillar, coughing in the dirt as the guardian unleashed his rage. When the barrage finally came to a stop Raiden peaked over the pillar.

But the guardian remained.

With the anti-magic sword still in his chest, the guardian was on his knees, the black spreading across his chest and back, threads climbing up his throat into his face. One eye had started to darken, while the other was bright with madness and fury. He grasped the hilt of the sword and pulled it free, screaming as it passed from his body. Then he tossed it away, the black sword bouncing across the dirt and disappearing.

The gaping shadow on its body remained but the guardian rose to his feet, his limbs shimmering with his remaining power. Raiden fought his rising fear. His anti-magic sword had been crafted to negate magic, and could take down even mighty entities with a well-placed strike. But the guardian had survived a wound that should have killed anything born of magic.

From across the chamber, Jester peeked out from behind his own hide. Raiden spotted him and their eyes met, and it was the first time Raiden saw fear in the assassin's gaze. The man had killed Verinai and beasts across Lumineia, but here they faced an adversary beyond anything they had encountered.

"Come to me, my little fleshies," the guardian said, "And I will end your suffering."

156

The guardian spoke like he would to a child, soft and sweet. He began to sing as he stalked Raiden, the words indecipherable yet the meaning clear. Raiden huddled behind the pillar, fear crawling up his gut. Unbidden, he thought of Alydian. He wondered if an oracle could stand against a guardian. As he listened to the crunch of gravel under the guardian's feet, he fought the rising desperation.

# Chapter 19: Herald of War

With fear raising the hackles on Raiden's neck, he crawled away from his hiding spot, slipping behind one of the few intact pillars as the guardian rounded the corner. Light shimmered in his palms as he looked upon the spot Raiden had been. Then he pressed on, his disturbing song reverberating through the now quiet great hall.

Raiden dropped to the floor and worked his way to another pile of debris until he spotted his discarded sword. Before he could reach it a burst of light shredded the floor around the sword, sending an explosion of stone and dust into the sword, knocking it away. It bounced against the wall and disappeared again.

"It's not nice to stab," the guardian scolded like a mother to an errant child.

Raiden rolled in another direction and sat up behind the foundation of a pillar, trying not to look at the charred remains of a Verinai nearby. The guardian continued to stalk the room, occasionally sending bursts of light into the stone. Raiden remained in place, struggling to control his breathing. Then he heard a scuff nearby and whirled.

Jester slid to a stop beside him and sank into a seat. "Only the Verinai would create such an abomination."

"He used to be a man," Raiden murmured.

"Anything human died in the enchanting," Jester said. "We need to kill it."

"Where are the king's soldiers?" Raiden whispered.

"Outside," Jester said, "trying to find a way in, I suspect. Last I saw the entrance was a pile of stones."

"We should never have brought it here," Raiden said.

Jester threw him a sharp look. "The Verinai built it."

"And we wielded it," Raiden said, his tone harsh.

"You didn't kill these men," Jester said. "That *thing* did. And it's going to kill more if we don't end it."

Raiden heard the crunch of rock as the guardian ambled in their direction, and he fought to put his guilt aside. There would be time to dwell on his mistakes later. If he survived. Wiping the blood from his mask, he nodded.

"Where's my sword?"

"In the dust by the west wall," Jester said. "I'll try to keep the guardian occupied while you find it."

"And then?" Raiden asked.

"We cut it to pieces."

The force to his statement was sufficient to drive Raiden to his feet. Jester stood as well, and then drew a throwing knife from his chest. With a flick of his wrist he sent it spinning into the cloudy air. It *pinged* on the other side of the hall, and the guardian swiveled in that direction. Without breaking his song, he glided toward the sound, his voice drowned out by the sudden crackling in his hands.

Raiden sprinted toward his lost sword and dived to the ground. Apparently hearing the motion, the guardian rotated and sent light lancing at Raiden's back. The magic seared a line across the wall, tearing through a decorative shield like it was parchment. As the shield clattered on the ground, Raiden dug through piles of dirt, desperately searching for his sword.

Jester darted through the smoke, cutting a line across the guardian's arm before disappearing. The guardian spun but wasn't fast enough, his strike missing Jester by inches. Instead of going after him, he continued his advance toward Raiden, still singing.

"Little fleshy, little fleshy," he sang. "I will kill you like the resty . . . ."

Raiden shifted a stone, grunting from the effort. Then he dug into the dirt and rubble, his fingers clawing through bits of stone. His efforts turned frantic as he heard the guardian's footsteps approach, and this time Jester could not distract him.

The guardian appeared around a pile of stones and spotted Raiden—just as Raiden spotted the glint of black in the dust. Diving for it, he yanked the sword free and fumbled for the hilt. His fingers closed on the steel and he spun, but the guardian was already pointing to him, his eyes alight with glee.

With no time to evade, Raiden raised his anti-magic sword. The searing lance of light blasted into the weapon and sheared apart, sending rays of magic arcing away. The impact drove Raiden's feet across the floor but he grimly held on, knowing that if he lost his grip he would be consumed.

The light brightened as the guardian advanced, forcing more magic into Raiden's sword. The black of the blade began to brighten, the enchantment unable to withstand the sheer volume of power. Recognizing he had only seconds, Raiden leaned into the attack and pressed forward, closing the gap.

His sword shimmered, the anti-magic brightening, the hilt turning warm. Ten paces became two, and then Raiden caught a glimpse of the guardian through the blinding streaks of light. In a single motion Raiden dropped into a crouch and spun away, the light exploding past him to detonate against the wall, leaving a hole to the gardens.

As the guardian swiveled to him Raiden kicked off the wall and slashed his sword across the guardian's hands. Veined with light and steaming, the anti-magic sword passed through the guardian's hands without cutting.

His hands went dark, the blast of light sputtering into sparks and ash. The guardian screamed in pain and turned, but Raiden did not stop. Swinging his sword across one of the guardian's legs, he cut a line of darkness in the light. By then Jester was on the opposite side, and together they attacked the guardian.

160

He retaliated with a fury. Light flowed from his flesh to form shields and swords, the lightcast blades held by hands of light conjured from the guardian's body. Relentless, Raiden stood his ground, deflecting the swords to find openings in the shields, driving his still-steaming sword into the guardian's body.

Each cut darkened his form, each wound killing part of his magic. Sensing defeat, the guardian stumbled away, attempting to retreat. Jester cut him off, his sword swinging for the guardian's throat. He managed to block it with a shield, but Raiden came from behind, striking deep into the neck.

The guardian crumpled, the light of his body flickering and dying. With dark wounds littering his form, the guardian collapsed to the floor, his shields and swords disintegrating. The magic drained away, the body turning back to flesh. Without wound or mark except for blackened skin where the anti-magic blades had cut, the man appeared oddly serene as he closed his eyes.

"Thank you," he breathed, and finally went still.

Raiden leaned against a fallen section of wall, his chest heaving. On the other side of the body Jester did the same, and for several moments the two gasped for breath. Raiden stared at the body of the guardian, his guilt slowly churning into rage.

Jester was right. Raiden had made a mistake by bringing the guardian here, but the Verinai had created an unstable weapon, one powerful enough to withstand even anti-magic weaponry. One was dangerous enough, but if they had an army of guardians . . .

"We must go," Jester said.

Raiden looked to him, and then heard it as well. Shouts and the distinct clatter of tools came from outside. A burst of magic echoed, and then sunlight filtered through the smoke near the front entrance.

Raiden wearily nodded and turned to the gaping hole the guardian had created it in the outer wall. Stumbling through the opening, they exited the castle into the gardens that surrounded it. Shouts and cries of alarm rang out, and thousands of soldiers struggled to shift through the rubble that blocked the entrance. Others raced about the gardens, their expressions panicked.

Raiden turned away from the army and slipped into the trees, working his way around the outer wall of the gardens to one of the gates that led to the city. He expected sentries but the gate was abandoned, and dozens of men and women stood on the threshold, gawking and pointing at the smoke rising from the king's great hall.

A woman squeaked in fear and surprise when Raiden stepped into the open, and the rest of the spectators surged back. Raiden ignored them and strode through the crowd. They recoiled, scrambling away.

Covered in burns, dust, and blood, Jester was hardly recognizable. His mask was cracked as well, and through the gap a cut marked his chin. Parts of his tunic were shredded, revealing burns on his torso. Raiden numbly wiped the dirt from his mask, but his hand had so much dirt that it merely smeared it.

"It's the Soldier!" someone cried out.

"Is it really him?"

"I don't believe it!"

"What happened?"

Jester came to a halt and turned to the crowd. "The Verinai forged an abomination with their magic," he said, his voice gravelly from the inhaled dust. "It killed the king's advisors and destroyed his castle."

"And King Talin?" a woman asked in a shrill voice.

"Dead," Raiden replied. "By Master Mineva's own hand."

Stunned to silence, they stared at him until Jester added, "The Soldier slew the guardian abomination—but the Verinai have crafted more."

"What will they do?" a woman cried.

"They will kill us all!" another shrieked.

"Will you save us?" a man in a merchant's clothing asked, stepping forward.

"I cannot," Raiden said. "Not from what comes. The people must rise up against the Verinai . . . or your children will become their slaves."

Someone cried out, and then another began to shout. Raiden turned away as the crowd dissolved into fearful argument, but a woman in a fine emerald dress hurried to catch up. She caught Raiden's arm and retreated when he turned.

"Where will you go?" she asked.

Raiden noticed others listening for his answer and said, "To expose the Verinai as traitors and tyrants," he growled. "Even if it must be by the sword."

Beyond the crowd a soldier appeared, and came to an abrupt halt as he spotted Raiden and Jester. He shouted for aid, and in seconds a score of soldiers rushed into view. Many in the crowd shifted to block their path, and the soldiers got lodged in the press.

Raiden nodded his gratitude and turned on his heel, striding into the street. Drawn to the spectacle, more and more people filled the streets of Terros. They parted for Raiden and Jester, whispering and pointing. Raiden had already sown the seeds of his own rumor, so he held his tongue.

A group followed them all the way to the southern district, and only stopped when he climbed to a roof. In the confines of the buildings they leaped to adjacent roofs, working their way to Ellie's shop. Once they had ensured they had not been followed, they dropped into the alley behind her shop and removed their masks.

Ellie appeared when they entered, her features lit with worry. Beckoning them to follow, she led them to the basement, and filled two tubs with hot water. Fretting like a nervous mother, she helped them remove their outer clothing and clean their wounds.

Wincing as Ellie stitched a gash, Raiden's thoughts turned to the king. After three years of striking from the shadows, the guardian's assault on the Terros castle could only be seen as a call to war. But would the people support Mineva's version? Or the Soldier's? More importantly, who would the princess follow? Raiden recognized the signs and knew the truth.

War was coming.

# Chapter 20: Rift

Alydian's death in the Requiem lasted only a moment, but Holan's punishment lasted for two days. Devkin still fumed at his betrayal, and tried to get him dismissed. Commander Othan refused.

They probably expected Alydian to come back timid and afraid, but when they next fought she did so with a fury. Sensing her desire to retaliate, Grogith allowed her to lead the charge in subsequent Crucibles. The defiance of their patrol did not earn the respect of the other Verinai acolytes, and instead it seemed to incite them to greater anger.

Against Devkin's advice but with his aid, she began sneaking into the training hall at night. With Devkin manipulating the memories, she fought against foes of every type—especially Verinai. She even took the role of the bandits in order to fight Verinai soldiers. Holan may have tried to intimidate her, but she was no longer the woman the Soldier had attacked. Alone in a Requiem she could unleash her full might, and cast spells that Alethean could not.

Within the Requiem she fought against Holan and his fire reaver, and his entire patrol, punishing him for his betrayal. She cast her memory of the Soldier's attack and fought him as herself, now powerful and fearless.

During the day she kept herself rigidly in check, but at night she unleashed Alydian. With Devkin's private lessons she learned how to fight with bows and knives, swords and spells. She began to wonder if someday she might one day match her mother, and cast a phoenix.

In an attempt to heal the widening chasm between the acolytes, Commander Othan placed all the acolytes into an elven training hall. Inside the Requiem the detail of the wood was flawless, the walls covered in a variety of ancient elven weaponry. Commander Othan spoke as he walked among them.

"Every magic has its weakness," Commander Othan said for the thousandth time. "Light cannot be cast in darkness, and plant magic is useless in a desert. You must learn to adapt to your surroundings as much as harness the magic—and you must learn to respect the power of your Runeguard companions, even if you do not care for them."

Alydian had heard before, so she pulled on the floor, causing it to swell and lift her a few inches. Earlier that day a dwarven Verinai had used his magic to glide around the training hall, the stone lifting and carrying him like a wave of the sea.

"Combat is movement," he'd called as the stone threw him into a flip, catching him and curving him in another direction. "Standing still can get you killed."

Like the other stone mages, Alydian had been instructed to attempt the spell, but she'd found it difficult to do so. Each time the stone lifted her off the ground, she felt the urge to panic and her magic dissipated. She was so focused that she didn't hear the approaching footfalls.

"Am I boring you, Alethean?" Commander Othan said.

She looked up and found him glaring at her. "No," she said hastily. "I just wanted to practice the glide spell from earlier."

Othan stabbed a finger toward the front, and Alydian heard snickers and laughter from the Verinai as she made her way to the front of the group. Coming to a halt at her side, Commander Othan gestured to the group.

"Since you apparently know everything about the weaknesses of magic," he said. "Perhaps you can instruct us. What is the weakness to body magic?"

"Temptation," Alydian replied. "Frequent uses—especially when combined with other body spells, weakens the flesh of the caster."

"And healing magic?" he asked. His tone was casual but his eyes were hard, indicating the threat was yet to come.

166

"Magic cannot be transferred," Alydian replied. "So a healer cannot use their own health to knit a wound. They can only draw on the energy within the wounded's body."

The questions came faster now, bombarding her with the other types of magic. She answered them all, and tried to keep the smile from her face. The commander had no way of knowing how much she truly knew.

"Fire is unpredictable and difficult to contain," she said, answering his latest question. "It can spread easily if the caster is not focused, and can even kill them."

Commander Othan folded his arms and regarded her. Then he asked, "And what is the weakness of combined magics?"

"Magics may be fused by a Verinai, or different casters," she replied, meeting his gaze. "For example, I can cast a stone golem and Toala can add a banshee hex to the stone."

"And anti-magic?" he asked, his tone still mild as he began to circle around her. The Verinai acolytes began to smirk.

"The most complex of the common magics," she said, her lips twitching as she glanced at Grogith. "Anti-magic absorbs all types of energy, but it requires enormous effort to shift it into solid form, or enchant it into any form of permanency."

"You clearly know the common magics," Commander Othan said with a humorless smile. "But what about the rares? Lightning, for example."

"No one studies the rare magics," Ferin protested. "You can't expect her to know anything about lightning."

Alydian did know about the rare magics, and uniques. Her studies had included every known branch of magic, even the ones that were considered myth. From birth it had been made clear to her that she would need to understand every type of magic, even if she was only skilled in a portion of them.

Alydian actually knew a great deal about lightning magic, and had begun to harness it in her nightly training with Devkin. She'd nearly lost her head for the initial efforts, but now she'd begun to control it. Unpredictable and almighty, lightning magic hadn't been witnessed in centuries. It would have been a unique except for the handful of documented casters in Lumineia's history.

"As a Runeguard you must know every type of magic," Commander Othan admonished, his expression triumphant. "And be prepared to stop them all. Since Alethean clearly has fallen to arrogance and believes she knows everything about magic, she will spend the rest of the day in the archives until she learns the weakness of lightning."

Alydian knew from experience that only a handful of tomes in the archives even mentioned lightning magic, let alone in detail. Fortunately, she'd read them all.

"Lightning magic harnesses a difference in power between the earth and the sky," she said, unable to keep the smile from her face. "The powers change constantly, making it nearly impossible to control exactly where lightning will strike unless one has tremendous focus and skill."

Her patrol stifled laughs while Commander Othan's face darkened with fury. Holan and his Verinai friends scowled. Alydian realized the commander sought to pull her from the acolytes in order to diminish the conflict. His effort to do so had been thwarted, and his nostrils flared. He took one step toward her but a woman spoke from the doorway.

"A flawless answer," she said, drawing all eyes to her.

Alydian turned, and her smile evaporated. Elenyr, First Sister on the Eldress Council, stood in the doorway. She didn't seem to notice Alydian's sudden fear, and her gaze remained on Commander Othan. He bowed his head and gestured to her.

"First Sister," he said. "I did not realize you had entered a Requiem."

"I didn't," she said, a smile on her lips. "I do not need a Requiem to enter your memory. I have watched much of your training in the last few weeks." Her eyes flicked to Alydian before returning to Othan.

"Would you honor us with a lesson?" Captain Barrows asked.

168

"Alas," she said. "I cannot stay. I must request the presence of Alethean."

"An acolyte?" Othan asked, his eyebrows rising. "Why would the high oracle wish to speak to her?"

Although it was clear he made an effort to control his voice, a trace of irritation seeped into his tone. Elenyr did not comment on it, and instead motioned to Alydian, who bowed and strode to her.

"She will return in the morning," she said. "I'm certain you can manage without her."

Othan scowled as Alydian faded from view, her vision returning to the interior of the Requiem. Her mouth dry with fear, Alydian exited the training hall to find Devkin in the courtyard, his expression sober. He gestured her to follow and guided her to Elenyr's private quarters at the top of the Elsheeria tower.

"May I know the reason for my summons?" she asked Devkin while they were in the ascender.

"I'm certain you can guess," Devkin said. "You are no fool."

Alydian saw worry in his eyes. Did Elenyr know of Alethean's identity? Had she divined it with her farsight? Or had she noticed Alydian's constant absence? She grappled with the questions as they ascended into the Elsheeria tower. Then they exited the ascender and advanced down the hall.

"It will be an honor to meet an oracle," Alydian said for the benefit of the guards they passed.

Devkin glanced her way as they strode down the hall. "Perhaps one day you will be her guard," and then his lips twitched with amusement. "Unless you are dismissed and have other duties to attend to."

They reached the door to Elenyr's private chambers and Devkin swung it open, allowing her to enter. Alydian knew the room intimately, but hung back. She did not need to feign fear.

Elenyr was sitting at the table in the corner of the room. The afternoon light cascaded upon her through an open window, making her appear beautiful and regal. Her blue dress added to the grace of her appearance, as did the pendent on her throat, which was simple silver shaped into the oracle's crest. She smiled at their appearance and gestured to the seats at the table.

"Acolyte Alethean," she said. "Would you care for some cha?"

Weldina approached and served them as they sat. Alethean took a nervous sip and tried to relax, but her tension mounted when Elenyr ordered the guards from the room, including Devkin. When they were gone she turned her gaze upon Alethean.

"Alydian," she said with a small smile. "Are you enjoying your time as an acolyte?"

Alydian flushed. "How long have you known?"

"I had my suspicions from the beginning," Elenyr admitted with a smile. "Your choice to be an acolyte is bold, and quite clever. I have taken measures to ensure your endeavor remains a mystery, especially from the council. They would undoubtedly be furious if they knew."

"Do you disapprove?" Alydian had expected condemnation, but her mother seemed to actually be pleased with her.

Elenyr sidestepped the question. "I especially enjoy your nightly training with Devkin. Your talent has grown significantly, particularly lightning magic. I always found that type challenging, but it appears you have a talent for it."

She raised her chin. "I nearly died when the Soldier attacked—and I never want to feel that way again. I don't want to be a coward."

Elenyr stared at her. "From what I understand, your Verinai acolytes wish to kill you."

Alydian scowled. "The Verinai—"

"Are the reason you are here," Elenyr said calmly. "Your guise of a Verinai was well considered, but your behavior is not in line with their practices."

"I cannot be what I am not," Alydian said bluntly.

170

"You could have pretended better," Elenyr said. "Now your presence has become a gaping rift between the acolytes."

"The rift was there before I arrived," Alydian shot back.

"But you have widened it," Elenyr pointed out.

Alydian cringed at the rebuke. "I don't understand," she said, facing her mother. "Are you angry because I did it? Or because of my behavior as an acolyte?"

"You are not the first oracle to secretly train with their magic," Elenyr said, her eyes sparkling with humor. "But the current climate is tense, and you have heightened that tension."

"Why did you summon me?" Alydian asked.

"The guildmaster of the Verinai has requested your return to her hall," Elenyr said, "and Elsin does not make a request without cause."

"Why?" Alydian asked. "I've done nothing to merit a dismissal."

"She thinks you a rogue Verinai," Elenyr said, "and has demanded your dismissal. She wants your head."

"For what?" Alydian demanded. "I've done nothing wrong."

"Being an oracle is more than right or wrong," Elenyr said quietly. "It's about understanding and accepting others—even when *they* are wrong. The principle applies when you are in another's persona."

"How can I understand the Verinai when they act with such arrogance?"

Elenyr sighed and passed a hand over her face. "You have always harbored resentment against the Verinai. I hoped that within the guard you would learn to appreciate them, which is why I permitted you to remain among them even when they began to target you."

"I'm sorry, mother," Alydian said softly. "I did not mean to incite such conflict."

"I will not admit it outside this room, but I'm proud of you," Elenyr said with a smile. "But we face a dilemma. Even if Alethean disappears,

171

Guildmaster Elsin will search until she finds her—and that hunt will lead to Alydian. The rift won't just be among the Runeguard, it will spread to the kingdoms. We cannot permit that thread to come to pass."

Alydian hadn't considered the potential ramifications of the enmity between her patrol and the Verinai. Now that she did, she realized her mother had used her farsight to do what Alydian should have done.

"I'm sorry, mother," she said. "I should have been more careful."

Elenyr regarded her with kind eyes. "Your effort to master your magic is admirable," she said, "but it does not take precedence over your calling as an oracle. The people, the kingdoms, and the guilds look to us for guidance and leadership. They trust us to balance the needs of different individuals and cultures. If an oracle acts out of self-interest, that faith will be broken."

"I understand," Alydian said, bowing her head. "But what do I do?"

Elenyr sat back, her eyes sparkling in sudden amusement. "You must die,"

# Chapter 21: Summoned

Alydian looked to her in surprise, but her mother's expression was one of amusement. "You are nearing the third trial," she said, "where you will journey out of Dawnskeep and face a real threat in Lumineia. With your farsight you should have no problem feigning death and slipping away. Guildmaster Elsin will be appeased, as will the Verinai."

"And I will no longer train with the Runeguard," Alydian said.

Elenyr's expression turned sympathetic. "Daughter, no one but I will know how much you have truly grown in the last few months, but you've reached the end of your intrigue. Under the current circumstances, this does seem to be the best thread for your future."

It was not meant as a rebuke, but Alydian recognized it as one. Her mother had searched the future on her behalf—an act she should have been doing for herself. Alydian had become so engrossed in her time as an acolyte that she'd forsaken her true calling.

"I will do as you request," she said.

"Then our business is concluded," Elenyr said. "You may return to your training."

"As you order, Mother," Alydian said, rising to her feet.

Elenyr's lips twitched with amusement. "After your return to Alydian, please visit me in my chambers. I would like to hear the tales of your last few days from your own lips, especially of lightning magic."

"Anything else?"

She smiled blithely. "Make sure you humble Holan."

"Are you encouraging me?" Alydian asked.

Elenyr grinned. "As an oracle I disapprove of your behavior. As a mother, I couldn't be prouder."

Buoyed by her mother's statement, Alydian turned and strode to the door. Before she reached it, Weldina swung it open. The look on her face shattered the levity of the room and drew Elenyr to her feet.

"Captain?" she asked.

"The king of Griffin has been killed," he said, and her features darkened. "By the Soldier."

"It cannot be," Alydian blurted. "He only hunts Verinai."

"Hold your tongue, acolyte," the captain snapped. "We just received a lightbird from Master Mineva herself, and sealed by Oracle Ciana."

"Who else was killed?" Elenyr asked.

"Two score Verinai," the elf replied. "A handful of others."

Elenyr went white and sank into her seat. "Guildmaster Elsin will want to hear of this."

"She is already on her way," the captain said. "She wished to speak with you immediately."

"The Soldier has escalated his attacks," Elenyr said, suddenly appearing weak. "First Alydian, now King Talin. Who will be his next target?"

"Acolyte Alethean," the captain said. "Return to your patrol. Your presence is no longer necessary."

"Leave her be, captain," Elenyr said.

Confusion washed across her face but she inclined her head. "As you order. Guildmaster Elsin wishes to speak to you. And Raine is here already."

He stepped aside, and Raine strode into the room. "I *warned* you that the Soldier was a threat. Now the king of Griffin is dead." Her eyes flicked to Alethean and then passed across her.

"What would you have me do?" Elenyr asked, her voice strained. "Teriah has sought him to no avail. We've dispatched patrols throughout Lumineia and they find nothing."

"Allow the Verinai to dispatch an army after him," Raine said. "They will not fail."

"The Verinai?" Alydian asked. "They will leave a swath of devastation behind them. They won't care who is harmed." Then she recalled that she was still Verinai and shut her mouth.

"They will find the Soldier," Raine insisted, her forehead knitting in confusion at an acolyte's presence.

"But not without causing bloodshed of their own," Elenyr said. "The acolyte is right. The Verinai will not show restraint."

"How else do you expect to stop him?" Raine asked. "How many does he have to kill before you will take action? Alydian will hardly leave her quarters because of him, and when I do get to see her she is quiet and fatigued." She passed a hand over her face.

"Alydian will recover from his attack," Elenyr said.

"But how many more hide in fear?" Raine asked. "We must act, before it's too late."

"Action without wisdom will lead to ruin," Elenyr said. "We need to consider our next thread carefully, and learn exactly what occurred in Terros."

"You want to *wait*?" Raine said, her voice rising. "The people will be clamoring for safety and you want to sit idle? If we do not act swiftly the kingdoms will fall to war."

"And if we act swiftly, we could cause it," Elenyr said.

Raine released an explosive breath and retreated to the balcony. In her absence Alydian stepped to her mother, whose face was drawn and white. She placed a hand on her shoulder and knelt.

"High Oracle," she said, "I do not believe the Soldier would have killed the king. He didn't even kill the magicless when he attacked Alydian's caravan, and spared Captain Devkin when he could have killed him."

"I agree," Elenyr said. "But my faith in Alydian's word is not enough. If the people of Griffin believe the Soldier killed their king, they will fall to fear. They will clamor for safety."

"And the Verinai will provide it?" Alydian asked.

"They are powerful enough to do so," Elenyr said. "But we must hold them in check."

"Then summon the council," Raine urged, returning to join them. "Tell them I will lead the search for the Soldier personally."

Elenyr's eyes widened in shock. "Oracles never lead the Runeguard."

"There has never been one like the Soldier," Raine said. "Let me find the one that hurt Alydian."

"You speak with bravery," Elenyr said. "I will consider your proposal."

"You have my gratitude," Raine said.

Elenyr nodded and gestured to the door. "Alethean, you may depart." Then she added mentally. *And return as Alydian.*

Alydian nodded and left, making her way to the guest quarters. Selecting a dress from the many in the closet, she pulled it over her shoulders and removed the Alethean necklace. She paused before a mirror and adjusted her hair before hurrying back to her mother's quarters. The sentries merely nodded to her as she slipped inside.

Raine glanced up at her presence and smiled. They embraced and it looked like Raine wanted to ask more, but instead fell silent and returned to the window. Elenyr's eyes were shut, indicating she was deep in her farsight. Alydian fought to calm her breathing and heart, and wiped the moisture from her brow.

The door swung open and Weldina appeared. Bowing to Elenyr, she said, "Guildmaster Elsin has arrived."

"Let her enter," Elenyr said.

Alydian stood and retreated as an elf entered the room. Tall and beautiful, the woman conveyed an aura of power that was intimidating. Her features were angular and sharp, while her eyes were a darker shade of blue than normal, suggesting human blood in her ancestry. The tattoo of a Verinai marked her neck, and nine symbols of magic graced her shoulder.

Alydian had met her before, but never realized just how much fear she inspired. The woman's power was legendary and rivaled that of the oracles, with some rumors claiming that she even harbored a tenth magic, a unique that none had yet discovered. She wore an azure dress crafted of interwoven light and threads. The material moved like silk but could bend at her will. Gliding forward, she bowed to Elenyr and smiled.

"Dear friend," she said, "it is a troubling time that we must endure."

"Elsin," Elenyr said. "Please, sit with me."

Elsin chose Alydian's former seat, her azure eyes flicking to Raine, and then to Alydian before returning to Elenyr. The way her gaze slid off made Alydian's lips tighten, but she held her tongue.

"Tell me what you know," Elenyr said.

"The Soldier stole a guardian while it was on route to Verisith," she said.

"A what?" Alydian asked.

Elsin looked to her. "A higher order of the sentient spell," Elsin said. "We have been experimenting with the spell and discovered a method to make them much more powerful—and permanent. We've begun selling them as guardians."

177

"New spells must be approved by the Eldress Council," Alydian said.

"It was," Raine replied. "Teriah observed the crafting personally, and assured the council it was perfectly sound."

Elenyr caught Alydian's eye and sent a message with mind magic. *Be silent, daughter, that you may learn.*

The words were not harsh, merely urgent, and Alydian did as requested. Elsin returned her attention to Elenyr and detailed how the Soldier took the guardian to the castle in Terros, and unleashed it upon the king.

As she described the damage to the castle and the list of dead, Alydian heard what was not said. The guardian killed over forty Verinai—alone. She doubted even an oracle could endure such a battle and live, suggesting that the guardian truly was as powerful as described.

"And how was the guardian slain?" Elenyr asked.

"Mineva risked her life to destroy it," Elsin said.

"And the Soldier?" Raine asked.

"Escaped," Elsin said. "He continues to elude us, but this action cannot be tolerated. The people's fear will lead to instability. Soon villages will arm themselves and defy entry to those they do not know. Merchants will remain home, and trade will suffer. The Soldier must be dealt with."

"I agree," Elenyr said. "But how?"

"For now," Raine said. "Perhaps Oracle Ciana and Mineva can assume control of Griffin. The people will trust an oracle, and Mineva can secure the castle."

Alydian made to protest but her mother threw her a sharp look and she held her tongue. Then Elenyr shook her head.

"An excellent solution but it is unnecessary. The princess is young, but intelligent and strong of will. Let her lead her people."

178

"And the Soldier?" Elsin asked.

Elenyr smiled. "Raine has offered to lead a command to seek him out."

The statement stunned Elsin, and Alydian fought to keep the smile from her face. It was a blatant refusal to allow the Verinai to intervene, while at the same time breaking senteniums of tradition. The oracles guided from afar, they did not risk their lives so blatantly.

"The Soldier attacked your daughter," Elsin said slowly. "And it has made her cower in her tower. The next time he may kill an oracle, and losing an entire bloodline would be an unprecedented tragedy."

"I have faith in Raine," Elenyr said. "And you. She will take her personal guard, and if you are willing, a command of Verinai as well."

Overcoming her surprise, Elsin looked to Raine. "She is capable, but I still think the risk too great."

"Perhaps," Elenyr said, her lips twitching. "And for that I will depend on your Verinai."

"How soon do we depart?" Raine asked.

"Four weeks," Elenyr said.

Raine rounded on her. "A *month*?"

"We need time for the inquisition into what occurred in Terros," Elenyr said firmly. "If we are to mete out justice, we must be certain it is deserved. Summon the oracles and we will convene. Then Raine will begin her hunt."

Elenyr's gaze flicked to Alydian, and she recognized why her mother had delayed the hunt. The time would give Alydian a chance to finish her training and kill Alethean. It wasn't much, but it was all Elenyr could give. Alydian recognized the gift for what it was and bowed.

"Prepare yourself," Elenyr admonished Raine. "This inquisition will be fraught with danger. Daughter, I suggest you return to your studies."

179

Alydian nodded and turned away, but Elsin's disturbing gaze followed her from the room. Her emotions in turmoil, Alydian made her way to her own quarters. She found her guards at her door, and the pair blinked in surprise when they saw her alone.

"Where is Captain Devkin?" one asked.

"Assisting the acolytes," Alydian said. "I wished to visit my mother before returning to my studies."

"You should not be without your guards," he replied, his tone one of admonishment.

"We're in Dawnskeep," she said wearily. "I'm surrounded by guards."

Before they could argue she stepped through the door and shut it behind herself. Closing her eyes, she leaned against the door, feeling the cool wood through her back. It felt like the world was disintegrating and she could not grasp the pieces. She sighed and opened her eyes, making her way across the room. Then a figure shifted and she turned—and froze.

The Soldier was in her room.

# Chapter 22: Alydian's Wrath

He stood near the door to block her exit, his silver mask obscuring his features. Dressed in a Runeguard's uniform, it was clear how he'd infiltrated Dawnskeep. He held his sword in hand, the angle low and ready. Alydian took it all in an instant and reacted.

"Alydian," the Soldier began, taking a step toward her.

She drew on her training and summoned her magic, calling on the ambient light in the room. The light orbs surrounding her chambers dimmed as she cast a warrior of pure light. It flowed into shape and hardened, swinging its sword as if eager, reflecting Alydian's burgeoning rage.

"You were a fool to come here," Alydian said.

The lightcast warrior leapt the length of the room and came down before the Soldier, swinging at his neck. The Soldier spun and deflected the strike, his anti-magic blade rotating back to slice a line across the warrior's back, darkening his body. The warrior parried the next attack and struck again. By then Alydian had reached the duel.

She'd cast her own lightcast weapon and added an asunder hex along the blade. The light orbs in the room were all but extinguished, their power drawn into Alydian's magic. Her sword ignited sparks along the blade, sending shadows dancing across the wall.

Coming at his flank, she drove her blade toward his gut. He leapt a couch and dived over the swinging blade, avoiding the warrior's swinging weapon as well. Unwilling to let him escape, Alydian drew on the stones of the floor, causing them to flow into tiny hands that reached for the Soldier's boots.

The Soldier leapt to a table and then a couch, his nimble path carrying him beyond the seeking hands. Alydian rushed at him from the opposite flank and pressed the attack the moment he landed again. The entity came at the Soldier's back, its blade driving for his heart.

The Soldier parried Alydian's blow and flicked his sword low, then he swung with his off-hand. Alydian flinched back, the fist coming inches from her nose. But the Soldier had not intended to land the blow. Instead he used the sudden space to whirl on the lightcast warrior. In a blur of dark steel he obliterated the warrior's defenses and plunged his anti-magic blade into the warrior's chest. With a deft spin he yanked it out and spun, severing the warrior's head and sending it bouncing across the room. It disintegrated, plunging the room into darkness.

Alydian called on the air, sending a gust charm at the Soldier's back. Unable to see it coming in the dim light, he was knocked sprawling, a clatter of steel indicating he'd dropped his blade. Alydian sprinted forward—and skidded to a halt.

The Soldier hadn't dropped his sword, he'd dropped a knife, using the ruse to draw her in. He rolled to his feet and lunged for her. On instinct she struck back, sending a barrage of fire at him. He whipped his sword up, catching the magic against the weapon.

The fires split against the blade and went to either side, parting as the anti-magic sword cleaved its way through the magic. The fire caught on a couch and table, scorching the cloth and wood. She pressed harder, forcing him back as she called on the bits of flame falling behind his body.

Beyond the Soldier the heat coagulated into small gremlins. The creatures resembled monkeys but carried tiny knives of fire. More and more appeared, until two became ten, and then she lost count. The room gained a chill as she used the heat, with frost appearing on the water in a pitcher, and creeping across the stone walls. When the focus to maintain them became too great she unleashed them with a triumphant shout and extinguished her attack. The moment she did the Soldier spun.

Dozens of tiny creatures leapt for him, tearing at his clothing, nicking his flesh. He growled and fought to strike at them but there were too many. His black sword whipped across them, rending three into

182

oblivion. Crying out, he went down amidst the horde of entities, their knives drawing blood, the fire of their forms igniting on his armor.

Alydian strode forward, flicking her lightcast blade in anticipation. As she rounded a corner she found the Soldier rolling across the floor, his black sword slicing through the entities as he went. More and more were killed but he kept rolling.

"Very clever, Alydian," the Soldier said, his voice strained as he rolled away. "Did you learn that as an acolyte?"

His statement brought a wave of confusion and fear, and most of the remaining entities disintegrated. Alydian ground her teeth together, recognizing his question as a calculated move intended to distract her. Before she could cast more he cut the last few apart and climbed to his feet.

Smoke and cinders littered his form, and small wounds bloodied his body. Some of the entities had dug their claws into his mask but the barrier had kept them at bay. Others had sliced against his armor, scorching the dark material.

"I don't know what you're talking about," she replied evenly.

He laughed. "Alethean? The name alone reveals your identity. That and your knowledge of magic gives it away. *No one* knows about lightning magic."

Alydian felt a surge of fear—but it burned into rage. How had he witnessed her answer in the Requiem? Had he been one of the trainers at the back of the training hall? It was a bold move to infiltrate the Runeguard, but to step into a Requiem to observe Alydian was truly daring.

"Or shadow magic," she replied. "But an oracle is still required to study it."

With the room and dark and cold, she called on the shadows. Like liquid smoke, they poured off the wall and crept toward the Soldier. He tried to dance away but the floor was his enemy, and the shadows climbed up his legs, attaching to his clothing and dragging him to the floor.

He struggled but the bonds just got thicker. Alydian plunged the searing sword into the floor and stalked forward, leaving the pool of light behind. Then she drew on the shadows, crafting a dagger of pure darkness. Striding to him, she found him bound and inert on the floor. His sword remained in his grip but his arm could not move, the shadows binding him to the floor. The muscles in his neck bulged but he was helpless.

Alydian straddled him and leaned down to place her dagger against his throat. Through the mask she saw his eyes, but they held no fear. Instead he seemed surprised and impressed. Alydian scowled at him.

"Even bound you are smug?"

"Last time you were a frightened kitten. Now you are an enraged dragon."

"I should cut your throat here and be done with it."

"But you're not a killer," he said.

She pressed on her dagger but the motion caused the shadow bindings to tremble, betraying her uncertainty. Grinding her teeth together, she growled and the shadows held their form.

"Alydian," he said softly. "I came to talk."

"I don't believe you," she said, and rose to her feet. "But I'll let the guards handle it. I wager Captain Devkin will enjoy a second conversation."

"Please," he said.

The pleading in his voice brought her to a halt, and she rotated. To her surprise he'd managed to turn his head and catch his mask against the foot of a table. With a twist he pulled it off, revealing his features.

He was elven, and only a few decades older than her. She'd expected scars but there were none, only a handsome face looking up at her. In the dim light his countenance was filled with a desperate hope. Attraction surged in her chest but she snuffed it as she would a stray ember fallen from the hearth.

184

"Why reveal yourself now?" she asked cautiously.

"I need you to trust me."

"I don't."

"I know," he said, pain abruptly twisting his features. "But you must."

Still guarded, Alydian could not contain her curiosity. "Speak."

"I did not kill King Talin."

"You wish to claim innocence?" she asked. "I already know how many you have killed."

"The Verinai are experimenting with magic," he said. "They've created a guardian spell that is more dangerous than anything you can imagine."

"I know," she said. "Oracle Teriah witnessed its creation and approved its use."

"The spell is created by infusing superheated magic directly with living tissue," he said. "They did it with a man, but the sheer power robbed him of wits. They killed him to create the weapon."

Alydian raised her hand, causing the shadows to lift the Soldier and drag him to a wall. Then she strode to him.

"You lie."

In halting words the Soldier revealed the events at the castle, his voice tinged with regret and guilt. He spoke of the guardian's madness and the king's captivity before detailing Mineva's act of betrayal. The more Alydian listened the more she wanted to argue, but heard the ring of disturbing truth to his words. He finished his tale by revealing the details of the Accord, and the Verinai's desire to build a Mage Empire. She wanted to dismiss his tale, but the haunted look to his eyes could not be denied.

"Then why reveal yourself to me?" she asked. "Now that I know your face, I could find you anywhere on Lumineia. You will never hide again."

"The Verinai are on the verge of casting down the kingdoms and replacing them with an empire—with themselves at the head. Single mages will be peasants, while the magicless will be slaves. Freedom will be extinguished. I have fought the Verinai for six years, but I cannot defeat a tyrant alone—and I cannot stop the rogue mage on your council."

"You want me to help you?" she asked. "After you came to kill me?"

"I misjudged you," he admitted. "And for that I am sorry. But the people need a hero . . . or perhaps they need a heroine." His lips twitched into a smile.

Alydian suddenly realized that the shadows binding him to the wall had dissipated, but she made no effort to replace them. Despite what he'd done, she sensed he would not harm her, not now. He was desperate and lethal, but not to her.

For the first time she saw him for what he was, a warrior that fought for the people. He killed the Verinai because they were the oppressors, the tyrants. In the past, the oracles were the force that protected the rights of the people, but in recent years the oracles had been subverted by the Verinai. The Soldier was merely performing the duty of an oracle, albeit with a sword rather than farsight.

Then she frowned, a nagging suspicion tugging at her thoughts. "Either Oracle Teriah did not witness the guardian spell . . ."

"Or she was complicit in its creation," the Soldier finished. "Perhaps she is your rogue mage."

Alydian's gaze was drawn to the tapestry of magic, to the symbol of an oracle at the center. Was it possible? Had Oracle Teriah betrayed them all? Her thoughts were interrupted when a soft knock came from the door.

On instinct she turned and pointed to the Soldier, drawing on the shadows once more. They engulfed him in an instant, obscuring him from view as the door swung open and Captain Devkin appeared. He came to an abrupt halt.

"Oracle," he drawled, his gaze sweeping across the room.

Darkened and chilly, the receiving room bore the scars of battle. Couches were cut and broken, flames licking at their remains, while Alydian's searing sword remained plunged in the stone, sputtering sparks. He stooped and picked up a small knife, the one the Soldier had thrown during the battle.

"Practicing in your chambers can be dangerous," he said.

"My apologies," she said wearily. "But I wanted to test some of the spells with other magics."

His eyes were suspicious but he accepted her excuse with a nod. "What did your mother know?"

Alydian sighed. "Everything." His eyebrows shot up, but before he could ask more she shook her head. "I'll explain in the morning. It's been a rather long day."

He regarded her for several moments. "As you order," he said, and then reluctantly withdrew.

When the door clicked shut Alydian turned to the wall where the Soldier remained. Dismissing the shadows with a flick of her wrist, she stooped and picked up his mask. Then she tossed it to him and pointed to the balcony.

"You should go."

"Why save me?"

She met his gaze, and after a moment said, "I don't know."

They were not close but it felt like they were inches from each other. Swallowing against the burgeoning emotions, she motioned to the balcony again.

"Don't get caught on the way down," she said.

"I won't," he replied, stepping to the railing. Then he paused and looked back. "My name is Raiden," he said quietly. Then he was gone. Alone, Alydian stared after him, still grappling with what had just happened.

She felt an inexplicable kinship with him. Knowing his name and face heightened the attraction she felt. But how could such a man draw her attention? She tried to use her farsight to determine a shared future, but no amount of magic would reveal her fate. And questions remained.

# Chapter 23: The Soldier's Heart

Raiden caught the edge of Alydian's balcony and descended. He'd borrowed Jester's shadow whip, and used its enchantment to attach to the shadows under the balcony. Thumbing the rune, he lowered himself to the balcony below before dropping into the streets of Horizon. He stuck to the shadows as he advanced through the city, hiding the litany of damage he'd sustained in his fight with Alydian. Stopping to retrieve his horse, he left the city behind and followed the road northward, where Jester stepped into view.

Jester grinned as he spotted his torn and burnt clothing. "I had a past lover do that to me."

Raiden smiled. "Only one?"

"Maybe two," Jester said. "Maybe more. I lose track."

"She's much stronger than in our last engagement," Raiden said.

Jester tossed him a change of clothes. "You favor her," he accused.

"My feelings regarding the woman are irrelevant," Raiden said, dismounting to change into merchant's garb. "What matters is that she believed me."

Jester began to laugh. "Deflection? So it's true. How long have you felt something for her?"

Realizing the man would not be dissuaded, Raiden grinned. "I think she's attractive."

"And?" Jester prompted.

"You aren't going to let this go, are you."

"Nope."

Raiden laughed. "When we attacked her the first time, she was terrified but managed to overcome that and stand with courage. I saw something then and felt drawn to her. Today, she could have killed me, but she stayed her hand. I've never met anyone like her."

"She's an oracle," Jester said with a snort. "There *is* no one like her."

Raiden shared the tale of his duel and conversation with Alydian. Jester's suspicion was accurate, but such attraction to an oracle would likely lead to ruin. Suppressing the emotion, Raiden finished the tale, and for several minutes they rode in silence through the dark countryside.

"How *much* do you favor her?"

"Is that all you have to ask?" Raiden asked. "You couldn't stop talking about how dangerous it would be to infiltrate Dawnskeep, and now you want to know the state of my heart?"

"Of course," Jester said, a sly smile spreading on his features. "Your heart died before I met you, so it's good to see a spark."

"The Soldier's purpose is not to find love," Raiden said caustically.

"Perhaps," Jester said with a shrug. "But a victory without love is no victory at all."

"I don't love her," Raiden protested.

"That's what everyone says . . . in the beginning," Jester said.

"Are you saying you have someone you care about?"

He smirked. "Of course."

"And why haven't you said anything?"

"Because you only talk about the Verinai."

190

His tone was not harsh, but his words sounded like a rebuke. Chastened, Raiden sighed. "I'm sorry, my friend. I've been so afraid of the oracles discovering us that I refused to look anywhere else."

"And now you've revealed yourself to one of them."

"I believe she will become a powerful ally," he said defensively.

"Ally?" Jester asked with a sniff. "Is that what you want to call her?"

Raiden laughed, and fleetingly realized it was the first moment of levity between them in months. Jester was right, and as much as they had fought together, they did not act like friends. Throughout the conversation he sensed a shift in their companionship.

"Tell me about your current love," he said.

"My current love is secret," Jester said with a smile, "but I'll tell you about my previous one."

Jester launched into a description of a raven haired beauty in the coastal city of Keese. As his companion spoke, Raiden relaxed in the saddle, laughing and smiling for the first time in years. Vaguely, he knew that to relax was dangerous. Thousands of Verinai and Griffin soldiers were hunting him, and if Alydian had betrayed him, they would arrive at any moment.

But they did not come.

Raiden's smile widened as he thought of her. Alydian might be an oracle, but she was valiant and courageous, fearless even against one like the Soldier. When anyone else would have tossed Raiden in a cell, she'd listened. More importantly, she'd believed.

The decision to sneak into Dawnskeep had been an impulsive one, but one he deemed necessary. On their flight out of Terros the rumors had been as thick as blood, spreading and changing with every telling. It quickly became evident that the people were divided, with many still believing in the Verinai's efforts to protect the king. By the time they had reached the refuge, Raiden had seen the truth, they could not remain free if the people turned against the Defiant.

Jester finished his description of his love and Raiden shook himself, forcing his thoughts to return to caution. Jester seemed to understand the moment of levity had passed and straightened in his saddle. The sun had set as they spoke and the countryside had plunged into darkness. Dawnskeep glowed in the distance, rising like a lighthouse to the kingdoms.

"What now?" Jester asked. "We may have an ally, but I don't have the slightest idea how to use her."

Raiden considered his answer but none came. He wasn't even certain he could call Alydian an ally. She'd believed his story and shielded him from Captain Devkin, but she'd made no mention of actually helping him. He frowned, wondering if he'd overstated Alydian's support for their cause.

"We wait," he said. "I think we sparked a measure of curiosity in her that will continue to bear fruit, but we need to give her time to seek her own answers."

"We can't just sit idle," Jester said.

"No. But we need to link up with Red. She should be back in the refuge any day now."

Jester nodded and they turned their horses off the road. Despite his faith in Alydian, Raiden kept his attention on their back trail, watching for patrols. Several times they were forced to work their way deeper into the hills to keep from being spotted by the abundant Verinai and Griffin patrols. But the real problem was the birds.

The Verinai had begun sending lightcast birds into the starless night. They flew in a grid intended to survey every inch of the terrain. Huddled in a small stand of trees, Raiden soothed his mount with soft words as one such bird banked above them.

When it departed, Raiden sighed in relief and mounted his horse. Jester did the same, and they eased their steeds out of the tree line. Just as they did, a rabbit burst into view, startling Raiden's horse into a whinny. The sound echoed over the dark countryside, and in the distance the lightcast bird swerved back.

192

Jester cursed under his breath. "It's got a listening charm on it," he said.

"Back into the trees," Raiden urged.

They worked their way into the dense foliage, reining their mounts just as the hawk appeared over a hill. It soared to them, curving to fly around the trees. Evidently its caster was suspicious, because the bird continued to circle. Raiden and Jester exchanged a look and they eased their swords free, and donned their masks. In the distance they heard the bark of an order.

Raiden realized they were coming and flicked the reins. His horse surged in response, leaping free of the trees just as the bird flew by. It tried to bank away from his sudden appearance it but was too close, and Raiden slashed across its wing. The glittering bird crumbled apart and died, plunging the trees into darkness. A shout rang out from its caster, close and urgent.

"The bird only saw me," Raiden hissed. "I'll lead them away and meet you at the refuge."

Jester nodded, the motion barely visible in the shadows. "Don't get caught," he replied, and smirked. "You have a girl now."

Raiden snorted and stabbed a finger north. The assassin led his horse into the open and sheathed his sword. Then he removed his mask and guided his steed away. Raiden waited until lights bobbed behind a hill to the west. Then he turned south, aiming his path toward the elven kingdom. If he could reach one of their cities he could hide among the populace.

He rode down a slope and up another, the rocky terrain preventing a full gallop. His horse was good, but it could still break a leg in an unseen hole. Above them a glimmer of light appeared, followed by another. The birds remained high but angled for him, clearly following his path.

The lightcast birds were shades of red, indicating they had been cast at sunset. Without a source of light, the Verinai would not be able to cast another bird before dawn, but that wouldn't matter if Raiden could not kill the ones already following him. A third bird appeared above him, and a fourth. Raiden scowled and risked picking up the pace.

The land east of Dawnskeep was barren and rough, the terrain marked by rolling hills and outcroppings of rock. Scattered trees afforded few places to hide, and Raiden doubted any refuge would endure more than a few hours.

He glanced up and spotted one of the birds turning away and swinging east, likely to inform another patrol of their quarry. The lack of urgency suggested they did not realize who they had caught, and perhaps thought he was merely a bandit that had gotten lucky enough to kill the lightcast bird.

He considered discarding his mask, but if it was found his identity would forever be known. If he got caught with the mask, however, they would learn the truth anyway. His only choice lay in escape, as the Soldier.

Dawnskeep and Horizon were visible in the west, the tower's light shining bright despite the lateness of the hour. Instinctively Raiden knew he could not survive if he turned to it. The birds would follow him there, and he would be trapped between his Verinai pursuers and the Runeguard.

He kept his pace even, his path due south. The hours slipped by and it seemed his trackers were in no rush to reach him. Other light birds appeared, and the growing flock indicated that other trackers had joined the hunt. They had him hemmed in, but they seemed content to wait until dawn to close the net.

Midnight came and went, and Raiden kept his pace unhurried until the first glimmerings of dawn touched the horizon. He was still half a day's ride from the nearest elven city, but once the sun came up the birds would spot him, and their casters would realize exactly who they were following. He lifted the mask and rubbed his eyes against his mounting fatigue, and drank from his water skin.

Raiden kept his head down as the sun touched the horizon, his skin crawling as he listened for the impending recognition. The minutes dragged by as the birds swirled closer, and then suddenly one shrieked, the sound shattering the still morning. Raiden yanked on the reins to point his horse toward the elven city and shouted, sending the horse surging across the hills. In seconds the shouts echoed in his wake, and the legion of soldiers flooded after him.

# Chapter 24: Death of the Soldier

Raiden accelerated into a gallop and hoped his horse wouldn't stumble. They streaked across the hills, rising and falling with the terrain as rocks gave way to scattered trees and streams. The birds gathered above and hundreds of soldiers appeared in his wake. Some of the birds soared past him, clearly aiming for Rualia, the northernmost city of the elven kingdom. Once the birds informed the Verinai in the city, he would be trapped.

He scowled but did not deviate from his course. His only hope lay in breaching the elven city before they caught up to him. With time against him, he maintained the gallop even when the trees began to thicken, and turned his mount onto a smaller road.

Lightcast birds flitted through the canopy as the Verinai tightened the net. As he neared the city he spotted soldiers just hundreds of feet away and knew it was time. He passed under a thicker canopy that briefly obscured his view of the sky. On impulse he slowed his horse and leapt off, rolling when he hit the ground. Rising into a run, he sprinted in a different direction.

The horse continued to follow the road, the sounds of its galloping hooves fading as Raiden wove his way through the trees. Elves were not known for endurance, but he'd trained extensively in his first century. Still, he managed his fatigue, setting a pace he could maintain. Then he crested a rise and the elven city of Rualia came into view.

Five hundred foot trees supported the city, their great branches as thick as a wagon. Homes, taverns, and inns lay nestled in the limbs, their walls formed from woven branches. More limbs shaped terraces and balconies that overlooked the forest floor, and lights from thousands of light orbs and entities illuminated the treetop city. The nature of the structures gave the city its name, the Living City.

Instead of walls, the city used open air as a defense. The bottom level of the city was a hundred feet off the ground, and the great trees that supported the city were completely smooth, with nary a branch, window, or platform. Battlements surrounded the trunks at the lowest level of the Living City and connected to neighboring trunks, forming an interconnected barrier that elves patrolled.

Some of the greater limbs bent to the earth, the boughs flattened to allow passage for horses and wagons. The entrance limbs curved in graceful spirals until merging with the lower cityscape. Larger caravans utilized the wide limbs for passage, while travelers on foot usually opted for the elven ascenders, branches enchanted to lift small groups of people into the city.

Inverted wells provided water and beauty to the city, the sparkling columns gracefully bending and twisting through the wondrous treeways. Defying the pull of earth, the water coursed upward, forming streams that gurgled up branches and through buildings, feeding fountains imbued with light.

Raiden stopped to catch his breath and scanned the slope below. His reckless separation from his mount had momentarily confused his pursuers, but the birds would find him in seconds. Again he considered removing his mask, but if he was spotted doing so the Soldier would be dead in days, even if they didn't catch him now. But if he didn't shed his persona, the moment he stepped into public the Verinai would find him and cut him apart. He needed a place to switch to himself, somewhere private.

As the birds circled closer, Raiden spotted a merchant caravan making its way up the road toward an entrance limb. Squat and long, the central wagon contained a collection of small barrels. More than a dozen dwarves guarded the wagon, their postures relaxed as they wound their way toward the city. Although the script on the barrels was not visible, there was only one thing the dwarves transported in barrels that size.

Stonesap.

Explosive and only handled safely by dwarves, the volatile liquid fueled dwarven machines across Lumineia. Likely destined for a dwarven smith in Rualia, the liquid was sufficient to last several years.

Raiden scanned the road ahead of the wagon and spotted a shallow bridge in its path. The bridge crossed a stream that gurgled its way into an inverted well. Its proximity to the city would suit his needs, but was a dangerous opportunity.

Raiden growled at the risk and stepped out of his hide before sprinting to the wagon, his appearance eliciting shrieks from the birds above. They converged on his location, some diving for him.

He spun and drew his sword, whipping it through a pair of birds. The blade sliced their bodies, shredding the magic and sending bits of light into the brush at his side. One lightcast bird dived for his eyes, but he reached up and caught the falcon by the neck and held on, ignoring its furious attempts to escape.

A score of soldiers appeared on the road behind the dwarven wagon and spotted him. Shouting, they surged into a charge. In the city beyond, another group of Verinai battlemages sprinted down the road, shoving their way through the crowd.

Still more appeared to the north, and then the south. With the net tightening like a noose, Raiden pushed his body to the limit, arriving at the dwarven caravan only moments before the Verinai. Confused by his charge, the dwarves shifted into a protective stance, their shields overlapping into a single barrier.

"Oi!" the caravan leader shouted. "What ye be on about?"

Raiden reached the shield wall and stepped on it, using it to leap over the dwarves. They cried out in surprise but he'd already landed on the back of the wagon. Darting over the barrels, he kicked the driver in the helm, sending him tumbling into the road below. With dwarves rushing to stop him he snatched the reins and whipped the horses.

The animals lunged against their restraints and the wagon bounced forward, the barrels clattering against the padding placed about them. Dwarves shouted and leapt in pursuit. Crossbow bolts streaked around Raiden and he ducked low on the seat. Then one of the dwarves gathered fire in his hands.

"Don't be a fool!" the caravan leader shouted, knocking him to the dirt. "Do ye wish to kill us all?"

Raiden pushed the horses as fast as he dared and other travelers scrambled off the road. Shouts and screams erupted from the crowd. The lightcast bird continued to flap in Raiden's hand and he slammed it on the bench. Drawing a knife, he plunged it through a wing and into the wood, pinning the enchanted bird to the driver's bench.

Soldiers swarmed towards him from all sides. Those descending from Rualia formed ranks and cast their magic, the earth rising to form a wall of stone. The sides of the road were already bound by stone, leaving Raiden trapped. He yanked on the reins, the horses bringing the wagon to a halt above the bridge. The soldiers from behind were quick to surround him, but kept their distance.

In a testament to how much they had come to fear him, the host of Verinai remained on the line and glanced about, clearly uncertain of how to proceed. The magicless and single mages also appeared conflicted, their expressions shifting between the Verinai and the Soldier.

"Soldier," a voice said, and Raiden looked down at the bird. It had gone still, the voice coming from its castor.

"Mineva," Raiden said, his voice laced with hatred. "Does the elven queen know a murderer hides in her realm?"

Through the enchantment of the bird, Mineva laughed scornfully. "I was traveling to Verisith when I heard the news. The Soldier was being herded to Rualia. It was something I wanted to see for myself."

"Your arrogance will be your downfall," he said.

Her laugh was long and mocking. "Is a dragon's arrogance folly? Or well deserved?"

It was Raiden's turn to laugh, and the sound caused the ring of soldiers to ready themselves for battle. Entities blossomed into view and blades were drawn. Raiden glanced about, measuring his foes.

"Dragons may be mighty," he said, "but their pride is the very poison that brings them down."

"The Verinai have more power than all the dragons," Mineva said. "And nothing in Lumineia can bring us down."

"Except my blade to your heart," he growled back.

Raiden looked over the heads of the soldiers on the road and spotted Mineva among the crowd at the base of Rualia's entrance. She stood with a trio of Verinai masters, her features triumphant. A crowd of merchants had formed behind her and they shifted uncertainly, torn between supporting the Soldier and condemning him.

Moving slowly, Raiden rose and stepped onto the barrels. They had him trapped but the soldiers retreated, their eyes dropping to the *Danger, Explosive Stonesap* engraved on the sides of the barrels. Turning a wide circle, he raised his voice so it could be heard.

"Do you not see what you have wrought?" he called. "The Verinai stand on the verge of destroying your queen yet you stand idle! Your kingdom will be no more, and the elven people will be enslaved to the Verinai! I represent the last vestige of freedom! The last bastion of hope! Will you now slay me, and silence the voice against oppression?"

His voice boomed all the way to the city, where thousands of elves lined the streets and paths of the upper city. His challenge echoed into silence and the soldiers around the dwarven wagon cast about, confusion and doubt on their faces. Then Mineva called to them, her voice crisp and tinged with a smile.

"A condemned man speaks his final words," she said.

She motioned to the side and a pair of lightcast birds plunged at the wagon's bench, crashing through the horses' bindings. Abruptly free, the horses whinnied in fear and bolted, leaving Raiden bereft of escape. Mineva's smile widened.

"Cut him to pieces and display his remains outside the city."

The Verinai drifted forward, but the bulk of the soldiers remained in place. Noticing this, the Verinai hesitated, and Mineva shouted to her Verinai.

"Kill him, you fools! If the barren will not do it they do not deserve to be soldiers!"

200

It was the first time a master in the Verinai had publicly called the magicless barren, and there was an audible gasp. Recognizing her mistake, Mineva forced a smile and gestured to Raiden.

"The execution order must be upheld," she cried. "He has murdered hundreds. Have you forgotten the blood on his hands?"

The Verinai drifted forward once again but an elven soldier raised his sword. "Let the Verinai deal with their own enemy!"

His voice elicited cries of agreement and the other soldiers nodded. The captain's ploy was a desperate one. If he moved in to strike at Raiden—who stood over a pile of stonesap—he was just as likely to lose men as he was to take the Soldier. His choice to leave Raiden to the Verinai could be recognized as tacit support of his actions, or a captain allowing one of greater authority to apprehend the criminal. It was a dangerous tactic, and Raiden had no doubt he would be reprimanded for it.

"You are not my foe, Captain," Raiden said. "But the Verinai I gladly kill."

Whipping his sword free, he sliced the wing off the lightcast bird, and then struck the barrel, leaving a notch that liquid trickled from. Sparks crackled from the bird's wound, falling toward the stonesap. The rings of soldiers surged back as Raiden dived off the wagon and rolled under it. Soldiers, dwarves, and Verinai all dived away . . .

The detonation obliterated the wagon, engulfing the Verinai that had drawn too close. Their burning bodies were flung into the trees, setting them ablaze. One barrel was knocked upward where it detonated in the canopy above, swallowing a pair of trees in the ensuing fireball.

Men and women screamed and scrambled away from the carnage. Billowing smoke and cinders rose from the scattered flames amid shrieks of the dying. Surviving mages called for aid and they drew from the stream beneath the bridge, using its water to extinguish the flames before they could spread. The smoke gradually cleared, revealing a gaping hole in the bridge. The Verinai searched for the body but as the hours passed it became clear.

The Soldier was gone.

# Chapter 25: The Living City

Battlemages hunted among the trees, the dead Verinai, and the scorched earth around the destroyed wagon, but their efforts were futile. Mineva herself came and sought for his body, her orders increasingly harsh as they found no sign of the Soldier's corpse.

"Perhaps the fires consumed him," a Verinai said.

"The Soldier was not made of paper," Mineva snarled. "Now find him."

"As you order," he replied.

Mineva's expression gradually changed from triumph to doubt, but she refused to believe the Soldier had slipped through her fingers. Her demands growing more fervent, she drove the soldiers to greater efforts.

Raiden watched the display from the balcony of a tavern in the city above, a small smile on his face. He had no doubt they would figure out what he'd done eventually, but for now, they didn't want to admit he'd slipped through their fingers.

With the stonesap set to explode he'd rolled beneath the wagon— and right off the edge of the bridge. Catching the lip, he'd swung himself into the darkness below just as the stonesap had blown.

He'd huddled in the dark just feet from the massive explosion, the sheer force cracking the bridge to its foundation. For an eternal moment he thought it would cave in, but then the earth stopped trembling. Rising, he removed his mask and cloak before stumbling into the haze of smoke and dust.

Elven soldiers scrambled to extinguish the flames before they could spread, but in the billowing smoke they did not notice an elf dressed as a merchant slip through their ranks. From there it had been easy to ascend into the city. Raiden had even passed within feet of Mineva, who had surveyed the carnage with an expression of smug triumph, unaware that the Soldier was within spitting distance.

"Do you think they killed him?" the servant elf asked.

Raiden looked up and saw the concern written on her features. "The Soldier has proven adept at escape," he replied with a smile of assurance. "I'm sure we'll see him again in the future."

"You care about that criminal?" an elf nearby asked. "He was nothing but a murderer and a thief."

"The Verinai are worse," the elf maiden said. "Word is they killed King Talin."

"A lie!" The elf said. "They sought to protect him!"

She muttered and departed, leaving him to rant in her absence. Many of the other tavern's patrons harbored the same divided sentiment. The people seemed uncertain whether to celebrate or mourn the Soldier's death, or even believe he'd been killed. Some of the disagreements turned violent, forcing the elven guard to step in.

All around the tavern, elves and a smattering of humans spoke in tense undertones, their words laced with worry and doubt. Many of the common folk believed that the Verinai used their power to build and support the people, but those who had experienced Verinai arrogance were vocal in their opposition.

Raiden's smile faded as he watched them. Known for serenity and peace, the elven populace was on edge. Behind forced smiles and casual greetings, an undercurrent of anger and suspicion was rising. Fueled by Verinai oppression and the Soldier's increasingly public defiance, the people sensed a line was being drawn, and the day would come when they would be forced to pick a side.

Raiden sighed and looked to the destroyed road below, wondering how it had come to this. Although no one knew it, he'd tried to forestall the Verinai through legal means prior to becoming the Soldier, and even petitioned the Eldress Council for aid. He'd had a family then, a brother who stood with him.

The Verinai had tolerated him as they denied his accusations, but when the people began to listen, they had come for him. And his brother had paid the price. Raiden grimaced at the memory and turned his attention to his ale, staring at the cup as if the contents had answers. Raiden had become the Soldier to punish the Verinai and force the people to see the truth. But his actions had led the people to war, a war they could not win.

If the Verinai were allied with Oracle Teriah they would be nearly unstoppable, and all the armies of Lumineia would be for naught. The common folk may have outnumbered the Verinai by a thousand to one, but they would never overpower the guild of Verinai. Even if the other mage guilds joined the common folk, how could they triumph?

*Alydian.*

The answer came as he thought the question. The only chance they had of preventing a mage war was for Alydian to join the Soldier. Together they could humble the Verinai before the races dissolved into a bloody war—a war that had already begun with the murder of the Griffin king.

Dropping a few coins on the table, he rose and exited the open-air tavern, making his way up an arcing branch that led to a higher level. The treeways were packed with elves all craning for a look at the devastated road, and soldiers were in abundance. They paid no mind to an elf walking among them.

He'd managed to change out of his dusty clothing in the tavern privy but needed a bath and a bed. However, staying in Rualia would be risky. Once Mineva accepted that he'd escaped, she would be out for blood, and the city would be the first place she would look. She might not know the Soldier's identity, but she knew enough to track him.

He worked his way to the opposite side of the city to an elven ascender, but when he reached it the people were crowded around the exit. On a terrace lined with smaller branches, dozens of elves were clamoring for answers. Beyond them an elven guard stood before the lift.

A long slender branch extended from the main tree and held a cage. Large enough for several people to stand in, the cage provided a graceful descent to the ground a hundred feet below. But the cage was bound to the trunk, its doors shuttered and barricaded.

"What's the meaning of this?" a woman demanded.

"The queen is not permitting us to leave?" a man echoed.

"Please have patience," the guard shouted, attempting to drown out their complaints. "The Verinai have ordered the city closed while they perform a search for the Soldier."

"He was killed in the explosion!" an irate human shouted. "What purpose can you have to search the city?"

"The Soldier's body has not been found," he said. "They want to ensure he did not slip into the city."

"How long do you plan on keeping us here?"

"As long as it takes," the guard insisted.

"The queen will not stand for this!" an elven woman cried.

Raiden slipped away before he was spotted. Shuttering the city was a dangerous move, one that incited the ire of the elven people. It also superseded the queen's authority. When she learned of the Verinai trapping an entire city she would be furious—if she wasn't already under Verinai control.

He worked his way to another exit, his pace hurried, as if he were on an important errand. It too was blocked, and the next. As word spread of the Verinai blockade the elves began to push toward the exits, demanding to be released. The rising tide of anger mounted as the guards began their search, systematically moving through the city.

Elves cried out in dismay as they were forced to endure a search by the Verinai, but their shouts of protest went ignored. Those that resisted were shackled and dragged away, and in minutes the city was in an uproar.

Raiden pushed his way through the struggling crowd, evading knots of soldiers fighting to carry out their orders. Raiden knew they were looking for the Soldier's mask and considered discarding it. Then he heard what they were truly searching for.

"What is the meaning of this?" a human demanded as a Verinai stood in front of him.

"Quiet," the elf barked, and leaned in.

"What are you doing?" the man shouted, recoiling from the inspection. Another guard caught his arm and held him fast.

"Detonated stonesap leaves a residue," the Verinai said. "If you were anywhere near the explosion an earth mage will see the dust all over you." He passed a hand over the man, a flicker of light on his fingertips. "It can linger in the flesh for hours, even days."

"I'm a simple merchant from Griffin," the man shouted, indignant.

"He's clean," the Verinai said, waving in dismissal. "Bring the next."

An elven woman was forced to stand before her. "The Soldier is male, you dolt," she snapped.

"Master Mineva isn't taking any chances," the Verinai said with a thinly veiled sneer.

Raiden tightened his grip on the mask in its hidden pouch and drifted away, mingling with a dour group of elven water mages. When another group of soldiers appeared, Raiden took a small path to a higher level.

The branch led him to a quieter section of the city. Larger limbs held aloft great houses, the walls and ceilings built of living branches. Prolific light orbs adorned the homes of the wealthy, and streams curved among the treetops.

The serenity of the upper terraces was marred by the shouts and screams from below, and Raiden drifted into the highest tavern he could find. Mineva had demonstrated a willingness to subdue the entire city to find him, and she wouldn't stop with the lower terraces.

207

The elves in the tavern lined the balcony, speaking in hushed tones. Their food sat on the polished wooden tables, steam dissipating as the plates cooled. Even the bartender stood against the rail, shaking his head at the near riots unfolding below.

Raiden made his way to the rear where the tavern clung to the side of a great trunk. He tried not to pace but he could feel the trap closing about him. After the events of the morning it was an altogether familiar sentiment, and he doubted he could escape a second time.

He considered his options but none were appealing. He could try and snag a rope to lower himself to the forest, but he would be spotted and killed long before reaching the ground. Or he could attempt to hide and hope they did not find him. Neither boded well for his survival.

The shouts drew closer as the Verinai gradually ascended through the city, driving their quarry to where he could not escape. Raiden scowled and paced at the rear of the tavern, casting about for any avenue of escape.

A flutter of light drew his gaze.

He paused, his gaze drawn to a tiny lightcast hummingbird. It hovered in an obscure corner, nearly invisible unless someone was skulking in the rear of the tavern. His curiosity got the best of him and he reached for it. At his touch it unfolded into a note.

*R,*

*Clever ploy with the wagon. There's a secret door behind you that will take you out of the city. Be well.*

*A*

The bird's wings turned red and burned before his eyes, the ashes crumbling to his feet. He began to laugh as he stepped to the great tree. Now that he knew where to look, he spotted a curious knot in the bark of the tree. He pressed a finger to it—and a section of the bark swung inward, revealing a hidden staircase illuminated by a handful of light orbs. Raiden breathed a sigh of relief as he stepped into it and the door shut behind him.

"You have my gratitude, Alydian," he murmured, and then disappeared down the staircase.

# Chapter 26: The Third Trial

Deep in her farsight, Alydian watched Raiden slip into the Thieves Guild escape route. She remained in her magic long enough to verify he escaped the city before relinquishing it with a sigh.

When she'd heard that the Verinai had located the Soldier, she'd taken the first opportunity of privacy to dive into her farsight. She'd seen his face and knew his name, so it hadn't taken long to locate his tree, and she followed his future to see the wagon explode. Even through the magic she flinched, her heart gripping with fear. But his tree continued to grow beyond the moment, indicating he'd survived.

She'd watched him escape the explosion with piercing relief. But her doubt turned to anger when she'd witnessed the Verinai bind and search the people of Rualia. Such an action superseded law and inquisition, forcing the people to relinquish their freedom by force. Her anger rising, Alydian watched the elves endure the scrutiny of the Verinai, and then she spotted Mineva through Raiden's eyes.

Although clean and dressed in expensive garb, the woman reminded Alydian of oil. She'd spoken respectfully to the oracles, including Alydian when they'd met, but her tone turned condescending to everyone else. She'd even tried to order Captain Devkin to retrieve a cup of cha for her, an action that had made Alydian's blood boil in her veins. If her mother had not been there, Alydian would likely have done something rash.

Through Raiden's eyes, Alydian watched the hate and barely suppressed rage in Mineva's features. She would search every corner of the city to find the Soldier, even if it meant shattering legal precedent and shackling innocent people. On impulse, Alydian had cast the hummingbird and sent it soaring away.

Alydian let her magic fade and strode to the balcony that overlooked the city. Rualia lay in the heart of Orláknia, and was just a day's ride from Dawnskeep. The hills obscured her view, but a dark haze still rose in the distance, smudging the horizon and marring the blue sky. On impulse she made her way to the door and swung it open to find Yaria and Bathic outside.

"Any news?" she asked.

At her back, Yaria answered, "Master Mineva trapped the Soldier outside of Rualia but he escaped into the city. She's searching it now."

"How are the people reacting?" she asked.

There was a moment's pause, and then Bathic replied, "Many are cooperating with the Verinai and elven guard, although a few have resisted the effort to find the criminal."

It was carefully worded to sound true, but obscure the truth. *Many* could have been the majority or just a large group, and the choice to say that instead of *most* indicated her guards knew exactly what the Verinai were doing in Rualia—but they didn't want to admit it to an oracle. Alydian's lips tightened as she recognized that her guards protected her, but they were Verinai first.

Misunderstanding her expression, Bathic said, "Mineva has sworn to find him, my lady."

She turned away so they wouldn't see her slight smile. Mineva had no idea that Raiden was already slipping from her grasp, and Mineva's frustration would only mount. Then Alydian's smile faded and she turned to her guards.

"How many were killed when the wagon detonated?"

"Thirteen," Yaria said, her tone dark.

Alydian didn't respond, and shut the door again before returning to the balcony, fighting the surge of guilt. She'd aided The Soldier after he'd killed again, and felt as if she'd crossed an invisible line. Why was she helping him?

211

She turned back when Captain Devkin entered, bringing her morning meal. He nodded to Yaria and Bathic before deftly shutting the door. He placed the tray on the table and moved to stand beside her.

"Were you going to tell me the Soldier paid you a visit?"

The blunt question should have been shocking, but it wasn't. Captain Devkin was clever and relentless, and he'd clearly been suspicious when he'd seen the damage to her quarters. Sinking into a seat by the tray of food, she rubbed her neck.

"Can we discuss this later?" she asked. "Today is my only day of respite before I embark on my third trial as an acolyte, where we both know I'm supposed to die."

He jerked his head and folded his arms. "We discuss it now."

She leaned back in her chair and met his gaze without flinching. Fleetingly she realized that their relationship had changed over the last few months. Devkin had been her guardian for some time, but now she viewed him as an equal, rather than her protector.

"He wanted to tell his side of the events in Terros," she said.

"That he didn't kill the king?"

"Why do you say that?" She asked.

He snorted scornfully. "The Verinai claim he killed King Talin, but that makes as much sense as the rumor of your mother turning into a dragon."

She laughed without humor. "The Verinai have begun experimenting with magic," she said. "They created a new spell, one so powerful that it nearly destroyed the castle at Terros."

"And it killed King Talin?"

"No," she said. "Master Mineva did that with her own hand."

Devkin regarded her for several moments. "Tell me everything."

She left nothing out, even what she'd done regarding the note to get him out of Rualia. When she finished, Devkin's expression was pensive,

212

and he leaned back into his seat. While he sat silent she took a citrus off the tray and methodically peeled it.

"You aided a criminal," he said slowly.

"I know," she said quietly.

"Why?"

She stared at the peel in her hand, and noticed the contrast to the bruises on her skin from her confrontation with the Soldier. She did not have an answer so she just shook her head. When he did not respond, she looked up.

"He is not evil," she said quietly.

"He's killed hundreds," he said.

"Yet he acts with honor," she replied. "I cannot explain further."

"Then what now?"

"I don't know."

"You are an oracle," he pointed out. "Have you not used your farsight to examine the possibilities?"

"The events of my third trial are clouded by indecision," she said. "And even my mother has remarked on how unusually dense it is."

"Do you see evil in the Verinai?" he asked.

She sucked in her breath. "A frightening amount," she said, "in most of them."

"Then your choices should be clear," he replied. "Do you ally yourself with those that are filled with malice . . . or honor?"

Her eyes widened. "You would have me publicly support the Soldier?"

"Not the Soldier," he said. "The Soldier's cause."

It was a fine line, but a clever tactic. If she began to publicly question the Verinai's actions, and even launch an inquisition, it would shine light upon the secretive guild. A smile spread on her face. The single mage guilds, the magicless, even the kingdoms of Lumineia would collectively demand answers. But how would the Verinai react to such opposition? How would Teriah?

Her smile faded. They would retaliate, that much was certain. They would never be cowed by those they called barren. For them to submit would require force, meaning Alydian needed the support of the entire Eldress Council.

"What about Teriah?" she asked. "She claimed to have verified the Verinai's creation of the guardian spell, and all signs indicate she is a rogue mage in the council, the betrayer the Soldier spoke of."

"The Verinai could have falsified their work to Teriah," he mused.

"It is nearly impossible to deceive an oracle," she said with a shake of her head. "And if Teriah has signed the Accord to create a Mage Empire . . .?"

"If Teriah has betrayed the council, wouldn't your mother know of it?" he asked.

"Her health declines by the week," she said, her stomach tightening with worry. "She has relied more and more on the other Sisters."

"Then we must tread carefully," Devkin said. "But speak to your mother first. She will want to hear of this."

Alydian hesitated. She had yet to tell her mother of Devkin's visit, and found herself reluctant to do so. Her mother had been lenient when she'd discovered Alydian's true training, but she would likely be disappointed upon hearing Alydian had allowed the Soldier to escape. It would also mean admitting her affection for him.

"She's resting," Alydian replied. "I will speak to her upon my return from the third trial. With Alethean dead, I will be free to carry forward as Alydian." *And bring the Verinai to their knees*, she mentally added.

Her jaw tightened. Now that she knew her course, she began to ask questions about the third trial. As one of the captains tasked with training the acolytes, Devkin was privy to the third trial plans. Acolytes were not supposed to know the events of the trial, so she would have to feign ignorance among her friends.

The next morning Alydian rose early and, as per her usual routine, made her way to the library first before donning her Alethean persona. She arrived at the gates of Dawnskeep just as the other acolytes appeared. Ignoring the baleful looks from the remaining two patrols of Verinai, she joined her own patrol.

Grogith, Toala, and Ferin had all finished the second trial, and all but Grogith smiled at her approach. With two elves, a gnome, and a human, their group was the most varied of the acolytes, and the smallest.

"Glad you could make it," Toala said, inclining her head to Alydian.

Ferin grinned and tapped his newly issued armor. "I admit I like the new gear. It's shiny."

They had been training in armor for the last few weeks now, and although it still showed blue highlights, it resembled the white and blue of the standard Runeguard uniform. Alydian smiled in turn.

"Do we know anything about our target?"

They shook their heads, and Alydian managed to keep the smile from her face. Their target was a bandit camp in the western province of Griffin. Led by a man known as the Black Shroud, the group preyed on caravans traveling to and from the city of Herosian, the largest of the western cities.

Devkin and Alydian had done what research they could into the group but found very little beyond an area they preferred to operate in. Fortunately, a recent attack had been foiled, and a bandit had been captured. He'd promised to lead the Runeguard to the camp in exchange for freedom and gold, both of which he would never get.

215

Alydian didn't care for the subterfuge, but the reports on the group indicated they were particularly ruthless. Dozens of bodies had been found, with several caravans stripped bare, their merchant owners and guards left to rot in the road. Grief stricken wives had demanded retribution, and the Runeguard had offered to deal with them in place of the regular Griffin army.

Commander Othan stood at the head of the group and ordered them to march, and Alydian fell into step with her patrol. It was her final days as a Runeguard soldier, but a ghost of a smile appeared on her face as she exited Dawnskeep. She looked about herself, free of guards, free of restraints. For the first time in her life she walked as her own woman and, for the fleetest of moments, she felt free.

# Chapter 27: Mistkeep

With Commander Othan and a pair of captains to lead them, the fourteen remaining acolytes made their way through the rolling hills and into the Sea of Grass, so named for its endless vista of waist high grass. The expanse flowed in the breeze, beautiful and serene, if a bit melancholy.

They camped in the open, and Alydian watched the stars drift across the sky. Several times she slipped into her farsight to look at her own future, but the impending battle was still shrouded in uncertainty. Although she tried to resist the impulse, she frequently found herself using her magic to track Raiden.

He made his way north, bypassing Dawnskeep as Alydian traveled southwest. Even though she was not present, a part of her wanted him to return to her quarters. He paused and watched the fortress, and she flushed as if he were looking at her. Gratified but conflicted, she extinguished her magic and relaxed into slumber.

The acolytes rose at dawn and continued their journey. Drifting to the rear of the force, she spoke in undertones with Ferin and Toala, and Grogith when he decided to speak. They talked and laughed, and Alydian relished the final moments as Alethean. As an acolyte she'd turned into a warrior, and enjoyed friendship and unity. As Alydian she was revered and respected, but could count no one but Raine a friend.

As they neared the southern part of the region, they crested a rise and the Evermist came into view. The sprawling swamp lay shrouded in greenish mist. The swamp had been gradually encroaching on Griffin lands for ages, so they had permitted the Verinai to build a guildhall on a lake that bordered the swamp. The Verinai used their magic to contain the swamp, and in turn the guild had a stronghold in Griffin.

"We'll stop in Mistkeep for the night," Commander Othan said, gesturing to the fortress in the distance.

Alydian glanced at her friends, who bore expressions of curiosity mingled with apprehension. Even the gnome seemed nervous. Aside from Verisith, which was more city than guildhall, the Verinai strongholds allowed few outsiders into their walls.

The group followed the path downhill until it joined a large roadway. The region seemed deserted except for the castle, which rose from an island on a lake. The fortress lay shrouded in the greenish fog that seeped from the swamp. Its walls were high and strong, and several turrets rose above the landscape, providing an unparalleled view of the Evermist and its surroundings. As large as the late King Talin's castle, Mistkeep had been built by magic, its foundation sunk deep into the swamp until it fastened to the bedrock beneath.

The road came to an abrupt halt at the lake, where murky water separated them from the fortress. With the sun setting, the guards on the battlements were clearly visible, and one raised a hand, casting an eagle of pure light. It dived to the water and soared across it, sweeping around them before alighting on Commander Othan's outstretched arm.

"Commander Othan and Runeguard acolytes," he said. "All are Verinai except three."

"You may enter," the bird said, the voice and accent distinctly human. "We will prepare quarters for your group."

It stretched its wings before soaring back to its caster, circling to watch them as they waited. Alydian glanced at Toala but the woman smiled, the expression one of nervous excitement. Then a deep clanking rumbled from beneath the water, and a large shape materialized. Breaching the surface, the bridge locked into place, the water draining off through channels built into the bridge's walls.

The bridge had been built of white granite, pristine despite having been deep in the sludge of the lake. As they crossed, Alydian spotted numerous alligators on lake's surface. She swallowed and realized why the lake had been chosen for the location of Mistkeep.

The large portcullis was raised and the acolytes were led inside. The Verinai guards greeted Commander Othan warmly, while their eyes slid across the acolytes until they spotted Alydian with her three companions.

"This way," the dwarf said. "We are preparing quarters for you now."

The interior of the citadel was just as bright as the exterior. White granite and marble shaped the foundation, the walls illuminated by expensive gremlins of light rather than the cheaper orbs produced by the elven guild of light.

The clawed gremlins prowled the ceiling, clinging to poles bracketed into the corners. They scowled down at the newcomers, their thick claws scratching the steel as they kept pace with Alydian. Both for light and defense, the gremlins were the size of a badger, but were strong enough to take down an armored knight. When Alydian had learned how to craft that particular entity, she'd seen it cut through solid plate armor with its claws.

"Those don't look friendly," Ferin murmured, eyeing the gremlins.

"They aren't," Alydian said.

They followed the corridor to the first of three great halls in the fortress. Obviously intended as a waypoint for the travel of goods, the great hall contained stables on one side and crates and barrels throughout. Small light entities crafted to resemble mythical fairies fluttered in cages, the creatures bound for wealthy homes and nobles.

The scent of horses was overpowered by the produce and spices grown by Verinai plant mages. Cinnamon, peppers, salt, and other ingredients filtered into the air, a pleasant aroma that caused Grogith to sneeze.

"Your quarters are this way," the Verinai captain said, gesturing them down a hall. "The Verinai are welcome throughout the castle, but for their own safety, any non-Verinai are restricted to this hall and the guest quarters."

"Sounds like we're being caged," Ferin murmured.

"It's just one night," Toala said.

They followed the group to the guest quarters. One side of the corridor contained lavish quarters, the doors open to reveal private bathing chambers, large beds, and crackling fires. The opposite side was evidently reserved for servants, and accommodations were far more modest.

"The meal hall is on the far end of the corridor," he Verinai guard captain said. "You may join us for the evening repast."

The Verinai acolytes were quick to claim a room, but when Alydian and her patrol reached the end of the line the Mistkeep captain brought them to a halt and gestured to the opposite side of the hall. Although his voice was mild, his expression bordered on a smirk.

"I'm afraid the rest of the dignitary quarters are being renovated," he said. "I fear you will have to make do with the servant's quarters."

His gaze flicked to Alydian, narrowing slightly as their eyes met. Alydian saw the recognition in his eyes, and realized the dwarf knew exactly who Alethean was, and who she'd chosen as her acolyte companions.

"Your hospitality is—as always—legendary," Alydian said, but her smile carried more scorn than gratitude.

Turning on her heel, she entered the nearest servant's quarters and removed her pack, placing it on the small bed. Removing her armor, she donned acolyte blues, and used the water in the tiny sink to wash. Then she exited and joined the other acolytes making their way to dinner.

As she stepped through the threshold into the meal hall, her gaze lifted to the vaulted space. Large balconies overlooked the main hall, evidently reserved for the upper ranked Verinai. Instead of a chandelier, an entire dragon of light hovered in the center of the chamber. She stepped towards an empty table but a hand caught her elbow, causing her to turn.

"You have been requested to sit at a different table," Commander Othan said.

"By whom?"

"You have your orders, acolyte."

Alydian suppressed the surge of curiosity and followed the guard at Othan's side upward into the fortress. Grogith caught her eye and the gnome's expression turned into a scowl. Following the guard, Alydian ascended into the fortress. She had not anticipated this, and managed to force a glimpse of her farsight. Her heart sank when she realized who had summoned her.

The upper levels of the fortress were a maze of corridors and training rooms. Sources of magic were abundant, both for training as well as producing goods for export. Through an open door she noticed a large garden, the corn stalks well over ten feet tall and boasting dozens of ears rather than one. A trio of plant mages walked among them, using their magic to sprout even more.

Another room contained a group of Verinai crafting entities. The wolves were larger than reality, their coats threaded with fire and sound, their bodies built from fluid stone. Capable of breathing fire and communicating with their masters, the sentients would be powerful defenders when complete. She guessed the mages were four years into the ten it would take to finish the quartet of wolves, but the profit when they were sold would more than balance the investment.

Everywhere she looked she saw signs of the wealth the Verinai had accumulated, and wondered how the guild had become so powerful. The guild contained only fifty thousand members, but it seemed they were everywhere in the kingdoms. Their presence was felt in every facet of commerce, government, and the military.

And they were all loyal to the guild of Verinai.

She shuddered, realizing for the first time that the Verinai had placed their members into key positions in every kingdom. If the Soldier had not taken notice and tried to stop them, the Verinai might have forged their Mage Empire without opposition.

They ascended a large staircase to a set of double doors. Flanked by two lower ranked Verinai, the doors were polished and built of a single tree, the limbs and roots woven together into a seamless barrier. At their command, the tree uncoiled, opening the way for Alydian and her guide to enter.

221

Alydian stepped into the spacious receiving room. A trio of doors were placed on the opposite walls, while the main room contained couches and tables carefully placed to accentuate the curving walls of the space. At the center, a small dining table had been set for two, and one seat was already occupied.

By Elsin, guildmaster of Verinai.

"Alethean," she said, gesturing to the seat across from her. "It would please me for you to join my table."

Alydian saw the malice behind the smile, the scorn in her arched eyebrows. The elven woman exuded power, as if it leaked from every pore. She was supremely confident, the most powerful woman in all of Lumineia. Alydian gathered her courage and strode to the table, taking a seat.

"Guildmaster," she said, inclining her head. "I am grateful for your summons."

"Excellent," Elsin replied, her eyes glittering. "We have much to discuss."

# Chapter 28: Elsin's Offer

Alydian knew she should lower her gaze and act submissive, but the oracle in her refused to bow. She held the guildmaster's gaze until Elsin cocked her head to the side. Her expression turned curious as they sat in silence. The way she blinked indicated she was examining Alydian with her magesight, making Alydian glad she'd taken measures to shield other mages from seeing all the magics she truly wielded.

"I have wanted to speak with you for some time," the guildmaster said.

Elsin swept her hand at the table and then took a bite. Alydian cautiously followed her example, uncertain as to the sudden shift in mood. The vegetables were perfectly steamed, no doubt prepared by magic to ensure the various types were cooked well without turning to mush.

"I'm simply a humble acolyte," Alydian replied. "For what cause would you wish to speak to me?"

"Come now," Elsin said. "The tales from your group of acolytes have reached the breadth of the guild."

Alydian's gut tightened but she kept her tone light. "Tales of training are hardly interesting."

"Oh, but they are," she said, tearing a roll apart and spreading cinnamon butter on the interior. Her gaze never left Alydian as she passed a hand over the bread, a flicker of fire searing the bread to a perfect golden tint, the butter melting into the bread. "Your choice in friends is . . . surprising."

"They are honest and not arrogant," Alydian replied, deciding that a touch of honesty might glean more from the guildmaster.

Elsin laughed lightly. "Arrogance without talent deserves to be humbled," she said, "while arrogance with talent deserves a reward."

The statement carried the ring of repetition, and Alydian wondered if it came from Verinai training. She frowned, wondering why the guildmaster would quote it—unless she was baiting her.

"I have several talents," Alydian said, "but I deserve no pride." She sipped from the water, which held spheres of ice and wedges of lemon.

"Your mother must be proud of you," Elsin said. "For even among the Verinai there are few quinmages."

Alydian heard the edge of curiosity and realized the guildmaster was circling a single issue, Alydian's identity. She had probably tried to have her followed to her supposed family home in Horizon, but her efforts had been futile. Now she must have decided to come directly to the source. But why?

"My mother is proud of my choice to join the Runeguard," Alydian replied, slicing a piece off the perfectly seasoned potatoes. "But then, it is an honor for anyone to protect an oracle."

"They are the best of us," she said.

It was the first statement the woman said with full honesty, and Alydian realized the guildmaster truly believed it. She may be haughty, but she believed the oracles represented the pinnacle of magic.

"Without them we would all be lost," Alydian agreed.

"Did one lend their farsight to your family?" Elsin asked. "Is that what drove you to become an acolyte?"

The guildmaster was steering the conversation back to Alydian's family. Alydian chewed slowly, giving herself time to consider an answer. So far, she had spoken truthfully, albeit deceptively, but the more she answered the harder it would be.

"Yes," she said. "Without Elenyr I would not be here."

She managed to keep her smile earnest. Elsin smiled in turn, the motion brightening her flawless features. Beautiful was an understatement, and Alydian suppressed the touch of jealousy.

"Tell me about your family," Elsin asked.

Alydian put her fork down, abruptly tiring of the interplay. "Perhaps it would be best if you simply asked what you wish, Guildmaster."

Elsin regarded her for several moments before placing her own utensil on her plate. "As you desire. I wish to know how your family regard the Verinai."

The question set Alydian back. She'd expected the woman to ask who she was, or why she'd overtly refused to join the other Verinai acolytes. Alydian had thought the Verinai would be angry at her abandoning their principles. But Elsin wanted to know if Alethean's family had betrayed the guild, if they had *taught* Alethean to deny Verinai authority. And in that question Alydian realized an opening she hadn't seen before.

"They do not care for the guild," Alydian admitted.

"Are they single mages?" she asked, her eyebrows pulling together.

"My mother was never trained by a mage guild," she said. "And my father died when I was a young. He was a single mage from the elven guild."

She continued to speak the truth, but the first statement stretched it. The oracles trained themselves, so Elenyr had never participated in the training of another guild. Elsin nodded as if she'd expected it, and for the first time in the meal, relaxed.

"You are Verinai but trained outside our halls," she said, her tone now sympathetic.

"My parents did not trust the guild," Alydian admitted. "They felt it best I train my magics on my own."

"Their mistrust is misplaced," Elsin said. "But they must have had a great deal of authority to train you in secret."

225

"At present, I am not permitted to reveal my parentage," she replied.

Elsin nodded as if she understood. "Come with me, young one."

She rose and strode to one of the doors set against the wall, and Alydian fell into step behind her. The guildmaster gestured to the door and it swung open, the metal hinges turning at her command. Then she ascended a spiral staircase to another door. It too opened at her will, and they stepped onto a broad balcony that connected to another turret.

At a hundred feet off the lake's surface, the platform provided a stunning view of the swamp and the western end of Griffin. The line marking the edge of the Evermist was distinct, and she noticed tendrils of magic along the edge, the supports in the earth that kept the ground from sinking and adding to the bog.

The sun had set but the colors lingered on the horizon, the deep red and purple just managing to illuminate the region. The lights reflected off the scattered clouds, staining them in vibrant colors as the sun relinquished its hold on the sky.

"I must apologize for your treatment," Elsin said, turning to face her. "The Verinai acolytes did not know you had been trained outside the guild."

"Why would a different upbringing deserve their ire?" Alydian asked.

She swept her hand at the expanse. "Throughout Lumineia, it is an honor to be Verinai. Gnomes and trolls journey from the northland, elves and humans from the south and east, and dwarves come from the northwest. Even the occasional giant will travel months to reach our gates. All know, to be Verinai is a gift."

"Your guild members despise me," Alydian said pointedly. "And I have yet to understand why."

"They assumed you were trained as they had been," Elsin said. "You must forgive their mistake."

"Are they trained to punish friendship with those that are not Verinai?" Alydian asked.

226

Elsin's features tightened and she sidestepped the loaded question. "The kingdoms of Lumineia are ever in turmoil," she said. "The kings and nobles squabble over coin and land, and they send their troops to spill blood over their petty greed. Everywhere you look the people suffer."

"The oracles help maintain the peace," Alydian said.

"Their efforts are undeniable," Elsin said, her eyes on the Sea of Grass to the north of the fortress. "But they are too few. They speak but the people do not hear."

"All respect the Eldress Council," Alydian said with a frown.

"But respect does not equate to obedience," Elsin said, turning to face her. "Nor does it build discipline. The people inevitably return to their baser instincts."

"It is the way of the world," Alydian said. "Another may encourage and uplift, but the choice to rise comes from within."

"Only in the absence of a true leader," she replied. "And as I said, the oracles cannot be everywhere."

"But the Verinai can."

She couldn't keep the rancor from her voice, and Elsin's features hardened. "We are the mightiest of guilds, and not even the armies of man can offer challenge to our power. In time, perhaps the kingdoms will see us as more than builders and enchanters."

"What do you want from me?" Alydian asked.

"An answer," Elsin said. "One with five talents deserves a place of highest honor among our masters—especially for one as powerful as you."

"You have not asked a question," Alydian pointed out.

"Join the guild," she said, "and be trained as you deserve."

"And if I refuse?"

"Then I'll know your loyalty lies elsewhere."

The guildmaster's voice was mild, but it did not soften the threat. Alydian recognized the question for what it was, an opportunity to join the Verinai and become like the guildmaster. She was offering honor, prestige, and power, in return for unwavering loyalty. When Alydian did not answer, the guildmaster gestured to the door.

"You may return to your acolyte companions, but know that I expect an answer upon your return from your current assignment. Disappointing me would be unwise."

"Is that a threat?"

"Not from me, of course, but there are those in the guild that may consider your actions treasonous, and respond in kind. They might slip poison into your ale." Elsin laughed, the sound light and mocking.

Grateful that Alethean was about to die, Alydian offered a short bow. "I assure you, I will have an answer by then."

"Excellent," Elsin said. "And do remember that your choices reflect on those around you. I'm certain you would not want to put anyone you love in danger."

Alydian resisted the urge to rip the Alethean necklace form her throat and challenge the woman, but she turned and strode away, hardly noticing when a Verinai guard fell into step beside her.

She reached the meal hall but found many of the Verinai on their feet, all huddled around someone on the ground. Alydian pushed her way through to find Commander Othan kneeling beside Toala, who coughed and clenched her stomach.

"You are well," the captain said. "You must have eaten something that did not agree with you." His gaze swept the gathering. "You may return to your meal."

Alydian focused on the flushed woman and blinked into her magesight, instantly noticing the dark tinge to her belly, the mark of poison. The dosage was minimal, just enough to cause illness without death.

Alydian turned away and strode to her quarters, but found that her belongings had been moved to another room, one of the dignitary suites.

228

Although it was built for comfort, she did not feel comfortable. She entered and shut the door before scanning the room for signs of magical observation. When she was certain she was alone she sank into a chair by the hearth and pulled her knees to her chest, fighting to control her rage and fear.

The guildmaster had poisoned her friend as a warning, and in the same moment given her a gift. Even without words the message was clear. Alethean was being given the chance to be a Verinai, or become an enemy. It was her choice.

"I choose death," she muttered, relieved that her persona was about to end.

# Chapter 29: Greenwood

The next morning they departed Mistkeep shortly after dawn and made their way back into the Sea of Grass. Alydian remained at Toala's side but the woman looked no worse for wear after being poisoned.

"I don't know what it was," she said. "I was eating with the others when suddenly my throat closed up and I couldn't breathe."

"You should take smaller bites," Ferin said with a smile.

"Maybe it was poison," Grogith said.

His scowl implied it wasn't a joke, but others took it as one, and even Alydian forced a laugh. When it subsided Toala changed the topic, and Alydian didn't press the issue. She looked back as the fortress faded from sight and swore she spotted the guildmaster standing on the battlements.

The group made their way west, following the road until it reached Greenwood. The stretch of forest merged directly with the Evermist swamp, and the mist spread into the dark trees. Miles long, the strip of trees was dark and foreboding, and more than one traveler had been lost in its depths.

The southern highway bordered it for several miles, and the Black Shroud used the proximity to strike. His bandits attacked caravans before taking their reward back into Greenwood, where the Griffin army had been unable to find his lair.

Alydian recalled that at one time Greenwood had been bright and open, and much larger. But the ground beneath the forest was soft . Underground streams weakened the earth, causing the entire forest to gradually sink. When it did, the swamp waters expanded, swallowing the trees trunk by trunk.

Commander Othan brought them to a halt at the edge of the forest. "Our informant has detailed the Black Shroud's camp," he said. "A triangular ravine lies in the heart of Greenwood, and that's where the Black Shroud calls home. Each acolyte patrol will attack from a different entrance to the ravine. If the bandits submit to capture, they will hang in the Herosian square. Otherwise, their executions have been ordered. You are free to carry them out."

He turned and entered Greenwood, the mist swallowing his form. Alydian entered behind Grogith and used her magic to scan the region ahead. Although the cloud of indecision blanketed the impending attack, the next several hours were clear.

"Blasted mist," Grogith muttered.

"They could be waiting to ambush us," Toala agreed.

"They won't," Alydian said calmly.

"And how can you be so certain?" Ferin asked, casting her a strange look.

Realizing she'd spoken too confidently, she shrugged. "They don't know we're coming," she said.

"Perhaps," Ferin replied, and then pointed to the dense mist. "But I think I'll hold onto my caution."

"Her reasoning is sound," Grogith said with a grunt.

"Does our gnome actually have a friend?" Ferin asked, a smile spreading on his face.

"No."

The answer was hardly more than a grunt. Still, Alydian noticed a trace of another emotion in the gnome's dark eyes—respect. She grinned and inclined her head, but the gnome merely looked away.

The conversation remained light but a trace of nervousness was evident in their words. Although Alydian knew they would not fall upon hardship until the upcoming battle, the uncertainty of the battle instilled fear into her soul.

Aside from the Soldier's attack she'd never fought for her life, and never taken life except inside a Requiem. Now she would be required to do both against a foe that would undoubtedly be desperate to escape. Capture would certainly end in a noose, so they would be fighting for their lives.

The forest grew progressively darker as the mist thickened. The stench of rot filled the air, indicating they were drawing close to the Evermist. Grogith muttered under his breath about the reek and Ferin laughed lightly.

Ferin alone seemed at ease, his posture relaxed yet wary as he strode beside Toala, who fidgeted at every sound. Grogith kept a hand on the hilt of his dagger, a weapon he rarely used except to fight mages, which their informant had made clear the bandits were not. Anti-magic was tremendously powerful against mages, but useless against magicless.

Alydian's fears were magnified by the fate she knew would befall her. She wanted to protect her friends and endure the battle, but knew she was seeking the chance to feign death and slip away. Then she would journey back to Dawnskeep alone.

The Runeguard would undoubtedly seek to retrieve her body, so she had to perish in a way that made that impossible. Although she hadn't told her mother, she planned to use Holan. As lieutenant of the first patrol, he would lead the charge. His recklessness had injured several of the other acolytes during the Crucible, and if Alydian could find a way to let his favored flame entity strike her . . .

She stared into the dark trees without seeing them, irritated at her impending demise. She liked being Alethean, as much for the freedom she had as for the training she received. She recognized her mother's plan as the best course of action, but it rankled to abandon the identity. Alethean had learned more about the Verinai in six months than she had in decades as Alydian.

Her thoughts turned to the conversation with Elsin. The woman was pious and arrogant, but her words were not without truth. The kingdoms of Lumineia truly did struggle, and no amount of oracle intervention had prevented their petty wars and pride.

232

If the Verinai did take over, life for the magicless would be unbearable . . . wouldn't it? Perhaps they wouldn't have to go to war, and the wants of food and shelter would be all but negated. But was safety worth the loss of freedom? And could the Eldress Council keep the Verinai in check?

In her sixth decade, Alydian had journeyed to each of the kingdoms and met with kings and nobles from every race. All had sought to curry favor with her, but a glimpse into their futures had left her shaking in anger.

Most of the nobles would betray their families and kingdoms for coin, while the monarchs themselves had many secret arrangements to keep their power and line their pockets. Even the elven queen had her secrets, and Alydian had been shocked to learn them. When she voiced her feelings to her mother, the answer had been as sad as the truth.

"It has always been so," Elenyr said. "The honor of man is fleeting and weak, and few will ever master themselves."

"But they are leaders and nobles," Alydian had protested. "How can they be so regal on the outside and so vile inside?"

"A monarch is still mortal," she said. "Coin and corruption are always linked, even if the people do not know it."

"Then what do we do?" Alydian demanded, beginning to pace. "How can we stop what they will do?"

"We do not stop them," Elenyr said with a sad smile. "We guide and help, but the choice to rise or fall is always their own."

"But so many will fall," Alydian replied.

Elenyr rose and stepped to her, stopping her angry pacing. "One cannot rise unless one has fallen. Learning is more than receiving a lesson. It is gaining the discipline to *live* the lesson. Since the Dawn of Magic the kingdom of Griffin has endured—not because the kings were honorable—but because the oracles guided them to honor. The greatest privilege of an oracle is witnessing a person discover the honor that slumbers within."

Alydian shook her head and the forest of Greenwood returned to her eyes. Her mother had spoken the truth, but now she wondered if Teriah had fallen prey to the whisper of power. What could the other oracles even do? Never before had an oracle betrayed the council, and the need to discipline a traitor could very well lead to an end of the Eldress Council.

"Alethean?"

She blinked and turned to Toala, realizing as she did that the girl had called her name several times. The sound mage regarded her with disapproval but motioned forward, and Alydian followed her gaze.

The other acolytes had come to a halt on a ridge. As Alydian took her place among them she looked down the slope into a shallow valley. Mist pooled between the trees, but did not completely obscure the canyon below.

The triangular canyon was deepest at the center. It was not overly large, and each of the three points grew shallower until they merged with the valley floor. Light glowed from the canyon and spilled into the mist.

Commander Othan appeared at their side. "Grogith, take your patrol to the western point. The assault begins in ten minutes. Meet in the middle with any you have captured. If any escape you, your entire patrol will be dismissed. Is that clear?"

Grogith grunted in agreement. "As you order, Commander."

Othan sneered at Grogith's insolent tone. Without a word the gnome turned away and they began to circle the valley, working their way through the trees to the western point. Alydian expected sentries, but they were better hidden than even she expected. Only her farsight saved them, and she came to an abrupt halt and raised a hand to the trees ahead.

Limbs bent and spun, wrapping around a man hiding on a small platform high above the trail. He managed a squeak of surprise before the limbs closed off his mouth and dragged him to the forest floor. Alydian released her magic and the wood hardened, leaving the man bound and gagged.

234

"Well done," Ferin said, passing him by. "I didn't even see him."

"And I didn't hear him," Toala said, her eyes on Alydian.

"A plant mage has many friends," Alydian said, gesturing to the forest.

Grogith grunted. "Keep an eye out for more sentries."

They encountered one more sentry and Alydian did the same to her. Leaving her trapped, the group advanced to the end of the canyon, where the gnome brought them to a halt.

"There should be forty bandits," he said, his raspy voice annoyed yet somehow eager. "Cast your entities and send them out front. Alethean, use the canyon walls if they charge us."

Alydian called on a nearby tree and cast a treewalker. The small oak shuddered and pulled free from the earth, its roots tearing from the soil to leave a gaping hole in the ground. As the tree lumbered to the head of their group, Toala cast a large cat while Ferin drew his sword.

"I'll cover the rear flank," he said, drawing his dagger. If any get past you, I'll cut them down."

"Are we here to capture or kill?" Toala asked.

"Commander Othan said we have the option," Ferin said. "But it sounded like he'd prefer we carry out the execution orders."

Grogith's narrow face split into a rare smile. "If he wants us to kill, we capture."

Ferin smothered a laugh. "You won't make a very good Runeguard if you enjoy defying your officers."

Grogith almost smiled. Almost. Then he stabbed his dagger down into the canyon. "Don't get yourselves killed."

"A resounding speech, my captain," Ferin said with a quiet laugh.

Alydian smiled despite her nervousness and fell into step beside him. The treewalker groaned and creaked as it ambled down the canyon, its branches scratching against the walls. The ground had been cut to allow an easier egress for horses, and hoof prints were visible in the dirt. As they advanced Alydian's heart accelerated in her chest, thumping against her ribs as if it wanted to escape. Around a bend in the canyon a smattering of voices was audible, followed by an easy laugh. Then abruptly another sound shattered the stillness.

A scream.

# Chapter 30: Alethean's Choice

Ferin and Toala surged forward and Alydian followed suit, diving into the ethereal mists. Wreathed in the greenish fog, her treewalker lumbered around a bend in the deepening canyon and disappeared. Alydian reached the same corner and her footsteps faltered, her jaw falling open.

They'd expected less than forty bandits, but more than a hundred men and women stood around several campfires. The firelight pierced the mist and reflected off the dark walls of the canyon. Shouts rang out and someone barked orders.

Alydian saw rage, desperation, and fear in their eyes, but she was also oddly aware of their clothing. They wore makeshift armor from animal skins and pieces of metal, the garments a patchwork of broken gear intended to keep them protected from blades. Their hair was mottled and dirty, their hands darkened by soot and soil. Most were on their feet with sword in hand, still uncertain of the threat. As more caught sight of the treewalker another entity appeared on the opposite side, a huge reaver of pure fire. It snarled and pawed the ground even as an entity of rock appeared in the mist of the final canyon.

For an instant, the bandits stood rigid. Then their ranks exploded into chaos. They surged toward the three canyons, howling in desperate fury. Alydian directed her treewalker at the first line of men and the entity swung its limbs. They were knocked into the walls where they crumpled and fell, their swords falling from unconscious hands. But the sheer number of bandits swarmed the treewalker and hacked at its roots, splitting wood and causing the entity to stumble. Other bandits streamed past the battle and struck at Ferin and Toala.

Alydian turned her whole attention on the bandits cascading toward her. She'd expected to fight a handful but instead faced dozens, all screaming and swinging swords and axes. She went to cast a sword of light before remembering that Alethean could not use light magic. Stumbling back, she fought to remember her training, fear stripping her of magic. A man noticed her weakness and charged, swinging his sword for her chest.

Grogith grabbed her armor and yanked her back, stepping in to deflect the blow. In a smooth motion he darted in, plunging his dagger into the bandits' heart before twisting free and striking at another.

"Rise and fight!" he barked at Alydian.

The order galvanized her to action and she called upon her body magic. Although weaker than her other magics, she cast an agility charm. Then she called on the stones at her feet, summoning a giant spider of dirt. Four of the hands held swords, while the pincers themselves were as sharp as a blade. The spider assembled above her head, its legs as tall as she was. Clacking its pincers, it skittered across the ground, its swords spinning into groups of bandits.

Alydian leapt in pursuit, drawing on the earth once again, casting a sword in her hand. With the agility charm active, she deftly wove between their attacks, catching the stragglers that her spider had not knocked down. She struck at head and back, seeking to subdue rather than kill. Then a woman appeared.

She was young and short, her expression wild with fear and anger. Alydian hesitated, her charge faltering. She twisted to the side, permitting the woman an avenue of escape. Instead the bandit darted to Alydian, screaming as she drove a knife toward Alydian's side.

Alydian sucked in her breath and instinctively swung her weapon, the blade catching the woman on the head, sending her to the ground, lifeless. Alydian stared at the body, struggling with the sight of the kill. The oracle in her balked at what she'd done, but the acolyte in her hardened her heart. The woman had sought to kill her, and chosen her fate.

Alydian forced herself to turn away and return to the battle. Bandits were everywhere, and Ferin fought three at once, blood seeping from wounds on his shoulder and arm. Toala was on the ground behind him, holding her side as she used her cat entity to keep the bandits at bay. It shrieked, the sound reverberating in the confines of the canyon like a thunderclap, causing friend and foe to wince.

Grogith had taken refuge next to the spider, his dagger striking from the darkness at anyone attempting to down the giant arachnid. With the treewalker cut and on the ground, Alydian stood alone as a score of bandits rushed her.

Months of training had honed her reflexes and she yielded to them. She called on the stone beneath her feet, launching herself into the air. With the agility spell active she rebounded off the wall, striking at the bandits from above.

They cried out in surprise as her blows sent them to the earth. She alighted amid a trio of bandits and they came at her. She kicked the ground, causing a wave of dirt to send one slamming into the canyon wall, binding her fast. Then she spun and deflected an incoming sword, using the momentum to spin past him and strike the third. Dropping agility for speed, she overwhelmed their defenses just as another quartet reached her.

She looked to the ground at her feet and it opened, swallowing her as blades shredded her shadow. The dirt carried her to the side and then spit her out, directly behind the bandits. Dirt rose and trapped their feet, and she took advantage of their astonishment, striking them down before their blades could find her flesh.

She fought with skill and courage, and part of her relished the sense of freedom and triumph. But the emotion was marred by regret. For every one she managed to leave alive, two lay dead in her wake, and with each new corpse, a part of her died as well.

With the spider clearing the way, Alydian managed to reach the main camp, where a furious battle waged around the campfires. Tents were shredded and burning, while crates of food were shattered, their contents spilled and trodden into the bloody soil.

The other two acolyte patrols fought without mercy or reserve, their magic cutting the bandits asunder. Alydian struggled to suppress her hatred as she watched the Verinai acolytes kill, their expressions lit by dark excitement.

Alydian took half a step toward the Verinai but a bandit stepped into her path and swung a sword. She deflected it at the last moment. He persisted, growling as he drove his sword for her throat.

"I will not hang," he snarled.

"How many have you killed?" she countered.

"It's about to be one more," he snarled, and darted in.

The spider got to him first, catching him about the waist with its pincers. They closed once and then the spider tossed his remains aside before charging a knot of crossbow wielding bandits, forcing them to turn to the entity. The arrows dug into the spider but could not do enough damage to stop it. Alydian turned away as it struck.

The spider rampaged across the battlefield, by far the largest of the entities. Alydian wanted to dismiss the magic but knew she couldn't. Even with the dead bandits, the acolytes were still outnumbered by a wide margin, and two of the Verinai lay on the ground, unmoving.

Abruptly sick of the bloodshed, Alydian looked for an escape, and spotted Holan's reaver charging gleefully into a knot of bandits, striking at the large man in their midst. As it tore the Black Shroud apart, Alydian made her way toward the reaver, using her magic to reach out to the entity, calling it to her.

It turned, its head swiveling to the side like a dog hearing its master whistle. Out of the corner of her eye, Alydian saw Holan's expression turn confused as his entity disobeyed him, and Alydian felt a surge of vindication as her will overpowered Holan's.

She engaged a pair of bandits wielding clubs, striking at one as the reaver came at her. She prepared the magic that would flood her own flesh, keeping her from being burned even as the flames lifted and launched her out of the canyon. She counted the seconds, for the first time excited to abandon the acolyte persona.

Then she spotted her.

Across the distance a woman fought Commander Othan. With a savageness that rivaled any beast, she dived through the Verinai, her black sword cutting the entities apart and plunging into Verinai flesh.

They screamed in shock and pain and turned on her, bringing the might of their magic upon the bandit.

Amid the maelstrom of battle Alydian paused at the flicker of recognition. She didn't know her, but there was something about her movements that reminded her of someone. Her hair was such a striking red . . .

Alydian's surprise almost cost her magic. The last time Alydian had seen the woman she had been standing beside the Soldier, and she too had been wearing a mask. Only her hair had been visible. She was Red, Raiden's lieutenant and a member of the Defiant.

She instinctively took a step toward the woman before her hesitation brought her to a halt. In an instant Alydian recognized her decision. She could allow the fire reaver to engulf her and escape, or she could remain and save the woman's life. Surrounded by Verinai and wounded, Red shrieked her fury, and Alydian didn't need her farsight to see that her death was upon her. But the fire entity was nearly at her throat, and Alydian sensed she would not get a second chance.

She could save a life.

Or save her own.

Alydian's hesitation evaporated and she relinquished her hold on Holan's fire entity, leaving it to stumble in confusion. She knew instinctively that if she intervened to save Red's life the Verinai would brand Alethean a traitor, so she knelt and plunged her fists into the stone.

Her hands sank into rock as if it was soft cheese, and the ground rippled away from her. Gathering her might, Alydian called on the earth, summoning it to her will. The ground shuddered, trembling and rising.

Bandits shouted in triumph and converged on her kneeling form. Deep in the thrall of her sight, she saw the depths of the canyon in shocking clarity. Every pebble, every crack, all answered her summons.

Stone jaws exploded from the ground, rising and snapping shut on the bandits around her, encasing them in stone to the neck. Surging from the ground in an expanding ring, the jaws trapped the bandits where they stood.

Bandits cried out and sought to flee but more jaws opened beneath their feet, enshrouding them mid-step. Weapons tumbled from their hands as stone swallowed their arms, leaving fingers to wiggle helplessly.

The stone jaws engulfed bandits in every direction, shutting them into cages. Verinai leapt back in fear but the jaws did not reach for them. At the furthest from her position, the last jaws snapped shut around Red—just as Erona's sword struck her back. The lightcast blade shattered on the stone, leaving Red trapped but alive.

The battle came to an abrupt end as the Verinai stared about in astonishment. Some had been on the verge of a kill before the bandits were suddenly entombed. Other bandits lay on the ground, the stone closing off their wounds, keeping them alive. Bound in rock, the bandits struggled in vain.

All eyes turned to Alydian as she rose to her feet. The display of power far surpassed anything she'd done as an acolyte, or even as an oracle. Her pride was tempered when she spotted Commander Othan's features. The elf strode to her, his expression wary.

"Acolyte," he said. "Care to explain yourself?"

A wave of nausea flooded Alydian, the first sign of magesickness. Her vision blurred as the world began to spin. "Perhaps after I wake up," she said, and then slumped to the ground. The last image she saw was of Commander Othan standing over her, his expression inscrutable.

# Chapter 31: Seeking the Lost

Raiden rode north and passed Dawnskeep on the western side. After the harrowing escape from the elven fortress he should have been fidgety and nervous, but the idea that Alydian was keeping an eye on his future brought a sense of calm he had not felt in years.

He joined a merchant caravan headed northeast and shared meals with them. Because the tale of Rualia would spread soon enough, he shared his version of the events over the evening fire, making certain to paint the Verinai in the light they deserved.

With the rumors seeded among the travelers, he split off and made his way to the swamp directly north of Dawnskeep. From there he worked his way through the secret path until he arrived at the oak refuge. The moment he stepped onto the mound Jester intercepted him.

"Red has not returned."

Raiden's calm evaporated, and he gestured to the camp. "She should have returned a week ago. Are you certain she didn't leave a message?"

"Perhaps she found a love and decided to remain?" He laughed without humor.

"She could have been delayed," Raiden said, but doubted that to be true. Red was an unpredictable woman, but never failed to send a message. Then he spotted Jester's pack, still full and leaning against an oak tree.

"You want to go after her," he said.

"Don't you?" Jester asked, a frown creasing his features. "I'm not leaving her to the Verinai."

Raiden heard a flicker of evasiveness in the assassin's voice and wondered if he had an ulterior motive. On impulse, he agreed. "Let's go."

Jester stooped and gathered his pack before kicking dirt on the sputtering fire. By the time they exited the swamp and came to the road, the sky had darkened. By unspoken accord they did not halt, and pushed through the night.

Shortly before dawn they came to a small human village. Exhausted, they paid for rooms in the inn before pressing on the next morning, this time with a pair of rented steeds. As they worked their way southwest Raiden shared the tale of his escape, and Alydian's help.

He spoke in great detail, drawing out the tale as much as possible. When he finished, Jester speculated on Alydian's motivations and the two fell to talking about the oracle as an ally. Raiden recognized they were both avoiding talk of Red, but neither steered the conversation back to her.

Raiden had always expected one of them to perish, but they had escaped the jaws of death so many times that he'd secretly begun to think they would survive together. Despite his effort to distance himself from them, they were like his family. If Red had died . . .

He jerked his head and focused on the Sea of Grass, the green strands bending harshly as the wind picked up. The sky heralded a storm, and they just managed to reach Greenwood before it broke.

Huddling in the tree line, Raiden watched the storm unleash a deluge of rain upon the Sea of Grass. Without refuge or shelter, the Sea of Grass lay frighteningly empty, it's rolling hills left to bear the brunt of the storm's fury.

Raiden shifted his cloak and cowl so it covered more of him from the rain, and then entered the darkened trees of Greenwood. Visibility was hampered by the storm and mist. Cautious and slow, they worked their way through the mud.

Empowered by the rain, the mist seeped into Raiden's clothing, bringing a chill that sank to his bones. He shivered and focused on the image of Red appearing through the trees ahead of them, her expression annoyed that they had not waited for her. It was a vain hope but one he clung to.

They camped under a fallen tree, using its bulk for a makeshift shelter. Without magic, the drenched wood refused to light, forcing them to forego a fire. The night was dark and miserable, and they spoke little.

By dawn the storm had abated, to a degree, and they pressed on. Raiden chewed on a strip of cured meat as they pressed through the dismal forest. Jester had fallen silent, and a glance revealed his features rigid and dark, an expression uncharacteristic for the assassin.

The rain persisted throughout the day, and shortly after noon they came to the first sign of the bandit camp. Raiden had met the Black Shroud once as the Soldier, and knew where the sentry would be. But when they came to the tree they found it torn from the ground, leaving an impression in the earth. The hole had filled with water in the storm, and a flash of lightning reflected off the water's surface, revealing the imprint of a body.

They exchanged a look and slipped into the trees. In silence they advanced through misty forest until the ravine came into view. Instead of making their way to one of the three entrances, Raiden crept his way to the edge overlooking the heart of the camp, and eased himself forward until he could peer over.

The remnants of tents lay scattered around dead campfires, the cloth torn apart, the posts broken. Streaks of black lined the canyon wall and carried the scent of charred stone, the legacy of mage fire, while the once smooth ground was shredded, the broken remains of golems littering the earth.

There had been over a hundred in the bandit camp, all criminals that had escaped the noose in Griffin. They had preyed upon the weak and helpless, demonstrating with every murder their lack of valor. Still, they had been desperate people, ones that the Verinai had all but forced to a life of theft.

Raiden's jaw tightened as he saw the extent of the damage. Anyone left alive would have been carried away for a quick execution—and Red would have fought like a caged reaver. In the western channel of the canyon Raiden noticed a section of the walls scorched beyond recognition, but the damage appeared desperate, as if several mages had fought to quell a threat from within their ranks.

"This is the work of the Verinai," Raiden murmured.

"Not just the Verinai," Jester said.

Raiden followed the assassin's gaze to see a shard of a banner. The staff had broken and the cloth ripped, but the partial insignia of the Eldress Council was just visible. Raiden frowned and scanned the battlefield with new eyes.

"The third trial," he whispered. "They sent the Runeguard." Fear filled his veins as he thought of Alydian. Had she been present? Had she survived?

Jester looked surprised. "You think the acolytes did this? But why?"

Raiden wiped the rain from his face and peered at a section of ground protruding upward. The stone resembled a broken stump of a tree, the surface curved upward as if it had once connected about neck height . . .

"An entrapment spell," he said. Then he spotted the others and his eyes widened. "A powerful one."

"No acolyte could have done this," Jester said.

Raiden examined the sheer number of stone traps. The entrapment charm was meant to rise from the ground and close upon an individual, sealing them into a finger of rock. Although the spell was the same, each mage tended to cast it with slight variations, a bump here, a crack there. Yet all of those in the canyon showed the same distinct curve. There was also a clear epicenter to the spell, with those closest to it tilted slightly away as the magic had spread outward. Apparently coming to the same conclusion, Jester grunted.

"I doubt a master Verinai could have cast a spell of such magnitude," he murmured.

Raiden smiled. "What about an oracle?"

246

The assassin threw him a sharp look. "The oracles do not engage in combat—a fact we should be grateful for."

"Alydian was training with the Runeguard," Raiden admitted.

Jester's eyes widened. "Why?"

"After we attacked her, she wanted to learn to protect herself," he said.

"Why not tell me this before?"

Raiden shrugged, the motion causing rainwater to trickle down his shoulders. "I honestly didn't think it mattered. The oracles train to use their magic in their second century, and Alydian didn't want to wait."

"But the Runeguard?" Jester asked. "That's not just using magic, that's combat magic. They will turn her into a battlemage—an *oracle* battlemage."

Raiden's smile widened. "An even more powerful ally."

"Is that what you want to call her?" Jester whispered, his lips twitching into a smile.

"Don't start that again," Raiden replied. "We still don't know if we can trust her."

"Are you mad?" Jester swept a hand at the bandit camp. "Her character is on display. The Verinai guards came to slaughter, and she chose to trap them all, a feat that would have killed a lesser mage."

"Agreed," Raiden said, "But the question remains why? And what happened to Red? If she survived, the guards would have taken her back to Dawnskeep."

"Why?" Jester asked. "They are criminals of Griffin, and would have been taken to Herosian for execution."

"You know how she fights," Raiden said. "And she would have undoubtedly used her anti-magic sword. Even if she managed to discard her mask, the Verinai would suspect her identity."

Jester was nodding. "We'll know soon enough."

247

They rose and turned away from the canyon—but a sound brought them to a halt. For a long moment they listened to the patter of rain. Then Raiden heard it again.

Voices.

Curiosity drove Raiden back to the canyon and he peered at the battlefield. If a bandit had somehow survived, they might know more about Red's fate. Or it could be a soldier, one wounded and accidentally left for dead. Shrouded in darkness and soaked in rain, he squinted into the dim canyon, searching for the source of the sound.

A trio of figures appeared in the gloom, followed by a small collection of soldiers. The two in the lead picked their way through the uneven battlefield, their cowls thrown back to reveal their features. But the rain did not touch them. As if it feared to mar their flesh, the storm fall turned aside. Then Raiden recognized them.

Elsin, guildmaster of the Verinai, strode beside Teriah, Second Sister on the Eldress Council. The two elves were accompanied by a giant of a man, likely a barbarian. The way he walked, the way he ignored the rain, as if he did not even feel it, set Raiden on edge. Then he noticed the trace of madness in the man's eyes and realized what he was.

A guardian.

Raiden struggled to control his urge to flee. The opportunity to listen on the guildmaster herself was too great to pass up. Swallowing the knot of fear, he held himself in check, grateful he and Jester had spoken in undertones before. As he caught glimpses of other Verinai battlemages in the depths of the canyon, he craned his ears to listen . . .

# Chapter 32: Teriah's Secret

Guildmaster Elsin came to a halt where Alethean had stood, and placed her boots in the indentations left by the acolyte. She reached into the stone and felt its slumbering might. She tested the density of the stone and found it to be rigid. A scowl formed on her face as she relinquished her magic.

"Could you match her spell?" Teriah asked.

"Perhaps," Elsin said, turning to the oracle. "But it would likely leave me unconscious as it did her."

"Then the rumors are true," Teriah said. "And her power rivals your own."

Elsin bristled. "I doubt even you could have cast this."

"An oracle's power will always be more than a Verinai's," Teriah said, her eyes on the ring of entrapment charms. "You would do well to remember that."

"And you would do well to remember that I have bested you."

Teriah did not argue and kept her attention on the ground. "I want to know who she is," she said, her voice dangerously soft.

"You're asking me?" Elsin replied. "I told you, she was not trained by my guild."

"She was trained by someone," Teriah said.

"I have a dozen masters searching the records for her lineage," Elsin said, and then sniffed. "But I would think you, with all your farsight, could have divined her identity by now."

Teriah's lips curled upward, a decidedly unpleasant expression on the beautiful elf. "Need I remind you that my farsight has limits, limits that the Soldier has exploited quite well."

"Another thorn that threatens to pierce our plans," Elsin said, sweeping a hand at the rainy battlefield. "How many more are there?"

"Change has a way of creating adversaries," Teriah said. "And I suspect more will appear before our plans come to fruition."

"We are weeks away from the Accord going into effect," Elsin said, "and my forces are nearly in position to remove the kings. We cannot let Alethean prevent our Empire."

"Are you certain your Verinai forces can withstand any resistance from the populace?" Teriah asked.

Elsin sneered. "The barren pose no threat to my guild. When the monarchs fall, the people will kneel. But you still haven't told me how you intend to eliminate your own threat. We cannot move until Oracle Elenyr—"

"Leave her to me," Teriah said, a smile playing on her features. "The poison is nearing its completion now. When she succumbs to it, there will be none left to stop us."

"Except Alethean," Elsin said flatly. "If she sides against us, the people may follow her."

Teriah's silence spoke volumes, and Elsin did not press the issue. They both recognized how dangerous a rogue Verinai could be— especially one as strong as Alethean. If she decided to turn on the Verinai, it would take a small army to kill her.

Elsin looked back on her conversation with the Alethean. She'd been evasive but surprisingly composed. As guildmaster, Elsin was used to apprentice Verinai cowering before her. For a young Verinai to meet her gaze was disconcerting, which was why she had come personally to witness the spell Alethean had wrought.

A thought crossed her mind that made her scowl deepen. The girl was obviously talented in stone magic, but power usually focused onto an arc of the circle of magics. What if she had more magics than she claimed? But Elsin had examined her with her own sight, and seen the five magics she claimed to possess. Was she hiding more?

"What if Elenyr discovers the poison?" she asked.

"She is too weak, and it is too late," Teriah said absently, her attention on the battlefield.

"Are you certain Alydian will be more malleable than her mother?" Elsin pressed.

Teriah laughed lightly. "The girl has been reclusive since the Soldier nearly killed her. She is timid and frightened, and will do as I say when her mother passes."

"If Alydian does not join us," Elsin asked in a warning tone, "are you prepared to deal with her?"

"To lose an oracle bloodline would be tragic," Teriah said, passing a hand over her face as if in pain. "But we always knew that bringing peace to Lumineia would carry a heavy cost."

Elsin stepped to a shard of stone and picked it up, examining the smooth texture. If Elenyr had not been so resistant, the Mage Empire would have come to fruition decades ago. But the First Sister had proven to be adamant in her stance of neutrality, and ultimately Teriah had suggested she be eliminated.

"Do you have plans to deal with other rogue Verinai?" Teriah asked.

Elsin looked up in surprise. "My forces are all loyal to me."

"You have dissidents in your ranks," Teriah said, her tone becoming one of prophecy, "And soon they will unite. There is a shadowmage that will turn against you."

"Toron." She said the word like it was a curse.

"You have imprisoned him," Teriah admonished. "But his followers remain. I know what he once meant to you, but he's too dangerous to leave alive."

She looked away, her thoughts turning to Toron. He'd once been the staunchest of allies, more even, but he'd forsaken all because he couldn't see the greater purpose. Her lips tightened as doubt sparked in her heart. After what she'd done, had he betrayed her? Or had she betrayed him?

"Who follows Toron?" she asked, fleeing from the thought.

"I cannot say," Teriah said. "The future is ever dependent on choice."

"A fact the Soldier has exploited," Elsin said darkly. To her surprise the oracle smiled.

"The Soldier's time comes to an end," she replied. "For we finally have one of his closest allies, the woman they call Red."

This was news to Elsin, and she turned to the oracle. "Tell me."

"She was captured in this very camp," Teriah said, "and wielded an anti-magic blade."

"Weapons of such make are rare, but it does not guarantee she is his lieutenant," Elsin said.

"It does when her mask is also present."

Teriah turned away from Elsin and picked her way to a corner of the battlefield. Then she bent and caressed the muddy stone, and the rainwater curved into a swirl that washed the stone clean, digging into a crack in the rock. The water flowed out of view and reappeared a moment later, carrying a red mask.

"How did you find it?" Elsin breathed, moving to her and accepting the mask.

"You may see nine magics," Teriah replied. "But I see them all."

Elsin wiped the water from the mask and examined it. Imbued with anti-magic, the red material was shaped like a skull, intended to intimidate as much as obscure.

Elsin struggled to keep her excitement—and sudden irritation—in check. "You should have said this sooner."

"Why did you think I wished to come personally?" Teriah asked, and swept her hand at the rain pouring around her form. "A journey in this weather is not exactly pleasant, even if one manages to remain dry."

Elsin held the mask aloft. "The Soldier has been the bane of my guild for years and Red has killed many. But the Soldier is crafty, and will likely replace her."

"We can use Red to draw the Soldier out," Teriah said. "I've sent her to Verisith where she will await her execution."

"You intend to use her as bait," Elsin said, a smile on her face. "A clever plan."

"But not infallible," Teriah said. "You will need to keep your Verinai ready to capture the Soldier."

"Mineva is well suited to the task," Elsin said. "Her hatred for the Soldier has grown since King Talin's death, where she let him slip through her fingers."

For a moment there was silence, and Elsin recognized it as the oracle examining the future. Then Teriah released a long breath.

"Your decision to appoint her is a sound one, but carries an unclear future."

"She is my guild's second," Elsin said, her tone confident. "She will deal with him."

Teriah nodded in agreement. "Once the Soldier is dead, his rebellion will crumble. But before his end there is a final task he must complete."

Elsin noticed the flicker of uncertainty in the woman's voice and met her gaze. "What aren't you telling me?"

"An oracle—"

"Don't feed me that," Elsin snapped. "The moment we wrote the Accord we were joined in treason. No more secrets, or the Mage Empire will be vulnerable from its inception."

Teriah regarded her for several moments, anger simmering in her eyes. Then abruptly it dissipated and the oracle relented.

"Six months ago our victory was certain," she said. "And nearly every choice led to our empire."

"And then?" Elsin prompted.

"Then it all went dark," the oracle admitted, her expression tightening with confusion. "I have never seen a future so clouded."

"Then find the choice that will define our victory," Elsin said.

"I could spend a century in meditation and still not find the right choice," she replied. "What you ask cannot be given."

Elsin looked away, her lips tightening. Teriah had been certain of their victory from the beginning, but now she lacked faith in their future triumph. Elsin was loath to admit it, but she'd come to rely on Teriah's farsight.

She jerked her head, reminding herself that their plan was sound. Alethean may be an enigma and the Soldier was still free, but they were two against the guild of Verinai, a force of mages unmatched across the globe. And with Teriah at their side, they were unstoppable.

"It matters not," Elsin said. "With the king of men dead, we just need the elven queen and the dwarven king to sign."

"And the other guilds? And nobles?"

"All but the mage guilds have agreed to the terms of the Accord," Elsin said. "But then, we didn't give them much choice. When the Verinai act, the age of kings will come to an end, and the era of magic will have its dawn."

The conversation shifted to the day of upheaval, when the Verinai would destroy the monarchies, but Elsin's thoughts remained on Teriah's admission. It was the first time that Elsin could recall the

254

woman expressing any doubt, and it shook Elsin more than she cared to admit.

Elsin recalled the moment they had met, when Teriah had known so much about the Verinai's plans. At first Teriah had admonished her for such ambition, but then one day the oracle had admitted her own plans, and the Accord had been born. It had been nearly a hundred years since Teriah had agreed to support the Mage Empire, and everything that had followed had been based on that moment.

Elsin looked up at the dark sky. Visible between the great canopies, black clouds poured upon her, the drops veering away from her face to impact the ground nearby. She smiled, realizing how long it had been since she'd felt a storm.

As she lowered her gaze a small protrusion on the edge of the cliff caught her eye. In the gloom it was hardly visible, but the round shape was sufficient to give her pause. Then she recognized it as a head—two of them. She kept her voice casual as she stepped close to Teriah and lowered her voice.

"It appears we have guests," she murmured.

Teriah did not look to where she pointed. Instead she smiled. "I know."

Elsin raised an eyebrow, a spark of irritation seeping into her voice. "Have I mentioned I do not care for your secrets?"

"My apologies," Teriah said. "But in this case, telling you would have alerted them, and I really would like to speak to him."

"You know who they are?" Elsin asked.

"Only by reputation," Teriah said. "But then, so you do."

"I don't understand," Elsin said. "I assumed it was merely bandits that escaped the battle. Who are they?"

Teriah smiled and placed her palms together, gathering magic into her hand. Then she spun and pointed her fingers upward—and the rain parted. Like curtains being swept aside, the deluge swung open, allowing light to fall upon the two figures on the edge of the cliff.

"Hello, Soldier," Teriah called. "It was good of you to come."

# Chapter 33: Tidal

Raiden and Jester bolted into the trees. As they left the canyon behind he heard Elsin's voice. Although muffled by the storm and forest, the words were clearly audible.

"I want them alive!"

"We'll lose them in the swamp," Jester said.

Raiden nodded, and together they raced around the canyon and headed south, toward the Evermist. As they passed the eastern entrance to the ravine, a quartet of Verinai burst into view, already casting their magic.

Rainwater rose and shaped into sleek lions, and trees uprooted from the earth. The great cats surged into the trees and Raiden drew his anti-magic sword, holding it free as he ran. Jester drifted away but kept pace.

Like wraiths in the mist, Raiden and Jester darted through the trees, but the great cats were faster. The feline shapes were liquid, threading through tiny gaps and closing the distance. Raiden's boots splashed through puddles and snapped twigs, the sound of his passage muffled by the rain. In their wake the cats were quieter, their forms streaking through the mist.

Realizing they would have to fight, Raiden slowed, allowing Jester to take the lead. Then he ducked behind a great oak tree, his boots sliding in the mud. Righting himself, he listened to the approach of the cats, gauging his strike.

Water splashed on the opposite side of the tree and he spun into the open, leveling his sword as the lion streaked by. The lion reacted quickly but the blade pierced its flank, cutting from nose to tail.

The entity burst apart, drenching Raiden and knocking him into the muck. He managed to retain a grip on his sword and clawed his way to his feet in time to intercept the next entity. But it latched onto his cloak and pulled. Raiden released the tie on his cloak and let it plop to the ground, giving him the freedom to duck.

The second lion had been enchanted with threads of fire, the contrast beautiful yet lethal. With flames running inside the water, the beast opened its jaws, unleashing a burst of flames that set the drenched wood on fire.

Raiden managed to twist away from the blast, ducking behind a tree so the trunk accepted the blow. Then he surged into a sprint and passed Jester. As the cat followed him Jester leapt into view and struck at the lion. The beast twisted to avoid the blade, alighting on the ground before circling Jester.

Abruptly the lion began to shift, the fire pushing its way into the open, forcing a second head into view. It released a burst of fire at Jester as it solidified into shape, and then the two-headed cat split down the middle, forming two smaller entities. The water cat came for Raiden, while the fire cat lunged for Jester.

Raiden ducked as it leapt, but the claws raked across his shoulder. Even made of water, they were like shards of glass, and gouged lines in his flesh. Hissing in pain, Raiden rotated to keep the beast in front of him, pointing his sword at the cat.

"They're just slowing us down," Jester growled, stabbing at the fire cat.

"I know," Raiden growled back.

In the distance wood groaned as the treewalkers pushed their way through the forest. Branches snapped and leaves joined the falling rain. The great shapes lumbered through the gloom, resembling giants as they closed the gap.

It was a sound strategy, send the faster but more vulnerable entities to slow them down while the larger ones caught up. And there was still the guardian to deal with. Raiden's stomach clenched with fear and he fought to control it. They knew the identity of the betrayer on the council, and that information could not die with them.

Drawing his crossbow with his free hand, he feinted to the cat with his sword and it sprang back, right into the crossbow bolt. The anti-magic bolt plunged into the beast, darkening the liquid flesh like ink spilled into a cup.

It stumbled and Raiden closed, driving his sword into the creature's mouth. It burst apart, the water splashing onto the already drenched soil. Whirling, Raiden pointed his hand crossbow at Jester's foe, but the assassin was already rising, steam coming off his form as the flames died at his feet.

"Go!" Jester shouted, surging forward.

A treewalker exploded into view. Wreathed in mist and rain, it split the gap between two trees and reached down, catching Jester about the waist to lift his struggling form off the ground. The assassin cried out as the limb tightened on his waist and he stabbed at the wood. The treewalker withdrew into the mists taking Jester with it. Raiden took a step toward him but the second treewalker appeared, forcing him to dart away.

Growling, Raiden curved his sprint toward Jester, unwilling to leave him behind. Spotting the large form in the mist, he fired a crossbow bolt into the trunk, causing the tree to bend as if at the waist. The wood groaned and the limb loosened, allowing Jester to slice the remaining limb and fall. He struck the ground and limped away.

"Go, you fool!" Jester shouted.

The assassin turned away from the chance of escape and struck at the treewalker, plunging his blade deep into the trunk. The wood groaned as if in pain and recoiled, flailing its branches into nearby trees. Then Jester sent his whip at the second treewalker, the tip snapping wood, drawing its attention. Jester's attempted sacrifice was the only way for Raiden to escape. But it would leave him in the hands of the Verinai, where he would undoubtedly suffer the same fate as Red.

Snarling at the choice, Raiden sprinted toward Jester, but a crossbow bolt dug into the ground at his feet, bringing him to a halt. The assassin leapt behind a large tree, allowing the great trunk to accept a retaliating blow. Through the mist their eyes met, and Jester shook his head.

"What we witnessed must not die with us!" he shouted.

Raiden heard his own thoughts spoken and could not deny the truth. Snarling his rage, he spun and leapt into the trees, sprinting for the Evermist swamp. Every step was agony. Every shout a blow upon his soul. He fought against the urge to return—the people needed to know what they had overheard. Alydian needed to know what they had overheard.

The mist deepened the closer he came to the swamp, and he caught glimpses of the bog ahead. Threading through the trees, he raced for Evermist—but abruptly skidded to a halt. The small clearing bordered the swamp and the trees rose from uneven ground. The mist was so dense he could hardly see a dozen paces into the swamp, but it was sufficient to reveal the moss-covered trees and vines. And the figure standing on the threshold.

The guardian.

Raiden had sheathed his crossbow, so he put both hands on his sword, twisting in an attempt to rotate around the man. The guardian did not move except for his eyes, which followed Raiden's move with a trace of excitement.

"You don't have to do this," Raiden said.

"Even if the guildmaster did not hold my leash, I would relish the coming conflict," he replied.

The guardian swept his hands wide and the water exploded from his hands, streaking for Raiden. The torrent blasted into his chest and slammed him into a tree, crushing him as the deluge wrapped around him, tightening on his torso.

Engulfed in water, Raiden managed to twist his sword, the black blade absorbing a portion of the magic. The pressure lessened enough that he leaned to the side and the water pushed him up the curve of the trunk, knocking him into the trees beyond.

Groaning from the impact, Raiden coughed the water from his mouth and rose to find the guardian gliding toward him, a current of water lifting his translucent boots off the ground. He raised a hand and water surged forth, churning and shaping into a giant fist that came down on Raiden.

Raiden rolled away, but the impact sent mud and water onto his back, knocking him sprawling. He fought his way to his feet as the guardian circled, his eyes lit with a dark glow.

"Your blade stings my flesh," he said. "And since my new birth I have not known pain."

Raiden swiveled to keep the guardian in sight. "You're about to feel more."

The man burst into a laugh that chilled Raiden's blood—and then glided in. Raiden twisted and sliced his sword across the guardian's chest, rotating away so he faced the man again. The guardian sucked in his breath, the sound wet and delighted. He stood on the edge of the clearing and reached down to the wound. Raiden's sword had cut the clothing and sliced into his body, but instead of flesh there was only water. Ink stained the liquid but the guardian drew it out, wincing from the effort. When it was gone, the wound knit, and even the clothing closed. Smiling, the guardian hefted the ball of stained water and it straightened into a spear.

"I do not care for your weapon," the guardian said. "But I suspect you do not care for mine."

He flung the lance with such power that it pierced Raiden's arm and exited to shatter on a tree behind him. Crying out, Raiden fell back, grasping the wound. The guardian smirked and glided forward on his wave of water.

"A pity," he said. "The kill comes so easily now . . ."

Abruptly he came to a halt and a thread of blue light appeared on the ground. It touched his ankle and brightened, and the guardian stepped forward, wrapping a giant hand of water about Raiden's body, holding him fast.

"It appears my master wishes to kill you herself."

The wave under his boots swelled, lifting him off the ground and sending them into the trees. With shocking speed they blurred through Greenwood, slowing only long enough for the guardian to snatch Jester up as if he were a child. In less than a minute the guardian glided into the ravine and dropped them at the feet of Teriah and Elsin.

"Well done, Tidal," Teriah said.

"At last," Elsin said. "The Soldier lies at my feet."

Raiden struggled to rise but remained silent. Elsin sneered and strode forward, reaching for the mask to tear it from Raiden's features. As it tumbled to the ground she began to laugh, the sound echoing off the walls of the canyon.

"You are just a pitiful elf," she said, her voice full of scorn.

Raiden bared his bloodied teeth in a pained smile. "How many of your vaunted Verinai have we killed?"

"Don't ask her that," Jester protested. "She lacks the intelligence to count that high . . ." his mocking laugh caused Elsin to flush.

She stepped in and slapped Raiden, the force of the blow sending him into the mud. Then she drew on her magic, casting a whip of pure, blue fire. She snapped it once, the whip cracking on his back, drawing blood. Raiden stiffened and bit his lip to keep from crying out. Another *snap* and Jester fell next to him.

Jester spit blood into a puddle and smiled up at her. "There's no need hide your affections," he scolded. "If you want a kiss, just beg for it."

"She doesn't seem the type," Raiden said, forcing himself to his knees.

"Every woman is my type," Jester said, and winked at Teriah.

Elsin regarded them with unbridled hatred. "I do look forward to watching you suffer," she said.

"No," Teriah said.

Raiden wanted to enjoy the surprise and fury on the guildmaster's face, but the expression on the oracle sent a chill into his blood. She stared at him with a triumph that bordered on delight.

"Let them go," Teriah said.

Elsin stared at the oracle, her jaw open in disbelief. "You cannot expect me to—"

"Do it," Teriah said. "He will be more useful alive than dead. As I said, one more task and then he can die."

Slumped on the ground, Raiden watched Elsin's rage, and he wondered if she would strike at the oracle. Then abruptly Elsin reined her emotions. Stabbing a hand at the guardian, she spoke in a deathly calm.

"Let them go."

"No kiss goodbye?" Jester asked as the water bindings were withdrawn.

"It appears your suffering shall wait," Elsin growled.

Raiden caught up his mask and strode away. Then he turned and worked his way from the canyon. When he glanced back he saw Teriah's eyes still upon him, still lit with that same dark delight. Muddied, wounded, and barely alive, Raiden slipped into the trees.

He did not feel free.

# Chapter 34: Consequence

Alydian's eyes fluttered open, but it took several moments to recognize her surroundings. Then she noticed the walls inscribed with symbols of the Eldress Council underscored with the mage symbol for healing. She sat bolt upright—and immediately regretted it.

"Relax," Devkin said.

She groaned and laid back on the bed, pain spiking in her skull. After a moment of panic she realized she was still Alethean. "I'm back at Dawnskeep?" she asked.

"In the healing quarters of the acolytes," he replied. "You've been unconscious for five days."

She groaned and finally met his gaze. Although carefully controlled, his eyes held a mixture of anger, worry, and, surprisingly, pride. She glanced about the room and saw they were alone. She sighed and sank back into the bed.

"Is mother angry?"

"Yes," Devkin said, flashing a tight smile. "But she's also impressed. Rumors of your power have already begun to spread."

Alydian grimaced. "They were slaughtering them," she murmured.

"They were bandits," Devkin replied. "Do I need to remind you what they did to merchants on the southern roads? They murdered many in a quest for coin. They deserved their fate."

Alydian eased herself up, grateful the room had stopped spinning. "They were desperate people," she said. "They needed help, not hatred."

Devkin folded his arms and leaned against the wall, laughing wryly. "You know, I wasn't prepared for this."

Caught off guard, Alydian stared at him. "For what?"

"For you," he said, gesturing to her. "You were always strong, but Alethean has brought your power to the fore."

"I tried to die," Alydian said. "But I just . . . couldn't. If I didn't do what I did, they would have killed them all, butchered them like rabid wolves." She looked away as her voice trembled.

After a moment of silence his tone turned sympathetic. "Every soldier remembers their first battle . . . and their first kill."

"So you forgive me for Alethean surviving?"

"This isn't about forgiveness," Devkin said, pushing off the wall. "It's about consequence. You cast an entrapment spell more powerful than any mage in recorded history. More than forty bandits were captured in seconds, and Commander Othan isn't the only one asking questions."

She shook her head. "Just give me the worst of it."

"The Verinai are suspicious," he said, "and rightfully so. It's only a matter of time until they discover your identity."

"Any chance I can still let Alethean die?" she asked.

"No."

She'd expected the answer but it was still crushing. She closed her eyes and drew in a breath, struggling to bring her focus together so she could use her farsight, but it refused to come. She shook her head and looked at Devkin once more.

"What happened to the bandits?"

"All but one have been taken to Herosian and await their trails."

"The one?" she asked.

His eyes narrowed at the surge of hope in her voice. "The Verinai have taken her to Verisith, and have ordered her to be executed within the week."

She nodded even as her gut tightened. A regular bandit woman would not have merited a private execution, but one who had killed several Verinai in Greenwood would demand attention, and the Verinai would not rest until she was punished for her crimes. But did they know who she really was?

"She wielded an anti-magic sword," he said. "Much like a certain friend of yours."

"A friend of a friend," she hedged.

He grunted, his expression making it clear he knew exactly who she spoke of. Then he gestured to the door.

"We only have a few minutes before the healing mages return," he said. "I suggest you plan your strategy before they begin asking questions."

"What do you suggest?" she asked.

"Use your farsight," he said. "Right now, we need to know how the Verinai will react."

"I already know that," she said, releasing a held breath. Then she told him about her meal with Elsin. When she finished, Devkin's expression was almost scary.

"She threatened you?"

"She threatened Alethean," Alydian said.

He dismissed that with a jerk of his hand. "When she discovers your identity, there will be no end to her fury. She is not a woman that loves intrigue—unless she causes it."

Alydian managed to calm her heart enough to dive into her farsight. The tree appeared before her and she soared up the trunk, examining the branches of the next few days. A branch from a neighboring tree had appeared, one that had been absent before. The limb was bright and smooth on the exterior, but the wood was gnarled and twisted inside.

*Elsin.*

Alydian shuddered, her farsight flickering in response to her spike in fear. Containing it, Alydian examined the branches that wove together with the Verinai guildmaster. The woman already knew about Alydian's entrapment spell, and had dispatched a quartet of master level Verinai to find her lineage at all costs. Depending on where they went, Alydian had less than a week before they discovered the truth. Alydian saw them following Alethean from a distance, tracking her with lightcast birds and monitoring charms, which Yaria and Bathic would help place in her quarters.

Alydian watched her guards betray her and fought the tide of anger. When it cooled Alydian made decisions on how to delay the Verinai. The more she delayed them, the more the masters would become suspicious, and by the tenth day they would realize the truth. Alydian sighed and released her magic, and the room swirled back into view.

"A week," she said, "ten days at best. Then the Verinai know who I am."

"What will they do once they know?" Devkin asked.

"They will attempt to manipulate me," Alydian said, unable to contain the scowl. "But my response is too indecisive for me to see further. Whatever they offer, it will be something I'll want to accept."

"I don't like the sound of that," he said, his features darkening.

"I should reveal myself before then," Alydian said, "before the Verinai can make their attempt."

"Start with your patrol," he said. "After what you've brought upon them, they deserve the truth from your lips."

"When?"

"Never delay a difficult task," he said firmly. "If they will follow you, let them decide now."

Footsteps heralded the arrival of the healing mages. Devkin gave Alydian a warning look as he reached to an orange sphere sticking to the door. Grasping it, he deactivated and pocketed it, and Alydian realized the man had suppressed any monitoring magic in the room. She blinked into her sight and examined the room, and wasn't surprised to find several dots of sound magic scattered around her, all intended to capture anything spoken in the room. She hadn't even considered the possibility, but Devkin clearly had.

The door swung open and healer Marin strode in. Dressed in a simple white dress with a pink band on the shoulder, she was an older human and a single talent mage, but the best of the healing mages in Dawnskeep. A smile spread on her face as she saw Alydian sitting up in the bed.

"It appears my patient has returned to the living once more."

"How bad was it?" Alydian asked.

Marin gave a cursory nod to Devkin and stepped to Alydian's side. "Your magesickness nearly cost you your life, dear one," she said kindly. "I would not recommend such a spell a second time."

"It needed to be done," Alydian replied.

"Perhaps," Marin said, and touched her arm, examining her flesh. "But even an oracle will perish if they attempt too much magic. The body simply cannot endure such power. Do not forget that magic is the power, the body the conduit."

Devkin's lips twitched as if he wanted to smile. Then he stepped to the door. "I'll inform Commander Othan that his acolyte has awoken."

"Thank you, Captain," Marin replied before her voice became stern. "And do inform Alydian that I would still like to see her. She may be an oracle, but her illness has kept her in her in seclusion for a fortnight. I am confident I can help."

Devkin met Alydian's gaze. "She improves daily," he replied. "I'm sure she can visit you when she is ready."

"But I can—"

"First Sister Elenyr is caring for her," Devkin said, slipping out of view.

Marin muttered under her breath. "If that man wasn't so handsome I would give him a tongue lashing for his attitude."

Alydian raised an eyebrow. "You favor him?"

The woman glanced up at her, her tone amused. "He may be a few years older than I, but he has the physique of a man in his youth."

Alydian laughed at that. "His wife died many years ago, so I wish you luck in courting him."

She sniffed. "For now, I'll just admire him from afar. Now, be on your way, and use magic sparingly for the next few days."

"As you order," Alydian said.

"Do not disobey the order," Marin said, looking like an angry bear. "Or I will have you dismissed as an acolyte before your magesickness makes you vomit."

Alydian heard the sincerity in her voice and inclined her head. "I will do as you ask. Thank you for your concern."

Alydian exited the healing chambers and made her way back to the courtyard. It quickly became clear that her notoriety had mounted while she'd been unconscious, and every guard she passed regarded her with thinly veiled curiosity. The Verinai guards stared at her with wariness and anger, oddly a welcome shift from the previous hatred.

As she stepped into the courtyard she realized she was an enigma to the Verinai, a powerful master capable of rising in their ranks, yet refusing to abide by their secrets. Her very existence threatened the guild of Verinai, and if allowed to live she could become a beacon for those dissatisfied within the guild's ranks.

She walked across the courtyard towards the acolyte quarters, uncomfortably aware of the many eyes resting upon her. She recalled a voyage to the azure islands, where the islanders had used a cow to display the dangers of local sharks. The beasts had circled the chunk of meat for several minutes until tearing it asunder. She'd thought the display bloody and pointless. She never imagined she'd feel an affinity for the carcass.

She reached the acolyte quarters and stepped inside, making her way down the empty halls to the one containing her patrol. Built into the outer wall of the citadel, the barracks contained bunkrooms that the acolytes were required to share. The long corridor branched into patrol chambers, each reserved for the patrols residing together. Banners and shields adorned the wall, both crafted from magic to illuminate the corridor. Word of her recovery had preceded her arrival, and she found her patrol standing in the doorway.

"May we speak inside?" Alydian asked.

They parted without a word, allowing her to enter. The click of the door shutting reverberated off the bare walls, harsh and grating before fading into silence. Alydian avoided eye contact, her eyes passing over the beds and privy at the back. Then she sighed and turned to face them.

"You lied to us," Toala said, her voice clipped and hard. "No normal Verinai could do what you did."

Alydian raised her hand and sent a flicker of orange magic about the room, silencing the monitoring magic that had been placed. The sight of her using a magic she was not supposed to have caused Ferin to raise an eyebrow.

"I am not who you think I am," Alydian hedged.

"Then who are you?" Ferin asked.

Alydian tried to voice it but the truth stuck in her throat. Ferin, Toala, and Grogith had become the closest thing she had to friends, and she'd lied to them from the beginning. Would they hate her? Refuse to help her? She'd broken more than one rule to become an acolyte, and it would be easy for them to perceive her actions as the pinnacle of arrogance. Then Grogith grunted and stabbed a long finger at her.

"She's an oracle."

# Chapter 35: A Test of Friendship

"You knew?" Alydian asked.

The gnome made a sound between a laugh and a snort. "You are not as gifted in subterfuge as you might think."

"I don't understand," Ferin said to Alydian. "Who *are* you?"

Alydian reached up and removed the Alethean necklace, and the magic faded from her features. Toala gasped, while Ferin began to laugh in chagrin.

"But why?" Toala asked. "You are an oracle, the very person we have come to protect. Why put yourself in danger to be an acolyte?"

"The Soldier," Alydian said simply. "When he sought to kill me I was helpless, and I never wanted to feel weak again. As an oracle I do not train with combat magics until my second century, so I joined the Runeguard." She offered a tentative smile, but Ferin shook his head.

"The Verinai thought you were one of them," he said, speaking slowly. "But you didn't act like them."

She grimaced. "It was never my intention to incite their ire upon you."

Toala looked away, her emotions washing across her face. Ferin seemed uncertain as well, while Grogith's features were as inscrutable as ever. The seconds passed in awkward silence until Toala turned and stabbed a finger at her.

"They hated us because of you."

"They would have hated us anyway," Ferin said, his expression unusually somber.

"Not like this," Toala said. "They did everything in their power to force us out."

"And we defied them," Grogith said.

"They will never respect us now," Toala said harshly. "And once they find out what you did we will be dismissed. They'll think we aided you."

Alydian swallowed, knowing that what she was about to ask might divide them further. But she desperately needed allies, and aside from Devkin, they were the only ones she trusted. Gathering her courage, she began.

"They cannot dismiss you if you join my personal guard."

Toala's eyes widened at that, the surprise draining her anger. "But new guards are never granted the honor of protecting one on the council."

"They can at the request of an oracle," Alydian said.

"You trust us that much?" Ferin asked.

"We have fought and bled together," Alydian said earnestly. "And right now most of my guards are Verinai. I would rather have those I trust than those with power."

Toala and Ferin exchanged a look, and then glanced at Grogith, who hadn't moved. He leaned against the wall with his arms folded, his black eyes hard and focused. Alydian turned to him.

"To join me will be fraught with peril," Alydian said.

"Why not seek the help of the other oracles?" Toala asked. "Surely they will help you."

"I do not know who I can trust," Alydian said. "For a betrayer lies on the council, and I know not their identity."

They exchanged a worried look, and Grogith scowled. Although the taciturn gnome kept his distance from the others, she thought he'd developed a gradual respect for her over the last few months. Ferin and

Toala had accepted him as their lieutenant, and would likely follow his example.

"I have no wish to see you killed," Alydian said softly, "but I need your aid."

Grogith held her gaze, his expression annoyed. "Was our loyalty ever in question?"

Alydian laughed wryly. "I did put you in danger."

"The Verinai did that on their own," he said with a scowl. "We came to protect the oracles, even if Runeguard are the threat."

His black eyes flicked to Ferin, and the elf began to nod. "I'd get to train with Captain Devkin—assuming you still trust him to lead your guard."

"I trust him with my life," Alydian said, turning to Toala.

The sound mage looked between the three of them, uncertainty warring with her anger. Then she looked to Alydian.

"Ferin is right," she said. "And I have no love for the Verinai after what they have done."

Alydian swallowed against the sudden knot in her throat. "You have my gratitude."

"It doesn't mean I've forgiven you," Toala warned.

"I know," Alydian replied.

Ferin gestured to her. "There is still something I don't understand. Why did you reveal your power in the bandit camp?"

Alydian shuddered as the image of the battle flashed across her mind. "I have revealed the truth about myself," she said. "But that is not my only truth to share."

Briefly she outlined what she'd learned about the Verinai, the Accord, and the Soldier. She kept Raiden's identity a secret, but held nothing else back. As she spoke Toala's expression hardened, and

Ferin's perpetual smile disappeared. When she finished Toala muttered a curse.

"Skorn-blasted mages," she growled. "And we were all set to fight alongside them."

"If they would even let us," Ferin said, his features tight with anger. "Once they took over they would likely cast us out like feral dogs."

"Their pride will be their downfall," Grogith said.

"Their pride is not without cause," Alydian said. "They truly command the most powerful army in Lumineia. If their plan is brought to pass, there will be little we can do. They will control the strongholds throughout Lumineia, and no amount of magicless or single mages will be able to breach them. We would all live under a new Mage Empire."

"The people will revolt," Toala said.

"They haven't," Ferin said. "They live by fear, and fighting a tyrant requires courage."

"The Soldier has inspired them," Alydian said. "And the people view him as a hero."

"And you believe the one you saved in the bandit camp is Red? His lieutenant?"

"I do," Alydian said. "Which is why I revealed myself to you this day. Her execution will take place in six days. And I wish to stop it."

"As Alydian?" Grogith asked slyly. "Or Alethean?"

"Both," Alydian said, returning the smile.

As she laid out her plan their expression changed to astonishment, and then anticipation. It was a bold move, but one that could bring the Verinai's advance to a grinding halt. It would also invite retribution.

"We'll stand with you," Ferin said. "After what you have said, we can do nothing less."

Toala hesitated, and then inclined her head. "When you look into our future, do we triumph?"

274

Alydian shook her head. "Since the Soldier attacked me, my future has grown progressively more clouded. Many do not know how they will react to the impending conflict, and their uncertainty flows into mine. For now, my farsight is all but useless."

The admission was a blow, one that caused Ferin to scowl. "So you have no idea if this plan will work?"

"I do not," Alydian said.

Grogith grunted, the sound exasperated. "The plan has merit, elf. You can't deny that."

"Grogith speaks the truth," Toala said, stepping to Ferin. "Even without knowing the outcome, Alydian's plan is sound."

"We will do our part," Grogith said. "Go and do yours."

"She's not your subordinate anymore," Ferin said, grinning at Grogith. "You now answer to her."

The gnome jerked his head and scowled, but did not argue. Alydian looked at the three of them, relief and gratitude bringing tears to her eyes. She'd become an acolyte to learn to find her courage. She'd never anticipated she'd find a friend.

She stepped to the door but paused on the threshold. "Do not forget," she warned, placing the amulet back about her shoulders. "If the Verinai know who I am . . ."

"They will move against you," Ferin said.

Alydian nodded. "You'll receive your orders by the end of the day. Do try to act like they are a surprise."

"They *are* a surprise," Ferin said with a laugh.

Alydian grinned and stepped into the hall. She closed the door and leaned against the wall, her relief so palpable she could taste it. When she'd stepped into the barracks she'd steeled herself for the worst, but her friends were still hers.

As she exited the barracks and made her way to the library she considered the lie she'd given. She had not been entirely truthful when she'd said her future was clouded, but the pieces that remained open to her were not worth sharing.

She entered the library as Alethean and exited as Alydian, returning to her quarters to ponder. Passing her Verinai guards, she arrived to find Devkin inside. The grizzled soldier rose to his feet.

"I take it things went well?"

"Send the order," she said. "They are to join my personal guard by the end of the day."

"Your Verinai guards will not be pleased," Devkin said, his lips twitching.

"Don't act so happy when you reassign them," Alydian said. "And the trouble is just beginning. My patrol's appointment to the protection of an oracle will inspire even more questions, and accelerate the Verinai discovering my identity. We must act quickly."

"Then we have work to do."

They started with her farsight, and Alydian pushed herself to the limit of exhaustion exploring every branch not obscured by indecision. With every detail gleaned, she added to a framework of her original idea.

The next day she was forced to return to Alethean and endure the intense scrutiny of her superiors. Having survived the third trial, they were now officially Runeguard, and received new armor and weaponry. The actual ceremony to appoint them would take place at the end of the week, but if things went according to plan Alethean would not be present. Their patrol had been assigned to protect Alydian with Captain Devkin, a fact that drew enormous criticism from other officers in the Runeguard, as well as the other acolytes.

Newly appointed Rightenant Holan sneered at them as they passed in the meal hall. "A barren guard for a barren oracle," he growled, eliciting laughter from Leftenant Erona.

"Alydian must have lost her wits," Erona said.

The soldiers laughed again, and Alydian noticed Toala's jaw tighten. "Your mother would want you as her guard," she shot back, "but only to keep the world from seeing your ugliness."

Ferin burst into a laugh as Holan's face turned red. The Verinai fell to muttering as Alydian's patrol accepted their bowls of stew and bread. Taking a seat at the far table, they ate quietly. Throughout the meal Alydian felt the many eyes upon her back and did her best not to look up.

Of the four of them, none had been promoted, and Grogith had lost his rank. Even though Alydian knew Devkin was going to promote the gnome to rightenant, it still stung. Surprisingly, Grogith didn't seem to care, and ate his stew without a glance at the glowering soldiers.

After the meal the foursome reported to the Elsheeria Tower, ascending to Alydian's quarters. When they reached Alydian's door, Bathic and Yaria scowled at them. They saluted Devkin and then ambled away, casting baleful looks over their shoulders. Only when they were gone did Devkin speak.

"If you'll come this way," he said. "I'm certain Alydian will be pleased to meet you."

They filed into the room and Alydian promptly removed her necklace. The door shut and Devkin began issuing orders. He'd turned one of the private receiving rooms into a training room, and in minutes he began testing them. They took turns, all exiting the room exhausted and lathered in sweat, always in defeat.

The next two days were a blur of the same, with Devkin training them at a feverish pace, even allowing Alydian to test her mettle. Alydian used the intervening time to craft a special lightcast bird, adding her magic with great care until the tiny falcon carried enough magic to convey the required message.

Squirreled away in her quarters, she still heard the rumors that she was weak and timid, unstable even. The Runeguard launched an inquisition, seeking the Council's aid to force Alydian into accepting Verinai into her guards. Alydian reached out to Raine for aid and she promptly ended the request. The conflict was nothing compared to what was happening in Horizon.

The streets were clogged with travelers clamoring for aid. The elves in Rualia demanded an inquisition while the humans from Griffin were terrified that the king's assassin would return. Word had spread of Red's capture and some of the populace wanted to witness her execution, but the Verinai refused to bring her out of Verisith. Rife with speculation and argument, the conflict in the streets of Horizon mounted to the breaking point.

Three days after waking in the healing ward Alydian finished her charm, adding the last few spells to complete the enchantment. Then she took a place in front of it and began to speak, her voice causing the lightcast falcon to spread its wings.

"I hope this message finds you in time," she said. "And if it does, I need your help. We both know what is going to happen and want to stop it. It's time we stepped out of the shadows . . ."

# Chapter 36: Crescent Moon Farm

Raiden and Jester limped their way through Greenwood until they reached the southern highway across Griffin. The storm ended shortly after they were on the road, but they were drenched to the bone, and their injuries slowed them further. Two days after the battle they came to a farm owned by a member of the Defiant. The farmer's wife took one look at them and stabbed a finger toward the barn.

"Your clothes stay outside," she said firmly. "I'm sure you want a meal but you'll have a bath first."

"Holly," the farmer implored her. "Don't be daft. Let them in."

She turned on him, her eyes flashing. "They'll drag mud and blood all over the house, and if a patrol happens to stop by we'll all be headed to the gallows."

"Yes dear," he said, lowering his gaze and stepping onto the porch.

"And John? Don't call me daft."

"Yes dear."

As tired as he was, Raiden managed a smile. Holly barely came to his shoulder, but the diminutive woman had as much spirit as Red. Round with child, she closed the door and shouted at their seven children, calling them to order like a general marshaling her troops. John descended the steps and gestured toward the barn in the back.

"You heard her," he said with a sigh. "Off to the barn with you."

"You have our gratitude, John," Jester said.

"As we've said before," the farmer replied with a dismissive wave. "Any friends of the Soldier are welcome at our door."

Raiden and Jester limped around the farm. Shaped like a crescent, the large farm bent between two rocky hills. Its position south of Herosian and its proximity to the highway made it a frequent stopping place for merchants. Travelers of every race knew the rules of Crescent Moon Farm. If you want to eat you contribute to the table, and if you want to sleep you had to help with the morning chores.

"Anyone visiting?" Raiden asked.

John shook his head. "A group of sailors stopped by on their way to Keese," he said, "but they departed this morning."

"We have no desire to bring harm to your house," Jester added.

John laughed. "Griffin soldiers may stop here, but just to join us for a meal. Only the Verinai would search our land. If they visit, you know where to hide."

"We do," Raiden said, recalling the secret room beneath the house.

They reached the barn, a well-built structure that housed a few horses and some equipment. When they entered, one of John's sons was working the handle of a pump, filling the basin above the privy. An inventive and curious man, John had fashioned the basin above a small room adjacent to the barn. The place afforded privacy so his children could wash standing up, a method that allowed them to get clean without the painstaking effort of filling and draining a tub. A second son, who appeared little more than a child, swatted at the pigs to move them away.

"Add a fireball," John said.

"Yes, father," the boy said, and opened a stone bin fastened against the wall. With a set of tongs, he pulled out a steaming sphere of aquaglass, which he dropped into the tub.

"You don't have to waste such expense on us," Raiden protested.

"Nonsense," John replied. "You're dirtier than the boys after planting."

The water began to steam, and Raiden pointed Jester to it. John directed his sons back to their chores as the assassin began to remove

280

his outer clothing. Layers of mud came away with crusted blood and leaves, and Jester growled as the movement laid bare his wounds. Blood welled up from the reopened injuries, dripping from his leg, arm, side, and forehead. Then he stepped into the privy and shut the door, hissing in pain as the warm water met his torn flesh.

"Blasted mages," he growled, his voice echoing from within the privy.

Raiden sank into a seat on the wall and closed his eyes. Too focused on surviving the storm and escaping the woods, they had spoken little regarding what they'd overheard, but it had weighed heavily on Raiden's mind. But now his fatigue got the better of him, and he slept for several minutes until Jester hissed again.

Raiden snapped awake, fumbling for his sword until he realized the assassin was merely exiting the privy. Blood streamed from his wounds, staining the clothing John had brought. He caught up a towel and pressed it against his side, muttering to himself. Raiden winced as he rose and stepped to him, noticing the whiteness to the man's face.

"Your wounds are more severe than you let on," Raiden said, his voice laced with disapproval.

"What am I, a whelp?" he demanded.

"Are you covered?" Holly called from outside the barn. "I have more towels if you need them." Without waiting for an answer, she strode inside.

She took one look at Jester and her face went rigid. "Warren," she called, "Bring my needle and thread, quickly."

"I'll be fine, woman," Jester said.

Holly was already at his side and forcing him to lie on the bench Raiden had vacated. "Don't be daft," she snapped.

Another of their sons appeared with a needle and thread, and she went to work on Jester's wounds. He clenched his jaw but did not cry out as she stitched the wound on his side. Then she moved to the gouge in his leg.

"Take your bath," she called over her shoulder. "I suspect you have injuries of your own lurking beneath all that mud. I promise to keep my back turned."

Raiden did as requested and gingerly stripped his own clothing. His weapons clattered softly onto the floor and he stepped into the privy before removing the last of his clothing. He sucked in a breath as his own wounds touched the stream of water. It was odd, as if bathing in a waterfall, and would have been pleasant if it didn't sting.

"You should have said you were injured," Holly called after a moment. "I would have let you in."

Her voice was hard and clipped, but the disapproval hid her worry. Raiden smiled at the motherly tone, and recalled how many times his own mother had sounded like that.

"You spoke with wisdom," he called back. "The bathhouse is easier to clean than the house."

"Perhaps," she replied. "But a dead body is hard to clean up from anywhere."

Jester grunted, and Raiden wondered if she'd tugged on the thread to emphasize her point. Knowing she would be waiting to stitch him up, Raiden lingered in the bathhouse until the water began to cool. Then he reluctantly exited and dried himself before dressing. He forewent the shirt and stepped back into the barn, where Holly looked him up and down.

"Not as bad as your friend," she said briskly, "But that mud will likely cause infection."

She pulled a bottle of pink liquid from a cupboard on the shelf and released a single drop on each of Jester's wounds. He sighed in relief as the liquid healing magic soothed his pain. Then he eased himself up, allowing Raiden to take his place.

"She's rather good for a magicless healer," he said. His face was drawn, but he managed a smile.

Holly sniffed. "Of course I am."

Raiden lay down and endured the stitching, managing not to cry out. When she'd finished, he sighed in relief and sat up to pull the shirt over his head. His muscles were sore but his injuries no longer ached with every motion.

"You have my gratitude," he said. "But you should not have used so much on our poor forms."

"Don't scold me on where I spend my coin," Holly said briskly, rising and wiping blood onto her apron. "Now come inside for dinner. My boys will handle the cleanup."

"Are you certain—"

"Don't argue," she said, turning on her heel and striding to the house.

Raiden and Jester exchanged a look and a smile.

"Why can't Holly lead the Verinai?" Jester lamented.

Raiden laughed. "I was thinking the same thing."

Jester grinned and they ascended the back steps to the house. Entering the kitchens, they took the offered seats and Raiden watched Holly bustle about the kitchen, cooking, cleaning, and directing her children with poise and skill. A moment later steaming piles of potatoes and seared meat were placed before them and they dug in.

They finished their plates, and extra helpings, just as Holly disappeared to put the kids to bed. The oldest three protested at the early hour, but Holly sent them to bed with a single word. With darkness falling outside and just a handful of light orbs to illuminate the interior of the house, John leaned forward.

"I think it's time we know what's going on."

Holly glanced over from where she was cleaning the stove. "Did the Soldier kill the king?" She shot the question at them as if she'd been holding it in for hours, prompting John to sigh.

"Holly—"

"We deserve the truth," she said. "Rumors are flying and no one knows truth from falsehood."

"The Soldier did not kill the king," Raiden said, exchanging a look with Jester. "A Verinai master wielded the blade."

Holly stopped, her cleaning rag hanging in her hand as she regarded him for several moments. Then abruptly she nodded and returned to cleaning, but her posture seemed more relaxed.

"Tell us everything," she said firmly. "We cannot help from ignorance."

"Holly," John said. "They don't need to—"

"They certainly do," she said, waving the rag at him like a dagger. "The people of Griffin are on the verge of revolt, and townsfolk are terrified and desperate. They are gearing for battle even though they don't know the foe. Only truth will stop a war."

"Your wife speaks with wisdom," Jester said, his tone amused.

"She always does," John said. "Even if she lacks restraint."

Holly's lips twitched but she did not smile. "Then it's settled. Out with it."

Raiden hesitated, and then realized that he'd been guarded for too long. Starting from the battle with Alydian, he shared the tale in its entirety, withholding only Alydian's role and the true identity of the Soldier.

As he spoke Holly and John listened. John sat behind the table, his long legs extended beneath while his arms were folded over his broad chest. He absently scratched his beard as he stared at Raiden.

At first Holly cleaned, but as the tale drew to a close she slowed her movement, until she sat with them. When Raiden finally fell silent she regarded Raiden, her expression tight with emotion. Then she looked to John, her tone soft for the first time.

"John?"

"I know," he said with a long sigh. "It appears the war has already begun."

# Chapter 37: Invitation

Raiden, Jester, Holly, and John talked deep into the night. Then Holly exhaled in exasperation and stabbed a finger toward the stairs.

"Talk won't forestall a war tonight. Time for bed."

Again, Raiden heard his mother's voice and flashed a weary smile. Following the woman's direction, he trudged down the stairs to the secret room John had built out of a corner in their cellar. Cramped and containing a pair of bunk beds, the room was hidden behind a stack of crates.

Raiden climbed into a bed and was asleep in seconds. He dreamed of the bandit gorge, and of Teriah's final expression. Then he fought the guardian and repeatedly failed, until a spike of aquaglass pierced his chest. He snapped awake, nearly striking Jester as he poked Raiden.

"Easy," Jester said, his features illuminated by a dim light orb.

Raiden ran a hand over his face and sighed. "My apologies," he said.

"Can't shake the oracle's expression?"

Raiden sat up with a groan. "No."

"I understand the sentiment," Jester said. "But Holly wants us to come up to eat. Apparently it's noonday, and she won't let us skip a second meal."

Raiden cracked a smile. "She's like a mother hen."

"More like a lion protecting her cubs," Jester said with a grin.

A muffled shout drew their attention to the ceiling, of Holly scolding an errant child. They exchanged another smile as they listened to Holly correct her son. When it subsided Raiden rolled out of bed and eased his shirt past his wounds. He grimaced as the motion pulled on the stitches but was pleased to find his wounds nearly healed, the healing magic aiding in the recovery.

They ascended the stairs to find Holly bustling in the kitchen, a daughter and a son working with her, both doing dishes and cooking. Raiden spotted the two remaining plates heaped with corn, potatoes, and bacon, and chose the nearest.

"I'll finish the chores," Holly said to her children. "Go out and help your father."

"But mother," they protested in unison, shooting looks at Raiden and Jester.

"Don't argue with me," Holly said sternly, flicking her towel like a whip. "Now move along."

Muttering, they exited the kitchens. Raiden threw the children an apologetic look as he dug into the meal. It had cooled but was still delicious, and he ate with an almost feverish appetite. Jester was no less enthusiastic for the meal.

Holly gave them space, and finished the dishes with deft motions before tackling a load of soiled linens by the door. Raiden noticed his own bloodstained clothing from the previous day and made to protest, but she glared at him.

"Do *you* know how to get blood out of leather armor?" she snorted triumphantly before exiting the room. In her absence, Jester lowered his tone.

"I'd rather fight a battlemage than Holly," Jester murmured. "She intimidates me."

"Me as well," Raiden said, lowering his tone when she returned for a second load.

They finished their meal and then took their dishes to the sink of water, scrubbing them clean before placing them beside the sink to dry.

Holly returned to collect the last of the linens, and gave an approving nod when she spotted Jester and Raiden washing their own plates. Then she disappeared again, and a moment later Raiden heard her turning the outside laundry tub, another of John's creations.

Raiden exited the house and strode onto the back lawn, his gaze immediately drawn to the activity in the field. John and several of his children worked with corn and wheat, with even the young ones assisting in the labor.

Clouds drifted across the sky, white and cottony against a striking blue. The sun warmed the air while the breeze cooled it, the contrast warm and pleasant, a pure summer day. Trees dotted the hills that surrounded Crescent Moon Farm, their canopies tugged by the wind as if it had a secret it wished to share.

The yard around the farm contained a handful of great oaks between the house and the edge of the planting fields. The barn sat to the left, and a pair of young men were visible inside, shoveling hay to the horses.

On the opposite side of the yard the oldest oak contained a small structure nestled in its limbs. Crafted with great care, the small ship was evidently intended for the children, and even boasted a helm and a prow. A spiral staircase ascended to the deck, providing an elegant entrance to the whimsical vessel.

Raiden made his way to the great oak and ascended the stairs, wincing as the climb pulled on the stitches in his leg. Shaded and cool, the retreat provided an unparalleled view of the planting fields, the house, and the road. With a sigh, Raiden sank onto a bench and Jester joined him.

The tranquility of the farm instilled a yearning in Raiden that he hadn't felt in decades, and he marveled at the peace that Holly and John had painstakingly cultivated. For several moments he considered where he would be if he'd never picked up a sword.

"Why did Teriah grant us our freedom?" Jester asked.

The question had obviously burned in the assassin's mind, and his tone reflected his need for an answer. Raiden sat in silence, reluctant to defile the peace of the scene with a conversation of blood. Then he finally shook his head.

"I cannot say."

"I don't like being used," Jester said, "at least not by a woman like her."

Raiden grinned. "I thought you liked all women."

Jester laughed lightly. "I said all women like *me*, not that I like them."

Raiden laughed with him but the levity passed quickly, and Raiden said, "I don't like being manipulated either."

"Does she think we'll go after Red?"

"Is that what we should do?"

Jester threw him a sharp look. "You would not?"

Raiden sighed. "It is the predictable course."

"But why not just kill us in the gorge?" Jester asked, curiosity burning in his voice. "Why wait until we go after Red?"

"She said I have one more task before my death," Raiden said.

"Blasted oracles," Jester said, rising to his feet and limping to the railing. "Our world would be better without them."

"They've served the kingdoms for over two senteniums," Raiden said. "They've never betrayed the people."

"All it takes is one," Jester said. "And after what we heard, Teriah is a traitor of the highest order."

"Do you really think she would kill Elenyr?" Raiden asked, folding his arms. "Or was their conversation merely a ploy? Teriah obviously knew we were there."

Jester frowned, and then jerked his head. "Teriah may have known, but Elsin's surprise was genuine."

Raiden was inclined to agree. The guildmaster's expression when she'd spotted Raiden and Jester had been surprise, anger, and a trace of fear. The woman didn't want their conversation known. But why would Teriah want them to hear it?

"How long has Elenyr been ill?" Raiden asked.

Jester shrugged. "Years, decades even. They've been planning this Accord for longer than we thought."

"But have we delayed it? Or aided it?"

"You can't possibly think they have *allowed* us to kill hundreds of Verinai. That's beyond callous."

"Callous? Or clever?" Raiden asked, rising to his feet to stretch his arm. "Our actions have distracted the people, making it easier for Elsin and Teriah to carry out their plan. Armies and patrols have sought the Soldier, and inquisitors from every kingdom have been inundated with calls for justice upon us."

Jester growled and looked away. "I refuse to believe that our efforts have been futile."

"We've fought and bled for this cause, but did not know they had an oracle guiding them. They could see the *future*, and we could hardly see our own target."

"Are you giving up?" the assassin said, his tone sharpening.

Within the idyllic setting of Crescent Moon Farm, he wanted to say yes, but he could not betray his vow to his brother. But doubt and regret would not be freed either. He stood and leaned against the rail.

"If Teriah knows what we intend, how can we make any decision?"

"We use Alydian," Jester said with a knowing smile. "A prospect that should please you."

Raiden laughed. "You know it would please me to work with Alydian. But we hardly know her—and she's still an oracle. She could be manipulating us just like Teriah."

"You know Alydian?"

The young voice caused them both to look up, and Raiden spotted a small girl wedged into a crook of a tree high above them. She was hardly more than five, but she'd climbed to the top of the tree without fear. The resemblance to her mother was striking.

"She's a friend," Raiden said.

The girl smiled and levered herself down from the branch, descending with ease. Reaching the deck of the boat, she came up to Raiden and pointed to the sword.

"Do you fight for her?"

Raiden and Jester exchanged an amused look, and Raiden found the answer was quick in coming.

"We do."

The girl put her hands on her hips and glared at Jester—a pose that matched Holly to perfection. "How can you doubt Alydian? If you've met her, you know you can trust her."

"We don't doubt her," Jester said, his tone amused.

"Liar," she said.

"Elba!" Holly called up. "Are you bothering our guests? Come down and help me with the laundry."

"Yes, mother!" Elba called, and then glanced at Jester. "Dishonestly doesn't look good on you."

Foregoing the stairs, she caught a rope and lowered herself to the ground before scampering away. Raiden laughed at the girl's dominating poise, and Jester joined him.

"I don't think the world can handle two of Holly."

"It will have to," Raiden said.

They watched the woman and her daughter hang clothing on a line before Jester spoke. "We've been dancing with Alydian for months. It's time we made a formal proposal."

"But what can she do?" Raiden asked.

"I don't care what she does," Jester said. "But I'm not leaving Red behind. She has saved my life too many times to count."

"I as well," Raiden said, and felt a trickle of foreboding. Had Teriah known they would not abandon their friend? Was this the course she was counting on?

Abruptly Jester caught his arm and yanked him to the trunk of the tree, stabbing a finger at the hilltop. Recognizing the urgency in his motions, Raiden followed his arm to spot the lightcast bird soaring down to the farm.

Had the Verinai decided to come after them anyway? Or had Teriah resolved to follow and kill them at the farm? The questions bombarded Raiden's thoughts as he scanned the area, searching for any hint of Verinai. There was none, but that didn't guarantee they were not present. In unison they yanked their anti-magic swords from their scabbards.

The bird abruptly banked toward them, as if it knew where they were. Raiden tensed, drifting into the shadows as he readied himself for battle. Then he noticed the bird was not entirely yellow. He squinted, and managed to make out the streaks of other colors, including the thread of white.

"Alydian?" he spoke aloud, rising and stepping into view.

The falcon swooped under the branches and alighted on the railing. A trace of light leapt from its eyes and brushed across Raiden's chest. On instinct he retreated, but the spell merely marked him. Then the bird cocked its head to the side and began to speak.

"I hope this message finds you in time," Alydian's distinct voice said. "And if it does, I need your help. We both know what is going to happen and want to stop it. It's time we stepped out of the shadows. When my message is complete the messenger will disintegrate, so please listen well. Our mutual friend has been taken by our mutual enemy, and it's time we fight together. I have an idea, one I think you're going to like . . ."

# Chapter 38: Unto the Enemy

Alydian departed Dawnskeep the morning after sending the message to Raiden. She'd kept the message purposefully vague on the chance a Verinai intercepted it. To ensure it went directly to Raiden, she'd added a trace of Raiden's unique energy drawn from her own memory, ensuring the falcon would fly directly to him. But she had no way of knowing he would get the message.

Dressed and armored as Alethean, she rode a horse next to Devkin and Grogith, slipping out a small entrance of Dawnskeep with little fanfare. Then passed through Horizon and then took their journey south. Ferin and Toala were tasked with making it appear as if Alydian were still ill, a task made difficult by the increased demands for her time. Fortunately, they had Elenyr's support.

Alydian recalled the conversation with her mother the previous evening, where Alydian had told her everything she knew. Elenyr had accepted the truth regarding the Soldier surprisingly well, but she'd disliked Alydian's plan. Ultimately she'd agreed but insisted Alydian take Grogith as well as Devkin.

"Swear to me you will return," Elenyr finally said.

"I will, mother."

For six days they rode hard, passing the city of Rualia before turning east. The forest gave way to mountains and they climbed the winding road that marked the border between Griffin and the elven realm.

The road was well traveled and maintained. They passed shipments of goods guarded by battlemages. The Verinai cast them curious looks, and some surreptitiously conjured lightcast birds that flitted back the way they had come.

"They know we are coming," Devkin murmured.

"They are suspicious of me," Alydian said softly. "But they do not know my persona."

"Not yet," Devkin said.

The road twisted between two mountains and then climbed into a high pass, traveling between two peaks before descending into the valley beyond. With a large lake at the side, the valley was ringed by mountains. Its position outside of any kingdom and the difficult terrain made the guildhall of the Verinai defensible and mysterious.

"Boulder Lake should be over the next ridge," Alydian said, pointing up the slope. "The city lies beyond it."

Alydian struggled to contain her worry. Verisith was a city that only a handful of non-Verinai had been permitted to enter. At one time the Verinai had welcomed all into their halls, and even helped train single mages. But that time had long since faded, and Verisith had been built after the Verinai had embraced their arrogance. Now Verisith was a city steeped in mystery and rumor.

Aside from Teriah, few of the council had visited Verisith in decades, not since Elenyr had journeyed to meet with Elsin about rising tensions between Verinai and the other mage guilds. Alydian wondered how Elenyr would be received now.

The road descended into the valley and wound through a dense forest before rising again, turning back on itself to negotiate an escarpment. They passed a wagon surrounded by Verinai battlemages and then reached the top of the ridge, and the edge of the lake.

Surrounded by cliffs, the lake was mirror smooth and reflected the neighboring peaks. A breeze found its way in and caressed the water, sending ripples across its surface. The ripples swept outward until they encountered the boulder that gave the lake its name.

As large as a farmhouse, the boulder rose from the water, providing the base for an enormous statue. Black and forbidding, the statue held a sword that touched his feet. Its opaque eyes seemed to follow them as they entered the valley.

Grogith's eyes lifted to the statue and he muttered a curse. "What a monstrosity."

"It may be stone," Alydian said, "but it watches the road. You can be certain Guildmaster Elsin can see us." She pulled on the reins and guided her horse around the lake.

On the south side of the lake the cliffs opened into a canyon. Like a great sword had sliced into the rock, the chasm threaded its way between massive peaks, its high walls climbing four hundred feet.

"The canyon of mages," Alydian said, motioning to the symbols on the sides of the canyon.

Devkin's scowl deepened as they entered the canyon, and Grogith appeared apprehensive. Although large light orbs were bracketed into the canyon walls, they could not overcome the sense of oppression the canyon exuded. The dark, cold walls felt like they could close at any moment, smashing them into oblivion. Alydian shuddered and blinked into her magesight to scan the stone, grateful she found no such magic present.

Shortly after entering the canyon they rounded a curve and a gate came into view. Built to span the gap, the gate contained a portcullis and a dozen battlemages. The captain brought them to a halt before the closed barrier.

"Runeguard," he said, "what is your business here?"

Alydian bristled at his condescending tone, but Devkin didn't seem deterred. "I am on direct errand from the Eldress Council and Alydian, here to speak with Master Mineva."

"I will seek the direction of my masters," he replied.

He spun his hand and a lightcast hummingbird appeared. It streaked away, leaving Alydian and her guards to wait. Her lips tightened at the delay. Elsin already knew they were there, but would want to communicate with her Verinai in Dawnskeep. They in turn would seek an audience with Alydian, whereupon Toala would mimic Alydian's voice to confirm the order.

"Patience," Devkin murmured. "Toala will do her part."

Alydian drew a breath and released it, and mentally recited the oracle's code as she waited. It was lengthy and boring, but passed the time as the portcullis was raised and lowered for another wagon to depart. After two hours she grew impatient, and even Devkin's calm did not settle her, especially with the amused looks by the Verinai on the battlements.

A lightcast bird appeared and alighted on the captain's shoulder. He listened to the order and then motioned to the guards.

"You are permitted to enter," he said. "Captain Devkin, you and your party will be led to the keep, where Master Mineva is waiting for you."

The way he said it, as if Devkin lacked the mental faculties to find it on his own, made Alydian's blood boil. But she nudged her horse forward as the portcullis lifted, and they passed the barrier under the scrutiny of the guards. When they had left the wall behind, Alydian looked back—and caught a glimpse of the enchantments on the steel, which veritably shimmered with magic.

"They are more fortified than they appear," Alydian said.

Devkin also looked back as the canyon took the wall from view. "They speak of peace yet prepare for war."

The next wall was more ornate, and resembled a young dragon chained to the canyon walls. Visceral and menacing, the dragon's stone features were so real that Alydian shuddered and looked away. They passed beneath the carving's wings to reach the opposite side.

"Entity?" Devkin murmured.

Alydian shook her head. "A sentient," she said. "A powerful one."

They continued down the canyon, the view darkening as they descended. The next wall was built out of twin bears that held aloft the battlements, their gigantic forms also chained to the wall. Alydian swallowed as she looked at one of the beasts, disturbed by the glint in its opaque eyes.

The final gate was made of fire and light, the enchantments binding the power into solid form. Built so the wall itself could send gouts of fire into attackers, the wall shone in the gloom of the canyon, a beacon of destructive power that slumbered under its Verinai masters.

Alydian and her companions fell silent as they passed beneath the wall, and she could feel the heat on her face. She had last visited Verisith in her youth, and the canyon had been empty. The sheer volume of fortifications—before they even reached the city—bespoke intent, as if the Verinai were preparing for a specific assault. Even combined, the armies of Lumineia would be slaughtered in the canyon.

The canyon turned a sharp right, bringing the city of Verisith into view. A final pair of sentries were still being attached at the canyon's end. At forty feet in height, the smooth black stone resembled great panthers, their features fixed in snarls of rage. They stood bound by long chains, allowing them to strike at anything in the breadth of the canyon.

Devkin threw Alydian an uneasy look, and she nodded in agreement. The world was just beginning to realize a war was coming, but the Verinai had been preparing for decades, and they intended to win. The fortifications, the training of their guild members, all showed that the Verinai had forged their guild into an army, and they had done so without anyone knowing.

Alydian passed between the two great panthers and the Verinai soldiers working to complete them, coming to a halt on a shelf of rock that faced a plunging ravine. The fissure fell away into darkness, and even with Alydian's magic she could not discern the bottom. On the opposite side of the gap the fortress of Verisith occupied another shelf of rock.

Backed by a mountain and surrounded by cliffs, the city was only accessible from the canyon of mages. A trio of waterfalls cascaded from holes in the cliffs, the water feeding sparkling streams and ornate fountains.

The entrance road split to either side and descended to twin bridges that spanned the chasm. Taking the right one, Alydian led her guards down the slope and over the bridge to the city wall. Instead of a portcullis, a wall of aquaglass barred the way. As thick as the battlements, the barrier drained into the ground to permit them entry.

298

When they entered the city a group of Verinai were waiting for them, with Mineva at their head. Garbed in a flowing dress of crimson accented with black, she was resplendent and intimidating.

"Captain Devkin," she said, her eyes flicking to Alydian. "Your messengers arrived shortly before you did." She motioned to the pair of Runeguard standing nearby. "But they declined to say the purpose of your visit."

Devkin smiled at Mineva. "Oracle Alydian sent me to speak to you regarding the events at Griffin. As I'm sure you are aware, the assassination of King Talin has incited the kingdom to rage. I hope that your recollection of those events will aid in locating the Soldier. The man attacked Alydian and nearly killed her, so she is keen on bringing him to justice."

Mineva studied him for a moment before smiling and gesturing behind her. "I'm sure you are tired from your journey. We can speak inside."

Alydian's eyes flicked to the pair of Runeguard that had preceded her, and across the gap their eyes met. Jester smirked, his eyes sparkling with mischief. At his side, Raiden smiled at Alydian and inclined his head, sending a flutter into Alydian's chest.

The Soldier had arrived.

# Chapter 39: Verisith

Alydian wanted to speak with Raiden, but with so many Verinai about, they were certain to be overheard. He too seemed eager to talk, and Alydian wondered what he had to say. His smile was fleeting but she sensed it was meant for her, and she struggled to keep her excitement from bleeding onto her features.

Then she noticed the rigidity to his frame, the faint note of force in his smile. Was he displeased to see her? Did he not feel as she did? Her excitement crumbled, and then he looked her way again and the fleeting smile returned. Relief flooded her. He *did* feel something—but why the tension? What else did he know?

Struggling to contain her impatience, Alydian turned her focus upon Verisith. The road curved away from the gate toward the center of the city. Alydian had only visited the city once in her youth, and despite her feelings toward the Verinai she found herself in awe. Buildings were elegant and beautiful, with walls of magically carved stone that lacked seam or joint.

Shops and factories dominated the street and bustled with activity. The factories resembled homes, yet they were full of enchanted plants grown for consumption and export. Stone mages crafted glass spheres at an astonishing rate, while the next factory imbued them with light.

The upper levels of the city were dedicated to homes, and broad terraces interconnected them with numerous arching pathways. A pair of streets sloped up from the city floor and curved to the upper levels, allowing wagons and riders to reach the higher levels of the city.

They reached the center throughway and turned toward the keep. Extending from the cliff at the rear of the city, the keep seemed to have grown directly from the mountain. The first two floors were open, with expansive pillars that supported the higher levels. Balconies were in abundance, their size suggesting they were private quarters for high-ranked officers in the guild.

The keep's structure curved in impossible sweeps, the supports seeming too frail to hold up the balconies. Light seeped from the stone to display beautiful figurines of Elsin and other Verinai in an epic victory over reavers and dragons. Then the light morphed and another image appeared, this time of a small force of Verinai overpowering an army of magicless.

One of the great waterfalls flowed out of the cliff above the keep and fell in graceful patterns, the streams of water twisting and curling before feeding the brooks that lined the city. The streams added a soft backdrop to the hum of industry.

"It is beautiful, is it not?" Mineva asked.

Alydian realized the question was directed at her. "Your city is wondrous."

Mineva stepped closer and lowered her tone. "I know Elsin invited you to the guild, Alethean," she said. "I am glad you have this opportunity to witness our power."

Alydian wondered if that was the reason the Runeguard had been allowed into Verisith. If Elsin wanted Alethean to be impressed, she was. But the contrast to common settlements in the other kingdoms was striking.

"Perhaps in time, all cities in Lumineia could be as beautiful," Alydian said.

Mineva smiled with a trace of smugness. "You speak our very desires."

"Then why does Elsin require so much coin for guild exports?" Devkin asked, gesturing to the nearby factories. "It's clear you are able to produce much with little."

Mineva pointed to a small building with a forge, where a pair of mages built swords and enchanted them. "Other guilds have to work together to blend their magics," she said. "A difficult and time-consuming task that requires mages to be trained in the complexities of combining magics. We are able to craft, enchant, and finish products in a fraction of the time it takes the single talent mages. Our guild members train for decades to master the skills required. Do we not deserve payment for our actions?"

"Elsin's predecessor did not seek wealth," Alydian said. "He sought to better the lives of every class."

"Perhaps," Mineva said, "but we lacked the resources to be innovative, to create new spells and push the boundary of what we know as magic. Elsin has shown us that we can do more . . . if we have more. This city used to be like any other, yet now it displays an abundance of spells that never before existed."

"Wealth and pride are ever allies," Devkin said. "And pride does not like to share."

Mineva's lips tightened. "I don't expect a magicless to understand, Captain Devkin, but the guild has been preparing for centuries to change our world."

"And how exactly do you plan on doing that?" Alydian asked. She almost asked about the Mage Empire but held the words in check.

"In due time," Mineva said with a smile.

Alydian exchanged a look with Devkin, whose carefully controlled features revealed nothing.

"How is Alydian?" Mineva asked, glancing at Devkin.

It was good she wasn't looking at Alydian, because her surprise would likely have given her away. Devkin flashed a disarming smile.

"After the Soldier's attack, she has thrown herself into studies."

"Rumor has it she is unwell," Mineva said. "But then, fear is an ailment that is hard to remedy."

"Fear of what?" Devkin asked innocently.

Mineva snorted. "Come now, Captain. She is not here and you do not need to protect her. We both know she has locked herself away since the Soldier attacked her. But she is not the first oracle to have a timid soul."

Alydian exchanged a look with Raiden and managed to keep the grin from her face. He too looked amused, his lips twitching before he looked away. Alydian wondered what Devkin would say, but Raiden spoke first.

"Power is all the greater when it is unexpected," he said. "And I suspect the girl will surprise you."

Alydian threw him a sharp look, but Mineva misunderstood. She nodded in agreement. "You speak with wisdom, Runeguard. Perhaps one day we will see if the girl has grit. But if the Verinai were permitted to protect her, she would not need it."

Raiden's eyes flicked to Alydian and a faint smile crossed his face. "One with that much power does not need to be guarded."

Alydian raised an eyebrow. "You imply her magic surpasses the Verinai?"

"And her beauty."

Alydian coughed and looked away to hide her flush. Jester smirked and nudged Raiden, while Devkin coughed, throwing a warning look at Raiden. Grogith scowled at the banter. Unperturbed, Raiden kept his expression bland, as if he'd made an offhand comment.

Mineva's eyes narrowed in irritation and confusion, and for a moment they walked in silence. When she spoke again it was about the city, and Alydian recognized it as an effort to shift the topic. But Alydian wondered if they had revealed too much.

The road curved gently upward until it reached the keep. Half buried into the cliff at the rear of the city, the keep's base levels were open, with pillars instead of walls. The grand hall at the bottom was stunning, with crystalline statues lining the exterior, all imbued with golden light. Adjacent to the hall, curving staircases swept upward to the second, smaller hall.

Mineva led them upstairs to the second level, a courtyard with a statue in the center. Alydian blinked in surprise at the vivid figure, a rock troll armed with gauntlets of spiked chains. The depiction was feral and visceral, and even though it was stone she felt a spark of fear. Then they ascended beyond it to reach the upper levels of the keep.

As they passed higher into the keep Mineva gestured to the corridor. "These are the apprentice halls, where masters provide private instruction. Apprentices that show promise are granted the honor of living here." She pointed to the doors on the left, the rooms that would overlook the city.

The group ascended to the journeyman levels, that were built much like the apprentice chambers. Passing them, they reached the master level of the keep, and Mineva made her way to one of the rooms on the left. A pair of guards stood at either end of the hall, and they nodded when Mineva strode by. Entering her quarters, Mineva gestured to the chairs in the spacious receiving hall.

"Have a seat," she said. "I'll send for a meal."

She cast a bird and it soared out the window, banking through the waterfall before disappearing. Alydian stepped to the balcony and looked at the city. From her vantage point the city veritably glowed, a bright jewel hidden in the mountains.

Although Mineva's words and actions were kind, her tone and expression were not. Her calculating gaze swept across them and flicked to Alydian. She was alone in the room with her visitors, but the door remained open, and the guards were just outside.

Devkin and Raiden stayed close to the door, while Grogith drifted to a position behind Mineva. Alydian ambled to the side, preparing herself for what was to come. Jester took up position on the opposite side of her. None took a seat.

Mineva noticed the ring around her and frowned. "Captain Devkin," she asked, her posture tightening. "What is your intent?"

"To find the truth," Devkin said, and nodded to Grogith.

The gnome caught Mineva's arms, yanking them behind her. Threads of anti-magic swirled from his fingers and wrapped around the woman's wrists, binding her in place. Startled, she just had time to shout before Alydian's muffling curse cut her off.

The sound drew the guards, but before they reached the door Raiden and Devkin leapt out. They struck hard and fast, overwhelming the surprised guards. Mineva screamed but no sound escaped her lips, and she fought her bonds until Jester put a sword on her chest.

"I don't like to harm beautiful women," he said with an easy smile, "but I won't hesitate to kill a snake."

The scuffle outside the room ended and Raiden dragged an unconscious form into the room. Devkin did the same, and soon all four guards were inside Mineva's receiving room. Alydian breathed a sigh of relief when the door clicked shut.

"No blood in the hall," Devkin said. "But we don't have a lot of time."

Alydian nodded. "Give me a moment and I will find you the best route to the dungeons."

"Wait," Raiden said. "There are things you must hear."

"Can't it wait?" Devkin asked. "A servant is going to bring food in a few minutes and we need to be done."

"No," Jester said. "Trust us."

Alydian gestured an invitation. "What do you know?"

"We found the Black Shroud camp," Raiden said. "Teriah and Elsin were there, together."

Alydian clenched a fist. "So she is the rogue mage on the council?" She'd expected as much, but to hear it confirmed elicited a wave of anger. The woman had abandoned her oaths and the Eldress Council, and she wondered how her mother would punish such a betrayal.

Raiden was nodding. "They spoke of the Accord and the Mage Empire. They were going to strike in a few weeks' time." He briefly described the fight with the water guardian, Tidal, and the revelations they had heard.

"All the more reason we need to act quickly," Devkin said.

"One more thing," Raiden said. "They spoke of poisoning Elenyr."

Alydian blinked in surprise and turned to Mineva. "Is that true?"

The woman sneered at her and looked away, all but confirming it. Alydian took a step toward her, rage pouring into her fist. Devkin saw her intention and caught her arm, speaking in a low tone.

"After. We must retrieve what we came for."

Alydian stared at the woman, seething. She'd witnessed her mother's decline in health and felt helpless, but resigned herself to the way of life. The other oracles had sought to heal her, with even Teriah expressing her deepest sympathies that the ailment was incurable.

"Alethean . . ." Raiden said, his voice urgent.

"I am well," she said aloud, and mentally added, *or I will be when I have Teriah.*

She fought to control her rage and closed her eyes. It took three tries until she managed to find Raiden's tree. Over the last few weeks it had become progressively brighter, with many of the branches vivid and easy to identify.

She followed the next several minutes and watched him scour the lower levels of the keep. Many of the paths ended in discovery and combat, so she followed the ones that didn't. The seconds slipped away and her tension mounted. Then she spotted Raiden arriving at the prison and finding Red.

"Below the keep," she said, opening her eyes. Speaking quickly, she detailed how he could find Red and get her out, even warning him about the prison door. While she'd been looking into his future, Raiden and Jester had donned a pair of guard uniforms and stepped to the door.

"Be safe," she said.

"You as well," Raiden said, his eyes flicking to the still struggling Mineva.

He hesitated, and it seemed like he wanted to say more. Then his mouth shut and he departed, leaving the three of them alone with Mineva. Alydian turned and regarded the woman. As a master of Verinai she was gifted and powerful, but now her face was flushed and her jaw worked.

"Hold her," Alydian said as she walked toward her. "Extracting a memory is difficult enough without a defiant host . . ."

# Chapter 40: The Shadowmage

Raiden and Jester stepped out the door and turned down the hallway, making their way to the stairs at the end of the hall. In the uniform of Verinai guards, they kept their pace natural and unhurried, and the guards on the stairs ignored them.

It was only a matter of time before someone discovered the guards' absence, or a servant arrived with the requested meal, and Raiden wanted to be gone before either occurred. When the Verinai realized their vaunted defenses had been breached they would be furious, and they would tear the intruders to pieces.

Descending the stairs, Raiden followed Alydian's path and tried to look like he belonged. Fortunately, it appeared the Verinai relied greatly on the outer fortifications of the city, and sentries were infrequent.

The rooms of the upper keep were evidently reserved for the highest masters in the guild. Much like Mineva's quarters, the rooms were placed at the front of the keep overlooking the city, while the opposite side of the corridor contained training halls. The aquaglass doors allowed Raiden to see the interior and served to muffle the explosion of miscast charms.

Through one such door Raiden spotted a master dueling with an apprentice, the young dwarf struggling to cast a fire shield. But the master's banshee curse ripped the shield apart and sent the dwarf tumbling away. The subsequent scolding was inaudible through the door.

Leaving the master levels behind, they dropped to the journeyman levels, passing the senior officer quarters before reaching the base of the keep. Raiden strode past the rock troll statue and turned down the stairs to the subterranean levels of the city.

While the surface of Verisith was filled with wonder and magic, the underground corridors were stark and barren. Walls were smooth, undecorated stone with light orbs placed against the ceiling.

Instead of storage rooms, the chambers on either side contained gardens. Lit by powerful sun-like light orbs at the center, the gardens grew every form of vegetable and fruit. Raiden paused at one, shocked to see a small storm brewing at the ceiling, the clouds just beginning to dump rain on the interior farm.

Jester made a disparaging sound in his throat. "What would our world be like if power was shared instead of hoarded?"

Raiden motioned to the storm. "When that day comes, I suspect the want of food will be eradicated."

A door shut behind them and they continued on, passing beyond the growing rooms to the dwarven ascender that took them down another level. They stepped off to find themselves in a small room facing a large, aquaglass door. Beyond it stood a pair of Verinai battlemages.

"Runeguard dispatched by Oracle Alydian have arrived to interrogate the prisoner," Raiden said, stepping forward and withdrawing a scrap of parchment from his side. "We are here to retrieve the criminal known as Red."

"We did not hear of your arrival," one said, bored. "We'll have to request a master's approval."

Jester shrugged—and then darted forward, drawing his sword and plunging it through the aquaglass barrier. As he cut a large hole the liquid hissed and dripped to the floor, burning holes into the stone. Raiden dived through the acidic barrier and rolled to his feet as the two Verinai recovered from their surprise.

Raiden struck one in the jaw, knocking him into the wall. The other was evidently a body mage and darted out of reach before Raiden could close the gap. Raiden withdrew his crossbow and fired, but the man spun away, sneering as he did.

"You are no Verinai—"

Jester's whip wrapped around his neck and yanked him to the floor, where Jester finished him. Raiden leaned down and smashed his fist into the first guard's cheek. He'd been fighting to rise, but the blow sent him to the ground for good. Raiden bent down and wrapped a black chord around his wrists while Jester stabbed a finger at the gaping hole in the door.

"Why can't the Verinai do anything normal?" he asked, exasperated.

"It's an acid door," Raiden said. "If anyone tried to breach it they would die horribly."

"We can't close it," Jester said. "The first guard ambles his way down here, the entire city will descend upon us. As much as I like attention, I don't care for that much."

Raiden slapped the guard several times until he roused. The man blinked and then his eyes focused on Raiden. He jerked, fire coursing on his arms only to be drawn away by the anti-magic bindings.

"How often do guards come down here?" Raiden asked.

"Every ten minutes," the man said, jutting his chin out. "You'll be killed before you can—"

Raiden's blow rocked his head back. "I don't care for lies," he said. "I can kill you right now, or you can tell your superiors that we knocked you out. It's your choice."

The man's eyes fell on his dead companion. "You'll kill me anyway."

"Certain death or possible death," Jester said with a smile. "Which do you prefer?"

The man glared at him so Raiden sighed and drew his sword, placing it on the man's heart.

"Wait!" he cried. "The shift won't change for another two hours."

"How many guards are in the dungeons?" Jester asked, drifting closer.

"Two," he said.

Raiden smashed him in the face, harder than before. "I told you, no lies."

"All right!" he growled, wiping his bloodied lip on his shoulder. "Four."

"Apprentice or journeyman?" Jester asked.

"Guards are always journeyman," the man said, and then his eyes narrowed. "Something you would know if you were Verinai."

"Which we aren't," Jester said, knocking him out with a blow to the skull.

Raiden let the unconscious man slump to the ground and then turned down the corridor. Drawing his sword, he advanced to where the corridor split in both directions. He peeked down the left corridor while Jester did the same on the right.

Shaped like a large T, the prison contained cells along the back hall. The corridors stretched away for a short distance and contained a quartet of doors on either side, with one on the end. Two guards were in view, both standing at the end, talking. Raiden withdrew his head before he could be spotted and looked to Jester.

"Two guards," Jester said, "Short corridor, four cells on either side, one on the end."

"Same," Raiden said. "Take them down, fast and quiet. Then we find Red."

They nodded, and in unison turned the corner. Raiden kept his sword behind his back and walked casually until they noticed him. When they did, the shorter one frowned.

"You aren't supposed to be here."

Raiden gestured vaguely toward the ceiling. "The guildmaster wants to speak with you, something about your request for mastership."

311

It was a gamble, but a good one. Journeymen in every guild fought for their mastership, the highest rank one could achieve short of becoming guildmaster. The man was human and the colors on his left shoulder indicated he had three talents.

But Raiden was wrong.

The man shook his head, his eyes turning suspicious. "I haven't sought for mastership yet."

Raiden shrugged. "Nevertheless, your presence has been requested."

The second guard glanced over Raiden's shoulder, his eyes going wide at the same time Raiden heard a snap of a whip and a cry of pain. Raiden surged forward, closing the gap in four steps.

He brought his sword up, striking at the man on the right. He responded quickly, calling forth a sword of fire to block the blow. His features shifted through surprise and then fear as he saw the black tint to Raiden's sword, but he was already committed. Raiden's sword sliced right through the enchantment and came down on his shoulder.

The man cried out as he went down, and Raiden turned to the second. Faster than the first, the dwarf dived past Raiden and turned. Then he called on the stone of the corridor. A blob pressed out from the wall and formed a face, then shoulders and arms appeared. The golem left a gash in the wall as it pulled itself free and stepped between them, its hands shaping into warhammers. The golem charged, trapping Raiden at the end of the corridor.

The golem swelled until it filled the breadth of the hall, obviously intent on crushing him. Raiden leapt up the wall and placed his foot on the door handle, leaping into a twist that carried him up and over the golem. It crashed into the end of the corridor, blasting through the prison door into the cell beyond. Raiden landed and rolled to his feet, his sword rising in an upward swing that cut into the dwarf's leg.

Growling, the dwarf scrambled back—right into Red's fist. Dressed in simple clothing and unarmed, she struck the dwarf in the skull, sending him to the floor. He did not rise. Red spit on his unconscious form.

"That's for saying I was barren," she growled.

"The fool," Jester said.

Red grinned, a wealth of emotion written on her expression. "You weren't supposed to come for me. We made an oath."

"And we broke it," Raiden said.

"How did you even get in?" Red asked. "This place is impregnable."

Raiden and Jester exchanged a look, and Raiden said. "Alydian has proven herself an ally of the Soldier. She's here as well, gathering the proof we need to end the Verinai."

A voice called out to them. "If you're killing Verinai, I want to help."

Raiden stepped to a cell and looked through the window in the door. In the dark cell he managed to make out a man bound in anti-magic chains. Disheveled and dirty, the elf was dressed in a tattered uniform of a Verinai master, one with three talents.

"Who are you?" Raiden asked.

"Toron," the man said, stepping to the limit of his chains. "Let me out."

Raiden had heard the name before, when Teriah had said the man was dangerous. But was he here because Teriah knew the Soldier would come? Was he even the real Toron? Or was he a potential ally? He exchanged a look with Jester and the assassin's expression revealed his doubt.

"You're one of them," Raiden said. "How can we trust you?"

Toron's lips curled into a feral scowl. "Because I want to kill Elsin."

"You would kill your own guildmaster?" Jester asked.

"With the utmost pleasure."

Raiden stepped closer to the window. "And if you succeeded, would you then turn on us?"

Toron's eyes flicked between them. "You are the Defiant, are you not?"

"We admit nothing," Jester said, and then grinned.

"I cannot promise I'll join your ranks," Toron said, "But the guild has followed a vile leader for too long. It cannot be redeemed."

Raiden exchanged a look with his lieutenants, and Red shrugged. "Anyone that hates the Verinai is fine by me."

Raiden stepped to the door and ran his sword along the edge. Several times a burst of sparks indicated he'd severed a curse, and when he was certain it was clean he swung it open. Then he stepped into the room.

"Find the key to his shackles," he said to Jester.

"Are you certain?" the assassin asked.

"Impulse, not decision," Raiden replied.

Jester reluctantly nodded and slipped away, returning a moment later with a set of glowing keys. Stepping to Toron, he unlocked the man's bindings and the chains fell away. Toron straightened and breathed out in relief, issuing a current of fire from his lips.

Raiden kept his sword in hand, and used it to point into the hall. "Red, Toron, find guard uniforms and change. We have a long way to go before we reach the exit. Let's not make it obvious, shall we?"

Red ducked away while Toron darted into the hall and dragged the body of a guard into his cell. Raiden made to step out into the hall but Toron clenched his fist and the shadows in the room condensed into a wall, closing off the view so he could change.

Raiden raised his eyebrow at that. Shadowmages were rare. Many considered it a mark of a dark mage, and most shadowmages inevitably ended up enchanting weapons and gear for those of nefarious intent. A moment later the shadows dissipated and Toron stepped into view.

314

Muscled and forbidding, the shadowmage used a blade of fire to slice his hair, leaving the dirty locks to fall to the floor. His eyes were filled with suppressed rage as he stepped to the door and glanced back.

"Let's go kill some Verinai."

Red stepped into view and her grin was wild. "I like him. Can we keep him?"

Jester laughed. "If he behaves."

# Chapter 41: Reunion

Instead of taking the lead, Raiden gestured to the shadowmage. "I assume you know the best way through the city?"

Toron smirked, making it clear he understood that Raiden didn't want him at his back. "This way," he said.

The man passed a hand over his face and the shadows bent, marring his features until he was unrecognizable. Then he stepped to the forefront of the group and made his way back to the dungeon entrance. He looked back approvingly when they reached the hole in the acid door and carefully stepped through.

They ascended the stairs and worked their way through the gardens. Raiden watched the corridors for guards but kept a portion of his attention on Toron. The man was a Verinai, but the hatred for his guild was evident and Raiden was inclined to trust him. Still, there was no guarantee he wouldn't betray them.

They paused at the end of the hall when Toron raised a hand, bringing them to a halt. Around the corner came the sounds of approaching boots, the pace unhurried and bored. Raiden reached for his sword and it came free in a whisper of sound, but Toron threw him a warning look and stabbed a finger toward a recessed door.

Raiden raised an eyebrow but did as requested, and the others follows suit. Then Toron joined them, squeezing into the space before bringing his hands together like he was shutting curtains. The shadows closed upon them, engulfing them in gloom just as a trio of guards ambled into view.

They talked and laughed as they strode by, oblivious to the four intruders just inches from them. Crammed into the tiny space, Raiden could smell the stench of dungeon on Red and Toron. Then the guards passed and Toron opened the shade.

"A useful trick," Jester murmured.

Toron gestured to where the guards had departed. "One of them is an old acquaintance, and I would have been recognized, even behind my mask. Short of killing them we would not have been able to escape."

"I would have preferred to kill them," Red said.

"As would I," Toron said, a faint smile tugging his lips. "But we need to time to escape, and the more bodies we leave in our wake, the less time we have. We need to keep moving."

Raiden motioned for him to continue, and they entered the corridor the guards had just vacated. At the end of the tunnel the stairs brought them to a small guardhouse manned by a pair of guards sitting beside a fire. Striding past them, Toron opened the door and led them into the street.

Night had fallen, with just a sliver of red still touching the mountains above. Magic had taken the sun's place, filling the breadth of the city with light. The waterfall that poured down the face of the keep was bright blue, the light shimmering off the mist rising from the falls.

The guardhouse sat adjacent to the keep and looked down on a side avenue. Shops lined the street, the signs wreathed in dancing flames, crackling lightning, and small entities that crawled across the wood. A sign for the *Lingering Light* had a trio of stunning butterflies perched on the rim, their wings fashioned of light while their bodies were crafted from vivid flames. Water trickled across their bodies giving a visceral tint to their forms. They flapped their wings and spoke to nearby shoppers in melodic tones, inviting them to visit the store.

Across the street, a sign was covered in a miniature storm, the water battering the wood before splitting to either side of the door. The arch of water sent mist rising into the street, both beautiful and invitingly cool in the summer air. *Storm and Shield* contained more clouds within, many raining upon tiny crops.

"I didn't realize your guild could do so much," Raiden whispered to Toron as they merged into the crowd.

"Our talent is without peer," Toron said. "As is our arrogance."

He pointed to a shop depicting a dwarven Verinai standing with a foot on a dragon's neck. The sign read *Dragonslayers and Kings* and showed a variety of enchanted weaponry floating above. Through the window Raiden spotted swords and axes made of fire and light and imbued with powerful curses. Beside the weaponry, jewels and magically crafted pendants sat with actual crowns.

"Why did Elsin keep you alive?" Jester asked.

"It doesn't matter," Toron replied evasively.

Raiden glanced his direction. The man was entitled to his secrets, but would they damage the Soldier? Whatever had transpired between Toron and Elsin had left an open wound, one that drove him to vengeance.

"How many others would betray the guild?" Red asked.

"More than you'd think," he replied, his eyes on a group of battlemages talking next to a shop of enchanted weapons. "But not many."

Raiden considered the answer. There were fifty thousand Verinai, but even a few potential allies could make an enormous difference. The information they could bring might prove invaluable, especially if they knew guild secrets, such as how to infiltrate the other guildhalls . . .

Raiden toyed with the tantalizing thought as they worked their way toward the exit. A trio of guards appeared at the end of the street, so Toron led them into an alley and up a flight of stairs to one of the high roads arcing above the city.

With statues on both sides, the road provided a scenic route free of the crowds below. The statues held light orbs on staffs which bathed the road in soft light. Music filtered up from a sound mage below, setting an almost romantic scene.

Verinai couples ambled along the road, talking and laughing. Many ushered children along, the sight reminding Raiden that the city contained families and little ones, children that would be caught up in the carnage of war. A sense of tranquility and peace permeated Verisith. The mages walked between shops and homes without fear, their pace unhurried, their expressions carefree.

"A veneer of light does not obscure the shadows beneath," Toron said.

Raiden looked to the shadowmage to find the man's eyes on him. "I imagined Verisith with more . . . brutality."

Toron motioned to a couple talking in a small park, their children playing on the trees. The limbs were low to the ground and built to contain small cottages, resembling the treeship in the Crescent Moon Farm.

"That's Yaro," Toron said. "He killed a farmer because he refused to give him his room to sleep. Yaro's wife burned the house to the ground when they left."

Toron gestured to another man. "He scarred a woman because she would not come to his bed. His wife knows but ignores the assaults."

As Toron detailed the crimes of everyone in sight, Raiden's stomach churned, his perspective of the city shifting to reality. The Verinai were vile, their crimes a disease that was taught to their children. Finally, Red growled at him.

"Enough," she said. "Or I will try to free the children from their putrid parents right now."

Raiden lowered his tone so only Toron could hear. "Red lost her husband because of the guild."

"A sad tale," Toron replied. "But too often repeated."

More guards appeared, and Toron led them to a set of stairs descending back into the city. The high road had taken them close to the southern entrance, and they circled a pond to reach the final approach.

"My face is known to many," Toron said, motioning Raiden forward. "It would be best if you lead us through the canyon. The gates are usually open, so just walk through as if it's normal."

Raiden slipped to the head of the group and they turned down the final street to the main gates. True to Toron's word the aquaglass gates were open, and a handful of guards stood next to it. Devkin had taken them through the north gate, but it appeared they were nearly identical. Raiden strode past them, his posture bland despite his tension. No one called out as he passed the guards, and he allowed himself to relax as he reached the opening . . .

In a rush of water, the aquaglass flowed upward, closing off the gap and sealing them in. Raiden whirled to find battlemages stepping into view, ten, twenty, a hundred. They stood above and on the street, on the steps and in the doors to the guardhouse. Red cursed as the trap snapped shut. Then a figure appeared behind the battlemages.

Teriah stepped out of the shadows, a triumphant smile on her face. "The Soldier, come to infiltrate our guildhall. It was good of you to come."

Surrounded by a company of battlemages, Raiden's heart sank. She had known he would come, and known where to trap him. That left only one question.

"Why?" he asked. "Why not kill me before?"

"Because you had an ally," Teriah said. "One I could not discern. I knew if I let you live, you would be kind enough to bring that ally here. I must say, I did not expect it to be Alethean. Tell me, did she infiltrate the Runeguard on your orders? Or did you recruit her after?"

Raiden took a step forward but magic blossomed into view. "What have you done to her?" he demanded.

"Guildmaster Elsin should be taking her as we speak," Teriah said, her eyes never leaving Raiden's. "I knew you would come for your lieutenant. You may carry an anti-magic blade, but you cannot stop magic. A tiny charm linked to the door of her cell activated the moment you freed her, and I knew you were here. I must say, I'm surprised you freed Toron."

320

"You know her?" Red demanded, turning to him.

"I tried to kill her," Toron said. "I wonder, do you still have the scar, Teriah?"

Teriah reached up to her throat before controlling the reflex. "At least you get to die here," she said coldly. "I think Elsin will agree that you are too dangerous to let live."

"Such high praise before I die," Toron said.

Teriah raised her finger to the captain at her side. "Kill them."

The Verinai captain smirked—but a sudden explosion drew all eyes to the keep. For an interminable moment the city went quiet, and Raiden could almost hear Alydian's fury. Then Toron snuffed the light orbs and Raiden drew his sword in the ensuing darkness. Even with Toron they would not escape, but maybe the distraction would be enough for Alydian to flee. Sword in hand, he lunged for Teriah.

# Chapter 42: Mineva's Memory

Devkin shut the door after Raiden and Jester departed, and Alydian turned to Mineva, who began to struggle in Grogith's bindings. Mineva's features were tight with fury, her mouth open as she shouted, but Alydian's curse barred her voice, leaving her to writhe in silence.

Thoughts of Teriah poisoning her mother dominated Alydian's thoughts, and she imagined what she would do when she saw Teriah again. To have a betrayer on the council was one thing, but for an oracle to kill another was unheard of. Alydian clenched her fists and forced her burgeoning rage aside.

"I wish we could use the Soldier's memory of you killing King Talin," Alydian said coldly, "but the people may call that a trick, so I must come to the source. Your memory will condemn your guild, and bring you to the noose you deserve."

Mineva's eyes widened in surprise and fear as Alydian withdrew a small glass orb from her pocket. The sphere was commonly used for light orbs as well as a dozen other purposes, but in a moment it would be filled with Mineva's memory.

"Hold her still," she said, and Devkin and Grogith caught her arms.

Alydian reached up and touched the woman's forehead, closing her eyes as she drew on memory magic. Unlike the overt magics, memories were subtle and convoluted, making casting memories into glass all the more challenging.

Verinai and other memory mages charged a great deal of coin for their work, especially when the charm contained not just moving light, but sound as well. Alydian had practiced the spell several times with Devkin, but doing so with a bound and furious captive would be vastly different.

Alydian willed her consciousness to cross the gap and into the woman's mind. Whereas Devkin's mind had been ordered and rigid, Mineva's mind was haughty and chaotic. The woman betrayed an initial shock at the contact, obviously unprepared for Alydian to possess memory magic. But she recovered in force, nearly ejecting her outright.

I WILL TEAR YOU ASUNDER!

Mineva's voice was bound, but her scream reverberated through Alydian's skull. She cringed and fought to hold onto her magic. Empowered by her simmering anger, she pushed deeper into the woman's memories.

Mineva fought, forcing her mind to images brutal and dark, memories of her training as a Verinai and time as a battlemage. She dredged up every battle, every conflict, showing Alydian in all the visceral detail the battles she'd engaged in. All the while she silently screamed, bellowing her inaudible rage.

Memories contained just as much power as fire or light, and painful memories caused more agony than a blade. Mineva had lived through her experiences and worked for years to accept the regret and loss, but Alydian had no such filter, and lived the woman's experiences as if they were her own.

From the eyes of Mineva she watched the woman cast a blade out of fire and drive it through the hand of a merchant, watched his wife and children shriek and flee, and felt herself suppress the guilt with a single phrase.

*They're just barren.*

Alydian felt the woman's emotions as she gazed on the sobbing man, his only crime that of trying to haggle on price. Mineva spoke through her sneer, refusing to acknowledge the guilt that grew quieter with every vile act.

"Next time, remember the Verinai are your betters."

Through their blended consciousness, Mineva smirked and shoved another memory at her, this one showing her battle against a family of giants in the far northeast. They were simply trying to protect their

323

kindred, but the Verinai battlemages slaughtered them, leaving their corpses to rot in the summer sun.

Guilt assailed Alydian, surging into her throat with the taste of bile. It didn't feel like Mineva who had killed the innocent, it felt like her, Alydian. She'd forsaken her vow to protect the people and become what she most despised . . .

*No.*

She spoke the word aloud. Although no more than a whisper, it sent a current through her body, churning the guilt into righteous wrath. Mineva had carried out atrocities in the name of her guild, and gradually silenced her doubt. She had committed crimes. And justice had come due.

Armed with her fury, Alydian surged into Mineva's mind, crushing the current memory of her beating a thief. She focused on the woman's pride, forcing her to watch the same memory from the view of the thief. Recalling her fear when the Soldier had attacked, she added her own emotion, empowering the memory until Mineva witnessed her own contorted features.

"Know your place, you barren rat!" Mineva shouted.

Mineva mentally recoiled and shoved another memory at Alydian, but Alydian did the same, twisting the memory so the woman had to witness her own spite. Again and again Alydian forced the woman to view her actions from the perspective of those she'd made suffer. Mineva clung to her arrogance but the sheer tide of emotion cracked the woman's veneer of perceived honor. The crack widened, and then shattered. All the guilt she'd suppressed rose like a great beast, rending her thoughts with a voice of thunder.

*See what you have wrought!*

Mineva managed to resist for a moment, but the reminder of all her crimes was too great and her guilt overpowered her pride. She crumpled like an empty suit of armor, crashing to the floor and falling apart. Distantly Alydian felt her slump, but Grogith and Devkin held her fast.

*What did you do to the king?* Alydian demanded.

324

The memory burst into her consciousness and Alydian reached for the glass orb. Light swirled up one arm and down the other before seeping into the orb. Even with her eyes closed she knew the orb had begun to speak, the image of King Talin coming into focus.

"Perhaps your daughter will be more malleable," Mineva snarled, before plunging her sword into his body.

Unable to convince herself of the morality of her choice, Mineva began to cry, the tears turning into racking sobs as she faced the full weight of the murder she had committed. Alydian held the link until the entire memory was complete, until it showed the Soldier fighting the guardian in order to save the castle.

Alydian severed the link and withdrew, stumbling as Mineva's thoughts separated from hers. Mineva threw herself backward, desperate to flee from the truth of what she had committed. Her magic surged and Grogith's bonds snapped. All moved to restrain her but she crashed through a table and crumpled to the floor, her eyes clenched against the agony of her unfiltered memories.

"Forgive me," she cried softly. "I did not . . . I was just . . ."

Devkin turned to Alydian. "What did you do?"

Alydian didn't take her eyes off Mineva. "I showed her the truth of what she'd done."

Mineva continued to weep and cling to the floor like it held her salvation. The pitiful display caused them all to stare at her for several moments, and Alydian took a step toward her.

"Don't," Devkin said. "She now faces the fate she has chosen."

Alydian nodded and picked up the glass orb. Now glowing softly, it contained the precious memory that would prove to the Eldress Council that the Soldier had not killed king Talin. With such evidence she would be able to turn the Eldress Council against Teriah. Wrapping the memory in cloth, she handed it to Devkin, who placed it into a pouch at his side.

"We should depart," he said.

"What about her?" Alydian asked, gesturing to the sobbing woman.

"There's nothing we can do for her now," Devkin said, turning to the door.

Mineva reached up and latched onto Grogith's arm. "Please," she pled. "End my life."

The gnome stared down at her before extricating himself. "Whether you consider it or not, consequence is accepted at the point of decision."

The pity in the gnome's voice elicited renewed sobs, and the woman sank to the floor again. Turning away from the sight, Alydian wove her way through the unconscious guards and stepped to the door. As she reached for the handle the door swung open.

And Elsin stepped into the room.

Alydian stumbled back as Verinai guards flooded into the room. Elsin regarded Alydian with thinly veiled contempt and came to a halt, her soldiers filling their hands with magic.

"I must say I'm disappointed, Alethean," she said. "I never expected you to be the Soldier's ally."

"The Verinai are tyrants," Alydian said, relief filling her when she realized her persona was still intact. "Your predecessor brought the Verinai to prosperity. You brought them to ruin."

"Is that who trained you?" Elsin gave a mocking laugh. "I have led the Verinai to their true purpose, one far grander than my aging predecessor. He believed that if we could free the magicless from hunger and greed, their wars would come to an end."

"A noble desire," Alydian said. "And a noble man."

"He was a fool," Elsin spat with sudden vehemence. "He spent two hundred years trying to aid the poor and needy, squandering our might for a pittance. Even with all his talents he could not see the truth."

Alydian shook her head. "He saved thousands in the Griffin insurrection, and helped end the human plague."

326

"The *barren* are the plague," Elsin said. "One without a cure. You may have the magic of a Verinai, but not our vision. The barren will never conquer their own natures."

"You claim a desire to aid the people," Alydian said, her voice rising, "but we both know you merely crave power. Tell me, will it ever be enough? If you reigned over the whole of Lumineia, would you finally fill the void in your soul?"

Alydian measured the guards around them, all of which were veteran battlemages with multiple talents. But it was the barbarian at Elsin's side that caught her eye. The man seemed to exude power, and she blinked into her magesight.

Instead of the customary combination of magics unique to each sentient life, there was a storm of water condensed into a human body. Gone were the emotions and complexities of life, leaving only a rudimentary vestige of what had once made him human. Raw power churned in his from, feral and explosive.

*Guardian.*

Raiden had told her enough about the events in the bandit gorge that he recognized the man as the same one Elsin had taken as protection. He resembled the man she'd seen in Mineva's memory, the guardian of light Raiden had fought in Terros. But she was unprepared for the sheer mass of power contained in his body.

"Surrender now," Elsin said, "and I promise I will spare the lives of your worthless friends."

"And me?" Alydian asked.

Elsin smiled. "I'm confident I can find a place to put you until you see the truth."

"Don't," Devkin murmured.

Alydian looked at the ring of Verinai. She managed to push past her fear and see their fate if they fought, of Devkin falling to an asunder hex, his form turning to ash, of Grogith's anti-magic shield shattering, and the guardian piercing his heart with a shard of aquaglass. Alydian shuddered and returned to the present.

327

"Leave them be," she said.

"Alethean—" Devkin growled.

"I'm not letting you die," Alydian said.

Elsin's expression turned triumphant. "Bind her," she said, and a guard stepped forward, a thread of anti-magic appearing in his hands. He coiled it around Alydian's wrists and she felt it tie against her magic.

"You have me captive," Alydian said. "Now let them go."

Elsin raised a hand as if in dismissal, and then her expression turned malicious. "I warned you of the consequence if you chose against me," she said. "Now you will witness it."

Alydian cursed herself for not using her farsight to ensure Elsin kept her word. She fought against her bonds but they would not yield. Elsin's smirk widened and she gestured to the guardian at her side.

"Kill them," she said coldly.

"NO!" a voice shrieked.

Forgotten on the ground, Mineva lurched to her feet. Her cheeks were stained with tears and her face blotched, but the force to her gaze was arresting and terrifying. She stumbled around a couch to Alydian's side.

"We must not shed more innocent blood!" she cried in a shrill voice.

"Master Mineva!" Elsin called, looking the disheveled woman up and down. "Control yourself."

"You do not understand!" she shrieked, her voice rising with panic. "And we must pay for our crimes."

Elsin's eyes widened as she registered the threat—but Mineva acted first. Whirling, she pointed to the floor and sent a burst of light into the stone, searing a line around Alydian and her friends. The stone crumbled, leaving them to fall into an explosion of dust and smoke.

Then Mineva screamed and unleashed her magic on the guards in the room.

# Chapter 43: Unmasked

Alydian landed on her side and coughed in the dust and smoke. Grogith landed on his feet and darted to her, snapping the bonds with ease. She stumbled to her feet but hesitated, torn between flight and aiding Mineva. Grogith made the choice for her. He grabbed her around the waist before bodily launching her toward the door.

"Go!" he barked.

They'd fallen into a journeyman's quarters, its occupant stunned against the wall, staring at the pile of debris that had formerly been his receiving room. Alydian stumbled over the stones and yanked the door open. Then she raced into the hall as the devastated chamber was pummeled with magical strikes from above. All the while Mineva fought for her life.

"She atoned for her mistakes," Devkin growled, anticipating her desire to turn back. "Leave her be."

A crash echoed in the hall behind them and Alydian looked back. Riding a wave of water down the spiral staircase, the guardian smashed into the wall, making it buckle and crack before correcting his direction and streaming after them. His eyes wild and manic, he raised his arms and his hands morphed into aquaglass spikes, turning sharp and glittery. Ahead, a group of Verinai appeared at the opposite stairs, closing off their escape.

Devkin darted to a door and kicked its handle, sending the wood tumbling into the room. They dived inside as the guardian hurled the spikes, grazing Alydian as she leapt through. Alydian turned and called on the stone floor, closing off the opening in a wall of stone. Then she added more supports, lifting angles into the barrier, reinforcing it against entry. An instant later the makeshift wall shuddered and a crack appeared.

"That won't hold for long," Devkin growled, leaping to the windows on the opposite side of the room. "We need an exit."

"Even if we can," Alydian said, darting to the windows and looking down. "How can we possibly escape the city? We don't stand a chance of getting through the canyon of mages."

Another blow caused the barrier to shudder and Alydian winced. This was her fault. She'd led them to Verisith thinking she could get them out, and now she had doomed them all. Elsin had planned ahead— or more likely—Teriah had used her farsight to prepare for the Soldier's arrival.

She squared her shoulders, reminding herself that the helpless girl the Soldier had attacked was gone. She was a Runeguard, one with the power of an oracle. Forcing her fear aside, she surged her magic into her farsight, counting the seconds as she decided on various actions and watched them play out. She examined the room, the windows, pushing her magesight through the walls and beyond, watched the guardian turn his arms into a spinning whirlwind of aquaglass that sparked against the stone, drilling through it with shocking speed. Then she saw it, and her eyes snapped open.

"Devkin, use your sword to mark the windows, make it look like we escaped that direction. Grogith, see what you can do to add anti-magic to his blade, we're going to need it."

Alydian stepped to the south wall and ran her finger along the edge, searching for the hidden rune she'd spotted. When she touched it, a section of wall slid open, revealing a secret passage to the adjacent room.

Devkin used his sword on the window, scraping a line in the stone before leaping to join Grogith in the secret corridor. The aquaglass drill appeared through the stone, sending cracks throughout the barricade. Alydian cast a final look at the room before slamming the secret door shut.

Alydian's barrier exploded, sending fragments of stone into rugs, furniture, and out the window. The concussive blast caused the door to shudder, and a moment later Elsin appeared through the cloud of dust.

Alydian slipped into her magesight and the door turned transparent. Elsin glared at the empty room, her battlemages flooding the space. They searched the demolished room before stepping to the window and peering out. It was a hundred feet to the ground below, but evidently the marks were sufficient to deceive the guards.

"It looks like they escaped through the window," a woman said.

"Close off every exit," Elsin said, "and send reinforcements to the canyon of the mages. Find her, but I want her alive."

"Do you want us to wake the other guardians?" the captain asked.

"No," she said. "The longer they are in the flesh the quicker they deteriorate, and Tidal should be more than a match for Alethean."

The soldiers surged from the room but Elsin abruptly called out for them to halt. She cocked her head to the side and turned toward the secret door. She took a step toward it and frowned, raising a finger to her ear to enhance her hearing.

Alydian spun her fingers and all sound in the corridor stopped, silencing even her pounding heart. Then she pointed downward and sent a current of orange light through the floor, angled so it went outside. Just as Elsin reached the barrier and raised a hand to it a shout came from outside.

"Intruder!"

The reflection charm was difficult under the best of circumstances—especially through walls, but Alydian managed for the sound to carry the right echo of surprise, anger, and urgency. Elsin whirled and darted to the window.

"Go," she shouted. "You may kill her companions, but do not let her escape."

The group flooded from the room, leaving only Tidal standing next to the door. He twitched as if he wanted to follow them but remained in place. The guildmaster gazed upon the city for several moments and then strode to the guardian.

Alydian's relief turned to foreboding when she saw her whisper to Tidal. Alydian saw what was coming and turned, bolting down the corridor. The others followed her example and together they raced to the other room. Devkin reached it first and pulled the latch, causing it to swing open into another receiving room. Just as they departed the tunnel the secret door shattered and Tidal burst into view. He snarled as he caught sight of them, Elsin appearing at her side.

"Clever girl," she said. "But you cannot escape."

"I'm not alone," Alydian said, retreating into the receiving room of a journeyman's private quarters.

Elsin laughed. "Captain Devkin is skilled, but he is no match for a guardian, and your little gnome friend is just a single mage." Then her smile faded and she leaned to Tidal. "Break Alethean . . . but kill the others."

His features contorted into a wild excitement and he surged forward, bounding down the corridor as water spilled from his hands, lifting and accelerating him into a thundering wave. He began to laugh, cackling as he closed the gap.

Alydian retreated in a rush, allowing her companions to spread out and ready themselves to flank the guardian. Alydian had no allusions about the impending battle. She'd seen the guardian's power and knew what it was capable of. Steeling herself, she gathered her magic and reached for the floor of the secret passage.

Abruptly Grogith stepped in front of Alydian. As Devkin barked at him to resume his place, the gnome darted to the door and snatched a decorative spear from the wall. Bracing it against the floor, he leaned it toward the charging guardian, and black magic burst from his fingers, engulfing the spear in dense ink.

Alydian's mouth fell open. A skilled anti-mage could cast a small amount of magic each day, and even a master would have been hard pressed to release so much power in an instant. Throughout their entire training as acolytes, Grogith had never displayed more than a fraction of what he cast now.

Grogith aimed the anti-magic spear at the guardian's heart and snarled. The guardian slammed into the spear and came to a grinding halt, the spear piercing his body until it protruded on the opposite side. Its horrendous scream shattered glass as water exploded outward, detonating with the force of a typhoon.

The impact knocked them all flying. Still holding the spear, Grogith took the brunt of the explosion and soared into the room, smashing through a couch and a table on his way to the opposite wall.

The stone walls shuddered from the blast and the water gushed out the windows, merging with the keep's waterfall before falling from view. Drenched and dazed, Alydian grabbed a fallen couch and dragged herself upward, her eyes flying to the guardian.

Impaled by the spear, Tidal's body had turned to water. He clawed at the staff but the contact made the water of his hands darken. His entire chest had gone dark, the inky water dripping to the floor at his feet. He shrieked again, the sound overpowering Elsin's bellow of rage.

Patches of aquaglass fused across the walls in curls of white and blue, the splashes frozen in perfect detail. As hard as steel, they held a couch off the floor and sealed the door to the hall. The secret corridor was filled with glittering shards of magically hardened water, blocking Elsin from reaching Tidal.

Alydian stumbled through the sodden and broken furniture to reach Grogith, dropping to her knees to lift his head. The impact had broken his bones and shards of glass were in his flesh. Alydian's throat tightened when she saw the extent of the damage. His eyes fluttered and he looked up to her.

"You must flee," he said, his voice distant and weak.

"Why did you hide your talent?" she demanded, her throat tight with emotion.

"I owed a debt to a friend," he said. "She asked me to fulfill it . . . by protecting you."

334

"Who?" Alydian asked.

"Elenyr," he said, his smile suddenly soft.

"My mother?" Alydian asked. "What does she have to do with this?"

"She foresaw it all," he said. "She saw you becoming an acolyte and wanted to keep you safe."

The life was fading from the gnome's eyes, and Alydian growled in helpless rage. How had she not known? How had he kept himself hidden? Then she realized how many times he'd hovered nearby, always ready to protect her. Even sick and dying, her mother had ensured Alydian would be safe.

"But you didn't like me," Alydian protested, wiping hot tears from her cheeks.

The gnome issued a coughing laugh. "You proved yourself to be a worthy successor to your mother. Do not forget that other races besides human, dwarf, and elf need your guidance . . ."

The gnome's body relaxed and Alydian stared at him. Dimly she was aware that Devkin was at her side, his hand on her shoulder.

"Alydian," he said urgently. "We must flee."

"Not yet," Alydian said, rising to her feet and turning to the guardian still struggling on the spear. Even with an anti-magic spear piercing his body he remained powerful, and tore at the spear, fighting to reach her like a rabid animal.

"We only have a few seconds—" Devkin said, trying to drag her toward the window.

Alydian yanked her arm free. "That's all I need."

"Alydian—"

Alydian threw him a look that caused the grizzled warrior to recoil. Then she turned to the struggling guardian and poured her emotion into magic, sparking fire in her palms. She stabbed a finger to the open

335

window and the waterfall beyond. The current slowed to a crawl, the water barely moving as it fell past the window.

"Go," she said. "It will take you to the city below."

"Have you forgotten what it is?" Devkin stepped into her path. "It's a destroyer."

"So am I."

Alydian gathered fire in her hand and began to suck the heat from the room. The aquaglass began to harden and crack, the fissures spreading across the frozen walls of the room. Devkin's breath turned white as she passed him.

"Go," she said.

Her voice was deathly quiet, and finally Devkin nodded. He stepped to the window and leapt out, diving into the waterfall. It gradually carried him from view. Alydian only had eyes on the guardian with the anti-magic spear through his body. His chest heaved against it, each breath a raspy cough.

Alydian drew every ounce of heat in the room. Ice appeared on the soaked carpet and furniture, spreading across the floor and up the guardian's legs. He finally looked up, but the ice reached all the way to his fingers, freezing his contorted features halfway between human and magic. With all the heat in her hands, the ball of fire had turned the supreme blue, and she plunged it into the guardian's chest.

Steam exploded from the contact, wreathing his frozen features as they shifted to agony and horror. Then Alydian turned and strode away, stepping to the window and diving free. As the waterfall carried her gently to the ground the compression charm detonated.

The entire room exploded in blue and yellow flames, the inferno expanding through the waterfall, sending a burst of steam outward. The blast rent the walls and sent stones soaring into the city. Fragments of the guardian's body were just visible before the raging flames consumed them, leaving boiling water to rain down on the square below.

Alydian accelerated the stream until she caught up to Devkin and they plunged into the pond at the base. Instead of swimming, she carried

336

them up and out of the water, depositing them on the stones of the square. Then she turned and looked up to see Elsin standing in the gaping hole of the keep. With flames still raging about her, she stood untouched by fire.

"You did not possess fire magic."

The words were laced with accusation and Alydian flashed a grim smile. Then she strode away, hurrying into a sprint. Verinai converged on all sides but she drew on the water coursing down the street and lifted them up. Devkin grunted in surprise when his feet came off the street and they were swept away.

Alydian focused the current, carrying them down a side street and under a bridge, banking away from a group of battlemages who appeared in their path. For several moments the river carried them through the city, their flight too swift for the Verinai to stop. Passing a stream, she gathered up the extra water and cast it behind them, forming a wall of ice to slow their pursuers. Then she curved them around a final bend—sending them careening into a pitched battle.

Raiden and Jester fought with Red and an unknown companion. All four were wounded but still on their feet. Surrounded by Verinai and pummeled by magic, they fought with a valor that took Alydian's breath.

Alydian split the remainder of their water and sent it to either side, slamming the river into the ranks of Verinai and knocking them sprawling. She stumbled to a stop beside Raiden as the water pulled away from them, and their eyes met.

"You were supposed to be gone," she said in a rush, and wearily called on her magic once more.

"They knew I would come," Raiden said, and used his sword to point to the figure standing behind the ranks of Verinai. "It was a trap."

Alydian followed his gesture to see Teriah, whose mouth was agape in astonishment. Alydian's anger surged as she saw her sister oracle and recalled what Raiden had said. Then Teriah recovered and took a step forward.

"Who *are* you?"

In the midst of foes Alydian spoke with a fury that made them all retreat. "Do you not recognize me?" she asked, reaching up to the necklace to remove it. The magic faded from her face, revealing her true identity. Teriah's eyes widened with shock and fear.

"Hello, Sister," Alydian said.

# Chapter 44: Alydian's Fury

Alydian's sudden appearance brought the entire battle to a grinding halt. Verinai on all sides stood agape, craning to see if it was true. Some were so astonished their magic disintegrated, leaving them to stand in mute shock.

"Alydian?" Teriah breathed. "Why?"

"My mother helped me start my training early," Alydian said. "And I became an acolyte for the Runeguard. It was there I endured the Verinai's brutality."

"But if they had known it was you . . ."

"My birthright may excuse me from their condescension," Alydian said, her voice hard. "But it is *everyone's* birthright to be free."

"Sister," Teriah said. "You don't understand. The Verinai will bring peace to Lumineia."

"Peace through bloodshed?" Alydian demanded. "Are you truly willing to pay the price?"

Teriah winced. "If man will not be honorable out of duty, I will make them honorable out of fear."

As they argued the Verinai shifted uncertainly, clearly unprepared to fight an oracle. Most had been taught to revere the oracles, and harming one went against everything they believed in. Alydian saw their hesitation but doubted it would last.

"Robbing them of freedom does not give them honor," Alydian called, her voice rising. "It merely makes them slaves."

"Sister," Teriah pleaded. "This is not the way I wanted you to find out about the Accord."

"When would have been the right time?" Alydian shouted. "A year from now? Ten? When the Accord was revealed and the people subjected to a Verinai army? When the Mage Empire rules the races?"

"Please," Teriah said, stepping out and raising a hand to her, "give me the chance to explain. You owe me that much."

"Will you explain why you're killing my mother?"

Alydian did not shout, but her question echoed like a roar. Teriah stared at the hatred in Alydian's eyes, and she slowly lowered her hand. The silence stretched between them for several agonizing seconds until Teriah sighed.

"If you ally yourself with him," Teriah said, gesturing to Raiden. "You will fracture the Eldress Council forever. Do not forget that if you die, your bloodline dies with you."

"Better dead than united with a betrayer," Alydian shot back.

Teriah flinched, and then her features tightened. Calling out for the Verinai, she barked orders for them to close ranks. Alydian retreated to her companions, for the first time aware of the volume rising from Verisith.

The city was in an uproar, with the echo of booted soldiers converging upon them. Alydian guessed it was only a matter of minutes before they were surrounded and taken down, and there was nothing she could do to stop it. She forced herself into her farsight but the next several minutes was a cloud of uncertainty, the only visible branches showing her holding her dead friends in her arms.

Instead of regret and fear, it was anger that pooled in her gut. She faced Teriah and reached skyward, where the dark clouds threatened a storm. Teriah's expression turned mocking when she saw what Alydian was attempting.

"Lightning?" she asked with a laugh. "Even your mother could not harness it."

340

A bolt of lightning streaked from the sky, slamming into the ground at Teriah's feet and sending her tumbling into the wall. Her head cracked on the stone and she slumped to the street. With blood on her face she struggled to rise, her features frozen in shock when she realized the bolt of lightning remained on the ground.

Where the lightning had struck, a man crawled from the hole. His body built of crackling power, the entity of lightning flexed its arms, sending bolts arcing above the ranks of Verinai. The powerful mages surged back as the entity turned on them.

Trembling from the effort to hold the entity together, Alydian called down a second bolt of lightning. She aimed to cut off the path of the reinforcements but hit the soldiers instead. Soldiers were blasted skyward, one even landing on a nearby roof. Others were sent through the windows of a shop, the glass shattering as they hurtled into the interior. Another entity climbed from the crater.

Hundreds of Verinai surrounded the courtyard but they recoiled from the threat. Rank upon rank of battlemages shifted uneasily as the two lightning entities barred their path. Then Teriah got to her feet.

"An impressive feat," she said, her bloody features twisted in anger. "But you cannot hold them for long."

"Long enough," Alydian said through clenched teeth. "All I have to do is get the truth to the Eldress Council, and the guild of Verinai will see its end."

Alydian edged backward, retreating toward the gate. Raiden and the shadowmage drifted toward the guardhouse. The Verinai within called on their magic, the tension spiking until Raiden leapt in, deflecting a strike with his sword and slashing the guard's chest. The killing drew a cry from the Verinai, and the ranks of battlemages flooded down the road.

The lightning entities reacted with blinding speed, arcing twenty paces with every step. The first struck a Verinai in the chest. The blast of lightning sent him hurtling into the men behind him, his armor charred, his body shaking. Another blow and another soldier slammed into a tavern wall, narrowly missing Teriah. Screaming, she flinched out of harm's way and retreated.

341

Blasts of every type of magic were unleashed upon the two entities but few landed, the entities moving so fast that the attacks struck the street, cracking the stones all the way to Alydian.

Alydian's breath came in ragged gasps as she fought to keep the volatile entities under control. She was distantly aware of Raiden and his companions cutting down the remaining Verinai around them, and then the gate began to open.

"Alydian!" Devkin shouted.

If she turned she would lose her tenuous hold, and the lightning entities were the only things keeping the horde of Verinai at bay. Their power burned into the ranks of battlemages, tearing through entities of fire and light with explosive power, sending bits of fire to die on the stones. Still Alydian retreated, each step uncertain as her fatigue mounted.

Teriah ducked a flying body and then rotated, her fury spilling into her own magic. She conjured her own entity from a stream nearby, turning the water into a hulking golem. The entity charged through the broken ranks of battlemages and caught a lightning entity. The water entity absorbed the lightning and exploded, sending shards of charged water into the soldiers. A captain screamed in dismay as a third of his men died in an instant, torn apart by the blast.

"You cannot cast another!" Teriah shrieked at Alydian, ignoring the captain's fury.

Alydian fought to control the remaining entity, using it to strike at the sudden surge of water entities aiming for it. The Verinai had learned from Teriah's attack, and kept their distance as they attacked the remaining soldier of lightning. Despite the entity's speed, the sheer volume of water golems drew closer, until finally one caught it.

The explosion shredded the swarm of water beasts and golems, leaving the street with a giant crater. Releasing a howl of victory the Verinai charged, sprinting for the open gate and the intruders.

Devkin caught Alydian's arm and spun her about, all but throwing her through the opening. Then he leapt into the guardhouse and yanked on the gate controls. Alydian screamed as she saw them begin to close, with Devkin still inside.

The man drew his sword up and swung, sheering the controls in two before whirling and leaping into the open. Dodging blasts of fire, he reached the rising gate of aquaglass and leapt through for the narrowing gap.

The aquaglass slammed shut, catching Devkin's leg as he passed through the opening. He cried out as it sliced across his shin, taking his foot in an instant. He landed hard and rolled, his foot gone.

Alydian stepped to him but the shadowmage was faster. He stooped, and sealed the stump with a burst of fire. Devkin screamed as the flames closed off the wound. Then Jester stooped and helped him to his remaining foot. His face white beneath his beard, Devkin managed to hold onto Jester as they hurried across the bridge.

"I feared you were going to stay behind," Alydian said.

"I'd rather lose my foot than my head," he hissed.

Alydian blinked away the tears. Then she saw what awaited them and came to a halt. On the opposite end of the bridge another army was arrayed against them, with a pair of bear guardians at their head. She recognized them as the giants that had protected the third gate in the canyon of mages, but here they were all flesh, their bodies swollen to unnatural proportions.

"You cannot escape!"

Alydian turned and spotted Elsin standing beside Teriah on the city wall. Soldiers lined the battlements, their magic spun into giant crossbows and ballistae. Alydian's heart sank when she saw that they were trapped on the bridge, with the only escape an endless abyss beneath them.

"Surrender now and I won't make you watch your friends die," Teriah called.

"Or you can witness them torn apart," Elsin snarled.

Alydian looked to her friends. Devkin still had his sword but without his foot he could not stand. Jester, Raiden, and Red were wounded, the blood staining their guard uniforms and trickling onto the bridge. The shadowmage had suffered a blow to his shoulder, his arm saved by the scorched and broken armor. Blood lined his face from another wound on his forehead. Yet all were defiant.

Alydian met their eyes and then turned to Elsin. "I choose victory."

Her words drew a round of laughter from both sides of the bridge, the humor swelling as the two bear guardians snapped their jaws and roared. Their laughter turned to dismay when Alydian leaned down and punched the bridge with all her strength. The bridge cracked . . . and then crumbled into the abyss.

Taking Alydian and her friends with it.

# Chapter 45: The Soldier's Tale

Alydian plummeted into the abyss and watched the bear guardians roar their frustration at being thwarted. Fear gripped her as the wind snatched her breath, tearing it from her lungs. With difficulty, she shouted to the shadowmage.

"I hope you're as strong as I think!"

"I am!"

The light from above shrank and the shadows enveloped them, the absolute darkness giving Toron enormous power. Alydian couldn't see it, but felt him catch the shadows and spread them into a massive net that hooked the walls of the canyon. She struck something soft and began to slow, the sensation like falling onto a massive pile of cotton.

She hoped the abyss was deep enough and cringed, imagining striking the bottom before Toron could bring them to a halt. The man grunted from the effort as he maintained the shadow net, the magic stretching with the weight.

From plummeting to their deaths, they began to slow, but Alydian's fear mounted with each passing second. They'd already fallen a thousand feet and still they fell. The shriek of the wind diminished as they continued to slow, and Alydian's back crawled as she imagined smashing into the unforgiving stone at the base of the chasm.

Red crowed with delight as they finally came to a stop. "A pleasantly terrifying fall."

"Not my only trick," Toron said, his voice strained.

"How far are we from the bottom?" Jester asked.

"Don't spark a light," Toron warned. "Shadow magic is versatile, but the weakest of any magic. Any light will cause my tremendous display to disintegrate."

Alydian blinked into her magesight and the surroundings turned awash with color. As fatigued as she was, she lacked the stamina to manipulate the stone walls, but a disturbingly short distance below was the base of the ravine, where a trickle of water gurgled over sharp rocks.

"Lower us down," she said, "slowly. Another fifty feet and we'll be able to walk out of here."

She winced when the words left her mouth, and immediately apologized to Devkin, who didn't respond. She looked his way with her magesight and saw that he was unconscious, the light of his life fading. She swallowed against her fear and urged Toron to hurry.

"You just said to go slow," he growled.

Alydian watched the ground draw painstakingly closer. When they were feet from the rocky stream she cast a dim light in her hand. She caught a glimpse of the thick bands of darkness before they crumbled, and she landed heavily on a boulder. She and Raiden leapt to the side and they caught Devkin's body together, easing him to the ground.

"Is he . . ."

She shook her head. "Not yet, but he will be if I don't hurry."

She wasn't nearly as talented with healing magic, but she managed to weave a thread of pink into the flesh by his leg. It took her remaining strength to close the gash and remove a measure of the pain. The light dimmed as she worked, until it was hardly more than a candle. Then she sighed and sank back, her vision blurring.

"He may yet survive if we get him to a real healer," she said.

"We will have to hurry," Raiden said, looking upward. "They will come after us."

"They probably think us dead," Red added.

346

Toron shook his head, sending his black hair dancing in the darkness. "Elsin will want the bodies."

Alydian squinted upward. They had fallen thousands of feet in seconds, and even with magic the Verinai would take time to descend to the base of the canyon. Still, if they didn't depart with haste, the Verinai would be able to catch them.

Jester and Raiden took turns carrying Devkin as they worked their way over the rocks of the stream. Too weary to assist, Alydian wrapped a bandage around a wound on her arm and tried not to think of the pain.

The rocks were slippery with moss and nearly invisible, and she stumbled often. Only Toron kept his footing. Taking the lead, he guided them downstream, the minutes stretching into hours. When Devkin awoke, he refused to be carried, and hobbled along with the others. Even with her magic his pain would be excruciating, but he did not voice a word of complaint.

The hours passed in near silence and Alydian continued to stumble forward in a haze of fatigue and regret. She thought often of Grogith and his sacrifice, and her mother, the regrets numbed by the need for slumber.

Light sparked above, marking the touch of dawn. Shortly afterward the canyon ended where the river cut into a tunnel. The cave continued for several hundred paces before opening onto a wondrous vista. Alydian stumbled into the open and blinked against the sunrise, shielding her eyes from the brilliance.

The trickling stream gurgled into a great forest of pine. In the distance a lake was visible, as well as a handful of tree homes on its shores. The sun rose from the mountains in the west, bathing the world in golden light. Birds added a sweet melody to the scene.

"We're in the elven kingdom," Toron said, gesturing to the elven homes in the distance. "If we can make it to the village, we may find shelter."

"I'm surprised the Verinai aren't here waiting for us," Raiden said.

347

"If they were," Toron said, "we'd already be dead. Be grateful they were too arrogant to think anyone could flee by this route. You can be certain they will take measures to seal it now."

"Come," Alydian said, her eyes flicking to Devkin. "We have wounds to tend to, and a truth to share."

They worked their way through the trees and to the elven village on the lake. Dried blood and dirt caked their bodies, drawing astonished looks from the village members. But the elves responded with care and compassion, leaping to attend to their various wounds. An aged healer cared for Devkin while her daughter closed the wounds on the others. A pair of village elders asked questions, but Alydian had donned the Alethean necklace and was evasive with her answers. They did not recognize her. When the healers were finished, they withdrew from the room.

Devkin lay on a bed while the others were sprawled about with bandages wrapped on their wounds. Healing magic sapped the injured's body, so they were all sleepy. But Raiden rubbed his face and leaned forward in his seat.

"The Verinai will be here soon," he said. "We must move on."

"Where?" Red asked, fingering the bandage on her arm.

Devkin removed the memory orb from the pouch at his side. "Once the Eldress Council sees this, they will discipline the guild of Verinai."

"They won't accept a rebuke," Toron said. "And do not forget, an oracle has betrayed the council. If Teriah stands with them, they may choose to fight."

"They won't," Alydian said. "Not against the rest of the council. With the kingdoms and guilds as allies, even the Verinai will not be able to stand against us."

"And the Soldier?" Raiden asked.

"Will be a hero," she said, holding his gaze. "The Soldier has fought a war the people did not know about, and its time the kingdoms acknowledge his sacrifice."

He smiled and stood. "We should hasten to Dawnskeep."

Alydian shook her head. "Any Verinai in the elven kingdom will be watching for us. Take Devkin and the others north and I will meet you there. The quicker we end this, the quicker the monarchs return to governing their own peoples."

"And we will be free," Jester said.

"I'll see you in Dawnskeep," Alydian said, and stepped to the door.

"Alydian?" Red called.

Alydian came to a halt and looked to the woman.

"I never got to thank you for saving me at the Black Shrouds' camp."

Alydian smiled. "I couldn't let a friend die."

"I'm glad to call you friend."

Alydian's smile widened. "I hope you'll continue to be so in the coming conflict."

Alydian nodded to Jester and Toron before slipping out the door. As she stepped onto the balcony, Raiden joined her, and for a moment they stood alone. Alydian wanted to speak, to share what she felt, but the words did not come. Raiden looked down at her, his eyes soft as he reached up and moved an errant hair from her face. She smiled, suddenly shy.

"You never told me why you became the Soldier," she said.

He flashed a wry smile. "It's a sad tale."

"I'd like to hear it," she said, "If you're willing to share."

He stepped to the balcony and looked out over the lake. "Ten years ago, my brother and I joined the Runeguard."

She raised an eyebrow at that. "That's how you knew so much about oracles."

He nodded. "We also learned a great deal about the Verinai, and witnessed them commit many crimes. My brother and I started an inquisition against them, but the Verinai had us dismissed. We refused to let the matter drop and began gathering support. Other Verinai crimes came to light and our combined voices demanded attention. That's when the Verinai tried to end our inquisition . . . by ending us."

"And your brother died?" Alydian asked.

Raiden turned to her. "They thought us both dead, and I realized the anonymity would be my armor. Our followers became the Defiant, and I became the Soldier."

"I remember that inquisition," Alydian said. "Teriah helped the Verinai end it, and I assumed it was baseless."

"The Verinai needed to be exposed," he said. "How could I not finish the cause my brother died for?"

She stepped close to him. "Some may have condemned your actions, but you acted with honor."

He raised an eyebrow. "You think I'm honorable?"

Suddenly nervous, she laughed. "I admit nothing."

He laughed in turn and pulled her close, wrapping an arm around her back. "I admit everything," he said.

The kiss sent shudders down her frame, and she wrapped her arms around his powerful shoulders. The seconds passed and she refused to withdraw, the extended contact only heightening her need. When he finally retreated, her head spun and she caught the balcony railing for support.

"I look forward to more of those," he said.

"As do I," she said fervently.

He grinned and kissed her again, before stepping back to the door. "Go," he said. "Claim our victory."

"Take care of Devkin," she said.

"I swear it," he replied.

She embraced him and then descended the stairs to the ground. After the events in Verisith she'd carried a crushing weight, but now it had vanished. She made her way through the village and paid for a horse, unable to keep the smile from her face. Abruptly eager to reach Dawnskeep, she mounted and flicked the reins, sending her steed north.

She drove her horse hard, and slept only when her body required it. She still wore the pendent of Alethean, and retained the persona to keep any questions at bay. Her smile remained throughout the weeklong journey.

She paused at an inn in Rualia to rest and clean up, not wanting to arrive soiled and reeking from the journey. At dusk the next day she reached Horizon, and she reigned in her horse on a nearby hill.

The daily sun had filled the top of Dawnskeep with light, making it resemble a grand lighthouse. The sun set behind it, making the beacon all the brighter. Alydian's smile faded, wondering how the people would react when they learned that Teriah had betrayed the council. Many of those in power would consider Alethean the rogue mage, but the people would finally know the truth.

Abruptly reluctant to speak to her mother, she took her time descending the slope, entering the city just as the gates were shut for the night. She slowed as she neared Dawnskeep at the heart of the city, and used her farsight to see that the Verinai would be watching for both Alethean and Alydian. She dismounted near a hidden entrance to the fortress and sent a hummingbird of light into the sky.

Several minutes later a faint scuffle erupted behind the wall, and then a door opened to reveal Ferin and Toala standing over an unconscious Runeguard. Alydian darted to them and they shut the door. In the dim light she grinned at them.

"I take it things went well?" Ferin whispered.

"I have the memory," she said, and then briefly outlined the events in Verisith. When she finished her friends nodded soberly.

"Grogith had his secret but he was always loyal," Ferin said.

"I'm sorry to hear of your mother," Toala said. "Do you wish to speak with her first?"

Alydian slipped into her farsight and saw her mother was asleep. "No," she said. "Let her have a few final moments of peace before I share the truth of her illness."

*Never delay a difficult task.*

Devkin's words came back to her but she shoved them aside. She knew she should go directly to her mother but wasn't ready to face her, not yet. It would mean accepting Teriah's betrayal. Instead she blinked into her farsight and stepped to Raine's tree, pleased to find her reading in the great library.

"Raine is in the library," Alydian said. "She'll help me summon the other oracles."

"We'll take care of your horse," Ferin said. "It's good to have you back."

Toala abruptly embraced her, and Alydian smiled, returning the gesture. Then she nodded to them and slipped away. She bypassed the Runeguard by using her farsight and caught an ascender to the library. It was late, and the tower had been shuttered to the public. Making her way through the great bookshelves, she breathed deep of the scent of pages and ink, her smile widening at the sense of security it inspired.

Alydian spotted Raine in her favorite chair by a hearth and wove her way around the tables. Raine looked up at her approach, whereupon Alydian reached up and removed the pendant. Raine's eyes widened, her question dying on her lips.

"Alydian?" she asked, rising to her feet.

Alydian laughed and sank into a seat across from her. "You should sit, for I have a tale to tell."

Raine grinned and resumed her seat, listening intently as Alydian shared the story of her becoming an acolyte, and what she'd learned of the Verinai. Raine's smile quickly faded, her expression darkening the more Alydian spoke. When Alydian finished with what she'd done in Verisith, Raine stood and began to pace.

352

"I can scarcely believe what you have done," she said.

"It's true," Alydian said. "And Mineva's memory proves it."

"May I see it?" Raine asked.

Alydian withdrew the orb and held it aloft, and Raine accepted it, activating it with a touch. Mineva's voice filled the library and the image of her assassinating King Talin appeared. Raine watched it for only a moment before she ended the magic and turned to Alydian.

"You have no idea what you have done," she breathed.

And threw the orb into the fire.

# Chapter 46: The Rogue Mage

Alydian stared in shock as the glass orb shattered against the stone, the memory consumed by the flames in a distorted burst of light and sound. Her eyes flew to Raine to find the woman's eyes on her, her expression one of pity.

"*Why?*" Alydian breathed.

"You may be an oracle," Raine said. "But you do not behave like one."

"Do you have any idea how much I went through to get that memory?" she cried. "How much it *cost?*"

Raine shook her head. "The cost of keeping that memory would be far greater."

"How can you say that?" Alydian demanded, her anger causing fire to spark across her arms. "Do you even know the war the Verinai are waging?"

"The Accord?" Raine asked. "Of course I know."

"How do you know about—"

"Because I signed it."

The admission rocked Alydian back. Raine was her friend, a woman as close to family as her own mother. She'd taught Alydian the honor of being an oracle, how their identity was to serve the people. They were protectors of every race and life, and Raine had always spoken with such fervor that Alydian could recall the moments in perfect clarity.

"How could you sign it?" Alydian asked softly. "It goes against everything we stand for."

"We stand for protecting the people of Lumineia," Raine said. "But they don't want to be protected."

"Of course they want to be protected."

She laughed, her tone laced with scorn. "A hundred years before your birth a warlord rose to power in eastern Griffin. For months he pillaged without mercy but the king refused our aid—or that of the Verinai. His troops were helpless to find him, and the man grew bolder with every week. When the king finally let us help, we found the man in three days, and the Verinai ended his reign of terror."

"Criminals rise like weeds," Alydian said.

"Yet the kings allow them to flourish," she said.

"That was one event," Alydian protested. "You cannot judge the whole of humanity on the foolishness of a single man. You cannot expect perfection."

"It's not just the race of man," she said, her voice hardening. "Ten years later a dwarven general lost a son to an orc bandit, and sparked a war that resulted in tens of thousands dead."

"One dwarf—"Alydian began but Raine cut her off.

"He didn't care that the orcs were not at fault, he blamed his son's death on the entire *race*. When we finally negotiated peace the rock trolls stepped in, their king attempting to take advantage of the disorganized orc nation to expand their lands."

"Rock trolls do not care about land."

"No," she said. "But just one in power was enough. Don't you see? The races cannot be trusted with power, for they inevitably abuse it."

"I cannot believe the elves would behave in such a way," she said.

"Then you know nothing," Raine said, her voice mocking. "On the surface our people are fair and generous, but those in power veritably worship intrigue. Their pride rivals that of the Verinai, and many of the poor suffer in their pursuit of perfection."

"Even if what you say is true," Alydian said. "The Accord gives power to the Verinai, and turning the races into a Mage Empire would grant them even more."

"True," she conceded, "but for all their faults they understand their place. They believe themselves better than the people, their guilds, and even the kingdoms . . . but they respect the oracles."

"You think they will serve you?" Alydian demanded. "They are brutes with power, and it will only be a matter of time before they come for the Eldress Council."

"Have you forgotten who we are?" Raine asked. "We will see it coming."

Alydian saw the unwavering confidence in the woman's expression, and realized she would not yield. Raine truly believed her own words, and was committed to creating a Mage Empire. Realizing the effort to convince her would be futile, Alydian straightened.

"You cannot do this without the council," she said. "I will speak to them, and they will never agree with you and Teriah."

"They already do," she said.

A chill spread on Alydian's flesh. Raine voice filled with pity, and all at once Alydian saw the past councils in a new light, of the other oracles biding their time until Elenyr died.

"You have all betrayed your oath," Alydian said in horror.

"Don't you see?" Raine asked. "Only your mother stood against us, and now that she is dying, you will be alone."

"I will *never* join you."

The vehemence to her statement robbed Raine of her smile, and for several moments the two regarded each other. Raine's expression carried a trace of pity mixed with surprise, as if she'd thought Alydian would simply agree. Still grappling with the realization that the entire

Eldress Council had betrayed their oaths, Alydian wanted to flee, to escape from what she'd thought was home.

"You have no choice," Raine said, her soft voice gaining a dangerous edge. "The council acts together or we are all lost. No oracle has ever betrayed the council."

"Then I am the first," Alydian said. "I thought Teriah the rogue, but if the council has abandoned its honor than I will gladly stand alone."

"You would publicly fracture the council?" she asked, her tone harsh.

Alydian hesitated, recognizing even without her farsight that she stood on a precipice. To defy the council would send shockwaves throughout the kingdoms, and the people's faith in the oracles would forever be damaged. But staying silent would permit the oracles to become tyrants, and would require her to break her own oath.

"I am a sworn protector of the people," she said. "Even if the enemy is one of my own."

Raine measured her response before her jaw tightened. "So be it."

Raine reached for the fire and yanked on the heat, sending a blast at Alydian. On instinct she ducked and the flames soared overhead, impacting a bookshelf. Charms lit up as they protected the books but the shelves burned as Alydian scrambled back.

"I thought you were a sister," Raine said as she advanced upon her. "An ally that would support me in every course."

After all her training Alydian recovered quickly. She accepted the next blast of fire and churned it into a fire golem at her side. It swelled as she poured heat into it, growing to the size of a rock troll. Raine came to a stop when she saw the spell and, surprisingly, laughed.

"I must say I'm impressed," she said. "I knew your mother was up to something but I never expected you were training with the Runeguard. She must have shielded you with her own choices to keep you hidden from us."

"What do you intend, Sister?" Alydian asked, her voice rigid. "My mother is near death and cannot bear another child. Killing me will end an oracle bloodline. Is my life the price of your empire?"

"I do not wish to kill you," Raine said, "but if your bloodline is not ready to adapt, then you leave me no choice."

Raine pointed to the golem and Alydian felt a tug through the entity as the woman sought to gain control. Alydian gritted her teeth and willed the entity to step toward Raine. It took a halting step forward, causing Raine's eyes to widen. She clenched her hand into a fist, her face reddening from the effort to wrest control of the fire entity.

"Your will has grown in your time as a Runeguard," she hissed through clenched teeth.

Alydian poured her anger and confusion into her magic, and the golem took another step toward Raine, extending a flaming arm. Raine cried out but held her ground, and the arm slowly came to a halt.

Standing ten paces apart with a giant golem between them, they fought for dominance over the entity. Like a war machine battering the gates of her mind, Alydian felt Raine's power attempt to tear through her control, yet she did not yield.

"I am no longer a child," Alydian growled.

The golem began to tremble, the flames on its body sparking and spilling away. Still they battled, and the golem stumbled to the side, a great foot stomping through a couch, snapping the wood. It's trembling mounted and the flames brightened, and Alydian realized what was coming. Relinquishing her hold, she dived to the side as the entity detonated.

Fire blasted into the bookshelves and floor, lancing into the stone like a heated sword. Couches, tables, and chairs were shredded into fragments of burning wood. A pair of aquaglass windows cracked from the heat, and rivulets of water ran in steaming lines into the burning carpet.

Alydian cast a fire shield about her body and rose to her feet, stunned and dismayed by the damage. Fires burned on all sides, eagerly devouring the remains of the library furniture. A bookshelf groaned as it fell, crashing into the ascender and sending a shudder into Dawnskeep.

"See what your disobedience has wrought!" Raine shouted, rising into view. Her hair was in disarray and her clothing torn but she held her focus, calling on the air. Twisting in a circle, she summoned a tornado and sent it hurtling at Alydian.

Alydian cast an entrapment charm. The stone floor rose and snapped shut upon the cyclone, cutting it off at the knees and leaving it to sputter and scatter shielded books. But Raine darted around the pillar of rock and slammed into her, striking a fist into her jaw.

Backed by a strength charm, the blow was brutal, intended to punish more than harm. Alydian reeled away and just managed to cast an agility charm. She ducked the next blow and called on the surrounding heat to craft a sword.

"You think yourself better than I?" Raine shouted. "I've been training for over two hundred years! No whelp is going to triumph over me." She cast her own sword and smashed it against Alydian's blade, sending sparks across both of them.

"*Devkin* is stronger than you," Alydian spat.

She shoved Raine away and reached out to the stone left from her entrapment charm, knocking it down between the two of them, forcing Raine back. Then she summoned the light, shaping it into a trio of gremlins. They dropped into the flames and charged, scaling the pillar with their claws before leaping over. Three bursts of light signaled Raine had dispatched the entities, and Raine climbed into view.

"You must have learned that trick in a Requiem," she said. "But you don't even understand your power."

She reached down and struck the pillar, sending cracks throughout the stone. It crumbled into dozens of stones which grew arms and legs, and then heads. The gremlins howled a grating war cry and charged.

Outnumbered, Alydian reached to the broken aquaglass window, using the crack to tear it apart. The glass cracked into hundreds of

359

shards that leapt across the gap, pummeling the gremlins and shattering them to dust. Raine strode through the rubble and, flicking her sword.

Raine sneered at her. "I thought you were my ally."

"I thought you were my friend."

A cracking in the floor signaled a break, and then the section where the fire entity had exploded broke, tumbling into the great hall below. Alydian used the distraction to leap forward and strike, and Raine deflected the blow.

For several seconds the two fought, their swords cutting through stone and shelf, wall and floor. Alydian drove her back before Raine retaliated in kind, screaming as she struck at Alydian with her free hand. Alydian twisted, and the blast of superheated light reached past her and smashed into the floor, carving another hole. Alydian continued her rotation and swung her sword high, hiding her true attack in her free hand.

The anti-magic thread streaked from her finger and wrapped around Raine's wrists. Alydian attached a spike to the bonds and sent it plunging into a burning table, yanking Raine to her knees. Raine smashed into the floor, fighting the bonds that sapped her magic.

On the verge of victory, Alydian saw Raine's face. Her features contorted with anger, she hardly resembled the woman Alydian had known. Yet Alydian saw the woman that had taught her, guided her, loved her.

"You were more than a friend," Alydian said. "You were family."

"Family doesn't betray each other," Raine snapped, yanking on her bonds.

"You're right," Alydian said. "But I didn't betray the council, the council betrayed me."

She turned and walked away, leaving Raine bound amid the burning library. "There is nowhere you can flee that we will not find you!" Raine shouted.

Alydian paused and looked back, and despite Raine's anger she flinched away from Alydian's expression.

"You won't need to find me," Alydian shouted. "Because I'll be coming for you. You and the council have turned against the whole of our purpose, and the next time we meet the line will be clear. Rest assured I will not hesitate to kill you."

She stepped onto a set of metal stairs and coiled the steel into a hand that lifted her upward, to the level above. But Raine gathered herself, shrieking as she snapped the anti-magic bonds. Then she reached her hands up to the metal staircase.

"You cannot escape!" she screamed.

Metal bent away from Alydian and pointed downward, but she was close enough to the ceiling to leap. She jumped to where the stairs ascended into the ceiling, relinquishing her hold on the metalwork.

Without opposition, Raine's magic whipped the staircase down. The twisted metal came down upon her, piercing her flesh and crushing her to the burning floor. Hanging above the devastated library, Alydian managed to pull herself up to the final step and turn.

Her breath caught as she saw Raine's impaled body. Alydian's strength failed her and she slumped onto the step, her magic faltering. Alydian stared, unable to tear herself from the sight of an oracle dead, an entire oracle bloodline extinguished forever.

Because of her.

"I'm sorry," she whispered, wrapping her arms about herself as if doing so would end the pain in her chest.

Distantly she was aware of a group of Runeguard rising into view through a hole in the floor. She wanted to call out to them but couldn't find her voice. Assailed by guilt and doubt she didn't feel the effects of the sleeping charm until it was too late.

Hands appeared from behind her and caught her shoulders, preventing her from tumbling into the library. She tried to fight the magic but it preyed on her fatigue and guilt, sapping her strength. She was carried up the final steps and laid upon the floor above. Her vision swam into focus and she saw Teriah standing over her, her expression one of horror.

"What have you done?"

Tears welled up in Alydian's eyes. "The council has betrayed the people," she mumbled. "Raine tried to stop me from revealing the truth . . ."

Teriah's expression turned frightening. "I will see your end for this," she hissed.

Alydian tried to argue but the sleeping charm was too strong, and she slipped into unconsciousness. The last image she saw was of Elsin and a pair of Verinai Runeguard appearing. Then she was lifted and carried away . . .

# Chapter 47: Lost

Alydian woke violently. She lurched to her feet and stumbled about, slamming her head into a curved wall before she managed to take in her surroundings. The pain brought sharp clarity—and she sucked in her breath.

She stood in a sphere, the walls of which were a smooth black. Only a single light orb illuminated the space and sat against the ceiling. A section of one wall curved out and formed a bed, while opposite it was a small table, also extending from the wall. With a start she recognized the chamber for what it was.

A cell.

Fighting to control the burgeoning panic, she searched the interior of the sphere for an exit. When she blinked into her magesight all she saw was solid anti-magic, the very walls of the sphere were built with it, making her magesight useless. She searched and searched, forcing herself to look again even when she knew it was futile.

"Welcome to your new home," a voice said, startling her.

She spun about, trying to identify where the voice had come from. Then she noticed a small hole that had been absent before. She stepped to it and looked out, her eyes widening when she saw open air beyond the cell.

The sphere hung in an underground chasm, with great chains holding it aloft. A guardhouse had been built into the wall of the abyss with a clear view of her cell. Flanked by Elsin and Ciana, Teriah gazed upon her with abject hatred.

"Teriah!" Alydian cried. "I did not mean to—"

"Kill her?" she asked. "Yet you did. An entire oracle bloodline, extinguished because of a rogue mage, *you*."

Alydian flinched. "Her own magic killed her."

"It matters not," Teriah said. "You may not have landed the blow, but you bear the burden."

"You have betrayed our oath!" Alydian shouted, her guilt burning into anger, "After what you've done I could not sit idle."

"Yet that is what you shall do," Teriah said. "Four oracles built this prison and I assure you, there will be no escape."

"Why not kill me?" Alydian asked, trying to keep her voice from faltering.

"The bloodline must continue," Teriah said. "And when this war is over you will either join me . . . or perish in your prison."

"I would have killed you," Ciana said coldly.

"You cannot do this!" Alydian shouted. "The people will not kneel before an oracle. They will not bow to your Mage Empire."

"They already do," Elsin said with a sneer. "Griffin and the elves yielded their thrones days ago, and the dwarves will fall in time."

"None can stop those who see the future," Teriah added.

"My mother will stop you."

"She is too weak to rise from her bed," Ciana said. "And will likely die before you ever see daylight again."

"You cannot trap an oracle!" Alydian said, her fear seeping into her voice. "I will escape!"

Teriah swept her hands wide. "You are welcome to try. The only source of energy in there is your light, and it isn't enough for you to even scratch the walls. I would say enjoy your solitude, but I honestly hope you don't."

The hole in the sphere began to close, a dark liquid filling the opening with shocking speed. She tried to reach through it but it pushed against her, forcing her back. With barely a whisper it shut, leaving her in the sphere alone.

She shouted and screamed, searching the sphere again and again, her fury driving her to strike at the walls with her bare fists. But she was helpless. She sucked every ounce of power from the light orb into her hand, plunging her cell into darkness. Then she cast a tiny asunder charm, blasting the sphere with every morsel of her strength. When the power faded she stumbled to the spot and rubbed her hand across it, but the wall remained smooth and cold. It took several hours before the orb began to brighten.

Her chest heaving, she slumped to the floor, struggling to control the panic constricting her chest. The sound of her ragged breathing marred the silence, and calm refused to come. When she managed to contain her emotions she closed her eyes and slipped into her farsight, pushing past the circle of anti-magic to see the familiar forest. The trees of Raiden, Elenyr, and her other friends remained. But hers had changed.

Every branch, every fork, every decision, gone as if it never existed. The sprawling tree that showed a life of hundreds of years had become a withered trunk rising into darkness. Four oracles had built a cell that would take her future, and her remaining life would now be spent shackled until she joined Teriah, or death claimed her.

She blinked back to reality, sending tears down her cheeks. It took three days before she was willing to try again, but still saw the same haunting tree. She fought against her fate but no decision altered the tree, proving that her cage was impenetrable.

Each day a small trapdoor opened in the ceiling, allowing food to enter. She expected Elsin or the oracles to gloat, but days passed without a word. Then a week. By the end of the second week she began to question her sanity, and it took all her willpower not to succumb to fear and madness.

They had taken her magic, her farsight, and her freedom, but there was one thing they could not steal. Trapped in a cell built to contain an

365

oracle, she was like any other magicless, like Raiden. But he'd survived against powerful foes, demonstrating time and again that it wasn't power that defined a person. It was their will.

She began to laugh, the sound reverberating off the walls of her sphere. The trapdoor opened and food fell unnoticed, her laughter rising as she clung to the tiny sense of strength. She didn't have magic, but she was far from helpless.

Alydian's humor subsided, her emotions hardening into a singular focus. Her allies had betrayed her, locked her in a cage and robbed her of her birthright. Those she loved fought alone in a war they could not win. She thought of escape, but deep inside another thought dominated her soul.

Vengeance.

# The Chronicles of Lumineia

By Ben Hale

## —The Age of Oracles—

The Rogue Mage
The Lost Mage
The Battle Mage

## —The Master Thief—

Jack of Thieves
Thief in the Myst
The God Thief

## —The Second Draeken War—

Elseerian
The Gathering
Seven Days
The List Unseen

## —The Warsworn—

The Flesh of War
The Age of War
The Heart of War

## —The White Mage Saga—

Assassin's Blade (Short story prequel)
The Last Oracle
The Sword of Elseerian
Descent Unto Dark
Impact of the Fallen
The Forge of Light

# Author Bio

Originally from Utah, Ben has grown up with a passion for learning almost everything. Driven particularly to reading caused him to be caught reading by flashlight under the covers at an early age. While still young, he practiced various sports, became an Eagle Scout, and taught himself to play the piano. This thirst for knowledge gained him excellent grades and helped him graduate college with honors, as well as become fluent in three languages after doing volunteer work in Brazil. After school, he started and ran several successful businesses that gave him time to work on his numerous writing projects. His greatest support and inspiration comes from his wonderful wife and six beautiful children. Currently he resides in Missouri while working on his Masters in Professional Writing.

To contact the author, discover more about Lumineia, or find out about the upcoming sequels, check out his website at Lumineia.com. You can also follow the author on twitter @ BenHale8 or Facebook.

Made in the USA
Columbia, SC
26 August 2019